Philadelphia-born author **Lindsay Faith Rech** studied writing and theater at Rider University, graduating with honors in 2000. Prior to the release of her debut novel, *Losing It,* she had her own column in a New Jersey newspaper and worked as an assistant editor for a chain of newsmagazines in Pennsylvania. Today, she lives in Bucks County with her husband, Scott. When not writing, she enjoys eighties music, *Knots Landing* reruns, good reality television and wasting time on the Internet. *Joyride* is her second novel.

joyride

Lindsay Faith Rech

First edition October 2004

JOYRIDE

A Red Dress Ink novel

ISBN 0-373-25072-X

www.RedDressInk.com

Printed in U.S.A.

To Jill
“Best Friends Forever”

Acknowledgments

For so long, becoming published was my biggest dream. Thank you so much to everyone who's gotten excited with me over the past two years. In particular, thanks to Daryle, for technical support and enthusiasm; Sue, for shopping and lunch; Scott, for continued patience and understanding; all the Resnicks and Allans; and Mo, MMD and PPL, for being your fabulous selves. And Dad, I am always grateful—you *are* my number one fan.

Thanks also to everyone at Red Dress Ink, especially my kind editor, Margaret Marbury, whose valuable guidance helped bring this book to print.

The Beginning

The moment. It happened when we were thirteen and had something to do with thighs, music and our mothers. We've never been able to describe it exactly. We only know that it transpired at some point during that conversation in the locker room. And that it changed our lives. During times of crisis, I suppose it's good to keep the beginning in mind—if only for something to hold on to as the world collapses around you. As I drove to the airport on that dark December morning, I filled my head with the memory of our first meeting, hoping to calm my fears with the sweet recollection of how simple adolescence could be.

"Do you think Mrs. Wilder knows she has cellulite on the back of her thighs?"

That was the first thing she ever said to me. She being the cool girl from my gym class who didn't seem the type to wonder about things like that. Probably because *I* was the type who wondered about things like that, and I definitely wasn't cool.

But there'd always been something different about this girl. She wasn't popular-cool—no one in the popular crowd stood out the way she did. This girl was intriguing. I think it was the way she wore her confidence—subtle, detached and full of power, like she just might be some kind of rebel. Who would've known that underneath it all, she wondered about cellulite, too?

"I like your shirt, by the way," she said, glancing down at my chest. Milli Vanilli hadn't become common fodder for comedy sketches yet.

"Thanks! I didn't actually go to the concert, though," I admitted. "I got it at the mall."

"Oh, well, that's probably better. Things are always way overpriced at concerts, anyway."

"True," I agreed, not that I knew. I'd only been to one in my entire lifetime—a Michael Jackson concert with my parents when I was eight. I wasn't quite sure how this ranked on the scales of seventh-grade coolness.

"I'm Emily, by the way," she said, flashing a smile of gums and dimples that was both inviting and, at the same time, too quick to let any visitors stay.

"I'm Stella," I said, smiling back, though I was sure with a little less charm. "My mom was *A Streetcar Named Desire* fanatic. She said I was conceived during that famous scene where Marlon Brando stands on the street screaming, 'Stella!'" This last part was a lie and my imitation was hideous, but I thought it made me sound interesting.

"That's sexy," Emily said, her voice slipping into a low and seductive key. And then she just kind of stared at me for a few seconds. I found the strange silence ironically cozy. "So, do you think she does?" she asked finally.

"Do I think who does what?"

Emily laughed. "Do you think Mrs. Wilder knows she has cellulite on the back of her thighs?" And there it was. The question that had started it all.

"She couldn't possibly," I reasoned. "Or she wouldn't wear her shorts so short."

"It's a shame," Emily said wistfully, "because she's pretty hot for a teacher. Don't you think?"

I had always found Mrs. Wilder uncannily attractive for Willowood Junior High, but I wasn't used to referring to other women as "hot." Emily, on the other hand, seemed to own a language untainted by overusage and unhindered by what other people thought.

"She *is* hot," I agreed, experimenting with the word. I felt liberated and embarrassed at the same time and knew by Emily's smile that she'd already embraced me as her devoted trainee. "I guess nobody's perfect," I added, wondering if Emily was.

"I guess not," Emily said with a shrug.

Just then, the bell rang, signifying the end of class.

"Do you have lunch now?" I asked.

"No, algebra," she said, rolling her eyes. "I'll see you Thursday. We can stare at Mrs. Wilder's cellulite together and secretly think she's hot."

"I can hardly wait," I said, using *my* best "do me" voice to let her know I shared her sense of humor.

"Stella," she said reflectively, before turning to walk away. "That's a really cool name. My mom was a Laura Nyro fanatic. She named me after the song 'Emmie' and died when I was three."

That afternoon, I discovered *Eli and the Thirteenth Confession*—or more precisely, my mother pulled the one Laura Nyro album she owned out of the dust stacks in our attack—and on it was the song that would forever remind me of the girl who, in one indescribable moment, left a lasting impression. There was just something about that conversation—something that made me feel more excited and alive than I actually knew was possible, more like the "me" I'd always wanted to be. Something that made me look *forward* to gym class.

I fell asleep that night with the song stuck in my head, wondering if Emily was thinking about *her* new friend from the locker room and if my parents would ever adopt her. It was that instinct right there—to care for Emily—that would accompany me through the next fifteen years of my life.

★ ★ ★

Fifteen years is a long time to know somebody. And no matter how old you are going in to knowing that person, you grow up. You change. God knows, Emily and I did. But the important thing is that we changed together and never actually grew apart. For all those years of change and growth and experience, I thought nothing could break us apart. But I wasn't prepared for Europe.

Emily's phone call came at four o'clock on that dark December morning, ripping me from sleep. It was nine o'clock in London, but that wasn't the point. The point was that things had changed in a way I could have never prepared myself for.

We always said we'd be best friends no matter what, right? she'd asked me in a tearful panic. A rhetorical question if ever I'd heard one, but that was before she told me the news. *Just promise me, Stella,* she'd begged. *Promise you'll never forget us.*

Emily, you're not making any sense. If you tell me what happened, then maybe I can—

And that's when she dropped her bombshell—just like that, from thousands of miles across the ocean—and my entire world came undone.

I arrived at the airport in a flood of fear and sadness. It didn't even matter about the wait, having to sit for all of those hours with nothing but my own mind for company. I had nowhere else to go, nothing else to do, no place else I *could* be. At least, at the airport, I was safe.

It would take me three flights to get to her. Taking off and landing. Connecting. And taking off again. The whole process dragging out and repeating until one day turned into the next. And in the meantime—the time that separated me from Emily's frightening reality overseas—all I could do was wait and think…as the seconds turned into minutes, turned into hours, and became my whole life.

Sisters of the Moon

Philadelphia International seemed the perfect place to come unglued. Nobody knew me. Nobody cared. Nothing in the atmosphere existed to remind me of Emily. But still, I thought of her. Though, I thought of the old Emily, the one that had never made a transatlantic phone call on a dark December morning we'd remember for the rest of our lives. I thought of thirteen-year-old Emily and the way we were at Willowood when times were simple. And somehow, these memories were enough to hold me together.

Tinkerbell. That's how I described Emily to my mother before they met. She reminded me of the little revolving Tinkerbell in my jewelry box from grade school. A tiny blue-eyed china doll. But one that carried whips and chains. I guess the contradiction was what I found most alluring. Here was a girl who couldn't have weighed more than a morsel, but had enough attitude to propel *both* of us through the murky shit-mine our school board liked to call junior high. Before her, I was just a miserable suburban kid dreading my first period and praying each night for boobs to balance out my thighs. Instead of boobs, I got Emily. The period followed soon after and my thighs continued to spread like yesterday's news.

We were only on our third gym class of staring at Mrs. Wilder's cellulite together and secretly thinking she was hot, anyway, when I realized that particular rite of passage had arrived—right in the middle of jumping jacks. I was horrified and had to act extra spastic in order to get Mrs. Wilder's attention, flailing my arms above the crowd and jumping sideways, until, finally, I caught her eye.

"Can I run to the bathroom?"

"Quickly."

As I hurried off to check out the damage, I heard Emily asking if she could go as well.

"When Stella gets back, you can go."

"But I have to go…*now!*"

As I opened the locker room door, I turned to see my new friend doubled over, grasping her crotch as if she might explode from holding it in. I heard Mrs. Wilder say it was okay just as the door closed behind me.

Inside the bathroom stall, I nearly fainted. Could a person really bleed *that* much? There was suddenly a tap at the door.

"Stella?" It was Emily.

"Yeah?"

"Do you want me to show you how to use a tampon?"

"How did you…?"

"I noticed some blood on the back of your shorts. *Don't worry,*" she said before I could ask. "I highly doubt anyone else was paying that close attention. But I know you better than they do, and I knew something wasn't right when you started jumping around all antsy out there. I figured it could be, you know, 'feminine trouble,'" Emily continued, adopting a different tone of voice for the euphemism. "I just knew where to look."

"It's my first one," I admitted.

"I figured that. Do you want me to show you how to use a tampon? It's really easy."

"I'm afraid to stick something inside of me," I confessed to the stall door.

"You won't feel it once it's in there if you put it in right," she explained. "And besides, pads feel like diapers, so the sooner you learn to wear a tampon, the better."

"I don't even have any money for the machine out there."

"You don't need money," Emily said. "I have plenty of tampons on me." She paused. "Stella, I have my period, too. So, now we are sisters of the moon." There was a whimsical tone in her voice and I smiled in spite of my situation. "And sisters of the moon should not have to communicate through closed doors. Open up. The sight of blood does not freak me out."

I stood there contemplating the idea. I had always prided myself on my discreet changing abilities in the locker room. It had been three years since my mother had seen me naked and four since my father had even seen me in a towel. Facing another person with my pants down was not exactly my cup of tea.

Emily peered through the crack in the stall. "I see you, my sexy moon goddess. Now, let me in and I'll show you mine."

"Emily!" I shrieked, covering myself with one hand as I unhooked the lock with the other. Though, I had to admit, the better part of me was grateful that I wasn't going through this alone.

"Oh, I'm just kidding, you little perv," she said, locking herself in the stall with me and handing over a tampon. I'd never held one before. "You're lucky I'm here, you know. I got my period in fifth grade. I was, like, the *only* one. I stuffed a bunch of toilet paper down there and walked around feeling like I'd crapped my pants all day." We both giggled.

"That's probably what I would've done if you hadn't come in."

Suddenly, Emily's eyes grew serious, and I could tell that her mood had changed. "Your mom will probably make a big deal out of this," she said. I nodded. She probably would. "Let her," she told me. "And then let me know what it's like."

The lesson worked on my third try, and Emily was right. Not only about the tampon—I didn't feel it once it was in there—

but also about my mother. She made a *very* big deal. Not that I didn't appreciate her making my favorite dinner that night or buying me the seventy-dollar sweater at the mall the next day. I just didn't see why my soiling my shorts during jumping jacks had earned me these things. Emily explained it to me the following week as we sat straddling a locker room bench before gym class, in typical conference position.

"Because, dear Stella, raven goddess of the moon," she said, running her fingers through my long dark hair until they got caught in tangles on both sides by my shoulders, "it's a big deal for a mother to watch her little girl grow up. And getting your period is step one in the long and beautiful journey to becoming a woman."

One thing I'd noticed about Emily was that she enjoyed saying corny things like this, but always with the most serious of expressions on her face and in tones very much like the narrating voice in a public television documentary. It never failed to make me laugh, and when I would laugh, she would laugh. On this particular day, we bumped foreheads as we giggled. Her hands were still stuck in my hair.

"Are you two lesbians?" The voice penetrated our laughter, stabbing our fun on purpose. It was Nelly Whiteman, a tomboyish, good-at-sports, popular girl who wasn't even pretty, but attracted lots of male attention due to her highly acceptable social status at Willowood. If you asked me, she was rather butch, and based upon my extremely provincial and retrospectively ignorant seventh-grade definition of the word *lesbian,* I didn't think she was exactly the pot to be calling our kettles black. But I didn't have the balls to say this to her. Emily, however, despite her Tinkerbell exterior, seemed to have been blessed with two very big brass ones.

"Are *you?*" she asked. But Nelly just stared at Emily blankly, as if the idea that either of us might have a comeback had never even occurred to her. After giving her a good ten seconds or so to respond, Emily turned back to me and, in the romantic tone of a black-and-white movie Don Juan, said, "Stella, you have the most elegant eyes I've ever seen. Can we make out now?" I leaned over and kissed her cheek. "That's *not* what I meant," she said, sounding scorned.

"You guys are freaks," Nelly said, dismissing us with a flick of her hand and stomping away in a hurried huff, like we were no longer worth her time.

"At least we don't have brooms up our asses!" Emily called after her.

"You really don't give a shit about being popular, do you?" I asked as I untangled my hair from her fingers.

"Am I supposed to care what Nelly Whiteman thinks just because a bunch of mindless idiots decided that this year she and her friends were the ones to worship?" I shrugged. She had a really good point. I just didn't know how she'd gotten the courage to arrive at it in seventh grade. "Besides," Emily said as she got up off of the bench, "I *am* popular…with you."

"That you are, my dear," I said, extending my hand for her to help me to my feet, as if we were once again in our own black-and-white movie and she was my leading man. But the bell was ringing, and people were beginning to breeze between us, killing the moment. So I stood up on my own and, together, we headed out to another dreaded game of volleyball.

At first, I didn't know where the music was coming from. The notes sprang up from my lap and almost seemed to meld with the memory, with the buzzing of that gym-class bell, until, finally, they pulled me out of it, stripping me from that seventh-grade locker room with my brass-balled Tinkerbell and dropping the crowded airport terminal upon me like a bomb.

"Landslide." Fleetwood Mac. Emily had been driven by her longtime love for Stevie Nicks to customize my cell phone ring. Every time somebody called me, no matter who it was, I thought of my best friend and smiled. And normally, I loved it. But now the present was an intrusion. The adult Emily—the one who had called me that morning, the one who knew about making cell phones ring music—she was here, merging with the past, overshadowing her former self. And my comfort was gone. I looked at the caller ID and got ready to tell my first lie about Europe.

"Hello?"

"Hi, honey. I drove by your place on my way to the deli, but your car wasn't there. Is everything okay?" To call my mother a nervous person would be an understatement. But everyone has reasons for being who they are. She wasn't always this way.

"Oh, everything's fine, Janey. I just left really early this morning. That's all."

A lot of people consider it disrespectful to call their parents by their first names. But Janey isn't my mother's first name, and in our case, it's affectionate. Her real name is Mary-Jane, but the only person who ever calls her that is my grandmother, Dora. Everyone else just calls her Mary. I'm not really sure why, but for some reason, I chose to fixate on the part that comes after the hyphen. It happened when I was about twelve and evolved into its own special title. Emily and I both call her Janey. It seems pretty absurd when I try to explain it to people, but nevertheless, that's what we call her. Occasionally, I will call her Mom, but only in times of nostalgia or need.

"Where are you?" she asked. "Do you have errands? We could meet for breakfast, maybe."

"Oh, I can't," I apologized. "See, I'm at the airport. I got a call from Emily and—"

"Oh, my God. Is everything all right?"

"Oh, absolutely," I lied. "She just thought it would be fun for me to come out and see her during my time off. It was so completely spur of the moment, I barely had time to pack." There. Now I was telling the truth. About the packing part, at least.

"You must be so excited."

"Oh, I definitely am," I gushed, cringing at how fake I sounded. "I mean, I've always wanted to go to Europe with Emily. Now I'm finally getting my chance."

"So, will you be gone your entire break, then?"

"I'm not exactly sure," I said. "I haven't even booked my flight yet." I lied because if I told her I'd already booked my flight, she'd want to know the details. Then she'd know about the wait. And she'd offer to come keep me company, meet me for breakfast, lunch. I'd have no choice but to hurt her feelings. The less she knew, the better. The longer I held out in giving her my travel information, the smaller the window for her offers, her questions, my guilt. I just wanted to be alone, anonymous, a stranger in a crowd.

"Oh, well, don't let me keep you, honey. And try to stay the entire break if you can. You deserve a vacation with all those screaming meshuganahs clamoring for your attention all day long."

I rolled my eyes. I work as a second-grade teacher at Forest Hills Elementary, the same school I attended when my family moved to the suburb of Scottsboro from northeast Philadelphia when I was ten, and I adore it. I've loved every student I've ever had, even the obnoxious ones, even the ones who have smelled funny, and even the ones whose parents I couldn't stand. I've never complained about a single one of them to my mother, which leads me to the conclusion that my sister, Blanche, and I must have been screaming meshuganahs in second grade since that is the image my mother seems to hold of all children at that age.

"Listen, Janey...I'd better get going."

"Oh, okay...Stella, I..."

"Yeah, what is it?"

"I wanted to remind you to light a candle for Blanche tomorrow at sundown if you can." My heart seemed to rip all over again in the places the glue had dried so many times before.

"I will, Mom," I said, becoming fifteen again, as the old familiar lump rose like fire in my throat.

In Judaism, we light *yahrzeit* candles to honor lost loved ones on the anniversaries of their death. But the anniversary is always commemorated in accordance with the Jewish calendar, which I don't know anything about. I always just wait for my mother to tell me when it's time. I think she gets some kind of card from the funeral home each year, either that or my great-grandfather, Zayde Max, lets her know. I've definitely gotten to the age where I should be aware of the approach of Blanche's *yahrzeit,* but sometimes I think it's better not to know until it's upon me. After thirteen years, I know it should have gotten easier. But if there's one thing I've learned, it's that nothing ever gets easier. When I was little, I remember seeing candles in my Grandma Dora's kitchen from time to time, but they seemed like something one lit for old people who had died long ago, people who had faded into the shadows of dusty albums and cobweb memories and were too far gone to summon any tears. They didn't seem to burn for seventeen-year-old sisters.

"Now, you go book that flight," my mother said, so obvious in her attempt to sound unbroken that I wanted to slap my own face for making her feel she ever had to be anything but herself.

"Okay. I love you. I'll call you when I get there and let you know what my plans are."

"No, baby. Call me after you book your flight so I have a ballpark of when you'll be landing." She wanted to know when she should start worrying.

"Okay," I said.

"And I won't keep you long. I know how you like to read your magazines while you wait places." Her kindness just made me sadder. If only my mother could be a bitch sometimes, like everybody else's.

When we hung up, I found a bathroom, locked myself in a stall and spent a half hour crying over the all-too-sudden death of my older sister, Blanche.

Swan Songs

I used to be jealous of Emily's relationship with Blanche. For the last two years of her life, my sister wore her hair in spikes and always seemed to have a Sex Pistols shirt on. Emily didn't care much for punk music, but they both seemed to gravitate toward each other's natural penchant for rebellion. The key difference between them was that Emily was nice. It's awful to speak ill of the dead, I know, and I loved my sister very much, but she prided herself on not being nice. It was her trademark. She wasn't even nice to her friends. The only person she *was* nice to was Emily.

"So when's that Martin chick coming back over here?" she asked, poking her head into my bedroom on the night of Emily's first visit.

"Why, Blanche? Do you want to torment her because she hasn't accepted Sid Vicious as her personal savior? You hadn't, either, at thirteen. Mom still has videotape of you dancing to Lisa Lisa and Cult Jam."

Blanche's eyes widened above their dark black liner at the threat of being exposed as a former pop fan. "Would you *relax?* Jeez, Stella, you've got just as much of a pin up your ass as everyone else in this fucking town! I only asked when she was coming back over because I'd like to see her again, you stupid bitch! You don't need to go threatening me like some six-year-old extortionist asshole!" She turned and walked away, sulking as if wounded by her own verbal attack.

"And why is that?" I called after her.

Blanche turned around in the hallway with exaggerated effort. "Why is *what?*"

"Why would you like so much to see her again?"

Blanche thought for a moment, considering which answer might be most upsetting to me. When she seemed to have settled on the most suitable one, she sauntered back into my bedroom, leaned uncomfortably close to my face, and whispered, "So I can molest her and make her my sex slave." Then, she flickered her tongue like a serpent just to make sure I'd gotten the point.

My sister was probably the only fifteen-year-old in Scottsboro with a tongue ring. She'd gotten it done behind my parents' backs using a fake ID that said she was eighteen. When they found out, she threatened to develop a drug problem and become like "the rest of the kids" she knew if they didn't let her keep it. I don't think they believed that for more than a millisecond, if even that long. Blanche simply seemed too autonomous to fall prey to any kind of dependency issues. Besides, who just suddenly announces they're going to *develop* a drug problem? Blanche, that was who. I think my parents just gave in because they were tired of hearing her bitch. Of course, Blanche was almost always bitching about something. But nothing was worse than the way she went on about needing that damn *Anarchy* tattoo. My parents refused to back down that time and had to call in Zayde Max for reinforcements. It only took him three minutes alone with Blanche to put an end to the two-week battle. I don't think anyone ever found out what he said to her. All I know is that from that day forward, my sister never mentioned the tattoo again, and I began to view Zayde Max with a different kind of respect, like he was our family's own little Yoda. The only difference being that in our *Star Wars,* Yoda spoke Yiddish and could scare the shit out of any teenage rebel smart-ass who tried to outwit her elders.

Although Blanche never said another word about the tattoo, she continued to torment my parents in a variety of other ways, most of which led to drama, none of which were significant, and all of which contributed to my general feeling of being largely unnoticed most of the time. Blanche thrived on my parents' negative attention, which left little attention behind for me. It's not that I ever felt unloved in the shadow of Blanche's antics, just boring. I never wanted to give my parents any more grief than they already had with my sister, so I learned to stay out of trouble, which made me a conformist dork in the eyes of Blanche and some kind of precious lollipop in the eyes of Emily.

"Stella is the sweetest, most perfect little piece of candy in the entire world," she told my mom one evening. She was staring at me from across the kitchen table, her face full of admiration, while my parents made dinner. "She never gets into an ounce of trouble, but she sticks around and waits for me, anyway, every Tuesday and Thursday while I serve my detentions."

I shot Emily a look of warning. Tuesdays and Thursdays were the two days a week that our school conducted detention, which basically consisted of all the "bad kids" sitting in the cafeteria for an hour and a half doing their homework. For nearly a year, I'd been telling my mother that Emily and I stayed after school on those days to study in the library, which is what I always did while I waited for her. Afterward, we'd take the late bus to my house and Emily would eat dinner with us. I think my mom prided herself on providing Emily with homecooked meals. She seemed to think that before coming into our lives, the poor girl hadn't eaten since she was three. But I liked the maternal instinct she had toward Emily. It was the same one I had. I just hoped she wouldn't use it as a license to lecture her now that my best friend had just revealed herself as one of the bad seeds of Willowood Junior High.

"Detention, huh?" my mother asked Emily, raising one eyebrow my way so I'd know I'd been caught in a lie. Behind her, I watched my father chuckle. It didn't take much to amuse him. He was one of those guys who simply got a kick out of life.

"It's never my fault, Janey," Emily said, looking up at my mother with her big, innocent blue eyes.

"I'm sure it isn't," my mom agreed, winking at her playfully. Just then, Blanche walked into the kitchen wearing a Sex Pistols T-shirt with a long-sleeved thermal underneath. Lately, she seemed to have something against showing too much skin, as if exposing one's forearms was just *way* too "establishment." Her hair was especially tall and her aura reeked of antisuburban belligerence until she spotted Emily at the table and visibly softened up. "It's never Blanche's fault, either," my mother said, smiling affectionately at what the cat had just dragged in and then back at Emily, as if *they* were her two daughters and not me. She'd never even commented on my being the most perfect piece of candy. Maybe there *was* something to this rebellion thing.

"Hello, sunshine," I said to annoy my sister, who, because of her rough exterior, despised being compared to anything positive, bright or even remotely associated with happiness.

"Fuck off!" Blanche retaliated, heading over to Emily.

"Daddy's little angel," my father teased, though his jabs were always more loving than irksome.

"Vivien Leigh would be so proud," my mother added, sighing and looking up to the ceiling, as if to God. She was referring, of course, to the actress who played "Blanche" in *A Streetcar Named Desire,* the character for whom my sister was named. My mom said this almost every time her firstborn cursed, burped, spit, shouted, or swore she was going to go out and become something my parents would regret, be it a drug addict, pregnant prostitute or the world's first anarchistic republican.

I watched as Blanche kissed Emily on the cheek. "How are you, sweetheart?" she asked, using a tone reserved exclusively for my best friend. Sometimes I wondered if she did it just to upset me, but Blanche really wasn't that malicious. She just truly didn't like people. That's where all the hostility came from. Well, maybe not all of it. Looking back now, after all that's happened, I don't know that Blanche was ever really *angry* at all. But even when I thought she was Pennsylvania's largest homegrown bitch, I never took her for calculating or malicious. Blanche was never cruel. It simply boiled down to what I said before, the fact that Blanche just didn't much care for people in general. Which is why she wouldn't have been able to stomach being nice to anyone unless it was for real. That's how I knew she really did like Emily. But then again, what wasn't to like? I just couldn't quite figure out why Emily liked her back.

"I'm okay," Emily said, tapping her finger lightly on one of my sister's spikes. It didn't move. "We were just discussing detention."

"Did *you* get a detention?" Blanche asked me, her eyes lighting up as if Sid Vicious had just resurrected in the middle of our kitchen and asked her to dance. I shook my head, embarrassed to admit how boring I was.

"Stella never has detention," Emily said, smiling at me proudly. "She's my hero."

"Yeah, Supernerd," Blanche said, sliding into the chair next to me and bumping my shoulder as she tried on the role of Playful Big Sister. Although, "big" wasn't exactly the right terminology, considering that she weighed about fifteen pounds less than me and was two inches shorter. Next to Blanche and Emily, I felt like the marshmallow man.

"I think nerds are sexy," Emily said, reaching out to grab my hand. Although it was hard to deny that my greatest fan on earth was essentially calling me a nerd, I couldn't help but laugh, anyway. And although joining in more or less meant she was "conforming" to the conformist dork on her right, Blanche couldn't help but laugh, either.

Emily had a way of doing that—of bridging the gap that had been growing between my sister and me ever since she dumped our childhood traditions for solitude and angst. We had once been close, doing all of those things that sisters do when they can still claim camaraderie but are too young to appreciate the meaning of the word. The kinds of things they're too embarrassed to even let their best friends know they do because they should have outgrown them years before. The kinds of things a girl can only do with someone who shares her bloodline, someone whose experience of the world—in sight, smell, taste and sound—has been almost identical to hers since birth. Things like acting out scenes from TV sitcoms with our Barbie dolls up until I was eleven and Blanche was thirteen. That was back when our arguments were based solely upon who got to be Blair when it came time to recreate that week's episode of *The Facts of Life*. Once Blanche started spiking her hair and becoming a tough girl, it wasn't so much the fact that she'd ever played with Barbie dolls that confounded me, but that she'd thrown such hissy fits over wanting to be *Blair.* But by then, I'd denounced girlhood games as babyish, too. Though I do admit, there was a huge part of me that knew—without even having to be prodded—how much I longed to play Barbies with my sister just one more time.

My mom gave all of that stuff to our little cousin not long after my fourteenth birthday, and I cried every morning in the shower for a week. When Emily asked why my eyes were puffy, I actually broke down and told her the truth. She hugged me but didn't say a word, although, from then on, the three of us began spending a considerable amount of time together. Apparently, upon hearing that my sister and I had not always been rivals, my best friend saw an opportunity to fix something she never even knew had been broken.

Spending more time with Blanche wasn't too difficult to manage because she was already so incredibly fond of Emily. And after a while, I started to feel like maybe, just maybe, my older sister was also becoming just a little bit fond of me. It was a different level of interaction than I was used to—we were both teenagers now—and while I knew we'd never be able to recapture our childhood closeness, Blanche was no longer the angry stranger she'd been for close to two years, either, and she seemed to respect me on a whole new plane. She would never think I was cool like Emily, but she *had* begun to like me again. While for so long, she'd chastised me for being one of the masses, she was beginning to show a certain admiration for the fact that I was a good kid. A good kid who got good grades and had good values. I just wasn't all that interesting. But this I knew. Blanche and Emily were both artsy types and I wasn't. And Blanche managed to be this way while blowing me into the shallow end of the academic pool. I still did well, but Blanche excelled, making straight A's in practically everything without even having to try. I couldn't complain, though. I may have felt bland in comparison to the company I kept, but at least I had my sister back.

I was no longer jealous of Emily and Blanche's relationship, either. That all changed once the three of us started spending so much time together. Pretty soon, it would just be Blanche and me alone in my room at night, without the glue, and I'd realize that what I'd really been jealous of all that time she'd been doting on Emily was that she hadn't been doting on me. I'd always thought I'd been afraid of losing my best friend to my much cooler big sister, with whom she seemed to have so much more in common. It wasn't until we'd been reconnected that I realized that all along, I'd been afraid of losing Blanche. But by the time winter break rolled around during Emily's and my final year at Willowood, all that insecurity seemed a genuine artifact and I wasn't afraid of losing anyone.

We'd settled rather comfortably into the Three Musketeers pattern we'd established, a pattern that thrived on the notion that good fortune to one meant good fortune to all. Such was the case when Blanche got her driver's license. She'd been sixteen for quite a while and would, in fact, be turning seventeen just a little over one week later, but had taken her time getting her license because, to put it frankly, she'd been lazy. I think it was her blossoming friendship with Emily and me, and the knowledge that it would still be another year before either of us could drive anywhere—another year of wandering aimlessly by foot amid our suburban seclusion—that finally gave her the incentive to get her ass behind the wheel. My parents said she could have my mother's car every Friday night. On the Tuesday before our first Friday night out, I turned fifteen. Blanche turned seventeen that Sunday. Winter break came just twelve days later. Our parents let us take the car to South Street to celebrate our first of ten school-less nights. It started out as the best night of my life.

I was surprised when Blanche didn't make us listen to the Sex Pistols or the Dead Kennedys on the ride downtown. Instead, she kept the radio tuned to Mix 91.3 FM and actually *sang along* to songs that will always remind me of that night. Roxette's "Joyride." "You're in Love" by Wilson Phillips. "Unbelievable" by EMF. At one point, I could swear I even spotted her moving her shoulders to C and C Music Factory. It made me wonder if in her private moments, she ever just whipped out her old Lisa Lisa and Cult Jam tapes and went nuts.

We spent our time breezing in and out of stores, stuffing our faces and freezing our asses off. Despite the cold, I couldn't have asked for a better night. I look back on that trip to South Street as the swan song of simplicity, of innocence, and of taking things for granted because you'd never once considered that one day, you wouldn't have the chance.

Emily was going to stay the night at our house, and as usual, we decided to sleep in Blanche's room because it was bigger. I think we were still on an adrenaline high from South Street and I don't remember whose idea it was—for all I know, it could have been mine—but we decided to play a game of truth, the type designed to expose each other's darkest hidden secrets. Of course, I didn't really think that any of us had any of those, but we decided to play, anyway, for the hell of it. The rule was that you could either come right out and reveal something juicy about yourself or wait to be asked a specific question.

I was put on the spot first and, within the course of five ridiculous minutes, had voluntarily unburdened my soul about weighing 132 pounds (a hefty and daring admission considering Blanche weighed 113 and Emily only 97). I also confessed to pulling on my boobs in the shower in hopes of stimulating some kind of growth spurt that would finally make me an hourglass. I felt like a complete jackass by the time my turn was over.

Emily's confessions were a little more scandalous. She came right out and confessed to a same-sex crush—on *me,* though she was speaking past tense.

"Back in seventh grade, long before we ever talked about Mrs. Wilder's thighs, I just remember looking at you and thinking, 'There she is.'"

"Miss America?" Blanche teased.

"No," Emily said, staring at me. "My bella donna."

"Your bella *who?*" Blanche asked.

"Donna," Emily said. "Woman." She smiled at me. "My beautiful woman."

"Oh, I get it," Blanche said. "Like the Stevie Nicks album."

"Otherwise known as the greatest solo debut in the history of the world," I said, quoting Emily, who winked at me proudly. I returned the gesture, adding, "And for what it's worth, moon sister, you can be my bella donna, too."

"Oh, great," Blanche said. "Now I have to go throw up."

Blanche. She had the tough act down to an art form, though until that night we'd never had any reason to suspect it was an act. I think we purposely saved her turn for last. Probably because she was older than we were and we actually had a specific question in mind. With hindsight being twenty-twenty, this is the part of the night I always wish I could go back and change. But asking a different question or ending the game probably wouldn't have made a difference in the long run. I'd have only been putting a Band-Aid on a wound that was larger than any of us. A wound we knew nothing about when we asked. We were only having fun, playing a game. Emily was actually the one to raise the question, but only because she was bolder. It was something we both wanted to know. After all, Blanche was seventeen. It was only logical that we'd be curious.

"How far have *I* gotten?" Blanche said, reiterating the question.

I imagined it couldn't have been very far, farther than Emily or I had, of course, and far enough to make a good story, but Blanche had never even had a boyfriend. Still, she had this charge in her eyes I had never seen before. It wasn't the same kind of gleam she got from pissing off my parents. This charge was frightening. I'm sure that looking back and knowing how things turned out, I've brought my own associations to that look—the longest look in the history of my life—which seemed to be telling me something even then. I just didn't know what it was. All I knew was that the look in Blanche's eyes made my heart beat a little faster, and I worried I might hear something I wasn't ready to know about the girl I'd grown up playing Barbie dolls with. But it was too late. She was going to relive the nightmare, and Emily and I were going along for the ride. She spoke softly at first.

"Remember how Keith Shay had that party at the end of the summer?"

Emily and I nodded.

Keith Shay was Blanche's attainable equivalent of Sid Vicious—a rare gem among mortals, an even scarcer find in suburbia. She'd had a giant crush on him her entire sophomore year at Summit Valley. Most of his friends were from the city, and Blanche always claimed to feel in her element when she was around them. For an entire year, it seemed all she ever talked about was what a saving grace Keith had been for her at Summit Valley and how without him there to keep her sane, she probably would have dropped out already. After his party that past summer, she'd never mentioned him again. I had a feeling we were about to find out why.

"Well, Nora Mills and I were the only girls there," she continued. Her eyes had become tranquil, and her voice hinted quietly at liberation. She seemed, in some strange way, to be relieved, as if this were a secret she'd been waiting for just the right opportunity to tell. "The guys were all smoking pot in the basement, except for Keith. And so it was just the three of us up in the living room. And Keith starts talking all sexy to her, like right in front of me, so I just kind of sit there, waiting for him to say he's kidding or whatever, or to maybe turn around and somehow transfer the attention on to me, but he doesn't. So, I get up and go over to his parents' bar and do a shot of whiskey."

"But, Blanche, you don't drink," I said.

My sister just looked at me with a sad but sort of condescending smile. She was like one of those stickers whose surfaces change in the light. She'd never seemed older. And at the same time, never younger. In a haunting way, her confessional gaze was like that of a middle-aged woman revealing a long-hidden addiction. And in another sense, she seemed like a little girl who'd never needed more protection. I'd always thought Blanche was smart enough to make the right decisions, tough enough to fight peer pressure. I guess I was just a little girl, too. I was embarrassed for having been so naive. I shouldn't have said anything at all.

"So what happened next?" Emily asked.

"Well, after I did the shot, I turned around, and Nora and Keith were kissing." Emily and I expressed our condolences in groans. "I know. It was awful, absolutely the last thing I wanted to see. So, I just turned around and did another shot." My stomach tightened. I'd never thought of myself as a goody-goody, but Blanche was my sister and I was keeping tabs on her consumption. I didn't know much about drinking then, but I imagined that two shots of whiskey were enough to have an effect on a 113-pound girl. "When I finished that one," she continued, "this guy, Aaron, came up from the basement to see if Keith had an extra lighter, and that tore him and Nora apart. He went downstairs with Aaron for a minute, and while they were down there, I did another shot so I wouldn't have to deal with talking to Nora, since, as you can imagine, I was pretty pissed off."

"Well, did Nora know that you liked Keith?" Emily asked.

"I never *told* her, but she would've been a complete moron not to have known. Everyone knew Keith and I had something going on. I mean, we'd never kissed or anything, but everyone at school just assumed we were boyfriend and girlfriend. We were building toward that, or so I thought."

"Yeah, but Nora doesn't go to school with you guys," I said. "She's from Philly, right?"

"Well, right," Blanche conceded. "But you didn't have to go to school with us to know what we were all about, Stella. I was just using that as an example."

"Sorry," I said.

"So, then what happened?" Emily asked.

"Well, Keith comes back upstairs with this guy, Orlando, whom I'd only just met that night. But he was pretty cute, so I figured that flirting with him would be a really good way to see if I could make Keith jealous or not."

"How'd you do it?" Emily wanted to know.

Blanche shrugged her shoulders. "Seducing guys is easy."

I couldn't believe this was my sister talking, the same sister who'd once told me she'd sooner lick a dog's butt than kiss a boy. Granted, she was eight at the time, but that was only nine years ago. She sure had changed a lot—in ways I hadn't even bothered to notice. Maybe Blanche had gone a whole lot farther than I thought.

"Did you guys kiss?" I asked tentatively.

"Kiss? We did a lot more than that," she said. But upon realizing she'd just left us dangling there, like a couple of petrified fish, she threw us back into the water and explained. "All right, see, at first, we *were* just kissing a little bit on the couch. But I could hear Keith and Nora totally making out on the love seat, so that only made me want to do more with Orlando—you know, to get back at Keith. So, I decided to lie down, and I pulled him on top of me." She paused for a second. "I think that's when he took off his shirt."

"He took off his shirt?" I asked. "Right there in front of Nora and Keith?"

"Believe me, I don't think they noticed," she said dryly. "Pretty soon, he had my shirt off, too, and he was kind of, like, feeling me, you know?" Blanche looked down at her lap. "Down there."

"Over or under your underwear?" Emily asked. I *never* would've thought to ask that. "Down there" seemed racy enough for me without getting into the technicality of it all.

"My underwear was kind of down around my thighs,"

Blanche said, her plush burgundy carpet muffling the crash of my jaw as it dropped to the floor.

"And your bra?" Emily asked.

"Unhooked, but still covering me. Anyway, Orlando starts kissing down my stomach trying to, you know..."

"Go down on you," Emily supplied.

"Right. But I totally didn't feel comfortable with that." I wondered why. She seemed to have felt comfortable with everything else. "I mean, maybe if we'd been alone, it would've been different, but not with Keith and Nora right there. We didn't even have a blanket or anything to cover ourselves with. So, I kept telling him no and trying to lift him back up toward my face, but somehow, he ended up down there, anyway."

"He forced you?" Emily asked.

"No," Blanche said firmly, and then she just stared at Emily, like perhaps she was offended by the question. But just when it was beginning to grow a little too weird in the room, she broke into a reminiscent smile, letting her head fall back a little. "It felt *amazing,*" she said. "He didn't force me at all. I mean, he pushed a little bit, but once he was doing it, I didn't want him to stop—*ever.*" Emily giggled, but I failed to see the humor in my sister's post oral sex euphoria.

"So then what happened?" I asked, wanting Blanche to get on with it. I had a pretty strong feeling we hadn't even tipped the iceberg yet and didn't appreciate the way she was dragging things out.

Blanche looked down at her hands. I hadn't realized it, but she'd clasped them tightly together, something she only did in doctors' and dentists' office waiting rooms. She was nervous. I made a conscious decision right then and there to ban all further expressions of shock from my face and, if nothing else, to stop judging her.

"Well, I had my eyes closed," Blanche resumed quietly, lifting her gaze to meet ours. She looked tired. "And while Orlando was still down there, I felt someone kissing me. It was Keith." My stomach dropped, but I smiled lightly to show my support. I suddenly knew where this was going—and I hated it. "So, I'm, like, still really into what's going on down there, and I'm so glad my plan worked—you know, that I'd managed to make Keith jealous by pairing off with Orlando. But then, I think it was after Keith took off my bra..." I swallowed hard, disturbingly aware of the buttered popcorn we'd been eating. I feared it was starting to come up.

"Yeah, it was definitely when he took off my bra because I remember him whispering in my ear—something about great tits." Blanche turned to me suddenly. "Well, I *do,* Stella!" I guess that somehow, without intention, I had let judgment or shock slip back onto my face, which my sister had read as my not believing in the beauty of her breasts (something I had never actually given any thought to).

"I didn't say you didn't!"

"Just wait for sweet sixteen, my dear," Blanche said omnisciently, looking a little too serious afterward, as if she knew it was the last bit of sisterly wisdom she would ever share with me. "Anyway," she continued, turning to include Emily, "it was after he took off my bra that I asked him where Nora was and he said she went upstairs to lie down because she wasn't feeling well. And then, somehow, all three of us ended up on the floor."

"You, Keith and Orlando?" Emily asked.

"Yeah," Blanche said, kind of losing volume for a second. I could swear I saw the whole left side of her face twitch when she answered, like some sort of terrible tic. I've never discussed it with Emily. "We were all just, like, kissing each other and stuff."

"Even Keith and Orlando?" Emily asked.

"I don't think so," Blanche said, "because I was in the middle. I think they were just doing stuff to me."

"What kind of stuff?" I asked, not really sure that I wanted to know.

"Everything," my sister said, raising her eyebrows and smiling unsurely, almost as if her answer were a question.

"You had *sex* with them?" I asked.

"Well, that's everything, Stella," Emily said, rescuing Blanche from having to say yes. But there was more. A lot more. And we were about to find that out. "Go ahead," she said to my sister. "We're listening."

"Keith was my first," Blanche said, almost proudly and a little defensively, too, as if she didn't want us thinking she'd lost her virginity in some kind of suburban-legend orgy since, technically, the actual moment of loss had occurred with the guy she'd thought was the love of her life. "But after Keith, well, Orlando just kind of climbed up on top of me, and Keith whispered, 'It's okay' in my ear." *It's okay?* Who the hell was he to make that judgment call? Especially when he knew how much my sister trusted him? "I heard people making noise in the background while Orlando and I were doing it," she continued, "so I figured the guys had started coming up from the basement."

"You mean, people were watching you?" I asked.

Blanche nodded and it looked like her eyes were filling up with tears. But the tears never fell. "I wanted to get up," she said, sounding meek, and looking, as she sat there, almost nothing like the rebellious sister I had once known. "But Orlando said not to worry, that nobody was watching. When he finished, I sat up to find my clothes, and Nate Sparks was suddenly standing over me, dangling my shirt over my head. He said he'd only give it to me if I gave him a kiss, so I figured, why not?"

Suddenly, in my head, I flashed back to *Pretty Woman* and raw sugar cookie dough. That's what Emily and I were doing the night of Keith Shay's end-of-summer party—wishing we were Julia Roberts and risking salmonella because we were too lazy to bake, all while Blanche squirmed around naked on some punk prick's living room carpet bargaining for the rights to her own clothes with sexual favors. I had a sickening feeling she had slept with Nate Sparks, too. I guess Emily had the same feeling.

"Did you guys do anything else besides kiss?" she asked Blanche.

Blanche shrugged her shoulders. "It just seemed to happen." She wasn't being defensive anymore. Not defensive and not ashamed. She just seemed tired, very very tired.

"Where was Keith while all of this was going on?" I asked.

"He was just standing there, doing shots and watching," Blanche said, as if she didn't feel a thing. She looked past us as she continued. "The rest of the guys had come up from the basement. I guess they'd heard what was going on upstairs. After Nate, there was Tommy, then Jake—no J.T.—*then* Jake. Jake was last."

Jake was last. Those words seemed to echo through the room for a long time. No one said anything for about three minutes, and the digits passed slowly on the clock, like broken feet struggling through quicksand, until Emily finally ended what I have come to call the eternal silence. It was only three minutes, but it felt like three-hundred-thousand years.

"How did it end?" she asked as the clock struck 3:01.

Blanche took her eyes off of the wall behind us, meeting our gaze directly for the first time since revealing that in one night, she'd slept with six different guys. She seemed genuinely confused by the question.

"How did what end?" she asked.

"The night," Emily reminded her gently.

"Blanche?" I asked, putting my hand on her shoulder. It felt exceptionally small. "Are you okay?"

My sister looked at me with an almost offended sense of bewilderment. "It was only *sex*, Stella."

"It sounds like gang rape to me," Emily said.

Blanche dismissed her with a laugh. "What are the sex-ed teachers at Willowood filling your heads with these days?"

"Blanche..." Emily began.

"Emily, look, you wanna know how the night ended? I'll tell you how it ended. It ended with me in a lot of pain with a lot of blood, cleaning myself up in the bathroom so I could pretend like nothing happened when our dad came to pick me up at midnight. I felt like shit. I came home. I threw up four times. I cried. And I went to sleep. I created a bad reputation for myself that was totally true, and Keith and I haven't spoken since. But it wasn't rape."

"But..."

"But, nothing," Blanche said matter-of-factly. She wasn't raising her voice and she wasn't angry. She no longer even seemed offended. In fact, she seemed more clearheaded than ever. "Look, I was there, Em. You weren't. I'm not a victim—I'm a slut. There's a difference. I *decided* to sleep with those guys. They didn't force me."

"You're not a slut," Emily told her. "Don't say that about yourself—ever. All right?"

"As long as you both promise not to think of me as a victim," Blanche said. "Okay? Please?"

Blanche's eyes were huge and pleading, and I honestly believed in my purest and most naive heart of hearts that if we could both just give her this one thing, besides our love, this one acknowledgment that she was not a victim, then everything would be all right. Maybe it could almost erase what had happened, even. I had so much to learn about life. But I'd still trade all the wisdom in the world for one more day of youthful ignorance, for just one more thought like that.

"Okay," I said, leaning over her in a rush of wide open arms and hugging her as tightly as I could.

"Thank you, Stella," she whispered, rubbing my head in a maternal way that felt completely foreign, but incredibly safe. Emily joined in a few seconds later. It should have lasted forever, but after less than a minute, we were all facing each other again.

"I just don't want anyone to think they can take advantage of you," Emily said to Blanche. There was apology in her tone as she made her position clear: her judgment was of *them*, not my sister.

"I know," Blanche said, rubbing Emily's arm as she stood up. I watched her stare at the bowl of popcorn on the floor. "Do you guys wanna go make some more of this? I'm sure that bowl's cold by now." She started walking toward the door.

"Yeah, okay," I said. "Where are you going?"

"I'm about to piss myself," Blanche said. "But I didn't want to interrupt my own story for a bathroom break. Now, don't you fuckers talk about me while I'm gone."

Emily and I smiled at each other, and I think we both felt the same sense of relief—that Blanche was back to her old self. But then there was that pause in the hallway. I'll always remember the way she stood there. It may have only been for two seconds, but in my mind, it's grown to hold eternal significance. And so has the way she turned around and came back into the doorway, the words she said next.

"I may not say it enough. But I really do appreciate you guys."

"We love you, too," Emily said.

"Do something for me, then? Always and no matter what happens, keep what I just said in here between the three of us. Don't ever tell anyone, okay? Promise?"

"Always and no matter what," I vowed. "Go pee."

Always and no matter what. Blanche said that all the time, ever since she was a little girl. In her eyes, the phrase made a promise a promise; the truth, the truth. It solidified that forever meant forever. Attaching it to a statement was like a hand on the Holy Bible for some, a wish upon a shooting star for others, and I could see the relief on her face when I echoed it back to her. I have since framed that look in my mind, that look of overwhelming relief before she slipped back out into the hallway. Of course, I didn't know at the time that that look would become one of my most precious memories. I had no idea when I saw the relief wash over her face that it was the last time I would ever see my sister alive.

Emily and I were in the kitchen making popcorn when we heard my mother scream. Most of what happened after that is a blur. I remember running upstairs, fighting to get past my mom while my dad stayed with Blanche in their bathroom. She had done it in their bathroom, and I wasn't allowed in to see her. It wouldn't do anyone any good if I saw her. The ambulance was on its way.

Blanche died in that ambulance, holding my mother's hand. But Emily and I were in the car with my father, listening to him talk about razors and blame. It was his blade, after all. His blade that had made all that blood.

We found my mom waiting by the emergency room doors. Her face was red and streaky and she couldn't stop wringing her hands. "They..." she began shakily. "They couldn't save her!"

Emily threw her arms around my mother, but I didn't understand. Not once during that whole crazy ride with my father had I ever accepted the possibility that Blanche would die. They were supposed to bandage her up and send her home. She wasn't supposed to *die.*

"But she told us to make popcorn," I said. "When she came out of the bathroom, we were supposed to..."

My mother pulled me close. She and Emily got pretty hysterical for a while, but I felt numb. I couldn't stop wondering about really stupid things, like if my sister had peed or not before she did it. She'd said she had to pee. Was that just an excuse to leave us? Or was that the last thing she did before she died? And where had my father gone?

"It'll be a closed casket ceremony," my mother said, clearing her throat. "The doctor said it's all right if you want to see her one last..." She couldn't say it. "You can probably go in and see her in a few minutes."

It just didn't make any sense. This was still the same night we drove downtown, singing songs about joyriding and being in love. Dawn had yet to break, but in that single stretch of darkness, death had stolen away with my sister. It was time to say goodbye now—forever.

Emily and I faced our final look at Blanche together. How long is appropriate for something like that—a *final* look? How do you say goodbye to someone who can't say it back? We stood there for a while just staring, and then I did something awful. I started shaking her. I just went over to the bed and started shaking the body. It didn't make any sense—nothing did. Emily seemed to think Blanche wasn't even dead.

"Stop it!" she begged. "You're hurting her!"

I let go of my sister and backed away. "Not more than she hurt me."

We were about to leave when it actually hit me: never again.

The three of us would never be together again. I looked at Emily. "So much for the Three Musketeers." She hugged me as tight as she could for as weak as she was, and then we left, closing the door on a world that had ended way too quickly—in less time than it takes to make popcorn. And then there were two.

I felt completely exhausted when I got out into the hallway. I didn't think I had any emotion left in me until I saw my dad. One of the nurses in Maternity had seen him breaking down in front of the babies in the nursery window. They had to bring him back down to Emergency in a wheelchair. The whole thing was being explained to my mother as he cried like some kind of wounded animal in her arms. I had never seen anyone cry like that. I guess I'd never really seen a man break before. Not in real life. Not my father. It scared the hell out of me. And that's the last thing I remember about the night my sister erased herself from our lives.

There were a lot of teachers from Willowood at her funeral, and I guess from Summit Valley, too, but I was too young to recognize any of them. Although a bit of a discipline problem when she was trying to be, Blanche had been an excellent student and had managed to stick out in many minds. There weren't many people her own age there that I noticed. My sister never did have many friends. Keith Shay was there, though. He came with his parents, looking like he'd been shot. But I didn't hate him anymore. Between all the love and sadness, my heart just didn't have the room.

My mom was fixated on the epitaph, *In Loving Memory of Blanche Elizabeth Gold, Who Always Depended on the Kindness of Strangers,* taken, of course, from Vivien Leigh's famous line at the end of *A Streetcar Named Desire.* The idea made my stomach turn. Emily's, too, but she wanted to help keep the peace.

"Stella," she said to me a few days after the funeral, "if it will make your mom happy, let her have her *Streetcar* now."

"But life is not a Tennessee Williams movie!" I wasn't angry at Emily. I was mad at my mother. She was making Blanche's epitaph about her, and it should've been about Blanche.

"I know, but, Stella, your mom tends to wish it was. She named her daughters Blanche and Stella, for God's sake. Don't take it away from her now. Your dad has checked out in a really bad way. You're all she has. Don't drive a dagger between you over something so small."

"Small!" I shouted. I was starting to tear at my hair. "These are the words that will preside over my sister's body for the rest of forever! That's not small!"

"I *know,* but...look, I just don't want you to screw things up with your mother over this." Her voice had begun to waver and that's when it hit me—the wording on an epitaph *was* small compared to losing a loved one. Emily seemed to think things would never be the same between us if I didn't let my mom grieve the way she needed to. She seemed to think all mothers could slip away as easily as hers did in that 1979 fire in Chicago.

"Fine," I said, smiling gently, "you win." And then—overcome by some unexplainable force that must be unique to the grieving—I started to laugh. Maniacally. "But, seriously, the kindness of strangers? Come on!"

"Stella."

"Stella," I mocked, my sides hurting from the way I'd thrown myself into the laughing fit, almost as if it were a tantrum. "You know it's true." I tried on a horribly clichéd southern accent. "I've always depended on the kindness of strangers." I laughed so hard this time, I snorted, throwing my head forward until I nearly collapsed.

"Stella!" Emily seized control of my shoulders.

When I looked back up at her, the tears were streaming down my face. I kept trying to laugh, but it wasn't working anymore. My voice was shrill, and it pained my throat to speak. So instead, I yelled. "She hated everybody! Blanche hated everybody! She even hated me until you fucking came along! The kindness of strangers? She'll roll over in her grave and slit her wrists all over again! If she believed so much in the kindness of strangers, then why did she—"

"Stella, your mom!" Emily finally blurted, spinning me

around to face my mother, who stood, white as a ghost, in my bedroom doorway.

"I'm heating up the casserole Ellen dropped off," she said, staring at me blankly. "It'll be ready for you girls in ten minutes." She needed the support of the banister to hold herself up as she made her way back down the stairs.

I suppose it was that question I had begun to ask Emily in my room—that question of "why"—that threatened to haunt all of us forever. Why did my sister kill herself? Yes, Emily and I had heard part of the story. But one highly regrettable night at Keith Shay's couldn't have been the only thing that was wrong in her life. There had to be more—a part of the story we didn't know—and when my mother was going through Blanche's things a couple of weeks after the funeral she found it: a diary full of self-loathing entries dating back to a year before my sister had even met Keith.

If only she'd asked for help, given us a clue before that night. Sure, there'd been clues that she was unhappy, but all teenagers are unhappy; at least the "deep" ones are. And that whole rebellion thing—we'd thought it was just part of her image. Her loud, anti-establishment, suburbia-sucks, punk-rock, typical teen-angst image. If only she'd just come to me *once* with even a *hint* that something was truly wrong, a real hint, something I could've recognized as out of the ordinary, I would have done anything to save her. But instead of asking for help, she medicated on her own—with alcohol, pills and self-mutilation. She drank whenever she could and had gotten her hands on drugs I hadn't even heard of, mostly prescription. But her biggest comfort had been in cutting. She said the release she felt from that was better than any drug, that by inflicting bodily pain, she could somehow escape the pain of living. It didn't make sense to me. The only thing that became clear was why she'd spent so much time covering her arms.

My sister meant to slit her wrists. That we are sure of. My mother wanted to believe that it was an accident at first, but it was hard to ignore that line in Blanche's diary about cutting: "It gives me such a sense of control." She knew where to cut and where not to cut. But she couldn't always be in control. She certainly wasn't the one calling the shots at Keith Shay's party. I think that, in many ways, that was the final straw for her. But by suppressing it—by not telling a soul—she was able to hold on a little longer. The night she finally told us her secret was the night she relinquished control and finally said enough to more than two years of silent suffering.

I don't know why my sister hated herself. I don't know why she was sad. Diaries aren't meant to be understood by outsiders—people struggling to make sense out of a life cut short when it's already too late to do anything. We'll never understand exactly why she did it. The only thing we'll ever understand is loss.

None of the sex stuff was mentioned in the diary. Blanche was probably too ashamed to put it in writing. When my mom asked what we were talking about the night she took her life, Emily and I just said, "the usual"—boys, music, *90210.* I didn't think my parents ever needed to know about Blanche's night with Keith, Orlando, Nate Sparks, and everybody else. As far as I was concerned, that story could fade into the chronicles of suburban legends of the early nineties and no one over eighteen would be the wiser before it had been buried by some other scandal. There are just some things parents should never have to hear about their kids. Besides, we'd promised Blanche we'd never tell. She'd gone to her death feeling relieved because of it. And honoring that last wish, that last look, somehow made me feel more connected to her.

As for the epitaph issue, I felt like a horrible monster after my mom witnessed me ripping her idea to shreds, but I never actually discussed it with her. In Judaism, we consecrate the headstone one year after a burial during a special unveiling ceremony. At this time, the cloth covering the headstone is removed for all the mourners to see. I was squeezing Emily's hand so hard the day of Blanche's unveiling, I thought I might break it, but she didn't seem to mind. She was probably thinking the same thing I was, wondering if my mother had actually gone through with the *Streetcar* inscription or come to her senses. But once the cloth was lifted, we knew we could exhale. *In Loving Memory of Blanche Elizabeth Gold (1974-1991)*, read the engraving, *Forever in Our Hearts—Always and No Matter What*.

I actually felt myself smiling when I saw it, sadly, ironically, and with tears, as I realized that even Blanche's last words to Emily and me had contained that favored phrase, the one thing about my sister that hadn't changed when she'd traded Barbie and Blair for Sex Pistols and spikes. My mom had decided to forgo *Streetcar*'s Blanche Dubois for an everlasting tribute to the real Blanche in her life, in all of our lives, and I loved her for it. If she had decided to go with Vivien Leigh, I'd have accepted it. I'd have even understood. And I definitely would have forgiven her. But *always and no matter what* suited our Blanche much better. My sister would have definitely approved.

When it was all over, I made my way through the gathering of relatives to my mother.

"Good job, Janey," I said, hugging her proudly. Despite our surroundings, it was the first time in a long time that things actually felt close to normal.

"Thank you," she said, looking around. "Stella, where's your father?" Well, so much for normal. But then again, over the past year, my father's bizarre behavior had become our "new normal."

Emily and I went searching for him and found him sitting cross-legged by my Grandpop Eddie's grave, talking out loud. I told him my mother was looking for him and that it was time to leave.

"Can't she see I'm talking to my dad?" he barked, as if it were a highly logical question.

I wasn't sure how to respond, so I said nothing at all. Instead, I moved closer to Emily and instinctively reached for her hand.

If someone had taken our picture right at that very moment, it could've been captioned with Blanche's immortal phrase, because that was the day I realized that, regardless of what was going on around me, I would always have Emily, and that, together as a team, we were unbreakable. The two of us. Always.

No matter what. And I felt that way for the next twelve years. Up until I got that frantic phone call from London that threatened to shatter everything.

Emmie

"Hello?"

"Em?"

"Oh, Stella! It's so good to hear your voice again. Are you calling from the airport?"

"Yeah. I was able to get a flight, but it's a lot of connecting and I don't even take off until two forty-five."

"Not till two forty-five? Can't you go home and wait?"

"At this point, I'd rather just stay here."

Emily sighed. "I feel like an asshole." I didn't say anything. "You could at least tell me I'm not."

"You're not an asshole, Emily. You're just…I don't know. We'll talk when I get there. You know I wouldn't be coming if—"

"I know. It's like I told you earlier—you never have let me down. I just wish…"

"What?"

"It's just that there are two sides to every story, and you never let me tell you why—"

"Drop it."

"But, Stella, can't I just—"

"How's Emmie? You never told me how they liked her."

Emily seemed to get the picture. "I couldn't have asked for a better night," she said proudly. "They did the nicest write-up in today's style section."

"That's terrific. I knew you had nothing to be nervous about."

"But, still, I always am. Anna's really excited you're flying out here, you know. I mean, she knows it's not exactly going to be all roses and sunshine, but—"

"You tell her I'm looking forward to seeing her, too."

I wasn't exactly sure if this was true or not. Anna Fontanella and I really had zilch in common except for Emily, the only link in our completely unparallel worlds. I wasn't exactly envious of her, despite the fact that she was gorgeous, rich, monumentally successful and my best friend's absolute idol. Okay, perhaps I was slightly envious. Who wouldn't be? But I still liked her. After all, she was the one who'd given Emily her start in the business.

Emily had followed Anna's career like a religion throughout college. And after four years at the Fashion Institute of Technology, she'd put her design degree on the shelf to clerk at one of Anna's swanky boutiques on the Upper East Side. She said it was more than just a "pay the bills" job because at Anna Fontanella (the name is the store) she could actually get up close and personal with the designs that had taken her idol from a young Italian woman with a dream and turned her into a legend within the industry. Emily said the environment inspired her, that being surrounded by Anna's creations was like being surrounded by fine art that you got paid by the hour to touch and smell and fantasize about filling your life with. She was obsessed. But it wasn't a bad thing because it gave her the drive to get ahead, even if it meant lying to unsuspecting event planners to get there.

Jenna Mazzarelli is the name of the charitable and faceless wonder who, to this day, can be credited with getting Emily to the right place at the proverbially right time. Perhaps it was only because Jenna wasn't a skeptic, or maybe she was just too busy. Either way, Jenna never checked into Emily's background, but instead believed that last-minute phone call from the "editor" of the hot, new online fashion magazine, *Fad,* who, for some mysterious and hurtful reason, had not received her press pass to Anna's upcoming show. Emily's name was added to the guest list, and Ms. Mazzarelli apologized for the oversight, citing that the Internet was a powerful arm of the journalistic community, blah, blah, blah. Emily didn't care. She was finally going to see her idol in person.

They locked eyes after the show when the then twenty-nine-year-old Anna was talking to reporters. Emily told herself to memorize the moment, for it could be as close to her personal hero as she'd ever get. But she had no idea what she was in for, not even when she saw Anna cross the room and begin her steady approach. She said that Emily had a great look and wanted to know who she was wearing.

"Emily Martin," my best friend replied, with the same poise and assurance an A-list celebrity would possess when crediting Armani or Chanel. Emily had always been that way. She figured if you could design clothes, then you were a designer, whether people had heard of you or not.

Anna looked down at Emily's name tag and back into her starstruck eyes. "You designed this outfit yourself?" Emily nodded, mesmerized by Anna's accent, her beauty, her being. "All right, little girl," the great one said. "How would you like to come work for me?"

"I *do* work for you," Emily said. "In your boutique—on the Upper East Side."

"Doing *what?*" Anna asked, looking practically appalled.

"Sales."

"No, no, no," Anna said. "It's wrong."

"Wrong?" Emily asked.

"You say you designed this outfit yourself?"

"Yes." Suddenly, a lightbulb went off in Emily's head and she began to understand where this was going. "I was a fashion design major at FIT. I graduated eight months ago."

"Do you have a portfolio?"

"Oh, absolutely." Emily patted the brown leather tote she was carrying and smiled. "I never leave home without it."

They ended up going back to Anna's place afterward for wine, cheese and a little old-fashioned ass-kissing. Emily told Anna how she had followed her amazing career ever since Anna came here from Italy armed with nothing more than a dream (and something like a million dollars left from the sale of her grandfather's vineyard, which Emily naturally found it distasteful to mention). Anna, in turn, told Emily that she reminded her a lot of herself not too long ago (with the exception, of course, of the unmentioned *denaro*) and that she would've loved to have had an Anna Fontanella to light *her* way when she was just starting out—someone who could've served as her mentor and saved her from those fears of NEVER MAKING IT IN THE BUSINESS.

In short, she was offering Emily a deal, the absolute chance of a lifetime, the opportunity to create her own line and see her designs on the runway. Anna's empire already included "Anna by Ashley" and "Anna by Zoe." As with the other lines, "Anna by Emily" would be sold in all of her American boutiques, and my friend would retain a percentage of all profits. In addition, there would be media appearances, which would help her gain exposure and recognition in the design world, a wonderful break for anyone wanting to make it and especially for someone so young. Emily agreed on the spot.

The collaboration worked beautifully, and three-and-a-half years later, Anna decided to cut her name from the line and just call it "Emily," awarding higher profits and more prestige to her protégé. It was a major high point in Emily's career, but she had one minor stipulation—that they call her line "Emmie" instead, as a tribute to Laura Nyro and her mom. Under its new name, the line continued to flourish, and a little over one year later, Emily packed her bags for Europe.

In Europe, she would help Anna establish her fourth boutique abroad. She would debut her line in places like Rome and Paris, make promotional appearances, learn about business and fashion and the media and how everything fit together in a variety of other cultures. A golden opportunity. Fast paced and exciting. A little nerve-racking, too. She'd been especially anxious for Emmie's London premiere which, according to today's style section, had gone extremely well. And now she was back in the belly of the beast. With all that gold, all that excitement, the nerves, the motion of everything, I never thought she'd have time for trouble. But trouble had found her and worked its way back to me. And here I was.

"Listen, Em," I said, "why don't you write down my flight information?"

"Let me grab a pen." As she rummaged around her hotel room for something to write with, she said, "I tried calling you at home a few hours ago, but you'd already left."

"You must have just missed me."

"Well, I left you a message in case you decided to check your voice mail from the airport. Anyway, I've got my pen ready, so go ahead." Once she had all the details written down, she said, "You know, it's crazy that it's still gonna be a whole day until we see each other."

"Well, multiple layovers will do that to you," I said. "Not to mention the time difference. Just be there waiting at 11:03 tomorrow morning when I land."

"Check."

"Oh, and Emily?"

"Yeah?"

"Be alone."

When we hung up, I realized I'd forgotten to ask her about getting a *yahrzeit* candle to light for Blanche. But I didn't feel like calling her back. Besides, I didn't expect Emily to know where to buy a *yahrzeit* candle here. How was she *possibly* supposed to know how to get one in a foreign country? It would simply have to be on the top of our list of things to do when I landed. But, we already had so much to work out when I arrived. And I still had plenty of time before my flight. I would just go buy the candle myself.

On my way out of the airport, I decided to call home and listen to Emily's message.

"I'm calling to remind you about Blanche's *yahrzeit,*" she said. "But if you forgot, don't worry. I have a candle here. We'll light it together."

Letting Go

My mother sounded upset. "Your flight doesn't take off until *two-forty-five?* Well, if you want, I can come sit with you—meet you for lunch." That was precisely what I *didn't* want.

"No. Don't do that…I mean, it wouldn't be a good idea because I have book reports to grade." *Liar.* "I promised the kids I'd return them when the break was over. But now that I'm gonna be gone the whole time…"

"And the last thing you want to be doing is grading papers in Europe!"

"Exactly." There. My trusting mother had fallen for my boldfaced lie. I *really* needed to get out of this conversation. "Okay, well listen, I'm gonna—"

"Oh, be sure to thank Emily for those blouses she sent me."

"Blouses?"

"Yeah, the ones from Italy. I'm sure she told you. I called and left a message at her hotel. But I really want to let her know how much I loved them."

"Were they for Hanukkah?"

"Yeah, you mean, she didn't tell you? That's odd. Emily hardly ever puts one foot in front of the other without consulting you first!"

That hardly seemed true anymore. *All I want to know is how the past six weeks went on behind my back,* I'd said to Emily that morning on the phone.

Stella, I didn't mean for it to—

"Stella?" My mother's voice pulled me back into the present. "Did you hear me? I said Emily hardly ever puts one foot in front of—"

"Yeah, yeah. I heard you," I said. "She's probably just had a lot on her mind."

"Oh, well. Just thank her for me, anyway, will you? Listen, honey, there's something I need to tell you—before you go away."

"What is it?"

"I wanted to tell you in person. It's not the kind of thing you tell someone over the phone. But I don't feel like I have a whole lot of choice, so I hope you'll forgive me. I don't want you to get back and find I've been keeping something from you just because I didn't get the chance to tell you like I planned."

"Janey, you're scaring me."

"Don't be scared, honey. It's not that kind of news. I mean, I'm not sick or anything. And nobody died."

"Well, what then? Tell me."

"I got a letter from your father yesterday."

Suddenly everything went quiet. And I didn't exist outside this bubble, this funnel that had seized control of my body, stripping me of my ability to feel anything but confusion. This couldn't be happening.

"You mean he's still alive?"

"Of *course* he's still alive!"

Nausea was taking over and I had started to sweat. My father's resurrection was real.

"Stella? Are you okay? Don't you want to know what the letter said?"

"I have to go."

It barely qualified as a whisper, but it got me off the phone—the same way I got myself into the bathroom, because I simply had no other choice. My legs were dull scissors slicing through dense blocks of steel, but somehow I managed to make it. I found my way to the stall that had been my home for tears over Blanche, but instead of crying this time, I got down on my knees and threw up.

Things were never the same between my parents after Blanche died. But then again, maybe that's normal. I don't really know. I'd never been given a definition for "normal" that attached itself to the sudden death of a daughter, a sister. I just knew that I blamed my father for all the tension. But how could I? He was sick. Then again, we were all sick, really. My father was just the only one who wore his sickness like a proud new suit in front of the world.

My mom had to plan Blanche's entire funeral herself. My father was missing the whole day, and when the doorbell rang at nine o'clock, we feared it might be more bad news, but it was only my dad, returned from the shadows, ready to settle in and call it an evening. There wasn't an ounce of apology in the way he removed his coat.

"How'd you make out?" was the first thing he said to my mother, as nonchalantly as if it were a community raffle she'd spent the day organizing as opposed to her firstborn's funeral. But my mom didn't have the strength to be offended.

"Why didn't you use your key?" she asked him.

"What?" He looked at her curiously, as if the question—and not he, himself, the man who'd disappeared the day after his daughter's death—were bizarre. My mother nodded toward the keys in his hand. He looked down at them and smiled, meeting her worried gaze with a shrug. "I don't know," he said. His face was full of stubble. "It's funny—the things you take for granted." And then, without another word, he turned to go upstairs.

"Steven…" my mother called out to him as he made his way up the steps. But he didn't seem to hear her. "Steven…"

"Dad!" I shouted from the couch. Finally, my father turned his head. "Mom wanted to ask you something."

He looked at her as if she were a stranger. "I'm sorry?"

"Where were you all day?"

It wasn't so much his words that I'll never forget, but the way he said them, like it was the most obvious answer in the world.

"At the movies."

And then he disappeared, as if he hadn't confused either of us, as if "at the movies" was where every grieving father had been that day, while every grieving mother picked out caskets.

My father's disappearances soon became so commonplace, we stopped asking altogether where he'd been. It wasn't that we'd stopped caring, just that his answers were always so vacant. As long as he came back—that was the important thing. And he wasn't missing all the time. He was quite capable of tormenting us from home base as well. His firm had allowed him a couple weeks off, and one of those days, he spent turning the house inside out in search of some old baseball card his dad had given him when he was ten. The same card he later traded for a catcher's mitt and cigarettes. But no matter how many times my mom reminded him of that, he wouldn't listen. He wasn't interested in *stories;* he just wanted his card. "If I could just make my way to that one unturned stone" seemed to be his mantra for the day.

The morning after his search, he was gone. Yet, the following morning, he sat at the breakfast table with my mother and me as if nothing had happened, as if he hadn't been missing for nearly twenty-four hours, as if he hadn't torn the house apart in search of something that didn't exist. As if he wasn't growing a beard.

Those mornings that he ate with us, my mother watched him like he was an hourglass—the final hour—studying each particle of sand carefully and with fear, and knowing when the last one dropped, there'd be absolutely nothing left. Nothing left of him, nothing left of their marriage, nothing left of herself. I worried about my mother, but she seemed to be holding up okay. As well as could be expected. Just as good as I was, at least. And certainly better than *he* was. What bothered me most was the eeriness of it all, this strange decomposition of my family that had begun with Blanche and was now devouring my father.

Fortunately, my dad went back to work after a while. This, of course, meant that my mother, who processed orders from home for a national catalog company, could "go back to work" as well. With my dad no longer distracting her—whether it was by lurking around the house in search of things that didn't exist, talking nonsense, or fading in and out of light and shadow with his frequent disappearances—my mom could finally breathe a little easier. Grief was apparent in everything she did, but at least that grief could exist alone while she worked, without having to duel with the constant strain of worry. Knowing where my father was for eight hours each day was a relief to her. It was only at night that she worried now, when dinnertime came and passed and my father still wasn't home yet. Other times, he'd come home on schedule and slip away in the middle of the night. Sometimes when I'd get up to use the bathroom, I'd find my mother pacing the hallway in her robe. She always looked so fragile and helpless, more fragile and helpless than me, and I'd want to hug her and tell her it would all be all right. But how did I know that? And besides, I never got around to it. She was always the one to say it first, to tell me to go back to bed, that things were fine. My mother of steel. I knew it couldn't last. But at least she was doing better than my father. We were all doing better than my father.

I did try talking to him, though I admit not so much. There was something creepy about this stranger, this man who refused love, therapy and logic. Mostly, I just waited for him to notice me. But he seemed to think I had died that night in the bathroom with Blanche. Soon, I decided that if he wanted to ignore me, he could. I still had my mother and Emily. The wolfman could ignore me if he wanted to.

My father, bearded and unemployed, moved out of our house one month after my sixteenth birthday to live with my

Grandmom Betty in Florida. I was relieved when he finally packed his bags.

For a year, I'd watched my mother struggle to preserve what remained of her family. And for a year, I'd watched my father drain her with his total lack of regard for the people who used to matter to him most. I could feel him chipping away at us. And I hated him for possessing that power of destruction.

In the beginning of his madness, I felt sorry for him. And sometimes, even when hating the hell out of him with fire in my heart, a small scrap of pity would flare up again. But it was all just too easy—to pity a man who used to be brave. A man who could once lift me onto his shoulders and show me the world. And now, here he stood, a mere shadow of his former self, lurking behind a beard that scared little children, a beard that scared even me. I could've cried oceans—my pity was so strong, and so was my disgust—for this man, this shadow. Forty-three years old and terrified of razors. How was he supposed to show me the world when he couldn't even show his face?

My mom tried buying him an electric shaver, a nice one, too, expensive. One of those "just because" gifts. She didn't want to push, so she simply left it on the sink, in its box with a little red ribbon. He never used it. At least not anywhere we could see. "Maybe he's shaving his legs with it," she joked one day. It was probably the only joke she made all year.

He wouldn't change. And he wouldn't listen to reason. He would barely talk to my mother. It was as if my father was trying to punish her for not sharing in his guilt. I mean, we all felt guilty, but with my mother and me, it was about missing the chance to save Blanche from taking that final walk into the bathroom. With my dad, it was as if he'd taken the razor to her himself. His blade, his blame. My mother wouldn't convict him, though. She even tried telling him it wasn't his fault, but it was like trying to teach logic to a stone.

My mother refused to condemn him, and I barely talked to the man because he barely talked to me. But the neighborhood had its own agenda. And I think he got off on their judgment because—finally—he'd found a jury that would hang him without remorse.

But he'd gotten it wrong. The neighborhood didn't blame my father for what had happened to Blanche. They blamed him for not standing by my mother when she needed him the most. I didn't have to hear it with my own ears to know what people said about him. It was evident in their eyes, in the way they moved aside on the street to let him pass. My father had become a circus freak. Or perhaps, I was as paranoid as he was. Then again, how could I not have been a little paranoid? I was sharing my house with a werewolf. I still remember the tremendous guilt and freedom that shook my body the first time I made that wish to God—if only it had been that crazy werewolf that had bled to death instead of my sister.

From behind his beard—his shield—the wolfman abused all his rights, his right to withhold love, speech and valuable information. His right to come and go without caring. We were doormats for way too long. It was only when our faces became too obscured by footprints to recognize that we were finally promoted to emotional punching bags. It happened around June.

Five months after resuming his responsibilities at the law firm, my father was fired. This was because he never actually *resumed* his responsibilities, but instead missed thirty-six days of work and two high-profile client meetings. But these were only contributing factors. It was his failure to show up for trial that ultimately pushed his boss, Kenny Avery, an old friend from law school, to cut the cord. Kenny had been more than tolerant, overlooking three-hour lunches, missed meetings, all those absences, not to mention my father's dilapidated physical appearance. He'd discussed these things with my father, of course, but had refused to fire him. He just couldn't bring himself to do that to someone who'd been with the firm for so long, someone he'd known for twenty years, someone who had just lost a child. But now the company was attracting negative publicity, losing clients, and my father refused to get help. Kenny had no choice. He had to let him go.

Kenny called my mother a few days later. He wanted to know if everything was okay, to make sure she understood. That was how we found out my father had lost his job. We wondered how long we would've stayed in the dark if Kenny *hadn't* taken the time to make that call.

My mother never said much to my father about being out of work. After all, the last thing she wanted to do was "push" him. But it didn't matter that he had no pressure. It didn't matter about severance and savings because without the dignity of a job, he turned mean. I call this phase two of his madness.

My father never raised his voice at us, let alone his hands. Sometimes, I wished he had. Not that I wanted to be physically abused. I only wanted to see his passion, to know that he was living again, that there was actually blood—warm blood—thawing out those frozen veins. But he was mean the same way he was cold. Distant. Even his verbal abuse took the form of distance. He'd stand there, malicious and cruel, a sunken shadow, a ghost of a man, taking aim at his punching bags with apathy. And it was the apathy that hurt more than his abrasion. It was the fact that he could say the words, make the attack, and not care, that meant that he was still dead. Agitated and cruel, but no pulse. No heartbeat. His delivery was as cool and distant as his former silence. Everything was still the same. This had become our normal. When my father was around, it was like we weren't even there. The fact that he talked to us now—the fact that he was mean—didn't change our insignificance. We were nothing.

He liked to tell my mother she couldn't cook, that he'd be home for dinner more often if the meals were better, that the way she babied him made him nauseous. With me, it was that I breathed too heavily, talked too loudly—whatever he could find to criticize, he would. And there was no point in challenging him. He didn't care what we thought of his criticisms. He didn't care about anything.

As far as I'm concerned, my father left us months before he actually packed his bags and walked out the door. The day he moved to Florida felt like permission to wake up from a bad dream. For so long, I'd been hoping for the return of a man who was never coming back. For months, I'd known he was gone, but now this stranger who had drained our grieving hearts for a year was finally taking his leave. And I could let go. He had let go a long time ago.

Steven Harris Gold, devoted husband of Mary-Jane, loving father of Stella and Blanche. He had died one year earlier in the middle of the night when three girls having a slumber party decided to play a game. The man who packed his bags wasn't my father. He was only a walking tomb. My father, my real father—the one who could once lift me onto his shoulders and show me the world—was dead. And his soul was in heaven with Blanche.

My mother and I watched him from the porch. Before he got into the taxicab, he waved. And like a couple of mindless seals, we waved back. It was unseasonably mild for January.

My mother went inside, but I just stood there, determined to watch the cab drive away, to know it was over, that he couldn't suck the life out of us anymore. But the oddest thing happened: I began to cry—real tears for a man I no longer knew. And when the cab stopped in the middle of the street and the man got out, I kept on crying. I watched him run to me. I let him hug me. I saw when he pulled away that he was crying, too. The stranger. The sick, sad man. The lonely shadow got smaller and disappeared into the cab again. He was always disappearing, but this time he was really gone. And all I had to do was dry my eyes and go inside. And my mother and I would be a family. A small one, but a real one, united and whole.

I found her on the couch in the living room and sat beside her without saying a word. She was watching the movie classics channel and, like her own little gift from God, they were having a Tennessee Williams marathon. *Cat on a Hot Tin Roof* was next, starring Elizabeth Taylor and Paul Newman. I put my head on her shoulder and got comfortable. I had always wondered what Elizabeth Taylor looked like in her twenties.

Although my father's absence had brought an unquestionable air of relief to the house, the walls still rang with an awkward sense of loneliness. I mean, I certainly didn't miss the man who'd left. But I guess my mother did. Or more likely, she hadn't yet buried the man whose soul had perished inside of him. She missed the person she'd married. Perhaps, the loneliness in the walls was just an echo of that heartache. But personally, I felt better. Lonely walls or not, the air was still cleaner, and my mother had color in her face again. But the house really had grown too big. And perhaps the walls would be less lonely, the air even cleaner, in a condo. It would certainly be more affordable.

We moved at the end of April. But long before moving, I realized that although my mother and I had lost a lot in a year, not every loss is pure tragedy. With some, there shines a light so powerful, we discover a blessing that helps us heal. My light, my blessing, was Emily. I knew it as soon as my father left, as soon as my mother and I were alone. I knew it because we weren't alone.

Emily made everything easier. Not just on me, but on my mom, which, in turn, made things twice as easy on me. With the wolfman gone, I think she was more comfortable spending time at the house and could finally be there for us in the way she'd wanted to be since Blanche died. She was always helping out with dinner, whether it was pitching in when my mother or I were cooking or shooing both of us away from the kitchen so we wouldn't have to lift a finger ourselves. She also kept us informed of promising TV movies and would always run out and buy a fun dessert for us to snack on while watching them. I hadn't gotten around to going for my driver's license yet. I really didn't see the point since Emily already had hers. She took me anywhere I needed to go, often suggesting we pick up groceries or the dry cleaning or anything else that might help my mother. Emily can even be credited with helping me find happiness again, right in my own backyard.

"What are we sitting around stuffing our faces for when it's absolutely gorgeous outside?" she asked me one day after school as we sat eating chocolates from the centerpiece bowl at my kitchen table. I'd become really good at after-school snacking since Blanche died. I must have gained twenty pounds.

"What's to do outside?" I asked, not bothering to swallow my food first.

"Well, for one, Ms. Big Tits..." We both looked down at my chest and laughed. Blanche had been right about the sweet-sixteen thing, though I couldn't be sure if the change was hormonal or a direct result of a year and four months of relentless after-school bingeing.

"That's just another place I got fat," I said.

"No, raven goddess. *Those* are the miracles you've been waiting for since you were thirteen." She smiled. "So, as I was saying, there's plenty to do outside."

Rather than devouring that entire bowl of chocolates, we ended up taking a walk around my new neighborhood. It was a beautiful spring day in early May and for the first time since before Blanche, the bingeing, the beard and the boobs, I actually felt good. The sun was soothing and sweet; the breeze, soft and perfect. And every flower was in bloom. The trees were bright green. The grass was bright green, smelling like grass is supposed to smell when the weather feels too good to stay inside. Some people were outside mowing their front lawns. Some people washed cars. Children were too noisy, but it only made me smile. Summer was coming. We knew it with all our senses. And we walked until the sun went down.

It was a cold December night in 1991 when the rug was pulled out from under me, so completely and without warning. And it was that walk with Emily on a warm spring afternoon in May of 1993 that proved promise still existed in my life. With or without rugs to stand on. I wasn't cured. There is no magical potion to swallow for the death of a sister. The foundation I lost when Blanche died, the only foundation I had ever known, was gone forever. And I'd never have that kind of security again, the luxurious security of taking for granted that families stayed together and seventeen-year-olds didn't die. And I'd always miss my sister. That hole in my heart would never go away. But my life would go on. Like spring, like summer, the beauty of the seasons, the sun, there was promise in that fact. There was hope. And I was happy because of it.

I knew it wouldn't last forever—we're not programmed to be happy all the time. But I was okay with that. I was okay with a lot of things, for the first time in a long time. I liked our new home. I liked that my mother and I had developed new routines, routines that made us feel like a real family. And I liked that Emily was part of them. I was ready to shed this weight, and I was thankful that I had a friend like Emily to support me. I was excited that school was almost out for the summer, and I was happy that I could finally feel inspired about my future, even if it was only the short-term I had in mind. For nearly a year and a half, just thinking minute to minute had been a strain. The discovery that I had things to look forward to, besides my next snack, that there were promises, hope, more spring walks, more summers, more days with Emily spent however I wanted, perhaps just like this, was enough to make me realize I was going to be all right. That, in fact, I was capable of even more than all right. I never would have guessed that day, when we decided to forgo chocolate for nature, that I'd actually find happiness—waiting just around the corner among the flowers and the sun.

My junior year at Summit Valley brought the arrival of many things, including my driver's license, my goal weight, and, most importantly, John Lixner. John was a blond-haired, blue-eyed genius from my physics class. He was about a quarter of an inch shorter than me—maybe a half—and very, very thin. Not scrawny thin, but rock-star thin. Though, he had too much innocence about him to have actually been a rock star. He caught my eye the moment he walked into class on that first day of school. At first, I admit, it was probably his striking resemblance to Kurt Cobain that grabbed me. But then, it was more than that. The teacher paired us up as lab partners. And, I know, how cheesy—falling in love with your lab partner. But it wasn't exactly *love*. I don't think I was ready to understand what that was yet. Though, I did adore John Lixner. At times, I found myself completely fascinated by him, and at other times, overwhelmed by affection.

John was a year younger than me due to the fact that he'd

skipped a grade in elementary school. He'd later qualified to skip another, but decided to stay with his friends from that point onward. One of the things I admired most about him was how remarkably unaffected he was by his legendary status at Summit Valley. Most people couldn't match the face to the boy, but everyone had heard of his name. John Lixner, who had never gotten a B. John Lixner, whose IQ was somewhere in the 170s. John Lixner, whose name rolled lovingly off the tongues of amorous teachers singing his praises in their classrooms. And then, there was that phrase made popular in backhanded compliments throughout the school: "Well, he's *no John Lixner,* but…"

I'll never forget how stunned I was to learn during roll call on that first day of physics class that the Kurt Cobain look-alike I'd been staring at was Summit Valley's own beloved boy wonder, John Lixner. I'd always envisioned a stereotypical nerd, and even worse than that, a cocky nerd who thought his superhuman intelligence made up for his lack of social skills. But John was gorgeous—in a nonthreatening, slightly unconventional and totally mysterious way. He was also shy, sweet, funny and extremely receptive to being my friend. We were friends for three months before we ever even kissed.

It happened during MTV's premier broadcast of Nirvana's Unplugged performance in New York. In the background, the band was playing their cover of David Bowie's "The Man Who Sold the World." To this day, whenever I hear that song, whether it's the Nirvana cover or the original, I think of that kiss and smile.

Before going home that night, John asked me to be his girlfriend. Like the boy, the proposal itself was sweet, shy and unassuming. I said yes immediately. I'd been wanting a boyfriend for a while, figuring that after three casual hookups that summer, including a second-base run-in with the gorgeous Warren Blakemen at Lisa Solomon's pool party, I was certainly ready for one. But I'd been holding out for John, because I knew he was the perfect guy for me. I felt it in the way he coached me through lab experiments, which for some reason, though never sexual, always seemed to fill me with butterflies. I felt it in the way he was cute on the phone and in the way I always wanted to hug him. But most especially, I knew that John was the perfect guy for me because of the way we made each other laugh. We laughed differently than Emily and I did. The volume was softer. *His* volume was softer. But that was one of the things I found most alluring about him.

At the heart of John's soft-spoken wit was a sense of humor almost identical to mine, and he adored seeing me smile. He always knew just how to make it happen. And somehow, despite my considerably lower IQ and undeniable lack of flare for impressing beautiful boys with my knack for spontaneous comedy, I could always make John smile, too. But we were like a pair of starry-eyed puppies. I don't think either of us was mature enough then to say we were in love. In order for two people to really fall in love, they have to experience more than just physics and Nirvana. But that's not to say I wouldn't have *maybe* slept with John if he'd asked me. Of course, he never asked me. Instead, we kissed a lot, laughed more, and took naps together almost every day after school. We cuddled as tightly as possible, but always kept our clothes on. His hair smelled like apple shampoo.

Friday, April 8, 1994—the day the world learned of Kurt Cobain's suicide. That evening, my mother, John, Emily and I sat huddled on the couch watching MTV rerun Nirvana's Unplugged show as a tribute to the fallen front man. I couldn't help but recognize the irony. Here was a show that, less than four months earlier, had symbolized nothing more than great music and first kisses, and now it was all about eerie subliminal messages and mourning. The whole thing made me think of Blanche and of that night on South Street when she seemed happy. What if someone had secretly videotaped her? Then, we could've scrutinized her later, searched her face for signs of what she may or may not have been planning to do. John knew all about Blanche. There wasn't much I didn't tell him. He looked really sad, sitting there on the couch, holding my hand. I noticed he was swallowing a lot, maybe trying to suppress the lump in his throat. I knew it was more than Kurt Cobain, the "voice of our generation." I knew he was thinking of me and the story I'd told him—about Blanche. I was sure we were all thinking about Blanche.

After a while, my mother broke the heavyhearted silence with an offer of drinks. She had just taken the first glass out of the kitchen cabinet when the phone rang. I watched her hit the speaker button. "Lake of Fire" was playing in the background.

"Hello."

"Hello, Mary?" It was my Grandmom Betty. She never called us. My father was dead.

"Yeah, Betty? What is it?" My mom didn't sound as worried as I thought she'd be. Instead, she continued to prepare the drinks. It was in that moment that I realized what a long way she'd come since my dad left.

"I'm calling because..." My grandmother's voice faded beneath the music. Or perhaps, it was the distance from Boca Raton to Scottsboro that made her sound so meager.

"Speak up, Betty. I'm right in the middle of getting drinks. I have you on speaker phone."

"Oh, okay. Well, I'm calling because..."

I pressed mute on the TV.

"Yes?" Everything became quiet for what seemed like forever.

"Steven would like a divorce."

My mom picked up the phone after that.

Calling Janey... I took a deep breath and drew my cell phone to my ear. I wasn't exactly in the mood to talk about my father's letter, but I suppose I was as ready as I'd ever be.

"Hello?"

"Hi."

"Are you okay, honey?" She sounded calmer than I'd expected, considering it had been more than an hour since I'd practically hung up on her.

"I'm fine now. It's just that hearing about, uh, him..." I trailed off. I had begun feeling sick again.

"Your father," she said gently, yet in a way that seemed almost like a correction, which completely pissed me off.

"Him," I countercorrected, like a rebellious teenager. "Anyway, I wasn't feeling well after you told me about the letter, but I'm okay now." We were both quiet for a few seconds and I knew she was waiting for me to ask what he'd written, but for some reason—nervousness, maybe pride—I just couldn't bring myself to raise the issue.

"Do you want me to read it to you?" my mother finally offered.

"Please."

She cleared her throat, as if addressing a large crowd from a podium, and it irritated me. My father's letter didn't deserve that kind of dignity. Then again, perhaps she was just nervous. I remained quiet as she spoke, barely breathing, waiting for bombs.

"'Dear Mary,'" my mother read. "'I know it's been a long time, and I'm sure this letter is arriving to you out of the blue. You probably haven't thought of me in years. I think about you and Stella every day, though, and hope that you are doing well. I heard you got remarried and I think that's really terrific. I mean that sincerely. I'm happy for you. I've wanted to get in touch for so long, but what finally gave me the nerve was the fact that last Wednesday would've been Blanche's thirtieth birthday. I've been feeling exceptionally sentimental since then. Thirty. God—can you believe how time flies? I know it's a cliché, but it really does seem like yesterday that we brought Stella home from the hospital. It was just a few days before Blanche turned two, so we gave her that doll and said it was an early birthday gift from the new baby. I'll never forget the look on your face when she didn't believe us. I guess it's the smart ones you have to watch out for, huh? They can break your heart.

"'I don't think Blanche meant to hurt us, though—with any of it. I spent a lot of years wondering why she chose our bathroom, my razor. Wondering why, as the man who could once protect her from anything, I hadn't been able to save her from that moment. And to be alone with her in the bathroom, waiting for the ambulance—I knew she was dying. I was holding her and I knew she was dying and that somehow, it was all my fault. But there was nothing I could do. What kind of father can't even protect his little girl? What kind of man can't save his family? I felt like some kind of poison. But I shouldn't have walked out on you and Stella. Leaving was the coward's way of dealing with things. But then again, that's exactly what I was—a coward. I've faced a lot of my demons in therapy since then, and I know now that Blanche's death was not my fault. I only regret that I had to lose everything that mattered before I could come to that. It's selfish of me to think that after all I put you and Stella through, either of you would ever consider letting me share in your lives again. But I do want you to know how sorry I am. It's a simple phrase and it's not enough, but there are no words to make up for what I did to the two of you, so all I can say is I'm sorry—for everything I was and for everything I wasn't at the time you and Stella needed me most. You may not be able to accept my apology. Just please know how much I mean it and that I'd give anything to undo the pain I caused.

"'I really hope life is good for you now, Mary. I imagine it is. As for me, I'm still living here in Florida, but doing a whole lot better. I'm even practicing law again at a firm called Segal and Schmidt. I've been there for about four years. Oh, and you'll probably be glad to hear I got rid of the beard. (I figured I'd let ZZ Top have their look back.) My mother, on the other hand, isn't doing so well. I know you and Stella have never been close to her, but she had her reasons for moving down here after my dad died. It's not that she didn't want to see her granddaughters grow up. She just needed a new place to start over. You remember how feisty she was. My feisty, old mom—I never thought I'd see the day when she wouldn't even know who I was. But that's what happens with Alzheimer's. She's living in a nursing home now. I visit her every day and try to help her remember things, but lately, she won't even look at me. It's incredibly sad, but she's my mother, and I'll visit her every day until she's gone, hanging on to that tiny ounce of foolish hope that maybe one day she'll remember her son.

"'I'm sorry to end things on such a depressing note, but aside from working and thinking about the family I left behind in Pennsylvania, visiting my mom is pretty much all my life consists of these days. Oh, and I also have a dog, a golden retriever named Tennessee. It would break his heart if he knew I'd forgotten to mention him. What do you think of the name? I thought you'd get a kick out of it.

"'Anyway, I guess I'll get going now. At the bottom of this page, you'll find my home and cell phone numbers as well as my e-mail address. Please forward them to Stella. I know I can't expect to walk back into your lives with a simple letter. I can only pray that it is a start. No matter what you decide, please know that I never stopped loving either of you. And I wish you nothing but the best. Love, Steven.'"

My father's closing words echoed in the silence, and for some reason, I waited for more. There had been mention of phone numbers, an e-mail address. It took me a few seconds to realize she wasn't going to read those. I wasn't sure why I wanted her to. Why did I care what my father's e-mail address was? It's not like I was going to take note of it and become his electronic pen pal. I guess I just wanted to know more about his life. Not because I cared about him, but because it was intriguing, because I was trapped in some kind of haze and couldn't help but stare at the little girl across from me who seemed fascinated by her shoes. But it was only a place to look. My mind was somewhere else, in between the pages of that letter, as if it were a choose-your-own-adventure storybook. The werewolf had chosen the taxicab and had ended up in Florida with a law career and a dog named Tennessee. If he'd stayed in Scottsboro, he may have killed us all. I couldn't believe how normal he'd sounded.

"Well," my mother said, "what do you think?"

"He didn't sound crazy."

"Well, he wasn't crazy. Not always, I mean. Not for the first twenty-two years that I knew him."

"Twenty-two years is a long time," I said.

"What about your Grandmom Betty? That's so sad, isn't it?"

"Yeah. Hearing stuff like that always makes me sad."

"And what about that dog? Can you believe he named it Tennessee?"

"I thought he didn't even like dogs."

"Well, he's probably so lonely now without his mother around."

"I was surprised to hear he's actually practicing law again."

"And that he got rid of the beard!" my mother joked, and together, we laughed softly. It felt good to break the ice. "I can't believe he thought I was still married to Kevin," she said.

I didn't say anything, but instead smiled warmly at the little girl with the shoes whose father had just sat down beside her.

First Times and Second Chances

My mother met her second husband, Kevin, through my second boyfriend, Dan, whom I dated for six months during my senior year of high school, and who, as the saying went in those halls, was definitely "no John Lixner." John and I were still friends, but he'd been accepted to spend our senior year at a prestigious private academy out in Los Angeles, which would help prepare him for the Ivy League. He left in August, and we both cried when we said goodbye—and then burst into an immediate fit of laughter for doing what they did in every movie we'd ever made fun of. But we'd been together for eight months and we'd miss each other, just as much as any celluloid couple ever had. However, we'd decided against long-distance commitment, a state of being John feared might lead to resentment. At least this way, we'd always be friends. Though I understood his reasoning and had clearly lent consent to the decision, because I *did* value our friendship above anything else we may have had, a part of me still wished I'd gotten the chance to "resent" John—because deep down, I knew I never could.

I met Dan Jacoby in my creative writing class that fall and found myself oddly attracted to his cocky jock attitude. I was missing John terribly, much more than I ever thought I would, and in an attempt to distract the heart, I focused solely on desire, lavishing my libido's attention onto his polar opposite. John and I still talked regularly, but I wanted the hope to go away. I needed to transfer my romantic feelings onto someone else. Dan, the wrestler, was a perfect choice.

My relationship with John was never about the physical. With Dan, it was as if we'd never heard of anything else. We made out all the time, and when we weren't making out, we were *talking* about making out. Together, we conquered a wealth of uncharted erotic terrain. I was still a virgin by the time we were through, but had begun to understand the post oral sex euphoria my sister had alluded to that night in her bedroom when she told us the awful story about Keith Shay and his friends. However, as for returning the favor, I just wasn't quite there yet. But that's not why he dumped me. He dumped me for old-fashioned reasons—because I wouldn't sleep with him and prom was coming up. He was dropping a lot of money on the limo, corsage and trip down the shore afterward, and didn't want to bother if I wasn't a sure thing.

Before Dan Jacoby revealed himself as Summit Valley's Most Villainous Prick, our roof began to leak, and he gave us the number of his family contractor, Kevin Kilbride. Kevin was thirty-one, had been born in Ireland, and had come to the United States at the age of eight when his father's job relocated the family to Boston. In high school, he developed an interest in painting and spent the next seven years honing his craft while making rent through a string of odd jobs, none of which, he said, were actually *interesting* enough to qualify as "odd."

Eventually, he grew restless in Boston and began traveling south, trying on a number of different cities until he stumbled upon Philadelphia, and the fit just felt right. One of his neighbors owned a contracting business and made building, installation and repairs sound worlds more worthwhile than anything in the string of not-so-odd-or-interesting jobs he'd already tried. So, he trained for his license and had been working for his neighbor's company for about a year.

Painting was still where Kevin's heart lay, but he'd finally found a career that made him happy in the meantime. Though, I was never quite sure what "the meantime" meant, because as far as I could see, he didn't have any aspirations of ever becoming a famous painter. He never even tried to sell his work anywhere. Regardless, Kevin seemed to have reached a settling point in his life by the time he met my mother. Once a frustrated drifter, dodging permanence and commitment, he was now a thirty-one-year-old man in one place with one job that made him happy. And then there was my mom—a forty-four-year-old woman who hid a hundred years of sorrow behind her Mrs. Robinson smile.

Of course, I'm only joking about the Anne Bancroft thing. The age difference between my mom and Kevin wasn't really *so* big. I knew we weren't exactly talking *The Graduate,* but still, it was fun to tease her.

"Coo-coo-ca-choo, Mrs. Robinson," I'd say when she'd emerge from her bedroom, decked out and gorgeous, or come home glowing from one of their dates. And then we'd dance around the room, infused with the spirit of Simon and Garfunkel, getting giddy on Jesus and Joe DiMaggio until we collapsed. I could see the way that ecstasy had overwhelmed her. And it was beautiful. She was falling in love.

I became jaded to men shortly after my mother and Kevin got serious, and I was only eighteen years old. I suppose it had something to do with Dan Jacoby dumping me just two weeks before the prom. I went with Warren Blakemen instead, the guy I'd gone to second base with at Lisa Solomon's pool party the summer before junior year. We were completely platonic friends by now, and I made him promise no funny business.

Our prom was held at a fancy hotel in Center City. Emily went with her boyfriend, Jason Neeley, and disappeared with him midway through the night to have sex in one of the suites.

Afterward, we held a little funeral for her virginity in the bathroom, the two of us standing together in the stall, kind of like the day I received my tampon lesson, only this time in fancy dresses and tears. This rite of passage was quite different than a first period. But we hadn't expected to cry. We'd only locked ourselves in that stall because the ladies' room was too crowded and best friends discussing something as important as the first time were entitled to as much privacy as a crowded prom night ladies' room could afford them. Emily's tears came first, along with a stream of disconnected thoughts that somehow still made sense to me—how her mother would never see her get married, how she wished we could sometimes talk about my sister because she'd never grown out of missing her, how sex had really hurt. I started crying somewhere around the mention of Blanche. Only I wasn't crying about Blanche. At least not completely. The majority of my tears, the ones that lasted beyond that stream of thoughts and fell silently as we hugged, were for the fact that I had known Emily since we were little girls. And Emily wasn't a little girl anymore. That's when the music started playing in my head.

"My mom was a Laura Nyro fanatic," she'd said the day we met. "She named me after the song 'Emmie' and died when I was three."

I don't know what came over me—bursting into song as if I were headlining a real-life musical, and of all places, in a bathroom stall, was never something I thought I'd do. I can't even sing. Neither can Emily. I guess that's what made it so extra special when she decided to join the choir.

"'Emmie,'" I began alone. And then it was the two of us.

"'Your mama's been a callin' you-oo. Who stole Mama's heart and cuddled in her garden? Darlin' Emmie, oo la la la—'"

"Oh, my *God!* It must be S&M!" The voice penetrated our harmony, killing our picturesque moment. It was Nelly Whiteman, the popular athletic bitch I couldn't stand in junior high. We were friends with her now, and she called us "S and *Em*" because she enjoyed the innuendo. "Where one goes, the other follows!" she teased, peering through the crack in the stall. We still had our arms around each other. "You guys are freaks," she joked, echoing her seventh-grade sentiments as she turned to walk away.

"At least we don't have brooms up our asses!" Emily called after her, though I think she said it more for my benefit than for Nelly's, knowing full well I'd remember the rebuttal. A virgin or not, she would always be my brass-balled Tinkerbell, sitting on a locker room bench.

"I just wanted to let you girls know," Nelly called back, "they're about to announce prom queen!"

Well, here's the shock of the century: I wasn't voted prom queen. Emily had never given a shit about things like that. She especially didn't care about trivial crowning contests that night. She was too busy looking sparkly and radiant and in love with Jason out on the dance floor. It was as if she'd never even broken down in the bathroom. She was over that dip in the roller coaster and back to feeling high. But knowing that I'd been there for the dip—the tears, the rambling, the shaky Laura Nyro tribute—made me feel relieved. It was good to know that the Big Cherry Pop hadn't come at the expense of a wall between us. I'd always feared that once Emily lost her virginity, I'd feel farther away from her, but instead, after that experience in the bathroom, I felt closer than ever. I guess I should've had more faith in our friendship. Then I wouldn't have spent so much time wondering and worrying about the line that would divide us once Emily finally did it. In a way, I was surprised she'd waited this long.

Emily had always been several steps closer to losing it than I had. She'd had her first kiss before we were even friends, had gotten to second before I'd gotten to first, and had a much more liberal definition of third than I did. To sum it all up, Emily was just a lot hornier and far less inhibited than I was. But I always knew she'd never lose her virginity in a random one-night stand. She'd at least have to be going with someone. More than "going." The relationship would have to be bordering on serious. Enter Jason Neeley, the summer before our senior year.

Emily and Jason met at a department store in the mall where

she had just started working as a cashier. She said the new job was okay, great if you counted the mannequin-display guy. That was Jason. When Emily first told me what he did, I couldn't help but picture the character Hollywood from the movie *Mannequin,* but she said it would be more accurate to visualize the Andrew McCarthy character instead, only not as eighties-icon-pretty-boy—"and he doesn't talk to the dummies." She and Jason fell in love pretty quickly that summer.

Jason didn't go to our high school. He went to Lincoln, which was about fifteen minutes away. And although neither of them kept their jobs at the mall during the school year, they still managed to see each other every day and always insisted that I join them. It wasn't long before we became a threesome (in the purest and unsexiest form of the word). Jason was one of the coolest guys I'd ever met and he didn't make me feel like a third wheel at all. *I* couldn't even make me feel like a third wheel—that's how comfortable things were. It was as if Jason had been our soul brother forever, and it always felt more like three best friends hanging out than one single girl and a couple. I knew that in their private moments, they got mushy, because Emily told me everything, but they never seemed in a rush to be alone when the three of us were together. It was incredible, really—how lucky I'd gotten. I'd actually survived Emily's first love without a broken heart.

The funny thing was that Dan Jacoby never quite fit in with us. I only brought him around Jason and Emily a few times because I sensed that he made them uncomfortable. Every joke, every innuendo, every reference to a movie, song or previous day had to be explained—and then explained again for its humor. Dan just didn't get the three of us, and the part that got me was that I felt most alive, most confident and most myself when I was around Emily and Jason. Not that I didn't have a good time with Dan one on one. It's just that there was never really much joking, talking or explaining to do because the better part of that relationship was spent lying down. But Emily and Jason were cool about Dan, and never said a single unkind word about my cocky jock stud who'd unfortunately been born with his funny bone—and half of his brain—shoved straight up his ass. At least, they never said an unkind word until he dumped me. Dan Jacoby–bashing became a really fun pastime after that.

Warren fit in monumentally better with the three of us than Dan had. It was apparent within the first five minutes of our limo ride to the prom, and I was glad I'd ended up bringing him. His role had changed a lot in three years, from Trigonometry Acquaintance to Make-Out Star to that gorgeous guy I'd see in the hallway and feel stupid around because he'd once touched my boobs in Lisa Solomon's swimming pool. But that was all before Ping-Pong made us buddies.

Neither Warren nor I harbored a particular penchant for athletics. This is probably why we both chose Ping-Pong as our elective sport for first marking period gym class. By virtue of not knowing anybody else—or making repeated eye contact during the partner selection process—we ended up playing against each other three mornings a week for the next two and a half months. It only took a few minutes of awkwardness during our very first game before I got past the whole boob thing, and by the end of the period, we had seriously bonded over our hilarious lack of coordination. I hadn't had that much fun in gym class since Emily and I were thirteen.

Warren and I picked all of our gym electives together when Ping-Pong was over—badminton, followed by fitness walking, followed by square dancing. Yes, our high school offered square dancing, and yes, we took it to get out of playing sports. I even got my first detention with Warren—and my second, third and fourth. We were always getting into trouble in one way or another, probably because we were always messing up and falling into uncontrollable fits of laughter about it.

There was still that small spark of sexual chemistry between us, despite our platonic context. But I was dating Dan throughout most of my senior year, and besides, Warren and I only hung out on school grounds, so we never really had a chance to do anything risky. And even if we had been given the chance, I thought it was best to keep our friendship untainted. We'd already made out once, so it wasn't as if we didn't know what we were missing out on. It wasn't like other boy-girl friendships that are weighted down in curiosity. All that lingered between us was some lust, and our friendship was worth a whole lot more to me than a little getting off. That's why I made him promise there would be no funny business on prom night. Maybe it was more of a promise to myself.

I'd been watching Emily and Jason out on the dance floor for a while when I turned to glance over at my date. He was talking to Holly Myers, but when our eyes met, he stopped to smile at me. Even though we weren't in love, it was definitely wonderful being there with Warren. In a sense, it was a perfect way to end the year, considering that my finest memories of twelfth grade would be mostly of him, anyway, and not jerk-off jocks named Dan who were only good for one thing. Turning back to stare at the happy dancers who had just made love for the first time, I realized how incredibly sweet they looked—Emily wearing Jason's tuxedo jacket because she was cold, Jason holding on to her like she was more precious than anything on earth. Emily saw me watching them and signed *I love you* from across the room. I gladly returned the gesture, meaning it more than she may have known, and wishing with every piece of my heart that I'd slept with John Lixner when I had the chance.

Jason, Emily, Warren and I spent prom weekend down the shore with Warren's friends, Sarah and Doug, and Doug's older brother, Sid, who came armed with beer, whiskey, wine and women. The women were two college juniors named Vanessa and Jen, who called themselves best friends but seemed to be in some sort of weird competition over Sid, who, for some reason, didn't seem to notice or care.

I hadn't planned on drinking anything at first. Emily and I had never actually discussed it, but I assumed she was just as leery about liquor as I was. Although it had been more than three years, I don't think Blanche and her pre-gang-bang whiskey shots were far from either of our minds when we stole that moment alone in the kitchen. The fun was just beginning out in the living room.

"Maybe if we just drink wine," Emily proposed.

The idea sounded reasonable enough, as wine was the sophisticated beverage of choice in most movies and rarely led to the violent kinds of scenes that beer and shots often did. And I really wanted to loosen up and have a good time with everybody else. Wine was fine, I assured myself. And boy, did that wine taste good!

At some point during the night, I told Warren I loved him, which I later regretted and didn't mean the way I feared it sounded, though I couldn't even remember my tone of voice after the alcohol wore off. I also told Sarah and Doug I loved them, which was quite generous of me, considering I'd only just met them that night. But they were polite enough, and I suppose drunk enough, to say it back. Emily and Jason eventually got busy loving *each other* as they recreated prom night on the kitchen sink, while we all sat in the living room making immature jokes about it and acting as if it were only *mildly* inappropriate. But who am I to talk about inappropriate? After six months of not being ready with Dan, I took the plunge with Sid Somebody, performing my very first blow job in the shore house bathroom. I was too drunk to be disgusted with myself at the time, and was just so relieved afterward—to finally be able to say I had done it—that I never actually experienced any guilt or shame. If it were sex, it would've been different, but this was just oral. I'd finally gotten it over with. And now I could die without ever having to do it again.

"You mean, you didn't like it?" Emily asked, her tired eyes bulging forth from their sockets. We were the only ones still awake from the night before and had gone to the pancake house down the street to stuff our faces before passing out for the day.

"What's to like?"

Emily looked at me funny, and then she started to smile, allowing a big glob of whipped cream to squirt through her teeth and drizzle down her chin onto the plate.

"That's what I love about you," I said. "How sexy you are in the morning." I reached across the table to wipe her chin. "Speaking of sexy, how'd you like doing it on the sink?"

"Oh, God!" Emily looked truly mortified.

"Hey, at least you're in love," I consoled her.

"You're in love, too."

"I am?"

She smiled at me. "With Sarah and Doug and Warren…"

Now it was my turn to be mortified. "Do you think he'll remember I said that?"

"Maybe. But I wouldn't worry about it. Warren's smart enough to know what you two are all about. He's not going to take a drunken comment out of context. Besides, you've got Sid Cocker to worry about now."

"That can't *seriously* be his last name." Could it?

"It's not," she said. "It's Altman. I took the liberty of asking Doug so you wouldn't have a complex for the rest of your life about not knowing the last name of the first guy you ever went down on."

"You're so good to me."

"Don't mention it. It really *was* a night of firsts, though, wasn't it? For both of us, I mean."

"Since you brought that up, I've kind of been wondering about something."

"Then why don't you kind of, like, ask me?" Emily teased.

"Okay. How come you and Jason waited so long? I mean, you've been together almost a year."

"I wanted to do it on prom night," she said plainly. But I remained quiet, waiting for more. "Okay, remember how Brenda and Dylan did it for the first time at the spring dance?"

"Umm-hmm." This could not possibly be her reasoning. I mean, I loved *90210* just as much as the next girl and had often looked to the Walsh family for examples, myself, but this was her *virginity* we were talking about here. Something was a little off.

"Well, we don't have formal dances like that, but we do have a prom, so I decided I'd wait to have sex with Dylan—"

"Jason," I corrected her.

"Jason, right…at the prom…because it was our only formal dance." I knew she was lying. I could see it in her eyes.

"What is it?" I asked.

"I just fed you a bunch of horse shit."

"I didn't buy it."

"I know."

"So, what is it, then, Emily?"

She sighed, leaning back against her seat. "That whole Brenda-Dylan thing is what I told Jason. He thought it was odd, but he humored me. The truth is that my parents did it for the first time on their prom night. I read all about it in the diary my mother used to keep in high school. And I want to be like her, you know—make the right choices in life. So, I thought for my first time with Jason to be most special, we should do it on prom night. And not because it's *prom night*—when everyone gets a room and screws each other's brains out—and not because Brenda and Dylan did it at their formal dance, but because my mom and dad were in love, the same way I think Jason and I are in love. And prom night worked for them. I just want to live my life the way she did." Emily looked at me hopefully. "My mother was so beautiful, Stella. She was just so perfect and beautiful. I just want to be a little bit like her if I can. Does that seem weird to you?"

"No," I said, reaching for her hand. "It doesn't seem weird at all."

Back at the shore house, we slept all day and drank all night. Though this night was mellower, free of kitchen sex and bathroom blow jobs. I spared Warren the details of what I had done with Sid, but asked if he'd be my pseudo-boyfriend to protect me from him. I wasn't feeling as generous toward Mr. Altman as I'd been the night before, but was too immature to deal with any kind of confrontation. I figured I could just take the easy way out by making him think Warren and I suddenly had something going on. As it turned out, I had no reason to worry. Sid spent the entire evening flirting with Vanessa and Jen, which lent further evidence to my theory that all men were jerks, excepting, of course, a very special few. However, there *was* another theory: maybe I just sucked at blow jobs (pardon the pun). But I refused to focus on any theory that made me feel bad about *me* when there was already a perfectly good one that made me feel bad about men.

However unnecessary it may have been, I upheld my act with Warren throughout the night, letting him put his arms around me as often as he wanted and pecking him softly on the lips whenever the desire struck. I wanted so badly to kiss him for real, and finally, after three glasses of wine, I did. He hadn't expected it, but he accepted my affections quite graciously. It happened in the living room, right in front of everybody, and was entirely G-rated, though still hot enough to make me reevaluate my virginity. John Lixner had been the perfect guy and I'd let him go. I hadn't been aggressive enough with him. Well, Warren was a pretty good runner-up to perfect. He was funny, damn good-looking and incredibly smart. Granted, our children might not have as great of a shot at Mensa, but…wait. Why was I thinking about children? There were no *children* involved here. But what if…I wasn't ready. My worries had drained my libido.

I arrived home late Sunday afternoon. My mom was wearing a white tank top with a pair of dark blue jeans. Her eyes were glowing. I didn't always appreciate how truly attractive she was. Emily only had pictures and vague memories. I had this beautiful, living and breathing reality in my here-and-now world, every day. I had missed her. We'd never been apart as long as forty-eight hours. I dropped my bags in the foyer and ran to give her a great, big hug.

There wasn't much I could tell her about that weekend. We'd already talked about the prom when I called her from the shore house to check in. As for the rest of the weekend, all I could really admit to was kissing Warren, which she thought was sweet. I was way more interested in hearing her talk, anyway. It was funny, and a little socially tragic, how my mother suddenly had a much more exciting life than I did. But I was happy for her. It was obvious that she'd had *quite* a weekend with Kevin. And I wanted to know all about it.

"Oh, sweetie, it was just so incredible," she gushed. "Saturday night, he picked me up here and we went to that Japanese place that just opened in Eduardo's Shopping Center. And then afterward, he insisted we go for cappuccinos at this little café near his house, so of course, that meant it was going to be a late night, but I didn't mind. When I'm around him, time just seems to fly and—" She must have realized she was talking a mile a minute because she stopped suddenly and laughed. "I'm sorry. I just feel so..."

"Alive."

"Whenever I'm around him."

"And whenever you talk about him."

She smiled gratefully. "So you understand?"

"Of course I do. I haven't seen you this happy in a long time, Janey."

"Well, you haven't heard the greatest part!"

"What's that?"

She reached down into her pocket and slid a diamond ring onto her finger. And then she looked at me expectantly. Her eyes were sparkling like crazy. "He wants to marry me, Stella! He proposed right outside the café. Can you believe it?" I shook my head, allowing my smile to do the talking—I couldn't seem to find my voice. "God, this ring," she said, glancing down at the glittering stone. "Isn't it gorgeous?" I nodded eagerly. Like the bride-to-be, it was stunning. Their whole relationship had been stunning, a study in sparks and devotion. And now, this incredible second chance for an entire lifetime of happiness.

"Now, the wedding will probably be in July, so it won't interfere with your graduation. And Kevin wants it to be a real celebration—not one of these teeny-tiny deals that women my age tend to throw when they've already been married before. I mean, it's not going to be over-the-top or anything. It'll be just perfect—you'll see. Everyone will have a great time." She paused to tuck a strand of hair behind my ear, and in the silence, her expression changed from giddy to concerned. "Honey, are you okay? You haven't said anything at all. What do you think about your old mom getting married again?"

At that moment, I found my voice, just as my tears began to fall. Reaching out to give her a hug, I smiled and whispered, "Coo-coo-ca-choo."

Dirty Dreams

Kevin and my mom were married in an outdoor ceremony by my grandparents' rabbi. They went to Puerto Rico for their honeymoon, and the following week my new stepfather moved in with us. It was weird having him around. Not weird in an uncomfortable way, just weird in a weird way. *Unfamiliar* is probably the word that best describes it. Having a new man around the house, especially one so young and good-looking, was *unfamiliar*, to say the least. Of course, thirty-one wasn't *that* young to me at eighteen. At least not until I started feeling different around him. It all began with something Emily said one night when she slept over, a couple weeks after Kevin moved in.

"Do you realize there's exactly the same number of years between you and Kevin as there is between Kevin and your mom?"

That was it. That was the line. I'd never thought about our ages like that before. But now that I had, it struck me as odd.

Not that I thought my mother's new husband was some kind of stepchild-molesting pervert, but from then on I was extra careful about the way I presented myself around him. For one, I began wearing bras underneath my lounge-around T-shirts. I'd never done that before, but suddenly going braless around the house just didn't seem like the most appropriate idea. I also started wearing pajama bottoms with my nightgowns, afraid that Kevin might see too much of my thighs otherwise or get an accidental flash of my underwear when I stood up from the couch.

This is hard to explain without sounding as if I had very little faith in my mother's choice of men, or like I found myself so desirable that my own stepfather wouldn't be able to resist me in lounge clothes and Tweety Bird nightgowns. It was just that Emily's comment made me see him as more of a peer—granted, a significantly more mature one—but still a peer on some level. Kevin suddenly seemed more like the kind of guy who'd be the cool, young teacher at school, the kind you might even want to hang out with. He just didn't seem like a father figure. I guess he never really did. But I'd thought the reason was because we didn't know each other well enough. Now, I realized that there just weren't enough years between us.

Aside from this realization, other things began to happen. I ran into Nelly Whiteman later that summer and learned she was dating a twenty-seven-year-old lawyer who worked in her father's practice. *Twenty-seven.* Less than a week after that, I saw Wendy Welsley, a girl from my twelfth-grade psychology class, at the mall. She told me she was engaged—to a thirty-three-year-old man! This meant that someone my age was pledging her life to someone two years older than my stepdad. The generation gap had narrowed severely since high school, and no one cared how old you were as long as they couldn't officially be deemed a pervert or criminal for sleeping with you. Not that I wanted to sleep with Kevin. And not that I was pompous enough to think Kevin wanted to sleep with me. But the fact that Nelly and Wendy were running around with men in their late twenties and early thirties—and doing so proudly and freely—made me realize that men Kevin's age saw girls my age as sexual beings. The discovery made me feel like less of a stepdaughter and more of a, well, *woman*. And sometimes, that feeling led to another kind of self-definition. To be a little more precise, I felt dirty in a good way. And feeling dirty in a good way often led to bad dreams.

Perhaps in acknowledging that I was no longer a little girl and could actually run with the big boys if I chose, I had opened a door in my subconscious that didn't necessarily want to be shut. My bad dreams were actually great dreams, but they made me feel like a gross, guilty pig the next morning—worse than a chocolate binge—and that's why they were bad. They were always about Kevin. And we were always having sex. In one particularly raunchy one, we were on the lawn, getting wet from the sprinkler, and he kept trying to untie my black lace-up bra with his teeth. So many times, I woke up sweaty, half conscious, but still ashamed. I wrote about the dreams in my diary because I was too mortified to even tell Emily about them, and I wanted to make sense of them somehow. Deep down, I knew I didn't *want* my stepfather. Yet my subconscious was definitely trying to tell me something. It took a little while, but I soon figured out what it was. It seemed I was finally ready to have sex.

Separation Anxiety

Life as a college freshman was often quite uneventful for me. Emily had been accepted to study fashion design at the Fashion Institute of Technology in New York, and for the first time since we'd met, we didn't see each other every day. I was majoring in elementary education at the University of Pennsylvania, but had decided to commute so I could still live at home. Of course, I'd made the decision before my mother and Kevin even got engaged, but his being around didn't make me wish I'd reconsidered. I seemed to lack that thirst for independence that flowed like wine from the pores of every other eighteen-year-old freshman I knew. And then, there was that whole thing about not wanting to leave my mother. Hey, I was only eighteen. I don't think that exactly qualified me for the Can't Leave the Nest Club. Besides, who said every girl must be ready to leave her mom at eighteen? Or that every girl is dying to get away from home? My mother and I had gone through a lot to create ours. I just wanted to hold on a little while longer. I didn't want to leave it behind yet, not even for a semester.

Saying goodbye to Emily tore my heart out. It was a bright and sunny Saturday morning when I drove to her house to do what we'd both been dreading all summer. Her father let me in. He said he was just leaving—there were so many errands to run before he took her to New York that afternoon. I knew Frank Martin just wanted Emily and me to have our time alone. I found her upstairs, and there were boxes everywhere. Piles of clothes, books, cassette tapes, CDs. She was leaving. My best friend, my anchor, was actually going away.

I thought about stuffing myself into one of the emptier boxes, not that anyone besides Emily was actually tiny enough to fit in them. But was it not worth a shot? I imagined hiding in a box full of Emily mementos, surprising her when she got to New York, never having to go a single day without her. But what possible place would I have had at FIT? Schools like that were for people like Emily—artsy, intriguing people with amazing talent. The only thing I was talented at was resisting change. And despite my personal resistance, change was still happening all around me. All my friends were leaving. But I was a rock, always resisting. Even as a little girl, I'd clung desperately to my first loose tooth, hoping it would never fall out. I didn't want to grow up then and I didn't want to grow up now. I just wanted to go back to that one day in the locker room with my Milli Vanilli T-shirt when all we seemed to care about was Mrs. Wilder's thighs.

"Remember when we were thirteen?" I asked, looking around the room.

Emily selected a shirt from the pile on the floor, folded it and placed it inside the open suitcase on her bed. "Let's go have pancakes," she said. I guess she wasn't in the mood to reminisce.

Emily's dad had recently ordered one of those perfect pancake makers from a TV infomercial, and Emily was all about showing the world what she could do with its help. I wasn't a stranger to her cooking. Some of the best dinners I'd ever had were the ones she'd made for my mom and me after my father left. But breakfasts didn't appear to be her forte, even with the aid of the Amazing Flapjack Flipper, and we sat eating our foam patties in silence.

"I'm sorry," Emily said finally, pushing her plate away. "These tasted like crap. Do you want something else?"

"That's okay." I had a stomachache, anyway. But it wasn't just from the pancakes. It was from the unspoken sentiment between us, from knowing what we were avoiding.

We went back upstairs, and while she packed, we talked about the usual. But it wasn't "the usual" because there was one thing we were purposely skipping over, one thing that had become part of our everyday conversation—and that was college and the dread of our impending separation. All summer long, our separation had seemed only a hypothetical, somewhere along the lines of *What if the world suddenly collapses? What if Stella and Emily should ever have to live apart?* Could such a reality ever actually *exist?*

Well, it was about to begin. The reality was here, and now. It had arrived. And although the topic had never been timelier, it had never seemed more forbidden. Why were we pretending this wasn't happening? This was not how I'd expected goodbye to be. And the worst part was that this was only the beginning. Our only knowledge of each other as friends was about to change forever, and I hated it. Why couldn't we freeze time? Or put a glass ceiling over our heads and fill the space in between with glitter and snow—a globe that played Laura Nyro while Emily twirled around inside like Tinkerbell? Because nothing ever stays the same, and realizing that can make a person sick. I threw up in the bathroom just before Jason arrived, but didn't say anything to Emily about it. Though I'm sure I could've just blamed the pancakes.

I wanted to give Emily and Jason their privacy. This was goodbye for them, too. Jason was leaving for the University of Florida the next day, so they'd *really* be far apart for a while. But they were both devoted to maintaining a successful long-distance relationship, being simply too in love to even think about reconsidering their commitment. About twenty minutes after he arrived, I decided to pull a Frank Martin and said I had errands to run.

"Give me a hug before I go," I told Jason. "I'm gonna miss you."

In a way, I felt bad that his leaving had been so overshadowed by Emily's. But then again, she'd managed to haunt my goodbye with Warren as well. Warren had left for NYU a day earlier, and we'd spent the entire afternoon before that throwing bread crumbs to the ducks that had wandered into the field by his house, the whole time reminiscing about the good old days of high school. As we talked about times that had nothing to do with Emily, I kept getting pangs of sadness for her, but suppressed them because I didn't want to cry in front of Warren. If I were to have cried about anyone, it should've been about him. After all, *he* was the one I was saying goodbye to. But I actually felt good about Warren and me. He'd become so much more to me than just a Ping-Pong partner, more than a great prom date or incredible kiss down the shore. And even though Warren's New York was the same as Emily's, a little distance between Warren and me just didn't seem like the end of an era, or the end of the world. There was something bittersweet about being duck feeders at the end of the summer before he went away. And I think we both knew it—that although this was goodbye, it was only the beginning of something greater. I think that by eighteen, we'd already realized that true friends were rare. And it seemed we both knew that however ambiguous it may have been at times, the friendship we'd built just might last forever.

I hadn't been so optimistic earlier in the week when John left for Yale. We'd spent a lot of time together since his return from the academy. He'd even been my date to my mother's wedding. Though we went as friends, of course. We'd never resumed our relationship. Were we supposed to just pick up where we'd left off, knowing that in a couple of months, he'd be leaving again? Like John, I feared losing our friendship, and I just couldn't fall into a pattern of seeing him when it was convenient and breaking things off when commitments felt too scary. There was even more at stake now. A lot had changed in a year. I'd experienced so many things—sexual things, another boyfriend—but it all came back to him. To John, whom I still cared so much about, who made me feel like no other guy ever had or, quite possibly, ever could. But I appreciated him even more now and we'd both grown up. We weren't puppies anymore, living in a land of Nirvana and physics labs. The time we spent together confirmed it—I was in love with him. And being "just friends" was enough to break my heart. I wasn't sure whether or not it hurt him, too. I wouldn't know until the night we said goodbye.

I thought about laying it all on the line as I drove to his house in the rain. Why *couldn't* we make it work? If the feelings between us were really so strong, was braving the long-distance barrier really that big of a problem? But as soon as I saw him, I lost all my nerve. I couldn't ask John about *us*. "Us" was such a presumptuous term. We'd been kidding ourselves all summer long that we were platonic, and I guess for one reason or another, John wanted to believe that. Who was I to go throwing presumption to the thundering winds at the eleventh hour? John was leaving. We were parting as friends. And that was all there was to it. We spent two hours in his room not talking about us, and we wouldn't. We couldn't. We were just friends. And then, he walked me outside.

It had stopped raining for a while, but as we stood there talking, the drops began to fall again, though they were warm like bath water, and we didn't mind getting wet. For some reason, we didn't laugh about it like we normally might, and neither of us made any kind of move to seek shelter. Instead, we got quiet, and only stood there, staring at each other in the pouring rain. Hoping the drops would obscure what my eyes were fighting so desperately to contain, I let myself cry. But my tears fell faster and a little less gracefully than Mother Nature's. Only John didn't seem to notice. He simply remained quiet, eyes red, nose red, swallowing like he might have a lump in his throat. It was as if our entire summer had climaxed in that wet, emotional stare, and without a single spoken word, we'd acknowledged the enormity of all that had gone unsaid. If he hadn't kissed me at that moment, I probably would have ruined it with speech.

I didn't know then what making love felt like, but I imagined John and I were pretty close with that kiss. If that wasn't kissing when you were in love, I couldn't imagine what was. Of all times for my tears to get the best of me.

John pulled away slowly. "Are you okay?"

"I'm just…"

"What is it?" He was smiling down at me—he'd grown at least an inch-and-a-half taller since we'd dated—and something in the sincerity of his eyes said it was all right to be honest.

"I'm just so in love with you!" I blurted. And then I waited for lightning to strike.

Only it didn't. Instead, something miraculous happened. John actually looked relieved and said it back. "I'm so in love with you, too, Stella. You have no idea."

We started kissing again, only this time, there weren't any tearful interruptions to slacken the pace. We ended up on the hood of my car. But John put an end to things before they got too serious.

"We need to talk," he said, still on top of me.

"Right now?"

"Yeah," he said, laughing sweetly. "Right now. Can we do it in your car?"

"Excuse me?"

"Talk—in your car."

And so John and I climbed, wet and horny, into the back seat to have the talk we'd been avoiding all summer. Only, he had taken the lead, not me, and I had no idea what direction the talk was going in, especially considering how the past half hour had changed things.

"Stella," he began. It was nearly dark in the car, but his blue eyes pierced right through me, in the way that only John's eyes could. "You know there's no one in my life more important to me than you are."

I reached for his hand, my heart floating from his words. "I didn't know that, actually."

John smiled sadly. "I guess that's because I don't tell you enough—or at all." He looked down at our hands. "I just don't want to hurt you."

"But you won't," I said. "What hurts is pretending we don't feel anything."

"People make promises all the time, Stella. If you and I ever became like all those people who *say* they're gonna stay together..." He looked up at me with urgency in his eyes. "I can't lose you, not because of something like that."

"But—"

"Did you know you were the first person in my entire life to ever treat me like I was normal?"

"What do you mean?"

"All my life," he said, turning to look out the window, "people have treated me differently—whether it's good or bad. Maybe they haven't even meant to, but they have. And then I met you." He turned to face me again. "And you're just..." John sighed. He seemed to be lost for words.

"John..."

"You're just the most genuine person I've ever known and I can't..." He trailed off suddenly, gripping his head in frustration. I wasn't quite sure what to say. Perhaps I should bring up long-distance commitment, explain that I could never resent him.

"John, New Haven isn't that far away. Maybe we could try—"

"I fucking wanna marry you, Stella! But I'm *seventeen!*" His voice cracked when he said his age, not in an awkward, pubescent Peter Brady way, but in a way that revealed just how vulnerable he really was and endeared him to me even more. Tears began spilling from his eyes, but he continued to yell, anyway, angrily, though not at me. "I wanted to stay at Summit Valley last year! I didn't want to leave you and go to L.A.! But I had all these people advising me to go to that friggin' academy...*fuck!*"

In his own private way, John seemed to be flipping out at the world. I suppose he'd been bottling it up for a long time, waiting for a moment when he felt safe to explode. This was about so much more than me. John was angry with his parents, his teachers, his academic advisors, anyone and everyone who'd ever made him wish he hadn't been born with gifts. I wanted to protect him from all of them, to take him away from everything, but by wanting so much from John—by wanting him all to myself—I was only adding to his pressure. I was becoming a part of the problem. For whatever reason, he couldn't handle a relationship with me. I was the only person he could really be himself with. I was the only safety, the only comfort he knew. If things didn't work out between us—and they might not, considering the pressure he was liable to face up in New Haven—our friendship might never be the same. I'd never resent him—I knew that in my heart—but things would definitely change. And maybe John feared change just as much as I did.

I held him in my arms in the back seat of my car, listening to the rain and his breathing for a while, and then we really did say goodbye. We parted as friends and victims to bad timing. We were in love, but it wasn't enough for happily ever after. John was on his way to Connecticut and I was on my way home to cry buckets on my pillowcase. But at least I understood things more clearly. I guess I'd never realized how much pressure John was under. And a lot of times, I did forget how young he was. But even if John Lixner was just a scared kid that night in the rain, letting his fears and frustrations out before he went away to college, I knew that as long as I lived—even after I was married with kids of my own—he would always hold a piece of my heart. Because no one can ever replace your first love if it's real.

When Jason and I pulled away from our hug, I turned to Emily and shrugged my shoulders. This was it.

"I'll walk you out," she said.

They say that before you die, your entire life flashes before your eyes. I never understood that. How can one replay multiple decades in a single car crash or the time it takes to flatline on a hospital bed? It made sense to me as Emily and I descended the stairs. With each step, I saw something new. Five things new, ten things. But they were actually old images. Emily crying in her prom dress. Tinkerbell and her raven goddess, straddling a locker room bench. Two fifteen-year-olds hugging in a hospital room, alone with the body of a dead girl. Blanche. Step. Step. Step.

I looked at her as we stood out by my car. She was so small, so skinny, so easy to stuff into my trunk and kidnap. I was going to miss the hell out of her.

"You need to bleach your mustache before you leave today," I said. I needed to say *something* to break the unfamiliar silence between us. And that was the first thing that came to mind. Emily followed my lead.

"You have a hair growing out of your cheek," she told me. "And it's not an eyelash. It's attached."

Neither of us said anything for a little while as some newborn hostility tested the waters between us. I was angry with her for leaving me. She was angry with me for making it hard. But trying to hurt each other with hairy accusations was really rather ridiculous, especially since neither of us even suffered from facial-fur complexes. I suppose we'd taken such weak shots because we didn't really want to hurt each other at all. We just didn't know how to say goodbye.

"Your mustache isn't really that noticeable," I admitted, breaking the quiet. "It's only because we're in the direct sunlight."

Emily smiled graciously, then said, "You really do have a giant hair growing out of your cheek." Now it was a *giant* hair?

"So, is this really it?" There. I'd said it.

"I guess so," she said, looking down for a second and then squinting up at me, almost as if she were in doubt.

"Well, I'm really gonna miss you."

Emily looked like she was about to start laughing, and I couldn't understand why she was doing this. I watched as she slammed her body against the side of my car, covering her face with her hands.

"God, what the hell is so—" I was going to say "funny," except I'd realized that nothing was. Emily was crying.

"I can't say goodbye to you!" she sobbed. "We've never been apart, Stella! What am I gonna do without you there?"

I suddenly found myself in the very unlikely position of downplaying our separation—telling Emily that her going away wasn't going to change things, that New York was hardly a trip. I didn't believe a word of my speech, but I wanted her to be happy when she left for school. As for my own tears, I saved them for home, falling asleep on my bedroom floor in a puddle of cakey mascara while listening to a mix tape that Emily made for me in tenth grade. I awoke that evening to a knock on the door. It was my mother, hoping that I was all right and wondering if I'd be interested in ordering dinner with her and Kevin. I pictured Emily—getting ready for her first crazy college party—and had to fight off jealous pangs of self-pity as I accepted her offer.

Before joining them, I went into the bathroom and located the hair on my cheek that Emily had pointed out that morning. Sure enough, it *was* giant. How long had it been there and why hadn't I noticed it before? Who would tell me these things now that Emily was gone? I removed my tweezers from the medicine cabinet and yanked it out in one clean motion. It hurt only slightly, but I cried like hell.

"Hello?" The voice on the other end of the phone was older and farther away than I wanted it to be. I wanted her to be the eighteen-year-old freshman in my memory, standing in the sunlight, crying because she was afraid to leave me.

"Hey, it's me. I'm still at the airport."

"Is everything okay?"

"Yeah. I was just thinking about when you went away to school for the first time."

Emily laughed. "Didn't you try to tell me I had a mustache or something?"

"Something like that. Anyway, I never told you this, but it killed me to say goodbye to you. I only acted strong because—"

"One of us had to be."

"Mmm-hmm."

"Kind of like now."

"You think I'm being strong about this?"

"You're handling it better than I thought you would."

"No, I'm not. I've just gotten a whole lot better at acting."

"Stella…"

"Look, I've gotta go, Em."

"All right," she said, sighing. "But if you need to talk while you're waiting…"

"I know where to reach you."

"I'm *sorry,* Stella."

"What's done is done, Emily. But let's not talk about it right now, okay?"

"Okay."

"Goodbye, Em."

"Bye."

Triangles

In March of my freshman year, something terrible happened. I was nineteen, heavily into my guilty, hot sex dreams (in which my primary partner was my stepfather), and horny as a celibate toad. Unfortunately, I was still a virgin. Worse yet, a virgin with absolutely zero prospects. I hadn't struck up any worthwhile relationships in college, platonic or otherwise, but I suppose that was mostly my fault. It had something to do with the way I defined life as a commuter student—going to classes and coming home. I didn't really see the point in forming new friendships on campus if I wasn't living there. It just seemed like too much of an effort. It's not that I was a snob, although I'm sure that's how I was perceived. I just wasn't used to having to try in order to make friends. The ones that were meant to be were supposed to just come easily, to fall into my life and feel like they'd always been there—like Emily, John and Warren had. Of course, I did have some crushes on campus, but I was forever waiting for them to approach *me,* which they never did. Apparently, the only place men wanted me was in my dreams, in which case it was generally one man and practically incest.

It seemed like everyone was having sex but me. Jason had gotten Emily a vibrator as a going-away present when they went their separate ways to college. I guess he thought it would keep her faithful. And it did. She was very faithful—to the vibrator and to Jason. They had plenty of sex over Thanksgiving break, then three days before Christmas, he dumped her for a girl he was falling in love with down in Florida. Emily's heart was shattered, and she made me take custody of the vibrator. She just couldn't bring herself to throw it away. Of course, I had to promise never to give it back to her unless *she* promised to destroy it. The thing was huge, purple and revolting, and I kept it in a shoe box under my bed. For as horny as I was, I was never once tempted to use it. I mean, Emily and I were close, but not *that* close, and besides, I wasn't so much craving the part as the real, live man attached to it.

Emily seemed to be craving both the part *and* the man, or something else entirely that is embodied in rebound sex, for she indulged in it quite frequently after being dumped. In January, she had a three-night fling with Drew Clarkey, whom she'd had a class or two with back in the fall. In February, she had four nights of fun spread out over two weeks with Sean Gigliotti, whom she met at a party at some friend's apartment while drinking rum and Cokes through a licorice straw. That same month, she enjoyed a one-afternoon stand with Gabe Kauffman, whom she met in a bookstore while sober but ended up getting drunk with later, prior to an hour of "mind-blowing sex," whatever that was.

And then March came along. She called me on a Saturday morning, whispering. Her phone call had woken me up.

"You won't believe who left my room a little while ago. I've been trying to go back to sleep, but I can't. I had to call you."

I yawned and tried to stretch without dropping the phone. "Go ahead," I mumbled. "I'm awake."

"Are you sure?"

"Yeah. Tell me. What's up?"

"I said you won't believe who left my room a little while ago."

"Yeah, I got that part. Who?"

"Warren."

I shot up in bed. "What?"

"Warren," she said plainly, as if I simply hadn't heard her. "You know, Warren Blakemen, your buddy—our friend from high school."

My heart slammed against my chest as the room spun around me. I'd gotten up way too fast and I was sweating. I took a deep breath and tried to act unaffected. "What happened?"

"Okay, well, I went to this NYU party last night with my friend, Rosie." That, right there, was something I hated. Since she'd moved to New York, I didn't know who Emily's friends were anymore. For years, no one's name ever needed to be prefaced with phrases like "my friend," and now it seemed that faceless funmongers like Rosie were everywhere, filling up her life, while I lay like a lard ass in bed waiting for updates to add to her sexual scorecard. "And we saw Warren there," she continued, "and, *Stella*..." Emily always drags out my name when she's about to announce how hot a certain guy is or how wonderful he is in bed. "Oh, my God, when was the last time you saw Warren?"

"Like six weeks ago, when he was home on winter break." It annoyed me that she'd even asked. My life wasn't really all that exciting. Emily knew every move I made. I suppose she just wasn't thinking straight. Unfortunately, I couldn't relate to such bubbleheaded euphoria. I was still, as I was all too well aware of now, a virgin.

"Oh, so you remember how good he looks, then?"

"I guess." The truth was that Warren looked even better now than he did in high school, and I was proud of having a hot, platonic guy friend whom I could even say I'd made out with a couple of times in the past. Why did Emily have to cheapen that?

"Well, anyway, I was just so glad to see him, and we immediately bonded, you know? It was like we were an instant couple or something."

"A couple?"

"Well, you know what I mean. We were just buddy-buddy all night, making fun of people together, holding each other's beers when the other one would go to the bathroom..." Emily sighed, as if the moments were too sweet to sully with hazy, morning-mouthed recollection.

"And?"

"And, he ended up coming back to school with me. Kimmy's visiting her boyfriend in Delaware this weekend, so I knew we'd have the room to ourselves."

"Were you guys drunk?" I asked hopefully.

"No. Isn't that the best? Neither of us was drunk at all. We just really wanted to be together after the party." The tears welled up in my eyes, so much that I couldn't see anything in front of me. And then they fell, silently, softly. "We really just cuddled at first, you know, lying in bed, watching TV. And then we just started kissing somehow. And, oh, my God, *Stella...*" She was doing it again—dragging out my name. "You were so right about what a good kisser Warren is." I put my hand over the mouthpiece so she wouldn't hear me sniffing and choking on tears. If she knew what she was doing, she would throw her arms around me and smother me in kisses and apologies. Emily would never hurt me on purpose. But how clueless could she be?

"We must have kissed for like a half hour without even touching," she continued, "but I was just too curious to be good." I realized then that I should've been taking notes for questions at the end. *Too curious to be good?* What the hell did that mean? "So, I ended up taking his pants off and going down on him. *Stella...*Warren is huge!" I shut my eyes, fighting the image. I didn't care if Warren was "huge." I didn't want to think of him like that. I didn't want to think about this at all. "We must've had sex seven or eight times throughout the night," Emily said. "I'm telling you, Stella, that boy can go on and on and on." Why was she telling me this? How was this supposed to make me feel? How would a "normal," nonpossessive, unemotional, nonvirgin react? Suddenly, my other line beeped. "So," Emily said expectantly, "I'm dying to know what you think. Tell me!" The line beeped again.

"That's my call waiting," I said, trying to control the waver in my voice. "I'll call you back later on."

"Okay." She sounded a little bit disappointed and maybe even somewhat hurt that I was blowing her off. I didn't even say goodbye.

When I clicked over to the other line, I heard The Cure playing in the background and knew exactly who it was. Warren and I had never had a phone conversation without them. My tears began to flow faster. I couldn't even handle the sound of his music. How on earth was I supposed to handle the sound of his voice?

"Stella?" I didn't answer him. I couldn't. I was crying too hard now, too hard to hide my sniffles and sobs behind a muffled mouthpiece. "Hey, are you okay?" I couldn't speak, so I kept on crying, louder now because it wasn't a secret. "What's the matter?" His voice was soothing and sincere, but I couldn't tell him. What would I say? How could I put into words how I felt when I wasn't even sure myself? "Did you talk to Emily this morning?"

"Uh-huh!" I sputtered. And then there was no turning back.

"And that's why you're so upset?" Why was he questioning me if he already knew the answers? If he didn't think I'd be upset, then why would he have called me this early? But his tone was gentle, caring, understanding, sensitive, nothing like Emily's had been. The fact was, however, that he *knew* he had done something hurtful. So, what was with the twenty questions?

"Why shouldn't I be upset?" I asked, raising my voice a little.

Warren sighed. "You know what the worst part is, Stella? I wish I was there right now to hold you, but I can never say things like that to you, can I? I mean, heaven forbid, right?"

What was this? Had he slept with Emily to get back at me for something? Something I didn't even know I'd done?

"What are you trying to say?"

"That's just it! I'm telling you I love you, that I've loved you for over a year, but I have to walk on friggin' eggshells to protect our friendship!"

"That's not true," I said, my mind reeling from his confession.

"It is *so* goddamned true, it's pathetic. Do you even realize how much you use me?"

"*Use* you?"

"'Oh, Warren,'" he mimicked, "'Dan Jacoby broke up with me because I wouldn't suck his dick—'"

"That's *not* why he broke up with me," I protested, becoming angry. "He broke up with me because—"

"Because you wouldn't sleep with him, then. Fine. 'So, okay, I'll take my good friend, *Warren,* to the prom, but first I'll reinforce, *a million times,* that that's *all* he is—a *friend*—so that, God forbid, he doesn't try anything with me while we're there.'"

"I kissed you that weekend!" I threw in defensively.

"Yeah, how *gracious* of you. That's when you were using me to pretend I was your boyfriend so you could avoid Sid Altman."

"I didn't hear you complaining that night."

"Yeah, well when you're fucking in love with somebody, you take what you can get. I thought you'd know that better than anyone."

"What's that supposed to mean?"

"Oh, I don't know," Warren said, his tone uncharacteristically cruel and evasive. "Does the name John Lixner ring a bell?"

His low blow knocked the wind out of me. John had been on some kind of enrichment program in France over winter break, but had been back for six weeks now. I was still waiting to hear from him. We hadn't even seen each other since that rainy goodbye in August. I'd been counting on Thanksgiving, but then his parents went away and John decided to spend the holiday in Connecticut with one of his friends from school. He could have spent it with me. I missed him all the time.

"Why would you say something like that to me, Warren?"

"Why would you string me along for a year and a half and constantly make me feel like I never measured up?"

I had reached my breaking point. *I* hadn't done anything wrong. I had merely been sleeping like a good little virgin when this entire situation blew up in my face. Yet here he was, trying to turn the whole thing around and make *me* look like the villain.

"Look, Warren, *you're* the one who slept with Emily!" I yelled. "So, why the fuck are you trying to make me feel bad about it?"

There was silence on the other end of the phone. When he finally spoke, his tone was cold and distant. "We're not a couple, Stella. I have nothing to feel bad about."

"That's right. We're not a couple," I said. He'd made me so angry. "We're not even friends."

"Oh, come on, Stella..." He sounded regretful, but it was too late. I was out for revenge.

"No, fuck you, Warren! How dare you have sex with *my* best friend and then act like I pushed you into it? Who the hell do you think you are?"

"Stella..."

"No! Don't try to be all nice and rational with me now. You're an asshole—calling here and attacking *me!* You're just like every other guy, and I hate you! You're all the same—you, Dan, Jason—"

"John," he added snidely.

"Fuck you!" I screamed, punching the bed as if it were him. "You have no right at all to mention him, and you know what?"

"What?" he asked mockingly.

"You were right. You never will measure up to him. So why don't you just leave me alone and go fuck yourself. Better yet, fuck Emily. Then you can always say it was my fault!"

I hung up trembling, and before I knew it, the cordless had

hit the wall on the other side of the room. My mother rushed in and found me with my face buried in my hands, sobbing hysterically. That morning, I experienced one of the true benefits of living home at nineteen—being able to cry on Mommy's shoulder every time your heart breaks.

She suggested I have a talk with Emily, not necessarily about Warren, but about her promiscuous behavior in general. She reminded me that Emily loved me more than anything and would rather hurt herself than cause me pain. In fact, she said that Emily *was* hurting herself by sleeping around, regardless of whether or not she was being careful. Then she said something that hurt me.

"You really need to get past your fixation on John, sweetie. He's a wonderful boy, and hopefully you'll always be friends. But it's not healthy to sit around longing for something that may not ever happen again. Believe me, I'm only saying this because I care about you. And I know how hard it is to get over a first love."

I wondered if she was talking about my father, but was too busy trying not to view her advice as a death sentence to bother with questions. In a way, I knew that John and I might never get together. I'd known it since he left for Yale, but my heart was seated in the slow section and couldn't quite comprehend the meaning of *improbable*. It was too busy crawling through notions of fate and true love to bother with cruelties of logic. I guess my mother just wanted me to help it along so I wouldn't imprison myself in the past. I told her I would try. But I knew that even in my heart's helper—the brain, where logic lived—I'd always be comparing new prospects to John and wishing they were him. I suppose that's why I'd always taken such comfort in Warren. He was such a good runner-up to John—something he'd *so* resent being described as. And aside from John, he was the only guy I could ever picture myself ending up with once this crazy parade of youth was over. More than anything, I thought he'd be my friend forever. And now, without any kind of warning, he'd been cut from my life.

"I don't think you've seen the last of him, sweetie," my

mother said. "Let him get over his pride, and be ready to take him back when he does. You'll hear from Warren soon. Just let him get over his pride."

Warren got over his pride three days later in the form of a surprise package that was sitting on the kitchen table when I came home from school. The box contained a teddy bear holding a Ping-Pong racket, a framed picture of us from prom weekend that I'd never seen before, a rubber duck and a very long letter of apology. I loved the symbolism of the gifts—that he valued, as much as I did, all the good times we'd had, and was sentimental enough to hold on to things I'd never forget, either, like that one bittersweet afternoon when we were duck feeders saying goodbye before college. But more important than any of that was his letter and one thing, in particular, that it made clear—he *hadn't* used Emily. I don't know how I could've forgiven him for that. He said that without getting technical, there had been an attraction, and that things like that were bound to happen at parties. His biggest regret was that it had hurt me.

I accepted Warren's apology that same afternoon. I really couldn't imagine my life without him. Of course, I would always see him differently. How could he be my perfect "fall back" guy when he'd already slept with my best friend? But, maybe it was better this way. I mean, it wasn't exactly fair of me to think of Warren as Mr. Second Choice, especially now, knowing how he felt. I didn't need to tell him how I felt. He knew I wasn't in love with him. He knew by how crazy I'd gotten when he mentioned John's name. He knew by the fact that I avoided the subject of *his* being in love with me like the plague when we made up. We never even discussed why I'd gotten so upset about him and Emily in the first place. I guess he figured I felt betrayed in some way and would leave it at that. After all, discussing what had happened between them was not exactly one of our strong points. But I couldn't stop thinking about it, probably because I'd realized that my tearful reaction to their fling had little to do with the way I felt about Warren and a whole lot to do with the way I felt about myself.

I was tired of being a virgin. But it wasn't so much the physical restrictions—those I'd been tired of for months. It was everything that being a virgin represented. All of my friends had gone away to school and were out living life on their own in exciting, new places. But not Stella. Not stable, stationary, sedentary, unbreakable, unshakable me. The last woman standing. Change happening all around her, but never consuming her flame. One lonely flame, burning by itself in a snowstorm, out of place and full of stubborn pride. Stubborn Stella, champion over change. In all reality, I was a champion of nothing. Because I was afraid to face anything. I was a little girl trapped in a young woman's body, a virgin not only to sex, but to everything. And maybe I *was* afraid to leave my mother.

Emily was everything I wanted to be, and as a result of that, she magnified all of my failures. Granted, she was sleeping around too much these days, but at least she had the courage to grow up, to have sex, to leave home. Hearing that she'd been with Warren just reinforced all my inadequacies, making me feel even more left behind. Here were two of my best friends from home, off in the big city, doing something I'd never done before, something that bonded them in a way I couldn't even understand, in a way I was sure had somehow diminished the closeness that *I* shared with Warren. Being left that far behind gave me a sense of loneliness I'd never known before, and the solitude of it all was blinding. It had made me angry with the wrong people, when the real person I was mad at was myself.

But Emily and I did need to talk. I'd never called her back after my argument with Warren, and had been screening my calls since Saturday. I knew that by now, she figured I was upset. And I did have some right to be. She should've been a little more sensitive. But that wasn't the point. The point was that I just hadn't felt like dealing with the problem. And we did have a problem—I had a paralyzing fear of change, and Emily was changing way too fast. We needed to find some sort of medium, together. And she needed to get off of this promiscuity kick before she got in too deep to recognize herself. I called her on

Tuesday, right after I made up with Warren. But the conversation didn't exactly go according to plan.

"What happened to *you* on Saturday?" she asked, making the question sound more like an accusation.

"I was upset, Emily," I admitted. "I needed time to myself."

"And time to talk to Warren? I called him to see if he'd heard from you after you completely neglected to call me back."

"Well, he beeped in on the other line when you and I were hanging up."

"And you felt like you could tell him how upset you were, but you couldn't tell me?"

"It wasn't like that. We talked more about us than anything you guys did."

"Oh, suddenly you and Warren are an 'us'?" Her tone was bordering on bitchy, but I tried to laugh it off.

"Would it be more accurate to say that *you* and Warren are an 'us'?" I did hope she realized that prior to the other night, she and Warren weren't even friends in their own right. They were merely friends through me, and not even very good ones at that.

"Well, we did have sex, Stella. And, obviously, you have a problem with that."

"To be honest, yes, I do."

"Stella, Warren isn't your boyfriend. He's not a guy you're in love with. He's not even someone you once dated. Does 'hands off' now apply to all of Stella's platonic male friends, too?"

"Emily, Warren and I have always been more to each other than friends, and you know it."

"Why? Because you kissed once—the summer before *eleventh grade?*" Her voice was dripping in sarcasm.

"It was more than once, Emily."

"Sorry," she said dryly. "I forgot prom weekend."

"What?" I snapped. "That doesn't count?"

"I don't know, Stella. Kissing somebody twice in a two-year period and then having nothing happen for, let's see… How many months has it been since the prom?"

"If I had slept with him, then would it have counted?"

"Look, do you want me to say I'm sorry for sleeping with Warren? Then fine, your holy highness, I'm sorry for sleeping with Warren."

"And all the others?" This was not how I'd planned to raise the promiscuity issue, but she'd taken the gloves off first. She was obviously in the mood to spar with me, and I wanted to show her that I could play just as dirty.

"What *others?* You mean you have more secret boyfriends I didn't know about?"

"I didn't say that."

"Well, then, why don't you just say what you mean?"

"I think you know what I mean."

"I'm not psychic, Stella. If I were, I'd have known to keep my hands off of Warren."

"Well, maybe you should just follow that rule in general from now on."

"With Warren? I think I learned my lesson. It wasn't worth all the grief I'm getting from you."

"I'm not just talking about Warren, Emily. Look, besides him and Jason, I haven't even *known* any of the guys you've slept with."

"That's right, you haven't."

"And neither have you."

My heart pounded in anticipation of her reply. But there was none. And we waited in silence as the minutes dragged on my VCR clock. In the background, I could hear Tori Amos, singing to spare us from the glaring static of dead air. I almost wished I'd never brought up the promiscuity thing at all.

"Does Tori ever remind you of Laura Nyro?" I asked suddenly, my voice sounding stupid and fake. I didn't really care what her answer was, at least not at that moment. I just wanted a reason to talk to her again, about something other than sex. But Emily wasn't ready to drop the subject so easily.

"For your information, Stella, I had two classes with Drew last semester," she said. "We have a lot of friends in common. It wasn't just some cheap, frivolous fling I stumbled into because I have no morals."

"I didn't say you have no morals." I *never* said she had no morals.

"I'm not done," she said, her voice breaking. "Sean was my friend, Casey's roommate. And it wasn't just sex, Stella. I can't make you understand every detail of my life when you're not here experiencing it with me, but I know how you think. He wasn't just some guy I bumped into at a party and decided to have sex with. I admit I did have sex with him the night we met, but he sent me flowers the next day—I *told* you that—and we had something going for two weeks."

"So, why'd you let him go, then?"

"He wasn't Jason."

"Emily..." Finally, we'd reached the root of the problem, and now we could talk about it, the way best friends were supposed to talk about everything. But Emily wasn't quite ready for that.

"You know, it's real easy for you to sit there in judgment of me, Stella—at home in Scottsboro, with Mommy and Kevin and your precious virginity in a jar under your bed." What? Where was this coming from? I thought the sparring match was over. "But here in New York," she continued, "I have no safety net. So, I make my own decisions. Maybe in retrospect, they weren't always the best ones, but they were *my* choices, ones I certainly shouldn't have to explain to some high-and-mighty virgin who sits around condemning other people when she's never done a single daring thing in her life."

Sometimes, the only thing more disabling than being hit below the belt in battle is being knocked over the head with the truth. I was aware of my shortcomings. I just didn't realize they were visible to the outside world. It took me a moment to recover. When I did, I fired back with the aid of a big purple dildo.

"I may not be as daring as you are, Emily, but as for keeping my virginity in a jar under my bed, I think we both know the only thing under my bed is a shoe box."

"You keep your virginity in a shoe box?"

"If virginity comes in purple and is shaped like a penis."

"Why did you have to bring that up?" Jason's pre-breakup

fidelity insurance was, after all, quite a sore subject with Emily. That's why I had custody of the damn thing in the first place.

"Oh, I don't know," I said spitefully. "I guess I just like to say what's on my mind."

"Well, *that's* something new."

"Speaking of new, that vibrator's been in hibernation such a long time, I bet it would feel like a novelty again. *Maybe* if you took it back, you'd be…" I stopped suddenly. I didn't want to finish that sentence. But it was too late—I'd already started it.

"I'd be what, Stella? Less of a slut?"

"I didn't say that."

"You didn't have to." There was silence as, I suppose, we both thought about where to proceed from there. And then Emily spoke, calmly, but with words that seemed to come out of nowhere. "Sex didn't kill Blanche, you know."

The unexpected mention of my sister's death gave me chills. "I know that," I said shakily.

"Do you? I mean, do you really know that?"

"Rationally, yes…but, Emily, you were there the night she talked about sex like it was nothing."

"I *never* talk about sex like it's nothing."

"But you don't talk about it like it's *something,* either. And isn't it supposed to be *something?* Wasn't it *something* when you did it with Jason?" She didn't answer me. "You saw what that night at Keith Shay's did to her."

"Yeah, but, Stella, Blanche was really screwed up. You saw the diary. You *know* it wasn't just the sex."

"But can't you see that the stuff in the diary—the way she felt about life and herself—led her to go *along* with the sex?"

"Well, that may have been Blanche, but it's not me."

"But how do you know?" I suddenly found myself desperate, craving some sort of concrete answer that would set Emily apart from girls who died for their mistakes.

"Because we're two different people, Blanche and me."

"Yeah, but—"

"Oh, Jesus Christ, Stella, it was a razor blade! Your sister didn't die on that floor having sex with six guys! She slit her wrists and she died! It's not gonna happen to me!"

"Yeah, but what proof is there?" I begged. "I mean...how do we—"

"You want proof of what killed Blanche?" she said, sounding as if she'd just about had it. "Why don't you go ask your father?"

Emily and I didn't speak for three weeks. She never even tried calling me back after I hung up on her. And I certainly wasn't going to call *her* back after what she'd said. I was well enough aware of why my father had run from razors without her scraping open old wounds. And what did my father's breakdown have to do with her sleeping around?

It was decided—I wouldn't speak to her. But I needed to talk to someone, and I couldn't go to my mother this time. It wasn't just that I couldn't tell her what Emily had said—I wasn't planning on telling anyone that. It was the fact that she thought of Emily too much like a daughter to stay out of our feud and would probably end up trying to mediate between us. That was the last thing I wanted. I couldn't talk to Warren about it, either—he was just too close to the whole situation. There was only one other person I could turn to. So I swallowed my pride and called him.

John was purer of heart than anyone I knew, and he'd always had the power to calm me just by listening. I needed that now more than anything. Of course, I was nervous to call. I'd been playing the waiting game ever since he returned from France. But this wasn't about "us" or whether I seemed desperate or overzealous. This was about needing a friend. And John was there for me—for five hours the night I finally threw in the towel and dialed his number.

We didn't actually discuss my fight with Emily for very long. I didn't really feel like being too explicit. Although I'd always been able to tell John anything, I just couldn't imagine telling him about my emotional response to her one-night stand with Warren. Not that I wasn't curious to see if he'd be jealous. But

I didn't want to play games. I just wanted to talk to him like we used to. And it was a tremendous comfort to know that I still could.

He apologized for not getting in touch sooner, said he'd been running himself down between course work and extracurriculars. But none of that mattered—he wanted to visit. Spring break began for both of us that weekend and he was wondering if he could come stay with me.

"Well, if you're gonna be in Scottsboro, won't your parents want you at home?" I asked.

"You didn't know? My mom got that job at the *Post*. They sold the house a month ago and moved down to D.C."

I couldn't believe it—my rainy August wish had finally come true. Seven months later, but it was actually happening. I was going to take John away from his world of pressure and obligation. I was going to have him all to myself, finally, and for a week. A week that was brimming with possibilities.

So much for my mother and Warren and their theories about John and me. He wouldn't be coming if there weren't still that chance for something wonderful between us, something more than just friends. And I didn't care how much it might hurt when he went back to New Haven—I was going to see to it that we fell in love again.

Young Love

I really hadn't expected John to be so tired, but college had completely worn him out. For the first two days of his visit, all he did was sleep. Most of the time, I cuddled with him on the bed, but I was too excited to fall asleep, too grateful to be lying there with him again, just like when we used to take naps together after school. Too happy that he breathed the same, smelled the same, right down to his apple shampoo. Yet, I knew that falling in love would have to wait until John had energy, or at least until he was conscious.

When John finally snapped out of his exhaustion, it was Monday afternoon. Kevin was out on a job somewhere, and my mom, who normally would've been working from home, had taken the day off—bless her heart—to go shopping with her friend, Ellen. We had the entire place to ourselves, and John was full of vigor. But all he wanted to do was talk about my fight with Emily.

"You never actually told me what it was about," he said.

"Yes, I did. Sort of."

"Okay, well then, let me see if I remember. You disagreed with some of her recent actions."

"Right."

"And so you decided to bring them to her attention."

"Uh-huh."

"And that's when things got ugly?"

"That's right," I said. John laughed. "What's so funny?"

"You are."

"Why?"

"Because you're protecting her, Stella. You're mad enough to say you're never speaking to her again, but you're still protecting her. Doesn't that tell you something?"

He was right. I was protecting her. But I was also protecting myself. I guess I could've gotten around the Warren issue somehow and still given John the gist of our argument. But I wouldn't have been able to stand it if anyone thought less of Emily for one terrible thing she said to me. I was the only one with that right. And she had a right to be angry, too. It's not as if I was completely innocent. But the details were delicate in that they could only be understood—and wildly distorted—by Emily and me. I could never share them with anyone, not even John. Especially when it meant wasting a precious opportunity alone on my bed when his primary aim wasn't sleep.

"I didn't say I'm *never* speaking to her again," I explained, in hopes of moving on. "I just said I was putting our friendship on hold for a while."

John smiled. "That's not what you said."

"Well, that's what I've decided."

"Just don't wait too long. She may start seeing other people."

"What do you mean?"

"While the two of you are on hold—she may start seeing other women." I smiled, remembering how he used to refer to Emily as "my girlfriend's wife" back in eleventh grade. And as punishment for teasing me, I hit him on the shoulder with my fat purple teddy bear, Marlayna. "Damn it, that hurt."

With all my courage, I leaned forward. "Let's see if I can make it up to you." And that's when I kissed him, without being invited or seduced.

When I pulled away, he looked happy—like, perhaps, he'd been waiting seven months for it, too. And then he grabbed my face and kissed *me,* in a way that made up for lost time and all my fears that we might never get together again.

John was in complete control. Summit Valley's boy wonder had grown into quite the sexy man since we'd met. I wondered if he'd been working out. Was that what made him so assertive? Either way, it was a good thing. And there we lay, shirtless and breathless under the covers, kissing as if we'd missed each other for seven *years* and yet with as much understanding as if no time had passed at all.

I don't remember all the details of getting naked. I just know that he was gentle, sweet, the same way he always was, regardless of what he was doing. I didn't feel nervous and it never once seemed like we were rushing things. There was only a thrill and a warmth and one overwhelming awareness that consumed us—knowing that, together, we were changing our lives.

"Are you okay?" he whispered, his breath tickling my ear.

I brought his face back to mine. "I want to."

The look in his eyes was priceless, but he still asked if I was sure. I reached into my nightstand drawer and handed him a condom. He didn't need any convincing after that.

When it was all over, John and I lay there cuddling, just like we were used to, only this time naked and with a new bond between us. The wall inside of me had finally crumbled. I was no longer a champion of nothing, but a girl who had just had sex with the boy who held her heart. Life could not get any sweeter.

"What are you thinking about?" he asked.

"I'm thinking we should probably wash these sheets before my mom gets back." Obviously that's not the *only* thing I was thinking about. I just didn't want to be sappy.

"Why? Does she normally inspect your sheets when you have boys over?"

"*No*... It's just that they feel all wet and sticky, and if she sees me washing them later, she might get suspicious."

"Well, anything you feel is from you," he said, pulling me closer.

"Ew, it is not."

"Wanna bet? I wore a condom, didn't I?"

"So."

"*So,*" he teased me. "Did you buy them yourself?"

"Umm-hmm."

"How embarrassed were you?"

"I was mortified. How did you know?"

"Because I know you," he said. And inside, I smiled—and thanked God and every star in the sky that I hadn't slept with Dan Jacoby senior year.

"John?"

"Yeah?"

"I'm glad we did that."

"Me, too."

"I'd never done it before."

John squeezed me tighter, kissing the back of my neck. "I know."

"Was it that obvious?"

He laughed. "No. Not at all. I just figured." And then we were both quiet. And I think a part of me knew the answer to my question before I even asked. But I guess it's only human nature to require confirmation.

"Was it your first time, too?"

John propped himself up on his elbow to face me, his eyes brimming with apology. "It wasn't anything like this."

"What does *that* mean?" I asked, my voice betraying me with its waver.

"I didn't love her."

All at once, I was in tears—messy, hysterical tears—and I didn't want to be around him anymore. This wasn't how it was supposed to be. I sat up in bed, struggling for cover. On TV, they always make it look so easy—wrapping oneself in a sheet to walk across the room. In real life, when you've just lost your virginity and the guy you're in love with tells you he's slept with somebody else, graceful exits aren't as likely. Especially when said Love of Life's leg is weighing down part of the sheet you are groping for, and the rest is twisted up with the bedspread. Not being able to see through your tears only adds to the confusion. Wasn't it just like sweet, gentle John to sit up and help me escape?

"I'm sorry," he said, gathering the sheet for me. "Stella, I'm sorry. It meant nothing. This was different." He put his hand on my shoulder, and for a moment I forgot my mission. His touch, his voice, everything about him was so soothing and genuine. I turned to him and let my head fall forward, resting it against his chin as I continued to cry. But as his arms tightened around me, I grew angry—to be receiving comfort from the one who'd hurt me in the first place, to have forgiven him so quickly. More than that, I was angry that he could still see me, that he'd become privy to my secret side—the side that was obviously still so hung up on him, I was crying like a possessive slob over the fact that he'd been with other girls. I jerked away suddenly, crashing into his nose, which instantly began gushing blood.

"Shit!" was about all I could manage to say. But before leaving the room, I grabbed a box of tissues from my desk. "Here," I said, tossing it onto the bed. "Don't forget to tilt your head back." It wasn't an apology, but it was the most I could muster at the time.

I'd been in the bathroom all of about thirty seconds when John's voice sounded outside the door.

"Stella, please let me explain."

"What's to explain? I understand everything now—perfectly."

"That's not fair. Come on."

"Fair? Was it *fair* to tell me you didn't want a commitment just so you could go around screwing other girls?"

"It was *one* other girl, Stella, and it was only one time."

"And why should I believe that?"

"Have I ever lied to you before?"

"Not that I know of."

"Stella..."

"No. I guess you haven't.... Who was she?"

"Just some girl I met last fall at a party. I'll probably never even see her again. She was only in town visiting a friend. It was stupid, Stella, really. I'm telling you, it meant nothing."

I was relieved to hear it hadn't been someone from school, some brilliant bitch that he actually saw on a regular basis. But she had to have been pretty. I mean, she had to have had *some* sort of redeeming quality for John to have made the admittedly stupid decision to have sex with her.

"What did she look like?"

John sighed. "I was drunk, Stella. I don't know."

"Was she thin?"

"This is weird, Stella. Do we really have to talk about what she looked like?"

"Yes."

John sighed again. "Fine. She was thin." Pass the salt, please. "And she had long, dark hair—like yours, but not as nice." Ha! Perhaps, we were even then. But, there was still one more thing.

"What about her chest?" I asked.

"Not as good as yours."

"How do I know you're not just saying that?"

"Have you *seen* your chest?"

I smiled, basking in my triumph over the anonymous hussy who'd gotten to John Lixner first. "So, what are you saying? That no one's are as good as mine?"

"Well, I don't know from *experience*, but I'd feel confident in making that claim, sure.... Will you come out of the bathroom now?"

"Well, wait. I'd like to hear you make that claim first."

"Stella, you have the most beautiful breasts in the world." We both laughed, but I felt unexpectedly aroused. John had never been this forward with sexual compliments. In fact, he'd never given me a sexual compliment at all. Of course, he *had* been coaxed into it, but what was a little coaxing among friends who made sheets wet and sticky?

"John? Can I ask you something else before I come out?"

"You can ask me anything."

"Why did you do it? Was it just to get your first time over with?"

"No. It wasn't even that calculated. I know the whole 'it just happened' excuse is a really bad cliché, but I don't know how else to describe it. I don't want to blame the alcohol because that's a total cop-out, but it definitely played its part. I'd erase it if I could, Stella. I'll always regret that my first time wasn't with you. I always thought it would be. But if it's any consolation, I'll never forget today. And not just because you tried to beat me up afterward."

"I didn't mean to hurt you," I said.

"Same here."

"I know."

"So, are you coming out or what?"

"Wait. You never told me her name."

"Does it matter?"

"I'm always gonna wonder."

"Stella."

"What?"

"Stella—that was her name."

"Oh, get serious."

"I mean it. That was her name. I was only checking her out because she kind of looked like you from the back. Then she comes over and says her name is Stella. I thought somebody put something in my drink. It shocked the hell out of me."

"That is kind of weird." And flattering, for two reasons. One, that John thought enough of my rear view to remember it fondly at parties. And two, because he'd told me this other Stella was thin.

"She was a nice girl, from what I remember, but her face looked nothing like yours. I don't want to be mean, but she had, like, one of those beakish bird noses—you know which kind I'm talking about? That shocked me, too. I just expected her face to match her body."

"You mean you expected her to look more like me?"

"I think so."

"So, am I supposed to take your sleeping with another girl as some really big but twisted form of flattery and leave it at that?"

"Please?"

"Brace yourself," I said. "I'm opening the door."

I came out to find John naked in the hallway, blotting his nose with a tissue.

"I think we should wash the bedding," he said. "There's blood all over the sheets...and I think some of it's yours."

I reached up and kissed him gently on the nose. "Not just yet."

We washed the sheets just before my mom got home and spent the rest of the week making them good and dirty again. By the time John left, we'd had sex seventeen times and had definitely recaptured our love. But distance and youth would prevent us from making it last in long-term reality—or even beyond spring break.

Just Duckie

One of the best things about losing my virginity was that it put an end to my spell of naughty dreams. It's a good thing I never sought psychological treatment for those—I doubt my therapist would've advised getting laid. But as it turned out, that's all I needed. One week alone with John and I was cured.

I secretly saved all seventeen of the condom wrappers that helped heal me. Some may have called this psychotic. I called it...psychotic. I knew I was nuts. But I couldn't help it. I treasured those empty wrappers. They were proof that my rainy August wish had come true. I *had* had John all to myself—seventeen times. And now I had a new wish, a goal. There were still nineteen condoms left over. Before they expired in May '99, John and I would use them all. In the meantime, I kept the empty wrappers tucked away in a little box on the top shelf of my closet, buried beneath some old letters John had written me from the academy in L.A. He'd never written me from Yale. Though he did start doing so shortly after we had sex. That was another good thing about losing my virginity—it inspired John to write more. His letters never said anything about being in love with me or wishing we could be together. But so what if we'd gone from red-hot lovers to pen pals? At least we were staying connected, and I always had something to add to my John Box.

I was still basking in the afterglow of my fallen chastity when Warren came home for spring break. I'd resumed classes a week earlier and didn't have a ton of free time to spend with him, but that was probably a good thing, for two reasons. For one, I feared it might be awkward as hell. I mean, after everything that had happened, we were okay on the phone, but I still hadn't been in a room with him since he'd confessed his true feelings for me. And then, there was the whole issue of my week alone with John. Of course, I'd taken the coward's way out of telling him about it, leaving a rude and idiotic message on his voice mail the day before John's arrival. I waited until I knew he'd be in class to call so I could drop the bombshell that his nemesis was coming without worrying about his response. I made it clear that he shouldn't call during John's visit, though in the most sugarcoated of ways. But I suppose ending the message with "I'll talk to you next week, then" was a pretty good way of saying, "Don't call me." Not that I really needed to go that far. The warning that John would be visiting had probably been enough. I don't think Warren was interested in rehashing our turmoil by putting both of us in another triangle situation. But the fact that there would've been a "situation" couldn't be ignored forever. And even with classes and schoolwork, I still saw a good deal of Warren over his break. Things weren't awkward as *hell,* like I'd feared, but the need to talk was obvious. I just didn't have the courage to open my mouth first.

But sometimes it's not about courage or the plans we make. Sometimes things happen spontaneously, and at the least expected moments we find resolution. At least, that's how it happened in this case, when Warren began his uncomfortable interrogation about John and me.

He was lying on my bed, flipping stations on the TV, while I sat at my desk, paging through one of my mother's catalogs.

"So, how's John?" he asked. "You never told me about his visit." He turned off the TV and sat up.

"He's good," I said, closing the catalog. And without glancing up, I began packing my schoolbag for the next day—anything to appear busy so I wouldn't actually have to look at him during this conversation.

"And you?"

"Me?"

"You."

"I'm good, too."

"And the two of you?"

"Hmm?"

"It won't fit."

I looked up at him suddenly. "What do you mean?"

"That book you're trying to stuff into your bag. You have too many in there. It won't fit."

I looked down and realized that he was right. In my attempt to appear unaffected, I'd mindlessly filled my bag with books I didn't even need. I put the one I was holding back onto my desk, and then, out of nowhere, I burst into tears. Within seconds, Warren was on his knees in front of me.

"Emily and I aren't friends anymore!" I cried, surprised at the words as they emerged. But I don't know why I should have been. Deep down, I knew how much our fight was hurting me, but I suppose I'd thought I could bury it, the same way I'd buried those condom wrappers with letters in the John Box, because so many good things had happened, too. But Emily hadn't been by my side to share in them. She didn't even know I'd lost my virginity. "So much has happened, Warren, and there are things I want to tell her. But we aren't friends!"

"Shh, it's okay," he whispered, hugging me. "Come on." He led me over to the bed and I rested my head on his chest, without worrying what it might imply. And for a few minutes, we didn't say anything. He just held me and let me cry. "It's not worth it, Stella," he said when I'd calmed down. "Look what it's doing to you. This isn't what either of you wants."

"You've talked to Emily about this?"

"Barely. I called her a couple weeks ago just to make sure she was okay with everything—you know, with her and me. She called me the day after it happened, but only to see if I'd heard from *you*—we pretty much avoided the topic of what she and I did. I just figured I should call her and make sure there were no bad feelings." He stopped suddenly. "Does it bother you that I'm talking about this?"

"No, go ahead. What did she say about me?"

"That's just it. She didn't say anything. This was during the week that John was visiting and I didn't talk to you. So, I asked her if *she'd* talked to you, and she just said you two had stopped speaking. She refused to tell me why. I haven't said anything to you about it because I know it's a bad subject. But, please tell me. Did it—"

"No. It didn't have anything to do with you."

In the strangest way, I suddenly felt forgiveness. To hear about Emily, on the other side of our silent war, giving Warren the same answers I had given John—which were pretty much no answers at all—made me feel like she was protecting us, too. We might always be different, but on the inside, where it counted, we both knew what mattered. We were even loyal to each other in combat. She'd always be my best friend, even if circumstances and stupidity, for a moment, eclipsed our common sense and made us enemies.

"Look," Warren said, "I don't care what it was about, but you're both being ridiculous. You, my dear, are stubborn as hell. And Emily, well, I don't know her well enough to say, but I think she's scared to call you. At least, that's the impression I got."

"Really?"

"Yes, really. Look, remember that little fight we had a few weeks ago?"

"*Little* fight?"

Warren squeezed my shoulder. "Well, obviously it wasn't big enough to be the end of us. Can you honestly say this thing between you and Emily was big enough to end your friendship for good?"

"No."

"So, you'll call her, then?"

"I'll call her."

"Promise?"

I took a deep breath. I couldn't lie to him. "I promise."

"Good girl."

"Warren?" I asked, suddenly feeling comfortable enough for honesty.

"Yeah?"

"I really am sorry about what happened—between us, I mean."

"I'm glad we're still friends," he said, rubbing my arm.

"Me, too."

"I mean that, you know. And friends tell each other things. They don't censor themselves because somebody made an ass of himself one morning on the phone."

"What are you talking about?"

"Stella, my feelings are my problem, not yours. I don't want you to feel like you can't tell me about the better part of your life—the good stuff, I mean, the stuff you *want* to talk about—because you're afraid of hurting my feelings. That's not a real friendship."

I turned over to face him. "But how could I not care about your feelings when you're one of my closest friends?"

"I'm not saying don't care. Just don't let it be all you think about when we're together. Because, believe me, as much as I *do* have feelings for you, it's not even all I think about. I'm still the same person I was last year, and last month, even. You just know a little more now than you did before." He smiled. "And I'm gonna get over you, Stella." The finality of his words made me unexpectedly sad—if he "got over" me, would we still have this bond?

"Not too soon, I hope." It was a selfish thing to say, but I needed some kind of assurance that we'd never lose what we had, that he'd never stop caring, that he'd always be around.

"Not too soon," Warren said, stroking my cheek. "In the meantime, I guess it's every guy's curse to be some woman's Duckie."

And there was my assurance, brilliantly packaged in a John Hughes movie analogy. No *Pretty in Pink* fan ever questions whether Duckie and Andie stay close after Blane. Andie and Blane may end up together, but Andie and Duckie are unquestionably bound forever through friendship. I wondered if Warren realized that most women were secretly in love with Duckie, anyway. It didn't matter. He had just found an acceptable way to define our relationship, and I loved him for doing so with my kind of role models. After all, before *90210,* there had been the brat pack, and like Brenda Walsh, Molly Ringwald had never let me down. I would just have to remember how Andie handled Duckie. And didn't every girl want a Duckie of her very own? I leaned over and kissed Warren on the cheek.

"What was that for?"

"I just appreciate you a lot," I told him. "More than you know." I laid my head back down on his chest.

"So?"

"So, what?" I asked him.

"Tell me about *Blane,*" he teased.

"Warren!"

"Sorry, I mean John."

It wasn't exactly easy, but he wanted me to tell him things, the good stuff, the better part of my life, and so I did. I told him I'd lost my virginity to John.

Warren's response was nothing like I would have pictured. He didn't act hurt or resentful, but instead seemed almost fatherly about the whole thing. He made me promise that John had worn a condom every time. And then he asked if it had been John's first time as well. It should have felt weird—telling Warren how upset I'd been about John's other Stella—but it didn't. It felt good to talk to someone about it. Though, I must admit I was shocked when Warren said he understood John's point of view. He said he could definitely see where I would've been hurt, but that sex wasn't always black and white. He said that while girls often saw it that way, there were so many shades of gray to consider.

"For instance," he said, "let's say I have sex with a girl I just met at a party. I'm not doing it because I love her or want to date her. That's why they call it a one-night stand. But then, let's say another girl comes along six months later and I fall in love with her. It would be a completely different situation with genuine feelings. The only similarity would be in the definition. It would still be sex. Guys are only human, Stella. We can't reinvent the body to create new physiological experiences for the women we love. Sex is sex, but when you're in love, it's different.... I can only imagine, I mean. I've never had sex with someone I loved before." He was quiet for a second. "I'm sure John knows how lucky he is."

"Thank you for saying that."

"Well, it's true. This Stella Birdnose girl couldn't have possibly held a candle to you."

Warren and I lay there in silence for a while after our talk. I had gotten a lot of things off of my chest and I felt relieved. But most of all, I felt grateful that after everything, he was still in my life, closer than ever, holding me without pressure or restraint. We were comfortable. There was no need for censors. Everything was out in the open. Well, almost everything. For something had crept up during the silence, something I couldn't exactly ignore but would never have the guts to talk to him about. And I doubted very highly that Andie and Duckie had ever had to deal with this problem. There was only one person who would know for sure.

"Of course, Duckie got boners around Andie!" Emily said. "But they're not gonna show you those parts in the *movie.*" I'd called her as soon as he left. After all, I'd promised Warren. But that wasn't the real reason. I called because I was ready. And then there was this whole matter of illegal boners among friends to discuss. "Could you see how big it was?" she asked. "Through his clothes, I mean?"

"I was trying *not* to look, Em."

"Stella, it's *me*. Do you expect me to believe you're not the slightest bit attracted to Warren anymore?"

"Promise not to tell?"

"Do you want me to hang up on you, Stella?"

"Why?"

"Because asking me to promise not to tell a secret is like saying I've forgotten how to be a best friend. I mean, we may not have spoken for a few weeks, but—"

"I can't believe it's been that long."

"I know," she said regretfully. "Listen, Stella, you were one-hundred-percent right about me and I was completely wrong to say...well, we both know what I said."

"I missed you *so* much! I don't care about what happened. I just want to know we won't ever go that long without talking again. No matter what happens, we should always be able to talk. I've been dying here the past couple of weeks."

"Well, you should have called me, you crazy bitch! I was just too chicken to call you after what I said."

"Forget about it," I told her.

"I'll try—if you make a promise."

"What's that?"

"That you'll never keep me in the dark for so long when you have such *major* things going on in your life!"

"Like what?" I teased. "Warren having boners?"

"Well, I was speaking more along the lines of John's, but now that you mention our pal, Warren—I promise not to tell. So, spill. Are you still attracted to him or not?"

"I am," I admitted, feeling guilty for two boys who meant everything to me in different ways. But then again, I wasn't committed to John, and what was merely *admitting* an attraction when he'd actually acted on his? Not that I hadn't forgiven him for Ms. Birdnose, but why should I have felt guilty when I hadn't even done anything to feel guilty about? But then, there was Warren. It was unfair of me to have this attraction. In a sense, whether he knew about it or not, I felt like I was leading him on.

"I knew it," Emily said smugly. "I could tell by the fact that you stayed in your bed cuddling with him even though he had a boner."

I laughed. "That's not why, Emily! I was scared of that boner. I was afraid that if I got up—"

"It might chase you across the room?"

"No! That Warren might realize I saw it and things would get weird again."

"But, tell me something, honey. What would've happened if you'd taken advantage of it?"

"Of Warren's boner?"

"Of your situation—of the fact that you were lying together in your bed, with Warren all turned on like that? You said it yourself—you're still attracted to him."

"And I might always be, but it's not so overwhelming that I can't control myself, and it's definitely not a good thing."

"Why, Stella? Are you and John married?"

"No, it's not that."

"Well, what, then?"

"Warren and I are just friends. I can't go changing the terms now. I don't even want to. I *want* him to be my Duckie."

"But, come *on,* Stella. Doesn't every girl secretly wanna sleep with Duckie, anyway?"

"Okay, forget the movie for a second. This is reality we're talking about, not John Hughes. You're getting as bad as my mother and her *Streetcar.*"

"How *is* Janey?"

"Now you're just off the subject completely," I said. "But she's doing well. Listen, I need to ask you something, something serious."

"What is it?"

"How do *you* feel about Warren?"

"Promise not to judge me?"

"I learned my lesson on that three weeks ago."

"I like him. I think of him as a friend."

"Why would I have had anything bad to say about that?"

"Because I know it would sound classier if I said I was in love with him."

"It would make things a lot more complicated, too. Don't you think?" I asked.

"Definitely. I'd probably have to hate you."

"Which would be so hard to reconcile, considering how much you love me."

"Completely hard. My best friend/the other woman. Both a contradiction *and* a cliché… Can I tell you a secret now?"

"Always."

"I'd sleep with him again in a heartbeat if—"

"I'm not stopping you." Of course, the idea didn't exactly thrill me, but that wasn't Emily's problem.

"Hey, even if I *believed* that load of bullshit, I still wouldn't sleep with him again. Because whether or not you mean to, you are stopping me, Stella."

"How is that?"

"Oh, come on, honey. Just friends or not, you and Warren have something to work out of your systems."

"Do not."

"Do, too, and I'd kill to be a fly on the wall when you finally go for it."

"You mean you'd wanna watch?"

"That'd be some hot sex."

"You're gross," I told her.

"I'm horny. I haven't had sex in over three weeks."

"Really?" I was happy to hear it.

"I don't ever want to go back to the way I was. You were right."

"It's not about me being right, Emily. I just didn't want to see you hurt yourself."

"And I was. I just didn't want to see it that way. But you know what I've decided?"

"What's that?"

"That it's all okay. I mean about Jason. It's okay that he wasn't the one and that we didn't end up like my parents. I don't have to continue on this rampage because of one mistake."

"Are you going to be all right?"

"I'll be fine. As long as you don't drop out of my life again."

"I won't," I said. "I promise."

"Oh, and I was thinking…any chance I could get my vibrator back?"

"I'll make you a deal. If you let me throw that thing away, I'll come visit you this weekend and we'll go shopping for a big, shiny new one. My treat."

"Deal," she said.

And just like that, we moved on from Jason and the one ridiculous fight that just wasn't big enough to be the end of us. But some things *are* big enough. Some things swallow friendships whole. And some things burn them alive. Our next big test would rise like a furious claw from the depths of the ocean between us and threaten to drown us in ashes.

As I sat there, listening to departure-and-arrival announcements, I could still see Emily and me, nineteen years old, making deals about dildos and moving on from that which didn't kill us. It had only made us stronger—our battle, our distance. And we'd promised never to let go again, not to let anything tear us apart, no matter what.

But time makes you bolder, even children get older…

It was a shame life couldn't stay that simple. But there was a world of difference between nineteen and twenty-eight.

"Miss? Is that your phone?"

"Landslide," Fleetwood Mac—my cell phone, of course. I looked at the caller ID and wanted to die. I'd forgotten to cancel dinner with Warren.

"Hello?"

"Hey! I was gonna leave for the train station now. Is that cool, or should I come later?"

"Warren, I can't. I am *so* sorry…I'm at the airport."

"The airport? Why? What's going on?"

"Emily invited me to come see her on a whim." I hated not telling Warren the truth. It was harder than not telling my mother. "I should've called you earlier. This was really important. I'm sorry. I really am."

"Don't be," he said. I could hear the hurt in his voice. "It really wasn't that important."

"Of course it was. We have a lot to talk about, Warren. And we *will*—as soon as I get back."

"Well, when will *that* be?" He was more than just hurt. Warren was pissed. Damn Emily.

"You're mad. Shit. I feel like such a jerk."

"I'm not angry, Stella. I'm just disappointed. But I understand. I mean, how often do you get to go to Europe, right?"

"I'd rather be with you."

"Well, you're a very sweet liar." If only he knew the half of it.

"I am sorry, though. I mean, this was all my idea, and—"

"Forget about it. Just go and be careful and have a good time. Say hi to Emily for me, okay?"

"You've got it."

"And we'll talk when you get back."

"Okay. I love you."

"I know you do. Have a safe flight, all right?"

"All right."

"And Stella?"

"Yeah?"

"I love you, too."

I hung up the phone feeling angry. Angry at the impossible choices people make for their lives. Angry at myself. Angry at Emily. Angry that I was sitting here lying to people I adored when I could have still been at home with the covers pulled up over my head.

Unmasking Mr. Fix-It: The Truth About Kevin Kilbride

I never suspected that my stepfather was anything less than perfect until the day Emily came over to help me pack my things for college.

"So, have you decided if you're taking Marlayna or not?" she asked me that afternoon.

"Um…" It was hard to decide anything in that heat. Kevin wasn't around to fix the air conditioning, and there weren't even any breezes coming in from the open window to cool us. "I guess I'll leave her here," I said, hoping the teddy bear I'd slept with since childhood would understand why I wasn't taking her with me to school.

"Are you sure?" Emily asked.

"Come on, Penn isn't *that* far away. I can always come back for her if the separation anxiety gets too ugly."

"Besides, she's what, fourteen now?" Emily asked. "Marlayna might even enjoy some time away from Mommy." But would

Mommy enjoy the time away from Marlayna? That was the important question.

As we continued to pack, I remembered the way Emily's bedroom had looked a year earlier when I'd gone over for foam pancakes and one very dreaded goodbye. Only in the past year, I'd learned that distance wasn't death. I had no desire to freeze time. I was excited about living on campus. For once, I had embraced my enemy—change—and it had made me a happier person.

I'd made the decision in the spring, right after all the drama settled. I should've been content—Emily and I were speaking again, Warren was my Duckie, and John and I had finally had sex. But instead, I was left feeling as if everyone had returned to their exciting lives, and I was somehow lurking in the shadows, waiting for the next big thing. Not that I craved more fighting or tension—and, of course, I'd be lying if I said I *didn't* crave more sex, but it wasn't about that, either. The drama of March had simply taught me that I wanted a life—outside of my high school friends. I didn't want to be the girl they came home to and then left again when breaks were over. I wanted to leave Scottsboro, too.

"Have you talked to Alison lately?" Emily asked.

"Yeah, yesterday. She's really excited."

"She should be. I'd lick the ground for a chance to live with you."

"Well, maybe if you aimed a little higher than the ground, I'd consider it."

"Ew, Stella! You're starting to sound like me."

"And it only took what? Six and a half years?"

"Something like that. All kidding aside, though, I'm glad you found Alison. And not just because she happens to share my passion for Stevie Nicks and Tori Amos."

"But you do admit that made you like her more."

"At first. But you've told me so much more about her since then, and I think she's going to be really good for you."

"I think so, too," I said. And then, for no reason, we hugged.

In actuality, Emily gave me too much credit. I didn't exactly "find" Alison Bruno. She'd been there all along. I'd just been too opposed to forming new friendships, too lazy to attempt conversation, to realize what was right in front of me. We'd had two classes together during the fall semester and another two in the spring, but it wasn't until we were paired up for a project in April that I realized what an amazing girl she was. And the friendship couldn't have come at a better time for either of us. Alison's roommate was transferring in the fall; I had just decided that I wanted to live on campus. It was perfect. The two of us would room together.

"So, what's the deal with this bachelor's weekend?" Emily asked. "Who does Kevin know who's getting married?"

I took a break from packing and flopped down onto the bed. "His name's Don," I said, wiping the sweat from my forehead. "Kevin went to high school with him in Boston."

Emily sat down beside me. "And your mom honestly doesn't mind him being gone all weekend? He sure picked a good one. It's hot as shit in here." She fell backward, fanning herself.

"Tell me about it," I said, lying beside her.

"It's hot as shit in here."

"Yeah, yeah. Anyway, in answer to your question, no, my mom doesn't mind. I mean, she misses him and everything, but it's not the kind of bachelor stuff you're thinking. Don's not interested in strippers."

"What kind of man isn't interested in strippers?"

"The kind who's had to postpone his wedding twice because his fiancée had cancer."

Emily gasped. "That's terrible! Oh, my God, Stella, how old are they?"

"Well, Don is Kevin's age, and Rita's even younger. She's only twenty-eight."

"Shit," Emily whispered as a dark cloud seemed to settle over the room.

"But she's okay now. She's actually doing really well. The doctors say they got it all. So, she's gonna be fine." But I could tell by Emily's silence that she wasn't thinking about Don and Rita anymore. Her mind was somewhere else. "What is it?"

Emily rolled over onto her side to face me. "You know, my mom was twenty-eight when she died. It was just like this trip Kevin's taking—to visit a friend from high school. Only my mom had never even been to Chicago. Her friend Jessie had just moved there a year earlier. My God, can you imagine if you and I ever went a year without seeing each other?" I shook my head. "Me, neither. They were best friends and everything, but my mom had a toddler, and Jessie lived more of a wild life.... It's just so strange."

"What is?"

"How things work out. I mean, what if my mom hadn't gone that weekend, you know? Or they'd had a little less to drink? What if my dad had gone with her? I could have stayed with a sitter, right?"

"I guess so."

"I mean, how do you just leave candles burning and in the path of the cat if you plan on passing out?"

"I guess they weren't thinking, Em."

"They must've been so wasted. No one can be that dumb. It's pretty fucked up when you think of it—curiosity killed the cat and the cat killed my mother."

"Emily..."

"Sorry to be such a downer," she said, sitting up. "It's just that I've been living in a world of 'what-ifs' since I was three."

"Believe me," I said, as I sat up to face her, "I *know* what that's like. It doesn't get us anywhere, though, does it?"

"I guess not." She was quiet for a second, and then she smiled. "Hey, I've got a packing question."

"What's that?"

"What are we doing with your condoms? Are you gonna take all nineteen with you or leave some here?" Despair washed over me, but Emily dismissed it. "Don't look like that, Stella. It was only one summer. You still have until May of '99."

I was back to missing John like crazy. We hadn't seen each other since spring break. The past few months had been impossibly hectic for him, but that wasn't exactly the reason we hadn't seen each other. The reason was me. John hadn't gone home to D.C. to live a relaxed summer life at his parents' house. Instead, he'd stayed in New Haven, where he was juggling two internships for his double major of literature and philosophy and a nights-and-weekends job to pay for his place. I was the one living the relaxed summer life. All I had was my new job at the day-care center, and that was it. No internships, no crazy hours, and my weekends were free. John could never get away, not even to see his family. But I could. I could get away virtually any weekend of the month. And I knew John wanted me to visit. He'd invited me several times. I just hadn't taken him up on his invitations. I'd simply been too afraid.

With John's schedule the way it was, we wouldn't have had much time to spend together, and I worried that the time we *would've* had wouldn't have measured up to spring break. I was afraid I'd spend my entire visit watching him sleep. Not that a part of me didn't long for that, but it wasn't enough, not after our last visit, which had been so magical, so memorable, so thrilling. How could I seize control of John's heart if I could barely fit into his plans? And even though he wanted to see me, had fitting me into his schedule just become another source of pressure? That was the last thing I ever wanted to be—a part of John's problems, one of his many obligations. I'd realized the danger for that the night he flipped out at the world as the rain fell hard against my car windows. I couldn't visit him and get in the way. I couldn't visit him and be ignored. I couldn't let anything take away from the time we'd spent together in the spring, without stress, without worry, only with excitement and love. That's why I couldn't visit him that summer.

But once school started in the fall, things would be different. His schedule would be freer and he'd actually be able to enjoy my visit. Or maybe he'd even want to come visit me at Penn when Alison was conveniently elsewhere. We'd make use of those nineteen condoms then. But for the time being, the mere mention of that little batch of hope was just one big reminder of what a failure I'd been. I had no one to blame for my sexless summer but myself. The only thing that could make it all right would be a whole lot of love in the fall.

"I guess I'll pack all nineteen," I told Emily as I lay back down on the bed. The heat had made me so lazy.

She leaned over and grabbed the handle on my nightstand drawer. "Is this where you keep them?"

"Yup."

Emily opened the drawer. "Wait…you said there were *nineteen* condoms in here? Are you sure?"

"Positive," I said, sitting up, my head swirling a little from John memories and sweat. Or maybe it was Emily's question. Of *course,* I knew how many condoms I had. But Emily had just finished counting.

"Stella, there are only nine condoms in here."

I looked over her shoulder and realized that the pile had shrunk considerably since the last time I'd seen it—about two weeks earlier when I'd gone in the drawer to retrieve my diary. But who would've stolen ten condoms? Certainly not Warren, and besides, he'd spent the last three weeks visiting his mother's family in Arizona. He'd only been back for two days and hadn't set foot in my room yet. And it obviously hadn't been Emily. But the only other people who had even been in my room in the past two weeks were…

"Looks like Kevin and your mom have been dipping into your stash, condom fairy. I guess I'll just pack the nine, then?"

I nodded. "Just the nine."

What Emily didn't know was that I'd just had the wind knocked out of me. But then again, I'd never told her about my mother's surgery. It wasn't something I typically gave much thought to. That was, until the discovery of those ten missing condoms made it impossible to shake from my mind. I guess it was because I couldn't help wondering why they needed them. My mother couldn't get pregnant. She'd had her tubes tied when I was twelve.

Kevin returned from his bachelor's weekend on Sunday night. My mom was at her friend Ellen's house in Philadelphia, saying goodbye to Ellen's daughter, who was leaving for college the next day, the same day I was leaving for Penn. I was supposed to go, too, but had faked not feeling well—"nauseous butterflies" for my first year of living away at school. Though the lie soon became true: I did start feeling sick. Not because of school, but because of the real reason I'd stayed behind—to have a talk with my stepfather. My mom had been through too much crap to have this marriage go bad. I needed to confront him about the condoms. I needed to find out the truth.

I hadn't said a word to Emily about my fears. How could I? Charming, handsome, younger men who rescued older women from their former lives of heartache—maybe they *were* too good to be true. But how could I go voicing doubts about his fidelity without knowing the facts? I wouldn't allow myself to degrade my own mother's marriage that way. She'd worked too hard to get where she was. I just needed to have a talk with the man. Perhaps it had all been an honest mistake.

I was standing at the mirror, pulling my hair into a ponytail, when Kevin's voice startled me from the doorway.

"You wanted to see me?" I whirled around to face him, letting my hair fall against my shoulders. "It looked pretty. You should wear it up more often." He began walking into the room. "It's hot," he said, wiping the sweat from his forehead. "I'll have a look at that air conditioner in the morning. Of course, you'll be leaving, so it won't make a difference to you. I'm sorry your last two days at home were so uncomfortable."

As he got closer, I found myself backing away. There was just something about his eyes and the way his sweat dripped in the heat of my room that told me my initial fears had been warranted—he was guilty as sin. But I wanted to hear it from him. And even though I was backing away, I wasn't going to back down. Not now, not when I'd set aside this time for us.

I sat on the bed and looked down at my hands. Ready or not, this was still scary. I wasn't sure where to begin. Before I could figure it out, Kevin had sat down beside me.

"Nervous?" he asked. He meant about the next day, but he'd provided my cue.

"Are *you?*" I shot back, looking straight into his eyes.

"Me? Well, I'm not the one going away to school for the first time tomorrow."

"And I'm not the one on trial."

Kevin laughed, that charming, delicious laugh that had put stars into my mother's sky again. It wasn't so charming anymore. "I didn't realize that's what this was."

"I was packing up my things for school yesterday when I noticed something missing from my nightstand drawer." I waited for him to say something, but he didn't. He only stared at me with an expression I couldn't read. "It was a handful of somethings, actually. I don't really think I need to be any more specific than that." Kevin lowered his head. "Do you have any idea why they were missing?"

I watched as he traced the pattern on my bedspread, saying nothing, and a horrible possibility began to take shape in my mind. What if I'd spoken too soon? What if my mother already knew about the condoms because Kevin had some sort of STD, a disease he'd contracted before even meeting her, and they used condoms all the time? What if I'd just gone and accused him of hurting her when all he'd been trying to do was protect her? But there was nothing heroic in Kevin's response.

"I took those," he said finally, still looking down, "because...well...because I knew they were there."

I lowered my face to his level so that he'd have no choice but to look at me. *"And?"*

"And," he said, making eye contact. "I just..." He trailed off, staring at me strangely.

"Yeah?" What was this? He couldn't even come up with a decent lie?

"I just..." His eyes scanned my chin, my neck, dropped lower, and came back up again, all within seconds, and suddenly I felt something—his hand on my knee.

"What are you—" But Kevin had grabbed hold of my face before I could get the question out. And he was kissing me. Hard.

I tried pushing him away, but couldn't. With one hand, he gripped my head, pulling my hair down from the scalp. With the other, he rubbed my breast—rough—like it wasn't attached to my body, like it didn't matter that it hurt. Like I'd better just shut up.

He forced me down onto the mattress and climbed on top of me, pressing into me with his hot, sweaty skin in my hot, sweaty room on that hot, sweaty night with no air-conditioning or mother. It didn't matter how hard I cried because no one was there. I was like that tree that falls in the forest, the kind that no one is around to hear. So, the question, then, remains: had I really made a sound? Maybe I was already dead. One thing was for sure: I couldn't breathe.

My wrists were bound together in one of his fists, pinned over my head against the mattress. He was unbuttoning my shirt, sucking on my neck, harder and harder, until he'd exposed me. And then he started kissing my chest. The sickness rose steadily inside of me and I begged him through my stream of tears to stop. But he was too busy tugging at my bra, his belt buckle. Hurting my ribs. Stealing pieces of me he should've never even seen.

Why was Kevin doing this? Why couldn't I breathe? It was only supposed to be a talk.

The hot, sweaty room spun around our bodies on the bed as I choked and pleaded with my stepfather for freedom. I saw whiskey shots and girls on living room carpets bargaining for their clothes. I saw Blanche dying in the ambulance, holding my mother's hand. It wasn't going to happen to me.

I didn't expect to scream so loud or to grab hold of Kevin's neck quite so hard. Maybe I would've strangled him if he hadn't jumped off of me. After all, I'd found the strength to free my wrists. But he did jump off of me—I had scared him—and this time, it was his turn to scream.

"Jesus!" he yelled. "What the hell's the matter with you? I thought this was what you wanted!"

"What I wanted?" I'd managed to fix my bra and was now trying to button my shirt. But, I couldn't do it—my fingers were trembling too badly. Kevin's eyes softened as he reached out to help me, like I was a little girl who couldn't tie her shoes. But I shrank from his hands. They were more frightening than fire. "Don't touch me!"

"Fine!" he screamed. "But if you *ever* think about running

to Mommy with this, I'll deny it. Better yet, I'll tell her *you* came on to me."

"She would never—"

"You wanna bet, sweetheart? Do you want to open the drawer and get the diary or should I?"

And that's when it all made sense. If something like that could ever make sense. I'd never told anyone about those dreams I'd had about Kevin. I'd only written about them in my diary, which I kept tucked away in the drawer with the condoms. And anyone who'd cheat on his wife with condoms he'd stolen from his stepdaughter would certainly read a private diary. Kevin thought I wanted him. But did that make what he'd done okay?

We both reached for the drawer at the same time, locking eyes.

"It's okay," he said. "I already know what you wrote. And so will your mother if you ever open your goddamned mouth." I couldn't tell my mother about this, anyway. I'd never tell anyone. It was too humiliating. I wished I'd never even been born. "And if you're thinking of destroying the thing, it won't help. For every good piece of literature, there's a copy." A copy? Kevin smiled. "Gets the job done better than a dirty magazine. But, don't worry. As long as you're good, nobody else will ever see it."

"Kevin," I begged. "Please go."

Suddenly his expression changed, and he actually seemed sorry, maybe even sad. "Stella…"

"Just go. *Please.*"

He reached forward, I suppose to touch my face, but I slapped his hand away—hard. That's when he grabbed me by the throat. I was afraid it would happen all over again, but he only stared at me in silence as my eyes glazed over with tears. And then he let me go. He walked across the room, turning around in the doorway. I was shaking.

"That's right," he said. "Just sit there trembling like a scared little girl."

"I'm not a little girl!" I cried. "I'm not!"

"No, I guess you're not. You're just a screwed-up whore

who's got everybody fooled but me." And then he left, slamming the door behind him.

My room felt different. The heat felt different. I was different. Me, the whore, Lolita. A little girl so afraid of being alone in the dark, she fell asleep on her last night at home behind a locked door with the lights on, clinging desperately to the childhood crutch she thought she'd outgrown. Maybe I needed Marlayna a lot more than I'd realized. Maybe I hadn't grown up at all.

And there I'd been, actually believing I was ready to conquer the world outside of Scottsboro. And here I was, afraid to leave my own bedroom for a drink of water. It was amazing what men could do.

But at least my father had warned us. When people start resembling wolves, we *know* to stay away. But who would've ever guessed that beneath Kevin's charming, clean-cut, Mr. Fix-It disguise beat the heart of Satan?

Denial

After only a few weeks away at school, nothing fit me anymore. But it wasn't a case of the "freshman fifteen," or whatever the term is for *sophomores* who leave home for the first time to live on cafeteria food, pizza and beer. It was actually the total opposite. My diet of denial, flashbacks and guilt had caused me to lose what others gained. Alison was dying to know my secret. That is, my secret to losing weight. *It's called the "Kevin Kilbride Sexual Assault Plan"—three weeks later, you still can't keep anything down.* I couldn't tell her that. I couldn't talk about it with anyone. So, instead I told her that my secret was euphoria—I was just so unspeakably happy living away. And in part, it was true. I loved living away. I'd made tons of friends already and thrived on the fact that I wasn't my own island anymore, that I'd become a part of something real. The only thing weighing me down was what had happened the night before I left, but that would've haunted me anywhere, and at least I had a new environment to help take my mind off of things. A lot of times, it did. At home, I wouldn't have had that. My assailant would've been everywhere. Even when he wasn't there, he would have been—his things, his smell, his eyes staring at me from behind phony pictures. I couldn't have gotten out of that condo at a better time.

Kevin was supposed to help with my move onto campus, but fell mysteriously ill in his sleep the night before and didn't want to get me or any of the other residents sick by coming along that day. How thoughtful. Conveniently enough, he was out like a light when my mother and I loaded our last box into the car. I never even had to say goodbye.

"Poor Kevin," my mother said as we made the drive downtown. "He really wanted to come today." She glanced over at me, smiling. "He says the two of you had *some* talk last night." Her words sent a panic straight through me and I shifted uncomfortably in my seat. My mother noticed, but fortunately misread my behavior. "Oh, Stella, don't get antsy. I'm not hinting to know what it was about. What goes on between you and Kevin is your own private business. I don't even want to know."

"You don't?"

My mother laughed. "Honey, I *want* you to have a special relationship with Kevin, and sometimes that might include having conversations I'm not privy to, and that's fine. It means you're getting closer. It's what he wants, you know." No kidding. "I know it's hard for you to think of him as a father figure when he's so young, but believe me, honey, there's a world of difference between nineteen and thirty-two. And I think there's a lot that Kevin could teach you if you'd let him in a little more often, like you did last night."

Kevin *had* taught me a lot. He'd taught me how to keep secrets, how to fear for my life, and how to feel disgusting. He'd taught me what it was like to feel powerless, to want to kill, to want to die. My stepfather was a wealth of information.

"Janey?"

"It's okay, honey," she said, patting my hand. "I'm through with my little lecture. It's just that..." She sighed and I saw that her face was filled with peace. "I love him so much, Stella. I really do. And I love *you* so much. And maybe I'm just feeling sentimental because you're going away, but I really feel like last night was a turning point for the two of you. He told me when I got back from Ellen's that your time alone together really made him feel a connection, almost as if you *were* his daughter. He'll never have that, you know—kids of his own. It just feels so good to know we made it through that first year of marriage—as a family. It took a little bit of time, but you've really opened your heart to Kevin and accepted him as a part of your life. And I just want to thank you for making him feel welcome. I don't know what I'd do if I ever lost him, Stella." She shook her head. "I can't even stand to think about it."

"Janey, could you pull over somewhere?" I interrupted. "I think I'm going to be sick."

I was able to blame it on jitters. After all, my mom had raised me. She knew I didn't have the strongest stomach in the world when it came to high-pressure situations. Not that I saw moving onto campus as a high-pressure situation. I saw it as a lucky escape. But my mother had no way of knowing that. So I let her think the tears that came afterward were about leaving Scottsboro, too. I let her hold me and calm fears I didn't have. My real fears—the truth—would have shattered her world. Kevin wouldn't hurt me again. I wouldn't let him. It was over. And when things were over, they could be trampled on, buried, spit upon, left to burn. There was no reason to bring my mother into the mess that Kevin had made, that I'd helped create by documenting dirty dreams, by having them in the first place. My mother was innocent. How could I make an innocent suffer for something she had nothing to do with? Kevin and I and our one evil night might burn forever on my soul, but it was my burden to bear, not my mother's. She'd already been through enough. She deserved an uncomplicated life.

As for my own life, things became a little less complicated when I realized the devil had left my body. It took a little over a month for him to vacate and I hadn't forgotten. I'd never forget. The feelings—the very real sensations of his grip on my hair, my breast, my throat—may have finally worked their way out of my system to become a violent memory, an awful nightmare, but I could still recall them at the drop of a hat. Still, it was better than being possessed. You can't shake free what's inside of you, gnawing at your nerves, chewing on your blood like a disease. But memories, bad dreams, they can be suppressed. And no one knew how to suppress a nightmare like I did. Immersing myself in books, beer and my blossoming friendship with Alison, I was the poster girl for denial. But that was the way I survived. My mother had Tennessee Williams. Emily had the trinity—Laura, Stevie and Tori. I had denial. It was my new religion.

And I wasn't just protecting my mother. If it were only about protecting my mother, I could have told Emily. She would've kept my secret, our secret—Kevin's and mine. But I couldn't tell Emily. It was the only thing about me she'd never know, that nobody would ever know, and that's because I was also protecting myself. If no one knew, it could be like it never happened. And that's what I wanted—for this whole thing with Kevin to simply disappear. To drop that dirty, evil night into a vat of acid and dispose of it like toxic waste. To be normal. But maybe I was meant to go crazy. Just like Blanche and my father. Kevin had interrupted the chain, but had ultimately set things in motion again. I would go crazy, then my mother. One big, crazy family.

No.

I wouldn't let it happen. I'd keep the secret. I'd live the lie. And soon I would get so used to it, it wouldn't even feel like lying. In the meantime, I had to accept Kevin for what he was—a man who had made a mistake. Weren't men the masters of mistakes, anyway? So what if Kevin was getting off easy for his? I couldn't punish him if it meant destroying my mother, exposing myself, surrendering the rest of those Golds to the crazy side. I had to be strong, and time heals all wounds—even the kind the devil carves himself. The kind that leave scars on the petrified souls of stepdaughters who can't decide whether they're little girls or whores.

Crossing the Line

A very wise woman once said, "Oh, come on, honey. Just friends or not, you and Warren have something to work out of your systems." The woman was Emily and, of course, she was talking to me. And, of course, I denied it. And, of course, she was right. It was early November of that first semester I lived away when Warren came down from NYU to pay me a visit. And for the first time in our friendship, all systems were go.

I'd had three make-out moments on campus prior to Warren's visit. Three inebriated encounters that were tons of fun, but meant absolutely nothing to me and, I presume, even less to the guys I was with. Guys number one and two both happened to be named Bill, so perhaps it was in the interest of fairness that I went equally far with each of them, which wasn't very far at all considering that they both seemed rather disappointed about the lack of action below their belts. I could've sworn that guy number three said to call him Chaka Khan, though I very much doubted this in the sober light of day. Regardless, I let him get a little further than the Bills. Maybe it was because "I Feel for You" was playing in my head the whole time. Maybe I didn't *want* to know what his real name was. Then again, it didn't really matter what any of their names were. I wasn't looking for a relationship with Bill, Bill *or* Chaka Khan. That's why I never had sex with any of my hookups and only returned favors by hand.

Sex with strangers just didn't seem like something I could ever have. Sex with a guy I'd purposely avoided doing it with for two years, however—that was workable. Especially when that guy would wake up the next morning still respecting me and go back to New York. Especially when that guy had never looked better. Especially when that guy really had no shot in hell of ever really being my Duckie. Of course, I didn't exactly see things that way when we first made our plans.

The only one at school who knew the full extent of my history with Warren was Alison. And based on everything I'd told her, she agreed with Emily about the systems thing. She wanted to give us the room to ourselves when he stayed over. But I told her no, that Warren was going to stay a friend and *only* a friend, no matter what. A "special" friend—that's how I'd described him to everybody else. *Everybody* being Lauren, Alexa, Maddie, Cara, Tammy and Erin, or in other words, The Six. That was how Alison and I referred to them when we were alone to save breath. We never went anywhere without The Six, and as eight, we were very obnoxious. Warren didn't think so, though. He loved my friends from the moment he met them. And they loved him right back. In fact, they could've eaten him up. With whipped cream and a cherry on top, if he'd been willing. I noticed this during the party we went to when the drunken Six plus Alison hung on his every word as if he were the next Messiah, though with these lingering, lustful gazes that said they were all going straight to hell. Or maybe I was just jealous. Not that I had any reason to be. Warren couldn't take his eyes off of me.

"And you've never done it with this guy *because?*" Maddie asked when Warren walked away to use the bathroom.

"I don't know," I said, searching for an answer myself. "We're friends."

"So?" Tammy chimed in.

"*I'll* be his friend," Erin teased.

But Alison came to my defense. "It's a complicated history. Don't give her any grief. It's complic—" She looked at me, suddenly confused, and started laughing. "It's really not all that complicated, Stella. I'm sorry. Go screw the boy, *please.*"

"If not, at least let one of us have him," Lauren said. Alison looked at me sharply, raising her eyebrows. I knew what she was thinking.

"You can't," I told Lauren. "I won't sleep with him, but I won't let any of my friends sleep with him, either."

"Well, *that's* fair," Alexa said, joking but making the point abundantly clear. I *was* unfair. Warren was a hot, available guy who wanted me in every way. I should either go for it or release him to the highest bidder. But I needed to stop this resistance dance. Did I really fear change that much? On one hand, I was afraid to sleep with Warren because it might change our friendship. And on the other hand, I was afraid to let him sleep with any of my friends because I might not have the same hold over him anymore. He might fall in love with someone else. But I wasn't in love with him, anyway. So what did it matter if he fell in love with somebody else? It's not like I kept a leash on him while he was at school. That's how he'd stumbled into Emily's bed. And look at all the other girls who'd gotten to be with him already. Look at all the girls who wanted to. Well, *I* wanted to, so why couldn't I? Hadn't I earned the right more than some one-night stand he might never even see again? Hadn't we waited long enough? So, why *couldn't* I sleep with him? Because of a friendship? Because he might get hurt? He knew the risks as well as I did. And he knew that I wasn't in love with him. He was the one who'd called himself Duckie. Was it *my* fault that the guy who'd fallen hopelessly in love with me also happened to be as hot as sin? Was it *my* fault I couldn't be Molly Ringwald after three beers and seven girlfriends telling me that I was crazy? It surely *was* my fault, because alcohol and public opinion really had nothing to do with it. I *wanted* to have sex with Warren.

"Listen, girls," I said. "Can Alison sleep in one of your rooms tonight?"

"Don't do it if you're not ready," Cara told me.

"Yeah, Stella, I'm sorry," Alison said. "Don't listen to me. We're all just jealous of you. I know what Warren means to you. Don't let us talk you into something you'll regret."

"The only thing I'll regret is losing this chance."

"Then go for it," Alison said, hugging me. "And be safe."

Warren came back from the bathroom to find everyone gathered around me in celebration of the wonderful sex I was about to have.

"What did I miss?" he asked.

"Nothing," I said. "Let's go, okay? I want to show you something in my room."

Warren didn't object to leaving, but once we were alone, sex seemed to be the farthest thing from his mind. Then again, how was he supposed to know the words *off limits* had suddenly been replaced by *come and get me?* I certainly wasn't giving off any signals—I'd lost every ounce of my sexual nerve on the walk to my room. How *did* one make a move on one of her best friends?

"So, what did you want to show me?" he asked cluelessly.

I probably should've just said "this" and went straight for the kiss, but even if I *had* been feeling that confident, Warren wasn't just some random hook-up boy. And this wasn't going to be a wham bam. I may not have been in love with him, but I loved him with all my heart. And for now, I just wanted to be alone with him, without all of his drooling admirers.

"I didn't want to show you anything," I admitted. "I just wanted to spend some time away from the noise, if that's okay with you."

"That's fine with me. Do you feel all right?"

"I feel fine." I sat down on Alison's and my futon couch, patting the space beside me so he'd sit, too. "I just wanted to make sure we got some time alone together. But if you'd rather go back to the party, we could—"

"I came to see *you,* Stella," Warren said, taking my hand. "I mean, I like your friends—your friends are great. But this is why I came—to visit with you."

"Good." I looked down at his hand. He'd already let go of mine. He had no idea what I was up to.

"Is there something you wanted to talk about?" I shrugged my shoulders, still looking down. "Hmm?" He cupped my chin between his thumb and forefinger, raising my face so I'd look at him. "I couldn't quite hear that."

I smiled—his touch had completely awakened my sexual nerve. "Do you want to go to bed?" But, of course, I said it more like I meant sleeping. After all, I needed *some* kind of safety net. And after being friends for so long without having sex, Warren made no attempt to read into it.

"I'm not really tired," he said. "Would it be okay if I watched TV?" Great—now, what could I do? I was really failing at this.

"Sure." Some seduction that had been. And now I was stuck going to bed early when there was a perfectly good party going on, a party I'd only left, apparently, so that I could make a complete fool out of myself. And poor Warren was probably wondering what the big deal about "alone time" had been if I was only going to konk out on him.

"Do you need to change?" he asked.

"Yeah."

"Go ahead. I'm not looking," Warren said, staring wide-eyed. And even though it was more of a joke than flirtation, his comment helped reassure me of his feelings—he *did* still want me. I suddenly had a brilliant idea. First, I made a face so he'd turn his head. Then I went over to Alison's dresser and put on her "bad girl" nightie—red silk, a little lacey, a little *oops, I didn't realize this was see-through,* but still sophisticated enough to be classy. Perfect seduction wear. She'd said I could borrow it anytime I wanted to impress a guy. Now was that time.

"Okay, I'm done," I said, trying to act nonchalant as I walked over to my bed and began turning down the covers. I was waiting for him to say something, but he didn't. When the silence finally forced me to face him, he looked stoned. "What?"

"You can't wear that."

"Why not?"

He glanced down at the floor, then back up at me, then down at the floor again. "Where am I supposed to look?"

"Wherever you want."

He stood up from the couch, his eyes grazing over my chest, though I could tell he was trying hard to stay focused on my face. "Well…what should I wear?"

"What do you mean?"

"I didn't know we were dressing up. I was just gonna sleep in my clothes."

I smiled. "You look fine."

He pulled off his sweater, tossing it onto the couch behind him. He still had his undershirt on, and although I'd seen him that way many times, this time was different. This time, I wanted to jump him.

"Where should I sleep?" he asked, looking around.

"Well, I could open up the futon for you."

"Sounds good."

"Or you could sleep in my bed with me." Had I really just said that? Oh, well. If he laughed, I could always say *Just kidding.*

Warren looked completely surprised, but in a good way. And he certainly didn't laugh. "Are you serious? Won't Alison think that's a little weird?"

"Alison's not coming back tonight."

"She's not?"

"She likes to sleep with Lauren and Alexa when she drinks."

"Oh, yeah?" He began walking closer.

"Not like that, Warren. Sorry to kill your fantasy." Warren shook his head, smiling like I'd done something silly. "What?"

"You don't know much about fantasies, do you?"

"Oh, come on. Three girls? What guy wouldn't want to see that?"

"Try one girl."

"*One* girl?"

"You."

We were standing close together as I looked up into his eyes—those eyes that could quite possibly smolder ice. Emily, Alison, The Six, they had all been right. They just didn't come much hotter than Warren. And to top it all off, he was actually a wonderful person. A wonderful person who thought the world of me. What on earth had I been waiting for? Permission from God?

"Warren?"

"Hmm?"

I put my arms around his neck. "I want to be with you."

He reached forward to stroke my face. "Will you get mad at me if I ask a question?" I shook my head. "Are you drunk?"

"No."

"Promise?"

"I promise. Are you?"

Warren smiled. "I hope not. I only had three beers."

"Can we, then?"

"Can we what?" he teased.

"Warren!" And just when I was expecting some kind of witty torture, he leaned down and kissed me.

I felt it with all of my senses and still wanted more. I suppose that's what two years of waiting can do. He slipped the spaghetti straps off of my shoulders and Alison's nightie fell to the floor in a pile of silk and achievement. It was happening—Warren and me. There was no turning back now. Or was there?

"How sure are you?" he asked suddenly, pulling away.

"One hundred percent."

"Why now?"

"I think we've waited long enough."

"But what if you regret it and blame me?"

I cupped his face in my hands. "I'd never blame you. I love you." Oops.

Warren didn't say it back, but instead started kissing me again, convinced of my certainty, and we ended up on the bed. Most girls would've felt stupid or crushed that their sentiments weren't returned. I felt relieved. It meant that Warren knew what kind of love I meant. And my underwear soon joined Alison's nightie on the floor.

Everything Emily said about Warren was true. He *was* huge and he *could* go all night. We used five condoms from the May '99 collection, which still left me with four to wish on. Not that I should've been remembering past partners as I fell asleep in Warren's arms on that rainy November morning. But I couldn't help thinking of John. It was Warren holding me, Warren's cologne on my skin and sheets, Warren who now knew me in a way nobody else ever had except John. But it wasn't Warren whom I thought of when I closed my eyes. John was all my heart wanted. All that I could see, all that I could feel. And without even having to try, I remembered the smell of his hair, the apple shampoo. That lost little boy look in his ocean-blue eyes. His stare in the rain. I remembered and I cried. Because I had just lost him forever.

I'd told Warren I loved him—during sex. It didn't matter what *kind* of love I meant. The point was that I'd gone and had sex with meaning. Sex had meant nothing to John with his Lady Stella Birdnose. Why couldn't I have just done it with Chaka Khan? Why did everything have to have significance in my life? Why *couldn't* I just chalk this one experience with Warren up to great sex and leave it at that? Why did it have to spell some kind of death for John and me?

Because I had cut the cord, that was why. The sacred cord connecting me to the one person in the world I'd ever made love to, and now I'd made love to someone else. I knew that Warren wasn't "the one," but I loved him. And maybe the fact that he was here and John wasn't, that I hadn't seen John in so long, made me feel like it just wasn't real anymore. That John and I were destined to become nothing more than a pocketful of painful memories. And all because I'd erased his imprint with Warren's. In this case, sex with love was a sin. Sex without it would have been so much easier to wash away. I would have become a prune in the shower trying. I would have run outside naked at dawn to lie in the rain. But nothing could have saved us—me and the boy who'd been slipping away for months—because I'd finally cut the cord. I'd never love anyone as much as John. And my eyes burned from missing him every time I tried to sleep.

It was probably the rain or my tears or the ocean in his eyes, thoughts of cutting the cord, womb, water…I dreamed that John and I were swimming naked with the fish while "The Man Who Sold the World," the song that had framed our first kiss, played on in the background. It was an appropriate symphony, appropriate that the song that gave us our beginning would also shelter our goodbye.

That memory of us in the water became real to me and was the last image I had of John for years—until I saw his picture on the back of a book. *Seventeen Stories* and *Bloodlines.* Both best-sellers, both riveting reads, and neither bearing any obvious—or even subtly implied—mention of me. Sometimes I prefer to think of myself as Camille in *Bloodlines* since the main character, Trevor, is in love with her. The only thing is that Camille is Trevor's cousin and she's got red hair and skinny legs. But since he's willing to risk his good name and fortune to be with her, I like to think that John was thinking of me when he wrote her. Even though we were never cousins. And all we really had to give up in order to be together was a little immaturity and fear.

I suppose that was the lethal combination that kept our young love from flourishing. Although we stayed connected through phone calls and letters, eventually replacing both with e-mail, we never actually got together again, face-to-face. It's not that we didn't *want* to see each other, just that neither of us tried very hard. John's schedule never did see freedom. He was always busy with school, his double major, clubs, internships, and his only real tie to Pennsylvania was me. There were no more *Maybe I'll see him when's.* The responsibility was on our shoulders and neither of us accepted it. In a way, though, I was relieved that I didn't have to see him. So much had changed since our last visit. I was a different person now, not only because of what I'd done with Warren, but because of what Kevin had done to me. And the idea of being alone with John was scary. The idea of feeling *safe* was scary—because feeling safe might lead to spilling secrets. And there was one secret I wanted to take to my grave. Facing John would have been a threat to that, and sometimes, it's just better not to face things.

John and I lost touch completely in 2000—two years before those *Seventeen Stories* gave me another face to know him by. An older face than I knew in college, but still those boyish eyes. Though they didn't look quite so lost anymore. His hair was shorter than I'd ever seen it, but I wondered if it still smelled like apple shampoo. I wondered how weekly e-mails could become monthly could become none. I wondered where feelings went, where love went when you still felt it after so many years, but knew it would never amount to anything real, when you'd just wrapped your heart around somebody else, somebody great, somebody new. I wondered why John still managed to haunt me when I was happy. I wondered how in the world I could've ever been so stupid as to let him slip away.

John Lixner lives in San Diego, the first line of his bio told me. California. The other side of the country. I figured he must have gone for a girl. That he must have been happy, too. A couple years later, I read *Bloodlines* and decided that the California cunt must have been Camille.

Aftershock

A few weeks after Warren and I shocked our systems, I went home for Thanksgiving to face Kevin. I'd managed to see my mom several times already, but all of our visits had been on my turf. I just had too much going on at school to drop everything and come back to Scottsboro, even if it was only for one day. Or, at least, that's what I made my mother think so that I wouldn't be forced into facing Kevin any sooner than I absolutely had to. And she really didn't mind making the trip downtown to spend time with me. My mother enjoyed our private girl-time in the city. But she often said it was a shame Kevin couldn't make it. Mysteriously enough, he always had something to do, but like the true gentleman that he was, he always managed to send his best.

But seeing Kevin wasn't the only scary thing about returning to Scottsboro. Like me, Warren would also be home for Thanksgiving break. And we'd had a falling out. We hadn't spoken since the morning after we crossed the line. Of course, I was more afraid of losing him than of facing him. But what could I say about the way we'd left things? Was this it? Had it all come down to sex? Would sex be the one thing that was big enough to spell the end of us?

I knew something wasn't right when I woke up that Sunday morning to find him in my desk chair, watching me with sadness in his eyes.

"What's the matter?" I asked. Warren shrugged, attempting a smile. "Don't you feel okay?"

"Do you *remember* what happened last night?"

"Of course I remember."

"And?"

"And what?" I asked, using the blanket to cover myself as I sat up.

"And you're not sorry?"

"Are *you?*"

Warren was quiet for a second. "I just thought this would feel better."

"Oh." I looked down at the bed.

"No, no, I didn't mean it like that. It was great. *You* were great. You're perfect, Stella. Last night was perfect. But this morning..." I glimpsed back up at him, wondering why he'd trailed off. "Do you wanna put something on so we could talk?" I looked at him strangely. Did it really matter? I was completely covered. "It would just be easier to talk about this if you were wearing clothes."

"Fine. Do you wanna hand me that robe behind you?"

Warren turned around and grabbed the only robe in sight. "This one?"

"*That's* the one."

He got up and walked over to the bed, handing me the robe with a degree of apology that was downright hurtful—as if I were some kind of prostitute that just didn't know enough to be ashamed. And wasn't it just like Warren to feel bad for seeing me that way? Dirty, desecrated, his fallen angel naked on the bed the morning after, needing to cover her body.

"Thanks." I waited for him to grant me some privacy, but he didn't. "Are you gonna watch?"

"Stella..."

"Just turn around, Warren."

As I dressed, I looked down at my chest, and lower, realizing everything Warren had seen, where he had touched me, what we had done. I remembered how we'd lain there afterward, in the wake of our heat, how I'd ached for somebody else. And now he wanted me covered. And still, as I tied the robe around my body, I remembered the incredible feeling of being together, the physical feeling, the one I hadn't wanted to end. What was wrong with me?

You're just a screwed-up whore who's got everybody fooled but me. I suppose my stepfather had been right.

I cleared my throat loudly to signify that I was finished. Warren turned around and looked at me. Again, those apologetic eyes. "I just feel like we crossed the line," he said.

I looked up at him incredulously. "*That's* your big epiphany? We 'crossed the line'?" Warren shrugged his shoulders and returned to his seat at my desk. "I don't mean to make fun of you. I just don't understand why you're stating the obvious."

"Because I feel like an asshole, that's why." The asshole and the whore, a match made in heaven.

"Why do you feel like an asshole?"

"I just don't think you were ready for what we did."

"Not ready? I was the one who—"

"I wasn't talking about that kind of ready."

"Well, what kind of 'ready' were you talking about, then? I wasn't exactly a virgin before last night, Warren."

"And you weren't exactly experienced, either."

"So, what are you saying? That you didn't enjoy it?"

"I already told you I did."

"So, what's your problem?"

"Please don't turn this into an argument, Stella."

"Then, please don't avoid my questions all day."

"I just meant that sex is new for you."

"Would you rather I'd already slept with a dozen guys before you?"

"No." He looked at me sternly. *"No."*

"So, what's your point?"

"My point—if you'd let me make it—is that I don't think you were ready for the kind of sex we had last night."

"The *kind* of sex we had? Is there something I should know about here?"

Warren smiled. "You're impossible."

"I'm just curious, Warren. I mean, apparently, there was some *different* kind of sex going on here last night. And, silly me, I just thought we were two friends having a good time."

"That's the problem."

"What is?"

"I just don't think you're ready for that."

"Ready for what? Having a good time? Forgive me, but who are you to make rules when it comes to whom I sleep with?"

"I'm not making rules. I'm just telling you how I feel."

"Like an asshole, I know. Because *I* wasn't ready to have a good time."

"Would you stop twisting everything, Stella?"

"Would you just say what you mean?"

"Fine." He stood up and walked toward the bed. "I don't want to fight, okay? It's just that I know you and I know how you are about things, *including* sex. And I feel like... You said it yourself, Stella—'two friends having a good time.' I just don't think you're ready to handle that."

"Handle *what,* Warren? Would you please friggin' say what you mean? I'm not ready for *what?*"

"Sex—"

"I've *had* sex."

"Sex with someone you're not in love with!"

Well, there I had it. I was officially a bully. As Warren stood there staring at me, his chest pounding in the painful silence, I suddenly felt terrible. But then again, I suppose one of us had to acknowledge it sooner or later—the fact that what we'd done had meant something a lot different to him than it had to me. But it had meant something to me, too. He had to have known that.

"Warren..." I moved to hug him, but he quickly pulled away. "Just forget it."

"No. Because it did mean something to me. It did."

"It's not the same," he said, turning to face the wall.

"You're right." I couldn't lie to him. "But it doesn't mean—"

"Look, just fuckin' forget about it, okay?" he yelled, whirling around. "This isn't about that!" He took a deep breath and seemed to calm down a little. "Believe me," he said, "I learned to deal with our relationship a long time ago."

"Then, what is this about?"

He took a few seconds to answer. When he did, he said, "Maturity."

"Maturity?"

"I just think that what we did requires a certain level of maturity."

"I don't know if I follow."

"See? That's exactly what I'm saying."

"Which *is?*"

"It takes a certain level of maturity to handle a one-night stand."

"Really? I didn't know it was such an advanced skill."

"You *know* what I mean."

"Honestly, I don't think I do. I guess I'm not mature enough."

"I didn't say you were immature. I just think I let my own feelings get in the way last night. I should have looked out for you. I shouldn't have let you do something you weren't ready for."

"God, would you stop treating me like I'm *ten?* I'm capable of making my own decisions, Warren. And I'm sorry I haven't slept around as much as some of the other girls you've been with, but I'm not a nun. I'm 'mature' enough, as you put it, to handle a one-night stand, if that's what you choose to call this."

"Like you honestly planned to sleep with me again after last night." I didn't say anything. "I rest my case."

"And which case is that, Warren? The case where I can't

make decisions for myself? Or the case you said you learned to deal with a long time ago?"

"Oh, throw *that* in my face. That's very considerate of you, thanks."

"Well, you're the one who started it by being all sarcastic about whether I'd sleep with you again."

"I'm the one *who started it?*" he mocked. "And you say you're not immature."

"It's hard to be mature when we're having such a childish argument."

"Well, it seems our arguments are always childish, Stella. But then again, what else should I expect when, underneath everything, you're still a little girl?"

That's right. Just sit there trembling like a scared little girl.

"Do me a favor, Warren," I said, "and get out."

Warren left that day without saying another word. And in the weeks that followed, the silence had only grown thicker. He hadn't even tried calling me once.

"*You* have to call him," Emily said. "You're the one with the upper hand."

"How do you figure?" I asked her.

"Stella, when it comes to Warren, you always have the upper hand. Now, come on. How many times are you gonna break that poor boy's heart?"

I didn't want to break his heart. I didn't want to be at odds. I hated the distance between us, but what could I do? I could do what I always did—avoid the hell out of the situation until it was right in front of me. I suppose I could've continued avoiding Warren straight through Thanksgiving break. Scottsboro may have been a tiny town, but it wasn't *that* small. We didn't necessarily have to see each other just because we were both home. But somewhere in the back of my mind, the holiday had been my deadline. Our fight was easier to bear that way, knowing that we always had Thanksgiving to work things out. After that, it really *would* have gone on too long, and I would've missed that one little window of opportunity I'd had to save us. But how could I save us?

I'd simply have to be honest and say what we both already knew—that if we wanted to stay friends, we really couldn't ever have sex again. That it had been great while it was happening, but apparently neither of us could deal with the consequences. And if we could see past our morning-after fight, we'd realize that the experience still *had* brought us closer, that we were better off for having tested those waters because now we could go on as friends without always wondering what we were missing out on. And like Warren had once said, he *would* get over me. But I probably wouldn't bring that last part up in my speech.

I'd just picked up the phone to call him when a knock sounded at my bedroom door. It was Kevin. I told him to come in and watched with anxious eyes as the doorknob made its final warning twist. And then we were in a room together, alone—for the first time since that night. Only Kevin didn't *look* like Lucifer. He was just a man, the same man he had always been. I would just talk to him like nothing had ever happened—the same way I always had.

"Hey," I greeted him from the bed, not getting up.

"Hi." He took a few steps into the room, closing the door. My heart began to race, but I tried to keep calm. My mother was home. He'd never get away with hurting me now.

"Did you just get home from work?"

"Yeah. How about you? What time did your mom bring you back?"

"Isn't she here?" I asked, trying to hide my panic. "Didn't you talk to her when you came in?"

"She fell asleep on the couch. I didn't want to wake her."

"Oh. Doesn't she feel all right?"

"I don't know. I didn't want to wake her, so I didn't ask."

"Oh, right," I said, laughing lightly at my own stupidity. "Duh." Kevin smiled and took a couple steps closer toward the bed.

"Have you lost weight?"

"A little." The truth was that I'd already gained back about half of what I'd lost. Though it didn't bother me a bit. It meant that Kevin no longer had a hold on how much I could eat and keep down. So, in a way, it gave me the feeling that he no longer had a hold on me.

"You look terrific." Sure, he *would* think so.

"Thanks."

"Stand up."

"What? Why?"

"I want you to come here for a second." He watched as I remained still, glued to the bed, eyeing him suspiciously. "Do you really think I would hurt you, Stella?" I didn't answer. "Stella, please come here."

I rose from the bed with unsteady legs and approached him with caution, shrinking back when he lifted his hands, but it was only to wipe his eyes. He stood there wiping his eyes for a while as I waited, and then, out of the blue, he threw his arms around me and proceeded to cry about the night that had never happened. He said he'd never meant to hurt me *or* my mother. He said he'd gotten carried away, that he'd been confused, that it would never happen again. He said it would kill my mother to ever know what *we'd* done. He said he'd been having trouble sleeping since that night and just really wanted to clear the air. He never once said that he was sorry.

But I didn't feel sorry, either, at least not for him. This blubbering, terrified coward acting as if the entire thing were all an honest mistake that *we'd* made. I suppose I just wanted him gone, for the whole thing to really be over. I thought it was the one thing we truly did have in common—wanting that night to be over, wanting to get as far away from it as possible, to think of it only as some sort of sadistic dream. So I put my arms around him, reluctantly, but to show that I could move forward, that I was as willing as he was to let the whole thing live in the past.

"Everything's going to be fine," I said. "Let's just forget about it."

Kevin pulled me closer and I wanted to break away, but was afraid to spoil the moment, this one chance we had to put that dreadful memory behind us and be normal. Or as close to normal as we could possibly get by living in secrecy and shame.

But maybe it was all an act. Maybe men like Kevin aren't capable of shame. Men who turn moments of reconciliation into field trips for their wandering hands. I jerked away as soon as I realized what he was up to. But of course, Kevin tried to make it seem like I imagined it.

"Relax," he said calmly. "Like I said, I'm not gonna hurt you. I just came in to make sure we were okay."

"We're fine," I said, trembling.

"I'm glad. I've been looking forward to seeing you. I just wanted to clear the air about what happened so we could enjoy Thanksgiving tomorrow. Let's make a deal never to mention it again. Okay?"

"Okay. Listen, I've got a call I need to make, so…"

"Sure," Kevin said, turning to go. "I guess I'll just see you at dinner." In the doorway, he paused to smile. "You know, I'm glad you were able to be an adult about this." And with a satisfied nod, he closed the door.

I started dialing as soon as I was alone again. I knew that Warren and I still had some things to resolve, but suddenly they didn't seem so huge anymore. I just wanted to hear his voice, to be with him—away from all of this. The rest we could work out later. That is, if he was willing to work things out at all. But this was Warren. He'd never really let our friendship go, no matter what came along to screw it up. Even if the screwing was literal.

"Hello?"

"Hey," I said. "Do you have plans for tonight?"

"Aren't we supposed to be on bad terms or something?"

"Or something." There was silence on the other end of the phone. Was he going to bring up our argument, the fact that I'd thrown him out of my room, that I could have called sooner, that I'd been a total bitch?

"What time?" he asked finally. I smiled so hard it shocked my face.

"Well, what are you doing for dinner?"

"Dinner?"

"Yeah."

"I'm going on a date."

"Oh," I said, trying not to sound disappointed. "With who?"

"With you...as friends."

"Friends," I echoed, liking the ring.

"The best."

"Always."

"So, *friend,* where the hell have you been hiding yourself?" he asked.

And that was how Warren and I got over the aftershock of our one night of passion and moved on with our young adult lives. As friends.

As for Kevin, he never tried anything funny after that "innocent" hug in my room and after a while, acting like nothing had ever happened became easy. In many ways, it really did seem as if the whole sweaty struggle on my bed had been nothing more than a vicious nightmare. That's how far I'd forced the memory, into a dark and distant cave where nightmares never died, but weren't close enough to fear. Though I did start having nightmares of another kind, dreams about car wrecks, plane crashes, or anything else that might kill me. Sometimes I dreamed of being held at knifepoint or gunpoint by a faceless aggressor. Sometimes I was strangled. And it didn't matter that I never saw my assailant, the pilot, the driver of the other car. I guess I always knew who it was. And although I said their source was school stress, occasionally lending blame to violent TV images, I knew it was something more, that these dreams were merely an outlet for the terror I'd never released, for the secret that had burned its own little hole in my soul, for the part of me that wanted to die the night that Kevin attacked me, and for the part of me that wanted to kill. Violence, threats, suspicion and death wove their way through my dreams for more than a year, beginning after that strange embrace in my room and fading out just in time for me to enjoy the rest of college—and its limitless hookup possibilities—without being afraid of the dark.

A Whole New Chapter

Emily's father married his girlfriend, Katherine, a month after we graduated from college. The two had been living together for a while but hadn't wanted to "seal the deal" until Emily was done with school. They said they just wanted to know what her plans were—to make sure she was settled before *they* got settled. But I think they just wanted to make sure she wouldn't be living at home after she graduated. "They" meaning Katherine, Katherine being only twenty-nine and presumably wanting all of Frank's attention to herself.

"So, do you think it's in our blood to lust after younger guys?" Emily asked me. "Not now, of course. We'd practically be child molesters. But once we hit middle age, do you think we'll start trying for guys we once baby-sat?" It was two nights before the wedding and she was calling from her new apartment in the Village, which she shared with Nick, a friend from FIT, who was single, gorgeous and gay.

"Give your father a break, Emily. The age difference isn't that huge."

"It's massive! Okay, your mom and Kevin are one thing. He's thirty-five. She's forty-eight. But my dad and Katherine…*ew!*"

"You're only saying that because it's your dad."

"He was eighteen when she was born, Stella."

"Yeah, well…"

"Do you know what it's like to think my *stepmother* was probably only in first or second grade when *I* was born?"

"Well, you don't have to think of her as your mom, Em. Think of her like a big sister."

"But don't you see how weird that is?"

"What *isn't* weird, Emily? Everything's weird."

"I guess. It doesn't really matter, anyway. It's not like anyone could ever replace *your* mom." She'd said it so naturally, she couldn't have possibly had such grand plans to move me. But she had, just with that one little comment, that one implication that we really *were* family. "What?" she asked. "Why'd you get quiet?"

"I just love you," I said.

"Well, by golly, a fine piece'a woman like you? I don't know what to say."

"Say you'll dance with me at the wedding."

"Only if you make it worth my while."

"Well, what did you have in mind?" I asked seductively.

"Hey, don't use that bedroom voice on me. I might actually get turned on. You know I have no sexual outlet right now." If *that* wasn't an understatement. Emily hadn't had sex since the freshman-year Warren fiasco. She'd been getting by on vibrators and a steady stream of respectable make-out flings. But the stream seemed to have dried up now that college was through—there just wasn't as much water to go around. And then, there was the water she couldn't drink.

"It must suck living with such a hot guy," I said.

"You mean because of the gay factor?"

"Precisely."

"It doesn't mean I can't fantasize."

"Be careful..."

"Be quiet... Oh, listen, I meant to ask if your mom and Kevin were coming with you to my dad's house on Saturday. There's room if they want to ride with us to the church." Frank's mother wanted to take pictures of everyone in Katherine's garden before the ceremony and had insisted that as Emily's oldest friend, I be included.

"No. They'll just meet me," I said. My mom had been looking forward to this wedding for weeks and if it were up to her, she probably would have wanted to witness the little photo session. But she was always thinking of Kevin first and standing around a garden watching Frank's mother take pictures hardly seemed like something he'd enjoy. Of course, he hadn't gotten a look at Katherine's cousin Monica, yet. But he'd make up for that later—in front of a table full of people at the reception.

Frank and Katherine had just finished cutting the cake when I decided to stop by my mother's table for a chat. Emily was off talking to some guy she'd been clinging to for nearly an hour and I was starting to feel like a bit of a loser, gabbing the night away with her drunk uncle Sheldon.

"Hey," I said, sliding into the empty seat next to my mother. "Are you having a good time?"

As she and I talked about what a beautiful wedding it had been so far, I couldn't help but notice Kevin turning to ogle one of the bridesmaids who was passing by their table. I immediately recognized her as Katherine's bombshell cousin from the garden.

"Oh, hi, Stella," she said cheerfully, taking notice of my stare.

"Hi."

"Are these your parents?" she asked, eyeing Kevin, who was obviously too young to be my real father.

"Uh, kind of. This is my mom—"

"And I'm her stepfather," Kevin said, cutting me off as he reached for her hand. "Kevin Kilbride."

Monica smiled briefly at my mother, who returned the gesture meagerly, but politely. I think we could both tell that this vixen was much more interested in Kevin. He had charmed her—instantly, the same way he charmed everybody else.

"It's nice to meet you," she told him, her eyes glittering. "Both of you," she added clumsily. "I'm Monica, Katherine's baby cousin." She smiled all cutesy-like when she said "baby." And at that moment, I decided I hated her.

Kevin's laugh was low and sultry. "You look pretty grown up to me."

"Well, I'm twenty-four," she said, cocking her head to one side as if she expected some kind of applause for knowing her age.

I looked over at my mother. She still had that same meager smile on her face.

"Twenty-four," Kevin said reflectively. "Now, I was just twenty-four…hmm, maybe I shouldn't tell you how long ago I was twenty-four." Monica giggled. "Uh-oh, now she's laughing at me," he said. "Is that good or bad?"

"I'm not laughing at you," Monica assured him. "I'm laughing with you. Only problem is you're not laughing."

Kevin chuckled softly. "Feel better?"

"Much."

"Good to know. So, cousin Monica, where are you from?"

"South Orange." Flashing a flawless white grin, she added, "And you?"

"All over," he said, his eyes traveling the length of her body.

"All over where?" she asked suggestively. I turned to see that everyone at the table was staring at Kevin, anxiously awaiting his reply.

"What kind of answer are you looking for?"

She laughed. "Any kind that won't get you in trouble with your wife." So maybe she *did* know when to quit—which meant she also knew that what they'd been doing was wrong. "I'm on my way up to the bar," she said, addressing me now. "Can I get anyone anything?"

I shook my head politely, looking at my mother, who was still wearing that same frozen grin. "I think we're both fine," I told Monica.

"I'll join you," Kevin said, standing up, and finally my mother's smile faded. She had every reason to look sad. She'd never seen her husband flirt with another woman before. I suppose it scared her, too. For if Kevin could flirt so openly in front of her, imagine the things he'd do when he wasn't right under her nose.

"No," I said, rising to stop him. "I mean, you can't. They're playing 'Endless Love.' You have to dance." Joining his hand with my mother's, I stepped back and watched them take their place out on the floor with all the other happy couples. Monica shrugged her shoulders and walked off.

Emily and that guy she'd been talking to were dancing also—and looking rather close, I might add. I wasn't about to break up their fun so she could help me analyze my mother's marriage. Her father's wedding wasn't the place for that anyway. What I really wanted was to be by myself.

I made my way out to the deserted cocktail lounge and listened to Ross and Richie sing about the greatest kind of love on earth from my lonely post on the corner couch. When they were finished, the DJ announced that it was time to toss the bouquet. I thought about going back inside, but what for? So I could *maybe* catch a bunch of flowers that, according to some old wives' tale, would mean I'd be the next to get married? And who would marry me? John, who I hadn't seen in three years? One of my random college hookups who probably wouldn't remember my name if I bit him on the ass with it? Emily's drunk uncle Sheldon? Or better yet, a man who would promise to love and cherish me and then flirt with another woman right under my nose?

I was still debating the merits of bouquets when Emily came rushing out from the reception room carrying flowers.

"Hey," I said, rising to greet her as I put on my best happy face. This was a *wedding*—damn it—not a funeral.

"There you are!" she exclaimed, falling into me, breathless. "Why are you out here all alone? Are you okay?"

"Yeah. I'm fine."

Emily raised her eyebrows. She knew me too well. "Are you *sure?*"

"Yeah," I said, hugging her. "Of course I am."

"Okay. Well, then, I've got something to tell you. Guess what?"

"I can see. You caught the bouquet. That's great."

"No, that's not the *news,* silly." Emily sat on the couch, pulling me down beside her. "Okay, are you ready for this? You're absolutely going to die."

I listened as Emily told the story of how two people had met and fallen in love at a wedding. Of course, one of the story's stars was Emily. The other—the mystery guy she'd been clinging to—was Rob Sellers, the youngest of three boys who'd grown up down the street from Katherine and her two younger sisters. Rob's parents and Katherine's parents had been friends for almost twenty-five years, and Katherine had always thought of him very much like a younger brother.

"Again, more evidence that my father is robbing the cradle," Emily joked. "I mean, if my *stepmom* thinks of my boyfriend as a kid brother—"

"Your *boyfriend?*" I interrupted. "Isn't that jumping the gun a little? You just met him."

"He's not like anybody I've ever met, Stella." There was a peaceful conviction in her tone, her eyes, her smile, that said this might be more than a giddy crush. Maybe love *could* come in one night. "He's so sensitive and artistic and funny and amazing and…" She sighed. "I just look at him and want to take care of him. I've never had that feeling with a guy before. Not even with Jason. I could honestly see myself marrying him, Stella."

Whoa. She *was* for real. Emily didn't just go around talking about marriage to amuse herself. This Rob Sellers could prove to be very important.

"Well, tell me more about him, damn it! What does he do? Where does he live?"

Rob did a lot of the artwork for *Pixie Playpen,* a line of toys featuring baby fairies, elves and other mystical creatures. He lived in Hoboken, New Jersey, with his friend, Malcolm, but took the bus into Manhattan every day for work.

"We're thinking of getting a place together when my lease is up next year," she said.

"Wait a minute. You mean you've already discussed *living* together?"

"Well, it's not etched in stone or anything because he's really stuck on bringing Malcolm to New York and having it be the three of us. And, while I'm sure this Malcolm guy is great and everything, I just wouldn't want to start out with Rob that way—domestically, I mean. You know, living with his friend. It just wouldn't be private enough." She was completely missing my point.

"But I mean, isn't it a little *soon* to be talking about that stuff at all?"

"Stella," she said, putting her hands on my shoulders. "You and I are entering a whole new chapter in our lives… Rob and I have already discussed getting married."

"What?" She said she could *see* herself marrying him. She never told me they'd *talked* about it.

"Come on. I want you to meet him."

As we walked arm in arm toward the reception room, Emily turned and handed me the bouquet. "Here, you take this," she said. "I still have my flowers from the ceremony. And besides, I already got *my* dose of good luck tonight. Maybe this bouquet will bring you some." I accepted it gratefully. To hell with my thoughts on old wives' tales. We could all use a little luck.

Emily and I soon found ourselves back in the reception room, nearing that special table, where the star of the new chapter in her life sat waiting to meet me.

"This," she said, wrapping her arms around him, "is Rob."

Whether or not he was *the* One, I couldn't say, but I knew right away that he was *some*one, someone who'd have a big impact on Emily. I could tell because he already had. In the time I spent talking to them, I became the third wheel. They finished each other's sentences. They already had little jokes. And I was all too mesmerized with what was happening right before my very eyes to even be annoyed. Emily really *was* falling in love—real world love—not the high school kind that led her to lose her virginity at the prom. And as we talked, Emily and Rob on one side, me on the other, I found myself clutching Katherine's bouquet with white knuckles. I guess I feared that if I let go, I would have somehow left the wedding with nothing.

Left Behind

Silence crept up on me and shook me hard the day Warren left for Queens, reminding me of the old nursery rhyme about cheese and being alone. Of course, I was happy for him. He'd been offered a staff position at a halfway house for drug and alcohol dependent mothers. It was the kind of work he really wanted to do. But it meant that our secret summer was over.

Or perhaps, I should say private summer. For we never did anything particularly scandalous. It was simply the fact that we owned that summer, that precious little pocket of time that existed between college and actual adulthood. Neither of us had "started" our lives yet. My teaching job wouldn't begin until the fall, and Warren was still searching and interviewing. In the meantime, we had the season to ourselves, our own private, special season that no one else could touch. We developed a unique bond that summer, waiting for our lives to start. It was as if we existed in our own sacred bubble—the only two souls left in Scottsboro. Or at least the only two souls that mattered.

Warren was working at his mom's real estate office. I was back at the day-care center that had employed me through three college summers. Every night after dinner, we'd drive around in his car, listening to The Cure and talking about our in-between jobs, our in-between lives, and nothing in particular. Sometimes, we'd go for a drink. Sometimes, we'd go for a few. Sometimes, we'd take long walks in the dark and hardly talk at all, except to point out the stars. My biggest fear was that he'd finally get the kind of job he wanted and our little bubble would burst. But then again, maybe it was only meant to last one summer. It would've been impossible to float away to eternity on a bond created out of sun and circumstance. But at least we'd always remember it—the last summer we could really call ourselves kids.

Warren once said he'd eventually get over me. That day had arrived and passed by the time he moved to Queens. I knew because our summer had been devoid of "moments," "us" talks and, best of all, ridiculous fights. I'd venture to say the drop-dead giveaway was the absence of lust. There were so many opportunities to feel something during those carefree summer nights, but the Fourth of July was as close as we got to fireworks. As for my part, there was no denying that Warren was one of the most attractive guys I'd ever known, but thinking of him "that way" had honestly become almost gross, like he was *too* old of a friend or something. I wasn't sure if he was quite at the gross-out level with me yet, though he did say one night in his car that I was the sister he'd never had. Unless Warren was kinkier—and more demented—than I'd ever imagined, that pretty much clarified things. It may have taken five years, but by the time he left for Queens, it seemed we'd finally mastered the art of being truly platonic.

Three months of owning the world, or at least our town, of being kids for one more summer, one more season, one last time. And then Warren left me—to start his real life and be a grown-up with an apartment in Queens. *The cheese stands alone.* Everyone eventually left me all alone. Scottsboro and me—people were born to leave us. Emily, John, Blanche, my father. And now Warren, to be a man in Queens. It was silent when he drove away, softer than it had been all summer, not what I'd expected the bursting of a bubble to sound like, the shattering of youth. And then I remembered the cheese and filled my head with the old nursery rhyme. It made me feel better in a way, less lonely to have beat out the silence. But the song soon exhausted itself, and it was still only me, the only soul left in Scottsboro. Me. The cheese. The silence. Alone.

Dear Warren,
I feel so bad about canceling our plans. I really do want to get together and talk—about everything. I promise I'll call as soon as I get back from Europe.
I miss you!
Love always,
Stella

Just what I was so sure he wanted—a postcard from Philadelphia. But at least the sentiment was there. Not that it meant all that much without the truth. I just couldn't give that to him right now. Emily had really made things impossible for me—in every imaginable way.

Wedding Bells

Emily had been dating Rob Sellers for four months when he surprised her at dinner with a marriage proposal.

"He just got down on one knee," she gushed, "right in the middle of the restaurant and asked me—in front of everyone!"

"Did people clap?" I asked. "Like in the movies?"

"They actually did!" she squealed. Her happiness was contagious.

"That's so cheesy, but I wish I was there! I would have cried!"

"I wish you were here, too. Rob wanted to go out and celebrate and I said, 'I have to go home first so I can call Stella.'"

"Oh, I *love* you!"

"I love *you!*"

"Put Rob on. I want to congratulate him."

"Okay, I've gotta go to the bathroom, anyway. My bladder's about to rupture."

"Mmm. Thanks for letting me know."

A few seconds later, Rob picked up.

"Stella!"

"We're gonna be in-laws!" Well, not technically, but I knew he'd get it.

"I know, Sister Stella, isn't it awesome?"

"*You're* the one who's awesome, Bobby Celery."

"Hey, how'd you know about that?"

"How do you think?"

"Man," he said. "Katherine's gonna shit a brick when she finds out I'm about to become her son-in-law, or stepson-in-law, or however the hell that works."

"It's gonna make her feel old, Rob."

He laughed. "I know."

"So, what are you guys gonna go do?"

"I don't know. We'll probably go get drunk or something. Emily thinks Nick will be back soon, so maybe we'll wait and tell him our news, and then we'll all go. We both really wish you were here."

"Not as much as I do," I said. "I feel like that's my curse. The good stuff always happens wherever I'm not."

"Aw, don't say that."

"It's true. A lot of times I wonder why I stay here."

"Well, from what I hear, you're amazing with kids, you've got a great job, and you really have no reason to move."

"Yeah, but…"

"Yeah, but," he mimicked. "Emily really envies the bond you have with your mom, you know. She thinks it's so cool that you can still live at home and have your own life. She wouldn't have that if she lived with Frank and Katherine. And besides, what the hell do you mean about good stuff happening without you? Sister Stella, you *are* the good stuff." I laughed. "You bring the party when you visit."

"I think you exaggerate."

"Don't be modest. You don't get a chance to see Emily when you're not around. I *do*. Either way, I love her. But she lights up like a little kid when you come around, and frankly, so do I."

"Oh, go on."

"I would," he said, "but my fiancée just came back. And she's trying to grab the phone."

"All right. Well, congratulations. And I love you for making Emily so happy."

"I love you, too, party girl. Here's Em."

When Emily returned, I gave her my full endorsement of Rob as a husband, which was completely different from my full endorsement of Rob as a boyfriend, which I had just given her two visits ago. The thing I liked most about him, aside from the obvious fact that he treated Emily like gold, was that he seemed to look at me the way she did, to appreciate things about me that I would've never stopped to think were valuable. And in addition to that, he was so easygoing. And he had a terrific sense of humor. I looked forward to having Rob in my life.

Growing up, I'd always imagined Emily's future husband as this faceless middle-aged man I would meet sometime in my thirties and feel stupid around, but Rob was so incredibly non-threatening, he made me want to dance. So, that's exactly what I did when I hung up with Emily. I danced around my room until I was dizzy, never once feeling sad that my best friend had just taken such a flying leap into adulthood. For engagement was bigger than burying chastity at the senior prom. Bigger than going away to school. Emily was about to get married. But for some reason, I only felt happy. For her, for Rob, for the fact that something was finally going right for one of us, and in a way, then, for both of us. I ran out to the living room to share the news with my mother and Kevin as soon as I regained equilibrium.

My mom had the same reaction that, I believe, Emily's real mother would've had. She gasped, she cried, she jumped up and down, she asked if I was *sure* Rob was a nice boy. And then she called Emily to congratulate her. While they were on the phone, Kevin turned to me and asked if I was next.

"There'd have to be a guy in my life first," I said.

"I'm surprised they're not banging the door down."

"Please."

"Oh, come on, Stella. You don't need an old guy like me to

tell you how pretty you are." It was comments like these that still made me uncomfortable.

My mom put her hand over the mouthpiece and looked at Kevin. "Do you *ever* stop flirting?" And comments like that which made me ill.

Kevin stuck his tongue out at my mother. She rolled her eyes at him, half joking. He winked at me playfully. I felt myself blush. My mother liked to think of us as a family. I think we were as odd as they came.

That night, I lay awake in bed thinking of the engagement and fell asleep remembering two girls in a locker room talking about thighs and how their mothers' fanatical obsessions had given birth to their first names.

Turbulence

Emily and Rob were planning on a June wedding. The timing would coincide perfectly with the expiration of her lease, and they couldn't wait to start out fresh together in a new place, preferably in SoHo. Fortunately, Rob had dropped the idea of having Malcolm, his roommate from Hoboken, join them in their first apartment. "I don't know what I was thinking," he said. "I want it to be just the two of us, forever."

Katherine was three months pregnant and taking care of all the arrangements. Perhaps being *with* child had made her less of one, herself. Emily was grateful for her helpful enthusiasm and really did like the new Katherine, though at first she was understandably embarrassed by the pregnancy, complaining that her father's taste for younger women had resulted in her being old enough to be her unborn sibling's mother. Emily eventually consoled herself by vowing to make them name the baby Laura if it were a girl (after Laura Nyro) and Eli if it were a boy (after the Laura Nyro album, *Eli and the Thirteenth Confession*). I never bothered to ask how she planned to force Frank and Katherine into compliance.

With the wedding preparations under way, life was both sweet and stable. For the first time, I really began to appreciate my new routine. Rob had been right—I really had no reason to move. I suppose that underneath it all, I actually did love Scottsboro. I could have applied for a teaching job anywhere, but I'd chosen Forest Hills. It was a strange revelation, realizing that just like people, a town could make a place in your heart. But then again, I'd always known the opposite were true, that one could hate a town, hailing it as the symbol of her stagnation, the one prison she couldn't break free from, no matter how many people left her. Only I knew now that I wasn't staying in Scottsboro because I feared change. I had simply grown up enough to realize that my tiny suburban town had never been the problem. For the first time in my life, I felt centered.

I usually spent at least one weekend a month in New York visiting Emily, Rob and Warren, who'd always take the subway in from Queens to meet up with us when I was in town. On the weekends I was home, I spent my time with Alison, who lived only forty minutes away in Bloomdale. Despite good intentions, we hadn't really kept in touch with The Six since graduation, with the exception of Lauren and Alexa, who occasionally met us for beer or coffee. All in all, it was a pretty calm life, made calmer by the fact that I wasn't on the market for a man. It seemed I should've been, with Emily about to tie the knot and everything. But I just wasn't interested in turbulence. I liked the sweet stability of my world and didn't want to rock it with commotion. And men were nothing if not the kings of commotion. Or the kings of causing it and then walking away. That's exactly what Kevin was beginning to do at home with my mother. Only the turbulence was wickedly slow. Tiny, random bombs were the kinds he would drop. In his own creepy, handsome, satanic, Kevin way.

It was just after New Year's when he started making those comments about going West to paint the desert. He said he'd never seen it and that it really *was* such a shame—to have gone this far in life without seeing the desert.

"Well, when can you get time off?" my mother asked him.

"I was talking about more of a *permanent* vacation," Kevin said, his eyes glued to the TV as he casually flipped stations with the remote control.

"As in quitting your job?"

"As in, what's for dinner, sweet Mary-Jane?" he asked, turning away from the screen to face her. "I'm starving." My mother looked at him strangely. "Something the matter?"

"It's just that you called me Mary-Jane. Only my mother calls me Mary-Jane."

Kevin shrugged. "I just wanted to make you smile. You seemed a little nervous there for a minute."

"I think she thought you were going to quit your job," I said.

"Stella," my mother cautioned, not wanting me to get involved.

"No, it's all right," Kevin said. "Stella's an adult now. She's twenty-three. She's a teacher."

"What's your point?" I snapped.

"Stella," my mother warned again.

"My point is that I'm starving," Kevin said, "and no one's told me what's for dinner yet." And then he got up and went into the kitchen.

Hurling missiles and walking away. This would be his pattern for close to three years. Sterilized commotion—quiet, tidy and cold. The slow unraveling of my mother's nerves that began with that first mention of the word *desert*. Turbulence had found me, despite my disinterest in men. But it wasn't violent or constant, and in between those patches of disturbance, my mom still managed to see a sky filled with sunshine. I suppose I should've been wiser, but I wanted her marriage to work, so I got myself a pair of rose-colored glasses, too, and together, without ever discussing it, the queens of denial shielded their eyes from what loomed, dodging missiles and bombs with a smile, for everything looked prettier in pink.

★ ★ ★

Not even rose-colored glasses could have shielded Emily from what happened in February. Katherine was in her seventh month when she went into premature labor and lost the baby. Frank left a message with Nick at the apartment, but Emily wouldn't be home for a while. She was in a cab bound for Rob's place in Hoboken, warming her lap with Chinese takeout and her heart with thoughts of how wonderful her life was. Just one month earlier, she'd been ringing up sales at Anna Fontanella, the store, and today, she was sharing studio space with the legend, herself. Just four months earlier, she was merely tolerating her stepmom for her father's sake, and today, they were actually friends, planning a wedding together—*her* wedding, which was happening just four months from now. Her life was only *beginning* to get wonderful. In June, she'd be married to the man of her dreams and living in SoHo, with a beautiful new baby in the family named either Laura or Eli.

Rob wasn't expecting Emily and he wasn't answering his door, so she used her key. But there were strange noises coming from Malcolm's bedroom and she wasn't quite sure what to do. She'd wanted to surprise Rob with dinner, and if he was coming home soon, she would wait for him, but how could she with all that noise? It made her feel like she was spying. And she really didn't want to embarrass Malcolm. She had to go. But, wait. She recognized that sound, that moan, that voice. And before she knew it, she was in the room, watching her fiancé and his roommate scramble around naked for their clothes.

"So, what did she do?" I asked Nick when he called me that night on the phone.

He'd called because he didn't know how to handle Emily. When she'd first burst through their apartment door in tears, he thought she knew about the baby. But all he could make out through her sobs was the name Rob. So, he'd waited for her to calm down, holding her, rocking her, stroking her hair, until finally, she was able to tell her story.

"She said she just dropped the Chinese food, threw her engagement ring at him and ran out of his place 'like a crazy person.' Stella, I don't know what to do with her. She said she wanted to call you, but that was before I told her about Katherine. I had to tell her, though, and now..." He sounded truly panicked.

"Now, what?"

"I don't know! Stella, please tell me what to do because I can't get through to her at all—she won't even look at me. She's just lying here on the floor singing some song about the Emmy's and a garden and—"

"It's Laura Nyro," I told him, shaking. "The song her mother...never mind. Hold on."

I ran out to the living room to get my mom's advice, but when I opened my mouth to explain things, I started crying. She had to get on the phone with Nick to find out exactly what had happened. While she was in my bedroom getting the details, Kevin tried to comfort me on the couch and I let him. It felt unnatural, but not as unnatural as what had happened between Emily and Rob, not as unnatural as babies dying. When my mother reappeared a few minutes later, Kevin was still hugging me. She cleared her throat loudly and we both broke away, but her eyes were fixed only on him.

"Feel like giving me a ride to New York?"

I ended up going with them. I didn't want to be alone. All I wanted was to be with Emily. We returned home with her in the middle of the night. The next morning, my mother called Anna Fontanella's secretary on Emily's behalf to request personal time for a family emergency, leaving a number where she could be reached. Anna called our place a few hours later to find out what really happened, and Emily told her the truth. Anna said she was extremely sorry and that Emily should definitely spend the week resting. Frank welcomed her to stay at his house, but my mother told him that taking care of Emily would be our pleasure, especially since he already had his hands full with Katherine. And it was a good thing she stayed with us. If Emily had stayed with them, she wouldn't have been able to mention her break-up with Rob at all. Frank already knew about it, not the specifics, of course, only the bottom line. But he didn't want to upset Katherine with the news that the wedding was off. He didn't think she was ready to handle another loss just yet. But then again, Emily would eventually get over Rob, whereas Katherine might never get over Eli—she'd given birth to a stillborn boy, and Emily would've had a baby brother. Children aren't replaceable, but the world is crawling with jerks. My best friend would get over the pain of this broken engagement in time. And one day, she'd find somebody else to break her heart.

"But how, Stella?" she asked me. "*How* am I supposed to get over him?" She'd just gotten off of the phone with Rob. He'd left a ton of messages for her on my answering machine, and she'd finally decided to call him back during my shower.

"Well, what exactly did he say on the phone?" I asked as I lay down beside her on the bed, propping my head up on my elbow.

"He said it meant nothing—that what he has with Malcolm in no way contaminates or changes what he feels for me."

"Did he actually say the word 'contaminates'?"

"He actually did. And he said that his love for me was always there—even when he was doing physical things with Malcolm. And because of that, he doesn't feel like he lied. Because the love was always there."

"But that only makes it worse! I mean, if he loved you, what was he doing sleeping with *anybody* else?" Emily was silent as she stared into Marlayna's trouble-free teddy bear eyes. "Sorry," I said. "How could you possibly know the answer to that?"

"Malcolm is not the mother of my children."

"What?"

She turned to look at me. "That's another thing he said on the phone. 'Malcolm is not the mother of my children. You are.'"

"Is that supposed to make you feel better?"

"Apparently."

"Well, how long has it been going on for? Did he, at least, tell you that much?"

"Five years."

"Five years?"

"For as long as they've known each other." Her eyes suddenly grew wide. "Do you think Malcolm was, like, Rob's *boyfriend?*"

"Well, what would that have made you?"

"I guess…I was nothing."

"You were *not* nothing," I said, taking hold of her arm.

Emily smiled lightly. "A hopeful distraction at best."

"Well, what do you think, Em? That Rob's gay and just doesn't want to accept it?"

"I don't know what to think anymore. He said he'd been meaning to stop, that he was calling it quits with Malcolm in June as a wedding present to himself—to *himself,* Stella—so that our marriage could be pure."

I shook my head. "I really have no idea what to say right now. This is just so…"

"Completely fucked up?"

"Yeah."

"Don't I know it. Just be glad it's not happening to you."

"But it *is* happening to me. I mean, not technically, but…"

She smiled gratefully. "I know."

"So, were there ever any other guys, or was it only Malcolm?"

"He says it was only Malcolm, that he and Malcolm have a bond that transcends orientation. 'So, why don't you marry fucking Malcolm?' I asked him."

"What did he say?"

"He said *I'm* the one he wanted to spend the rest of his life with."

"But was he honestly going to stand up there at the wedding and…wait a minute. Wasn't Malcolm supposed to be your best man?"

Emily snickered. "Yeah, the best man *Rob* ever had."

I looked at her seriously. "What are you going to do?"

Emily was silent for a moment. When she spoke, her voice was quiet. "Can I tell you something that won't leave this room?" I nodded. "I still love him. I mean, I could never marry him or anything, but I do still love him. It would be easier if I could just write him off as some kind of prick and hate him forever, but I don't think I can do that."

"So, then, what happens now?"

She shrugged. "I go on with my life and hope that one day we can be friends. I know it's a cliché, but gay men really do make the greatest friends."

"A cliché *and* a stereotype."

"And true," she said, getting up from the bed. She seemed to be in a better mood as she stood in front of the mirror, playing with her hair.

"Perhaps," I conceded. "But I suppose the trick is *remembering* that they're gay."

"Uh, the traumatizing visual is forever burned in my brain, thank you. I don't think I'll be forgetting."

She assumed we were still talking about Rob, but I hadn't been. My mind had already moved on from the ex-fiancé, and I worried that, without even knowing it, part of Emily's had, too. My words of warning had been about Nick.

Mr. Almost Right

Emily tested Nick's waters that spring. I realized her innocent attraction had reached the brink of a full-blown crush when she stayed the week at my house and spent half of her time talking about the guy who'd broken her heart and the other half going on about the wonderful friend who'd held her in his arms afterward, the friend she called every day to check in with, the friend who just might end up hurting her all over again if she wasn't careful. She hardly talked at all about her baby brother, though I did come home from work one afternoon to find her curled up on the floor by my CD player crying hysterically to the song "Eli's Comin." The last time *Eli and the Thirteenth Confession* had inspired such passionate grief was in April of 1997 when Laura Nyro died of ovarian cancer. But now the album was not only Emily's link to her mother but also to the little brother she'd never known. Her feelings were all over the place. Perhaps this whole crush on Nick would blow over when her grief subsided and she was finally able to see straight again.

Either way, I probably wouldn't have been able to talk her out of it. When Emily makes up her mind about something, proof tends to overpower reason. Nick was so attentive, supportive and sweet when she returned to New York. Gay or not, Emily was convinced that he was the perfect guy for her. The only thing missing from their relationship was the intimacy. Of course, she never came out and told me she'd found Mr. Almost Right. I guess she knew me well enough to know I'd try to reason with her. And this was one of those situations in which Emily had to be *proven* wrong. So, she kept the true extent of her feelings hidden and waited for an opportunity to show the world that reason meant nothing when it came to friends falling in love.

"Nick and I made out."

"What?" Her late-night phone call had woken me, but I was still pretty sure I'd heard her correctly. "But he's—"

"I know. It's so strange, I can't explain it."

"Try, Emily. Try *really* hard."

"All right, well, I had just gotten into the tub and Nick asked if he could come in and shave because he was going out tonight, so—"

"Wait. He wanted to come in while you were in the bath?"

"Yeah, he does that all the time. We're roommates."

"Yeah, but being roommates doesn't have to mean seeing each other *naked*."

"He doesn't see me *naked,* Stella. It's not like he's looking or like he'd even care, anyway. It's always just been like a brother-sister thing."

"Yeah, but what twenty-three-year-old brother-sister duos do *you* know who still bathe in front of each other?"

"We're getting off track, here, Stella. And I really need your advice.... Nick hates me. I think he really hates me!" She began to cry, and I suddenly felt like a beast for harping on the bathing issue.

"Oh, Emily, I'm sure he doesn't hate you. Just tell me what happened. You left off at shaving."

"Well, he never actually got around to that," she said, sniffing. "He'd just walked into the bathroom and we were talking and stuff, and, out of the blue, he asks if I've ever thought of becoming a model."

"A model?"

"It's okay. I thought it was far-fetched, too."

"No, it's not that. It just sounds like an odd time to bring it up, don't you think?"

"You mean while I was in the tub?"

"Well, yeah. I mean, I know you guys are laid back, but..."

"No, I thought it was strange, too. But as it turns out, he was leading up to a photography conversation. He thinks I'd be good for some shots he wants to add to his portfolio. So, I told him I'd think about it."

"Why not just do it?"

"I think I just felt funny, like I wouldn't live up to the pictures he has in his head or something. It was like I just got shy all of a sudden. And you know *that* doesn't happen very often."

"Could it have been because you have such a gigantic crush on him?"

"Is it really that obvious?"

"Well, I *know* you. Anyway, go on."

"Okay, so I said I'd think about it and he saw that I was kind of embarrassed, so he came over and knelt down by the tub and started to massage my shoulders—you know, like, trying to coax me. And at first, it was just really playful. But then, things started to change. He stopped talking about the pictures, but he kept massaging me. And neither of us said anything at all. It happened really quickly, just kidding around one second and then silent and serious the next."

"Serious how, though? You mean serious-*romantic?*"

"I *think* so. My heart was beating so fast, I couldn't tell. After a while, he rested his face against the back of my head, and I just couldn't wait anymore. I figured there was always that chance I could ruin the moment, but that if I didn't seize it soon, I could also lose it and never have the chance again."

"So, what did you do?"

"Well, I really didn't have a plan. I just wanted to see his face—to maybe see what was going on in his eyes—so I started to turn around, and we just kind of fell into this really slow and wonderful kiss."

"Wait, what do you mean 'just kind of fell into' it? Who made the first move, you or him?"

"Stella, it was the most mutual kiss of my life. I really can't say who started it. It was just…meant to be."

"Oh, Emily."

"Well, doesn't it *sound* perfect?"

"In *theory,* but—"

"I know, I know."

"So, how long did you kiss for?"

"I don't know. A little while, I guess. And it was really amazing. But then, all of a sudden he just tore away from me."

"Did he say anything?"

"No. He wouldn't even look at me. He was just sitting there with his head in his hands and when I asked him what was wrong, he wouldn't answer. So, I put my robe on and sat down next to him on the floor. And then I said we weren't leaving the bathroom until he told me what was bothering him."

"So, did he?"

"He just said we shouldn't have done that and that his head felt really fucked up. And then, he said he needed to get out for a while, so I told him I'd get dressed and go with him. But…"

"But, what, Em?"

"But that's when he yelled at me!" she cried. "He said he needed to get away from *me* because *I* was the problem!"

"Oh, sweetie, he didn't mean it. Nick loves you. You know that. He may not love you the way you want, but he *does* love you. He's just confused."

"No, he's not, Stella. He *really* hates me! I've never seen him that mad. And I don't even know what I did!"

"Nothing that he didn't do. You both made a mistake. It happens."

"Stella?" she asked quietly.

"Hmm?"

"I don't think it *was* a mistake."

"Oh, don't start that. Look at what happened afterward. I mean, I can understand your being glad that it happened. But treasure it as a memory and move on. I'm telling you, Emily, it's dangerous to try for anything else. You could end up losing the best friend you have in New York."

"But *why* do you think he did it?"

"Why do straight people experiment with the same sex? Curiosity, maybe? But one experience doesn't have to change who you are. And as big a fan of yours as I am, I don't think you have the power to turn a gay man straight."

"But don't you think it might be possible that what Nick and I have is so powerful, it transcends orientation?"

"Honey, if you start quoting Rob Sellers in times of trouble, we're all going straight to hell. He was a liar with convenient theories, not a prophet."

"But, Stella, the thing is, you're not around when it's just the two of us. You don't see how sweet he is to me all the time. We'd be so perfect together if only—"

"He weren't who he is."

"You frustrate the hell out of me when you're right."

"You need me, Emily. You're the passion. I'm the reason. We balance each other out. And speaking of passion, I *will* give you something."

"What's that?"

"I do think Nick loves you madly. I think he kissed you partly out of curiosity and partly because he *does* feel so close to you."

"You sound like you speak from experience."

"Well, not exactly. But it's not like I've never thought about it."

"Who's the lucky girl?"

"Who do you *think,* Tinkerbell?"

"Ooh, is this an open invitation?"

I laughed. "I'm glad to hear you're feeling better."

"You always make me feel better. I just wish I knew when Nick was coming back. I really don't want to fall asleep without talking to him."

"But if you do, you do. Emily, you and Nick are going to be fine. You'll talk when you talk. And before you know it, this will just be some crazy thing that happened one night in the spring of 2000. Listen, true friends always take each other back. Just give Nick a little bit of time. And *please* stop falling for men who like men. It's not a good pattern, my love."

"And the worst part is, I know it. Anyway, I'm gonna let you go back to sleep now. Thanks for dealing with me, Stella."

"That's my specialty. And you never have to thank me. I love you."

"I love you, too. Good night."

Emily awoke the next morning to a vase filled with yellow roses and a card that read, *I am an asshole—Nick*. She heard the shower running and immediately ran into the bathroom to thank him.

"I got your flowers," she said, sliding the shower door open. "I'm an asshole, too."

Nick bent down to give her a kiss on the forehead, and then he closed the door. "I think from now on," he called out to her, "we should only have one person in here at a time."

"Oh," she said, trying not to sound fazed. "Okay."

As she was leaving, Nick called out to her again. "Oh, Em? I got you croissants from that new bakery you like. And I made you coffee."

Emily thanked Nick again, this time without putting her face in the shower, and when she walked out of that bathroom, she closed the door on their one crazy night. Things went back to normal between them relatively quickly, the only major difference being that they stopped doing that whole "brother-sister" naked thing around the apartment. I suppose every relationship needs its boundaries. And though the circumstances were a little unconventional, Emily's tidy little heartbreak was exactly what the doctor ordered to get her over Rob. What her ex-fiancé did to her was shocking. What she really needed was to have her heart broken the old-fashioned way—by a healthy dose of rejection. Deep down, she knew she could never have Nick.

And at the same time, she also knew that no matter how much he hurt her, he'd be there to cushion the fall.

Emily and Nick. Extremely close friends who went a little out of bounds one spring night when they were twenty-three. Shit happens and love divides. But Emily was truly happy for Nick when he started seeing Evan. She just hadn't expected them to want to live together so quickly. Nick said the three of them could work something out—he didn't want Emily to worry. But she wouldn't let herself be a third wheel, especially when the new addition to the engine was as dangerously sexy as Evan was. She didn't want to be the girl who kept falling for gay men. And she didn't like herself for fantasizing about one of her best friend's boyfriends. Besides, she had a new roommate in mind already. Anna's Web designer was just dying to get out of her parents' basement in Jersey. She'd told Emily a couple of times how cool she thought it would be to room together. *Her. She.* A female. No men, no complications. Just someone to help pay the rent.

That June, Emily moved to SoHo to live with the very female Adriana Fernandez, knowing that she'd always stay close with Nick. Only from then on, there'd be no reason for rules, roses or regrets because their bathtub kiss truly was just some crazy thing that happened one night in the spring of 2000. And when all was said and done, they had patched things up and taken each other back. Just like true friends always did.

Independence

I was twenty-four years old when I left my mother's condo for a place of my own—an entire mile away. Due to its growing number of students, Forest Hills had been involved in some expansion efforts over the summer and a new crop of teachers had been hired. Alison was one of them. That fall, we'd be seeing each other every day again, just like college. Only it wouldn't be as much fun as college. Or could it be even better?

"Oh, come on. How perfect would it be, Stella Bella?" Alison asked, hoping to soften me with the nickname, which she claimed had nothing to do with a rhyme scheme and everything to do with how beautiful I was.

We were standing outside of Lauren and Alexa's new apartment in Center City. Seeing how they lived had made both of us jealous. It was just like college, only better because they weren't as poor and didn't have to worry about term papers and tests. I knew that Alison had been wanting to move out of her parents' house in Bloomdale for a while. She just hadn't been sure where to go. Her new job at Forest Hills had provided the location. All she needed now was a roommate. Preferably someone she already knew she could be comfortable living with. Someone like me.

"I'll think about it," I told her as we headed to my car.

The truth was that I didn't really need to think about it. I'd been fantasizing about having a place of my own for nearly a year. It all started with Warren and Emily.

During her first summer in SoHo, Emily began receiving frequent visits from Warren, who took the subway in from Queens every weekend under the pretense of "hanging out." I was way past the jealousy of my college freshman days—I was glad to hear they'd been spending time together. Yet, I suspected Warren was up to something. He'd never shown such interest in hanging out alone with her *before.* (With the exception, of course, of that one time they had sex.)

"So, what's with you going into Manhattan all the time?" I asked him one night on the phone. "You and Emily have hung out three weekends in a row now."

"Are you keeping score?"

"No. I'm just wondering."

"Oh, well, there's no big, mysterious reason. I just figured I should check in on her more often, you know? Especially now that Nick's not around. She's had a pretty weird year."

"Well, Nick's still *around,* just not as close by. It doesn't matter, though. I think it's really sweet of you to care so much."

"Yeah, well, I do what I can."

"And speaking of weird, how do you feel about her spending time with Rob again?"

Emily had run into Rob at a bar a couple weeks earlier and they'd struck up a rapidly growing but "strictly platonic" friendship. It had been five months since their breakup, and according to Emily, they were getting to know each other in a whole new way, without the complications of romance. Rob said he was no longer seeing Malcolm "like that." In fact, he wasn't seeing anybody at all. Emily's ex had taken on a vow of celibacy—probably another gift to himself—and although my best friend had never even hinted at it, I knew her well enough to fear that Rob's recent pledge made him all the more desirable.

"I don't trust that situation at all," Warren said. "I mean, Rob's a nice guy and everything, but he's shady. And I don't buy a word about that celibacy vow. It's bullshit to get in her pants and he knows it as well as I do."

"Do me a favor, then?"

"Anything for you."

"Don't stop going into SoHo to check up on my girl."

"I wouldn't dream of it. I have no social life here, remember?"

"Well, you're always working."

"True. Visiting Emily's a really good break from all that. It's actually become the highlight of my week."

"Good," I said. "Live it up."

And he did. He and Emily were on the road to developing a close friendship of their own, independent of me, and what would've once inspired jealousy now only fostered feelings of security. I didn't worry so much about Emily making the wrong decisions when Warren was around. But it was more than that. As we age, we tend to forget the people who seemed to matter so much to us once. I'd already lost touch with two-thirds of The Six. John Lixner and I hadn't e-mailed in three months. But Warren and Emily were still there, stronger than before. And by becoming such close friends in their own right, they'd created a new bond, not just with each other, but between the three of us. They'd made the line a circle. We were our own special force now, Emily, Warren and me—still standing after all these years. Survivors. Only survivors one and two seemed to be having a lot more fun than I was.

When Emily and Warren were drunk, which was pretty much every weekend, they missed the part of their circle that couldn't always be there. So, they'd call me to feel more complete. And hearing their voices always left me longing for change. I wasn't afraid to leave home. I stayed because things were comfortable there—I was used to the routine, and my mother didn't charge me a dime. I'd never actually felt the need for a place of my own. It was these calls from Warren and Emily that made me realize what I was missing out on. I was secure enough to know I'd made a lot of good decisions—one of them being to stay in Scottsboro—but my sweet-stability routine had begun to sour. I could hear the fun Warren and Emily were having in her apartment, with Rob, Nick, Evan, Adriana and all those people whose voices I didn't even recognize competing with the music in the background. And then I'd look around my bedroom, the same bedroom I'd had since I was sixteen years old, and wonder why I hadn't left it yet. Who said I had to stay there forever? Who ever said I had to be a monk? Twenty-somethings were *allowed* to call friends in the middle of the night spouting inebriated declarations of love. I wanted to be one of those twenty-somethings. I wanted to have parties of my *own,* a place that was mine. The desire took root inside of me and continued to grow, but I never took the initiative to fulfill it. Alison's new position at Forest Hills provided the perfect setup. And that visit to Lauren and Alexa's new apartment showed us what it could be like. I didn't need initiative. All I needed was to say yes.

"Break the news to your family tomorrow," I told Alison when I dropped her off at home that night. "We'll start looking for a place right away."

She was so happy, she grabbed my face and gave me a huge, wet kiss on the lips. I hoped Emily wouldn't be jealous.

"Of course, I'm jealous," Emily said later on the phone. She was drunk. "You know I've always wanted to live with you."

"I meant about the kiss, silly."

"It wasn't a *real* kiss. The whole world knows you're saving yourself for me. And Alison is well aware of the fact that you're my bitch. Hey, Warren!" she called out. "It's Stella. Tell her she's my bitch."

"Stella," he said, picking up the phone. "Emily says you're her bitch."

"So, I hear."

"What's this about you getting an apartment?"

"Alison and I—we're gonna move in together."

"Cool. So, I guess this means I'll be coming down there a lot more often then, right?"

"Sure. If you want to."

"If I *want* to? I remember the way you and Alison were in college. Don't tell me you're gonna live like nuns now that you have to pay for the place. I demand a party at least once a month."

"Woo-hoo!" Emily shouted in the background. "Party down!"

"That can be arranged," I said happily. "Just be sure to bring my bitch."

The fact that the apartment we ended up renting was only a mile away from my mother's condo didn't diminish my excitement. I had done it. I had finally moved out on my own. And I was ready to party down like a bitch.

Getting Wild

Our apartment quickly became a sanctuary of sin. Honoring Warren's demand, Alison and I threw at least one party a month. Our parties were almost as close to wild as we got. *Almost,* because while crazy, they were never X-rated. But that was because we only invited friends, and we had a thing about not getting naked with them. But then, there were the weekends when we *didn't* have parties.

Still hungering for an outlet between "almost" and the extreme, Alison and I turned to the casual sex we'd never had in college. I use the term loosely because I still had a thing about sex with strangers. Though to be more specific, I should say *intercourse,* since I'd pretty much opened myself up to everything else. A dry spell can do that to a woman. In the last two years, I'd only had contact with two guys—Jeremy, Emily and Adriana's cute stoner neighbor, who lost interest in me the minute his rolling papers arrived, and Maurice, the hotter-than-sex coat-check guy at the "Anna by Emily" launch party. Things got a little dirty with Maurice, but by the time we moved into McIntyre Suites, it still seemed like forever since I'd felt a man's touch. Alison wasn't exactly a wetland of activity, either. We'd both suffered through dry spells. But that's what bachelorette pads were for, aside from throwing killer parties.

So, Alison and I went on a binge of sorts. A man-eating binge. And *that* was as close to wild as we got. Though Alison got a little wilder than me. John and Warren were still the only guys I'd ever actually done it with. Sometimes I did crave sex, but my "Everything But" rule just made things simpler. Alison had a label, too. She was the "Everything But the Butt Girl." She thought it was a clever spin on my designation, but I told her never to use the term in public, as it sounded pretty trashy, no matter how true it was.

None of the guys we brought home were ever invited to any of our parties. We preferred to keep our sex lives separate from our social lives. It's not as if we were interested in building *relationships* with these guys. We were merely sowing those wild oats we'd been blessed with. And wasn't that every single twenty-something's God-given right?

Speaking of rights, Emily said it was *her* God-given right to sleep with whoever she wanted. Unfortunately, she was talking about Rob when she said it. Though, I must give her credit. The "just friends" thing lasted longer than any of us had predicted. For a year, Celibate Rob and his ambiguous ex-fiancée palled around without ever once falling victims to their past. But then Katherine got pregnant again. And during her third month, she miscarried. Rob was there when Emily heard the news, and that night, they fell into bed.

"He wasn't there for me last time," Emily said. "He wants to be there for me now. Please let him, Stella. I love him so much, and he's changed. That whole mess with Malcolm was a year-and-a-half ago. *I've* grown up since then. Why can't you believe that he has, too?"

"I didn't say I don't believe it. It's just that...Emily, he cheated on you the entire time you were together."

"That's all in the past now. Don't you want me to be happy?"

"Of course, I do."

"Then let me. *Please.*"

What choice did I have after that? Rob was her Achilles heel, and maybe she was mine. I'd always had a weakness for Emily. Until the day I have children, I'll think of her as my baby, even if she is one month older. There's always been that instinct to protect her, to steer her down the safer path. But even mothers have to let their little girls go eventually, and Emily would be twenty-five in three weeks.

Warren didn't like this new development in the Rob saga, either, but he managed to find comfort in the form of an exquisite goddess beauty named Giselle. Emily and I had begun to wonder if Warren would *ever* settle down with *any* girl. For as wonderful, sweet, sensitive and perfect as he was with the two of us, his apartment was pretty much known as the Heartbreak Hotel in single circles. One-night stands, one-week stands—it wasn't that he meant to hurt these women, just that he got bored so easily. Just as easily, it seemed, as the girls fell in love. But then Giselle came along. He met her at a club one night with the newly romantic Emily and Rob and their usual entourage of Nick, Evan and Adriana. As it turns out, Giselle Darley didn't just look like a model, she was one. But Warren wasn't superficial enough to date her for that reason alone. To have sex with her, certainly, but not to make her his first actual girlfriend. Though, that is what she became. So, I'm sure there was *something* to Giselle beyond her looks. I just never saw it. And I never wanted to insult Warren by asking him to identify what it was that made his girlfriend more than just a beautiful shell.

There *was* one thing I loved about Giselle, and that was the fact that she couldn't stand Emily or me. She flat-out told Warren she was jealous of how much he cared for us. She didn't like knowing that her boyfriend would drop everything—including *her*—to run to the aid of two women he wasn't even dating. I only knew this because Warren told me never to be offended by her snobbery. "It's just a front because she feels so insecure," he said. A *model* who felt insecure because of *me?* How could I not get off on that? I did try feeling sorry for her, but I knew her ultimate fantasy was to have Warren all to herself, with Emily and me cut from the picture completely, and that made me decide she *was* a bitch, which meant it was perfectly humane to get off on her insecurities. Not that my feelings toward Giselle really mattered. I knew that she and Warren weren't headed for the altar.

As for Emily and Rob, however, I could only pray. That boy was poison, and everyone seemed to know it but her. Once a snake, always a snake—isn't that how the saying goes? So what if his crawl had been slower, his hiss muffled by Katherine's miscarriage? So what if he'd colored himself celibate? Rob was the still the same snake. I was sure of it in my gut. But I was also sure of something else: no matter how much Giselle resented her boyfriend's "other women," no matter how much Warren and I doubted Rob, the three of us were a chain. And regardless of how many bitches and snakes came along spouting snobbery and poison, we'd stay that way. The Robs and Giselles of this world would come and go, but nothing could ever break our chain.

Settling Down

My personal slut streak ended in April when I broke the cardinal rule of my own code of conduct and had sex with a stranger on the living room rug. His name was Tony and I met him at a crowded party that this guy, Malik, was throwing on the third floor of our building. Tony was from South Philadelphia, but was in Scottsboro visiting "a friend of a friend" of Malik's. The details swirled around in my head, mingling with the vodka in my blood and telling me that this Tony guy seemed safe enough—and *definitely* cute enough—to hook up with later. I was drunk, maybe drunker than I'd ever been in my life, when I headed downstairs with definitely-cute-enough Tony only two steps behind me.

I'd trusted John Lixner. I'd trusted Warren. I didn't even know Tony. But for some reason, I kept telling myself it was okay. *It's just Tony from South Philly,* I thought as he put the condom on. *He knows people who know Malik.* But I hardly even knew Malik. I hadn't met him until that night. Like Tony from

South Philly, I, too, had been invited to the party by "a friend of a friend."

Lying on the floor with a stranger three times removed from a guy in my building whom I hadn't even met until that night, and so drunk my body had turned to butterflies—I still can't believe it came to that. People say rules were meant to be broken, but the circumstances weren't even special. They were just plain stupid. The rule, itself, was stupid—to think I could walk such a fine line between fire and certain death without getting burned. Tempting the flame was doing "everything but" what I thought might kill me. It had been more than ten years, but Blanche had never been far from my mind, not really. Those boys that night at Keith Shay's had killed a part of her and she'd let them. I just always had to be careful not to let them. With my rule, I thought I'd taken back control. For my sister. Because she couldn't. Because I'd never done anything to save her.

Sometimes I worried that they might get angry when I said no. That they might come home with me expecting sex and just go for it no matter what my rules were. But I always had Alison—right in the next bedroom. I could always just scream for her if things got out of hand. If some demanding prick tried to break my rule. But what if I were the one to break it willingly? What if Alison were still upstairs at a party when I realized my mistake? Who would I scream for then? Who would hear me?

I barely remember what Tony looked like, but I remember the sting of the rug. Blanche had done it with six guys on Keith Shay's living room carpet. And now I was doing it with them, too. Tony was heavy on top of me, and he was Kevin. They were all Kevin. And it wasn't a nightmare. I may have forced the memory into a cave and buried it in shadows. I may have whitewashed fear with denial. I might always live the lie, but my body knew what truth felt like. It felt like men on top of me, holding my wrists, when I was scared to death to be there. It felt like hot, sweaty, spinning rooms, wanting to scream, and memories of my sister. It felt like dying.

Blanche, the rebel who had never fought back. I screamed

because she couldn't. Because Kevin had really hurt me. Because Tony was making me burn.

"Jesus Christ, what the fuck is wrong with you?" he yelled, jumping up. He couldn't seem to get his clothes on fast enough.

"I don't know!" I sobbed, pulling a blanket off of the couch to cover myself with. "I don't know!"

"You're fucking crazy, that's what's wrong with you," he said before slamming the door.

You're just a screwed-up whore who's got everybody fooled but me.

After seeing Tony storm back into Malik's apartment and split with his friend, Gina, Alison knew that something bad had happened. She rushed immediately downstairs and found me in the living room—still lying on the floor in tears. Anyone could've jumped to the wrong conclusion.

"Stella, tell me what he did to you! Tell me and I'll kill him!"

Her panic soothed me. It was nice to be around someone who cared. "It was nothing like that, Al. Tony was just mad because… Look, I just don't think I can do this teacher by day, vixen by night routine anymore. Okay?"

"That's it? You mean he didn't hurt you?"

"Not the way you're thinking. We just…I…" I'd started to well up again.

"Oh, what is it, sweetie? Did you break your rule or something? Is that it?" I nodded. "Oh, it's *okay,*" she said, cupping my face in her hands. "We'll ditch the routine together, all right? I've been getting tired of it, too. And don't feel bad about breaking your rule. I broke mine last week. You know, 'Everything But the—'"

"I know," I said, hugging her. "Ew."

Alison and I spent the next month trying to erase the last eight with clean living. We still had parties and went to bars, but the only guys who came beyond the front door of our apartment, besides Warren and Rob, were our good friends from the building, Anthony, Marcus and Izzie. Marcus and Izzie were cousins, who roomed together down the hall, while Anthony lived in a one-bedroom upstairs. And in our minds, they didn't even count as guys because they *were* such good friends and, therefore, fell into the "off limits" category when it came to fooling around. It was part of that whole preference we shared for keeping sex and socialization separate. Only now our minds had left the gutter and sex wasn't all we thought about; an evolution was taking place. And the "asexual" trio we'd trained ourselves to treat like brothers was beginning to shine with promise. Izzie was the quiet one, while Marcus and Anthony tag-teamed as the life of every party. It wasn't until I took the time to slow down and breathe that I realized just how much I preferred the quiet.

Truth be told, I'd always been intrigued by Izzie. Part of it, I will admit, was the fact that he reminded me of John. I was immediately drawn to his gentle nature and soft-spoken sense of humor. But I hadn't even been face-to-face with John in six years. Izzie and I had a different dynamic. We were adults. And as an adult, I thought I'd found a guy that I could honestly wrap my heart around. As it turns out, I was right.

I no longer worried about mixing sex and friendship because I no longer wanted one without the other. I hadn't taken on a so-called vow of celibacy like Rob and I wasn't necessarily looking for a relationship. I just knew it was okay to have the feelings I was beginning to have for Izzie because they had nothing to do with conquest. If we got together, it wouldn't be a one-night stand. It would be something special, something real. And as he evolved from my intriguing pal down the hall to the guy I was actually falling for, I grew hopeful that he might care for me, too. Hints came in the way he looked at me during those early-morning conversations, in the fact that we were actually still talking, long after everyone else at the party had passed out, still talking and laughing as if time didn't matter, sharing a warm bottle of beer. And one of those mornings, he kissed me. The last thing either of us wanted to do after that was reverse our evolution.

Izzie Salvato was my first "real world" boyfriend and the greatest happiness I had known since that week I spent making love to John when I was nineteen. Following our lead, Alison began seeing Anthony, spending most of her nights upstairs in his apartment, which left our apartment free for Izzie and me. Anthony worked the middle shift in a warehouse and didn't get home until nine-thirty every night. That was generally the time my roommate would disappear and my boyfriend would show up at the front door. As a political cartoonist, Izzie did most of his work from home while I was teaching, so we could've spent even more time together if we'd wanted. But I liked that 4:00 to 9:30 was my time alone with Alison, even if all we did sometimes was sit in silence and grade tests. The last thing I wanted was to drift away from her just because we'd both settled down.

"It'll never happen, Stella Bella," she told me. It was Friday night and we were sitting at the kitchen table having coffee. "If Anthony and I eloped tomorrow, I'd *still* have my head up your ass."

"Now, *that's* a delicious visual."

"I just mean I'm not going anywhere."

"Glad to hear it. So, are you and Anthony discussing marriage already?"

"We've talked about it a couple of times, but it's not like he proposed or anything. It's only talk."

"Oh."

"Relax, Stella. You don't have to be having marriage conversations to know you're in a good relationship. You and Izzie are incredible together. And look what can happen to couples who discuss marriage too early. Isn't that what Emily and Rob decided their problem was?"

"Yeah, that and the fact that he was sleeping with a *guy* for four and a half years before he met her."

"No, but I mean, their recent talk, wasn't it all about—"

"Yeah, yeah. They shouldn't have jumped the gun."

"See."

"If you ask me, I still think their problems had a lot more to do with Malcolm than jumping the gun."

"Maybe that's what they meant—jumping *Malcolm's* gun."

"I don't think so, Alison. But the good thing is, at least they're not talking about marriage this time. They've been back together for eight months already and they're still taking it slow. I think that's good."

"Has it only been eight months?"

"Not counting the year and three months they spent as just friends."

"Okay, but technically, Rob's been back in her life for almost two years, and he's been nothing but good to her, right?"

"As far as I know."

"Then I'd ease up on the guy. Maybe he really *has* changed."

"I haven't wanted to admit it, but I think I eased up on him a while ago. It's hard to think someone's a jerk when they're so damn nice to you."

"Not to mention the fact that he hasn't *done* anything wrong."

"Except for break Emily's heart."

"Another lifetime ago. Forget about it."

"I've been trying."

"Hey, does this mean that Warren and Giselle are coming up on eight months, too?"

"Yup. And whoever thought *that* would last?"

"Well, aren't you the cynic?"

"How can I be a cynic when I'm so madly in love?"

"I'll get back to you on that one," she said, standing up from the table. She came over and gave me a hug. "Have fun with Izzie tonight, love bug."

"I guess I'll see you Monday morning, then?" I asked as she headed for the front door.

"*Monday morning?* You know I'll be coming back before then."

"You will?" I tried not to show my excitement.

"I always stop back in for *something,* don't I?"

My heart sank. "Yeah, I guess you do."

"But, I guess that's the beauty of dating someone in the building."

"And look at all that time we wasted—trying to keep our sex lives separate from our social lives."

"Go figure."

"Yeah, who knew, right?" She was standing in the doorway, waiting to leave. "Anyway, go, get out of here. Have fun, have sex, talk about marriage. Do whatever you and Anthony do. And I'll see you when I see you."

"I'll miss you, Stella Bella Love Bug," she said, smiling. And then she was gone.

It was probably for the best. With such different work schedules, weekends were like gold to Alison and Anthony. They treasured the time alone together, and I was glad they were able to have it. I just couldn't stand the loneliness on Saturdays. Guys' Day. The one day of every week that Izzie and Marcus set aside for Adam, their childhood friend from Center City. Sometimes it bothered me—the fact that Anthony was itching for more quality time with Alison while my own boyfriend was off devoting entire days of his weekend to the guys. But what could I do about it without sounding like one of "those" girlfriends? The kind who can't let their men have time alone with the guys without breathing down their necks about it. That's what I felt like the one time I dropped by to meet Adam. I'd expected a warm reception, but all I'd gotten was a lot of nervous energy, like none of them could understand what I was doing there. Needless to say, I never intruded on Guys' Day again. Izzie said they never did anything special, that it was more about "hanging"—just being able to watch movies, play video games and act dumb. Maybe *I'd* been dumb for making it out to mean something more, for thinking Izzie had to spend every waking minute with me on the weekends simply because that was what Alison and Anthony did. He enjoyed his days with his buddies. They invigorated him. And I reaped the rewards of his energy. Every Saturday night, he'd come over, completely renewed and itching to "consume" me, which of course meant that he was absolutely starving for sex, which I would always give to him, gladly and repeatedly until dawn. I just wished the hours leading up to that sweet reward weren't always so shadowed by loneliness.

But how could I really complain? Other than those solitary Saturday afternoons, my life was a dream come true. I had made it. I'd made it through Blanche, my father, that night in my room with Kevin. I'd even gotten over John Lixner. Well, almost. Seeing his name in the bookstore that day had honestly thrown me for a loop, sent my heart pounding, turned my knees to jelly. My reaction to his picture had been even worse. But how could I not fall in love again, seeing his eyes? How could I not wonder if it was a sign? I had just wrapped my heart around somebody new, for the first time since John. Izzie was the only guy I could *ever* see myself falling in love with, aside from the boy who'd first taught me what love was. And now, here was that boy again, only older, haunting my happiness from the back of a book. So, I'd e-mailed him, figuring there was no harm in e-mailing an old friend, even if I was falling for somebody new, even if John was so much more than an old friend. But the message was returned to me—"user unknown." I realized that he must've changed e-mail addresses without even bothering to tell me. Then again, we hadn't e-mailed each other in two years. And perhaps it was just as well. Maybe *that* was my sign—the fact that I couldn't reach him. And I really shouldn't have even tried. Because I *had* wrapped my heart around somebody new and he was wonderful.

I'd made it through so many rough spots, including Tony, the big bang that snapped me out of my slut phase and sparked my evolution with Izzie. And now I was exactly where I needed to be. Even everyday living felt magical.

"Sometimes—there's God—so quickly!" Vivien Leigh immortalized these words in *A Streetcar Named Desire.* Izzie gave them meaning for me. We were in bed one night at the end of July, listening to the rain, when he said he never thought his life could be that perfect.

"What do you mean?" I asked.

"I don't know," he said, becoming shy. "I just never thought…" He rolled over onto his side. "My parents' marriage was shit. And almost every guy I know complains about his girlfriend."

"So, what are you saying?"

"I never complain about you, Stella. Not even on Guys' Day."

"Well, I'm glad."

It was Saturday night, and still early. Our conversation had only been a break. There was still a lot more of me to consume. As we started getting into it again, Izzie whispered something in my ear. It didn't register at first, but once it had, I heard Vivien Leigh, loud and clear, making me cry. He told me that he would die for me.

And there *was* God, so quickly, just like that. And there was my life—passionate, prosperous and fulfilled. Everything made sense. And order surrounded the heaven I was in. Love didn't grow only in McIntyre Suites. Warren and Emily, my satellite hearts, were happy, too. All the stars were in line. It only stood to reason that at any minute, they could all come crashing down.

Brotherly Love

Emily took an early flight home from an L.A. fashion show one stormy August evening to find Rob and Adriana having sex in the shower. But there was no Chinese food to drop this time, no diamond ring to throw, not even any sexual-confusion labels to slap on his cheating behavior. And this time, Emily was more outraged than hurt. This time, Rob had just flat-out betrayed her—the traditional way. And she wasn't going to stand by and let there be a next time. She told Rob that they were through for good, meaning they'd never even be friends again, no matter how many vows of celibacy he took.

Of course, on the inside, she did bleed a little. But Warren said it wasn't as bad as we'd expected. And no one had a better view of the situation than he did, having taken over Adriana's lease and moved in with Emily just two weeks after Rob was ripped from the picture. Ms. Fernandez seemed to be suffering from acute postcoital anxiety and had thought it best that she move out. And since budget cuts at Warren's halfway house had led him to a job at the new community center in Chelsea, there was really nothing keeping him in Queens. He was more than thrilled to move into Adriana's room and begin a new life in Manhattan. Giselle, on the other hand, didn't find the opportunity quite as thrilling. She'd been living in the Village since Warren met her, and said that if he was so eager to live in Manhattan, they should get an apartment of their own.

"I don't think we're ready for that," he told her.

"But you're ready to move in with a woman you're *not* dating?"

"That's why I can move in with her," he said. "It's a stable relationship."

"And what we have isn't?"

"Apparently not."

That's when Giselle issued the do-or-die ultimatum. "It's her or me, Warren. If you move in with Emily, we're over."

"Then, I guess we're over," he said.

Emily saw Warren's moving in as a great big silver lining in the shit sandwich that was Rob Sellers.

"I realize now what a complete *ass* Rob was," she told me on the phone. "But look at what I got out of it. I got Warren. It's gonna be so great living with him. And I'm so glad he broke up with Giselle. I really couldn't stand her. And now Warren and I can be single together."

I could feel myself starting to worry. "Emily, Warren is one of your closest friends in the world. And you're not just taking a trip somewhere together. You've made a commitment to share an apartment."

"Why are you telling me things I already know?"

"I'm just saying, it's not like a fun little getaway where you guys can do something and go your separate ways when you come home. You *are* home, and if anything happens...and it *shouldn't,* Emily. Think of what you could lose. Warren isn't just your best friend's 'other best friend' anymore. You guys have gotten so incredibly close. I know you're on the rebound and he's going to comfort you and—"

"Stop, Stella," she said, laughing. "Would you just stop for a second? Who said *anything* about me getting together with Warren?"

"I thought you were implying that you wanted to."

"Please! Warren and I are *so* six years ago. We already did the sex thing. You, of all people, should remember that, Miss Hissy Fit."

"Oh, *I* remember. But I know you, Em. You get attached so easily, especially when you're on the rebound."

"Well, you don't have to worry. Honestly, Warren and I have become like brother and sister. We're not about getting it on."

"Yeah, but didn't you and your last brother used to go naked around each other?"

"That was different, silly. Nick was my *gay* brother."

"So, I guess you only make out with your gay relatives, then?"

"Oh, fuck *you*. Look, if you must know, I *am* still attracted to Warren. Hello—look at him! But that doesn't mean I'm a moron. I'd never mess with what we have for the physical thrill alone. Cheap thrills are a dime a dozen. If Warren and I ever did anything, it would be…I don't know. I don't want to make both of us vomit."

"No. Say it. It would be what?"

"It would be everything. I don't know—I can't phrase it right. I'm just saying you don't have to worry. The timing and every circumstance in the world would have to be perfect in order for me to sleep with that boy. He's just too special to me for anything less."

"Well, you deserve special. And if the next guy you date in any way reminds me of Rob, I'm gonna kick him in the balls *before* he hurts you."

"Well, there'll be a lot of sore balls in New York, then."

"Why? Are you planning a masochism spree?"

"No. But aren't all guys the same, really? Don't they all end up hurting us?"

"Not all of them," I said. "Not our brothers."

Lightning Strikes Again

My students had said I should dress as a witch for our class Halloween party. I preferred to think of it as "playing against type" and had gone out and bought a complete costume in preparation of the big day. I was already wearing it when the phone rang.

Izzie stumbled into the bathroom, half asleep, and found me spraying silver streaks into my hair. "It's your mom," he said, handing me the cordless. "You look beautiful." He was gone by the time I said hello.

"Janey?" There was silence on the other end of the phone. "Hello? Janey?"

"Yeah," she whispered, "I'm here."

"Oh, hi. What is it? I have to leave for work in a minute. We have our Halloween party today. I told you about that, didn't I?"

"Stella..." She was still whispering. She was crying.

"Janey, what is it?" She cried harder now, but didn't answer. "Mom? What's wrong?"

"It's...Kevin."

"What about Kevin, Mom? What did he do?"

The fact that I'd called her "Mom" had triggered something in Izzie, and he was back in the bathroom, holding my hand.

"He left me, Stella! Kevin's gone!"

I called out of work and rushed over to her condo in my witch's clothes. When I got there, she showed me the note.

We had seven years together, Mary. That's more than a lot of people have. But I have to close this chapter now. Save yourself a lot of time and strength, and don't look for me. This is just the way things have to be. I hope we both find happiness. —Kevin

"But, Janey, what does this mean?" I asked. We were sitting at the kitchen table—the note, two cups of coffee and a heavy cloud of pain between us. Pain, fear, secrets and confusion.

"I don't know," my mother said, shaking her head. "Who just leaves a note like that and takes off?"

"Were you two having problems?"

"No. Not for a couple of years, no. I mean, aside from all that nonsense about going West."

"Well, what do you mean 'not for a couple of years'? Did something happen a couple years ago?" My mother took a long sip of coffee. When she was done, she looked down at her cup. "Janey, whatever it is, you can tell me."

"He cheated on me," she said, looking up into my eyes, "with a younger woman."

I suppose it was crazy, but logic didn't stop my heart from shaking or my witch's legs from doing their petrified dance under the glass table. After all, *I* was a younger woman.

"Who was she?"

"Some woman whose roof he was fixing. Sound familiar?" Of course. It was exactly the way Kevin had fallen in love with my mother. The bastard.

"How did you find out about it?"

"I found a condom in his pants pocket and confronted him. He confessed to the whole affair."

I'd forgotten about those ten missing condoms. The ones he'd stolen from my nightstand drawer. *I took those because...well...because I knew they were there.* The night I confronted him was the night he attacked me. But, wait. That was six years ago.

"And when did you say this happened?"

"About two years ago. Why?"

"Oh, no reason." And there I had it—the fucking rat bastard had been cheating on her for years. Probably the entire time they'd been married. The night he attacked me and the condom-in-the-pocket confrontation were probably just the only two times he'd been caught. "I'm sorry, Janey," I said as I stood up to hug her.

"I'll be fine," she said, patting my arm. "I will." And then, she got up, too. "I just need to use the bathroom for a minute."

Moving aside, I watched her small, sunken body stagger across the room. When she reached the doorway, she turned and looked at me. An odd smile passed over her face. "You're a witch," she said. I didn't answer. Something in her tone and coloring alarmed me, and I could only stare. My mother giggled. "Your costume. I like it. It's sweet."

"Do you feel okay? Maybe you should lie down."

"I don't need to lie down. I just..." Her eyes caught sight of something in the distance—I wasn't sure what—and she stopped talking.

"Mom?" I asked, walking closer. "Are you all right?"

She looked at me calmly, too calmly, exhausted. "Well, my husband just left me." She turned to exit the room but lost her balance and stumbled sideways. I quickly seized hold of her shoulders.

"It's okay," I said, hugging her. "It's really okay."

My mother pulled away slowly, her eyes searching my face as if I were crazy. "I know it is, Blanche." And that was the moment my blood became ice.

"Mom," I said, trying not to cry. "It's me. Stella."

"Well, I know *that,*" she said, dismissing me with a laugh as she backed away toward the table. "That's what I said—Stella." She paused to look around the room, theatrically, as if we had an audience. "Stella for Star!" she burst out, laughing loudly. And then her eyes glowed with excitement, like a child's. "I can do it just like Vivien Leigh. Stella for Star! Stella for Star!"

"Mom, I think you should lie down."

"What I need to know, though, is why everyone leaves me. Could you tell me that, Miss Stella for Star? Could you tell me why everyone leaves me?"

"I don't know," I whispered.

"Good," she said. "Well, I suppose he'll finally get to see the desert." She started to reel backward but I caught her by the wrists.

"Mom!"

My mother laughed, releasing herself from my grip. "Your father gets the seven-year itch and a whole world of barren land, and I'm just barren. What do you think of that?"

"Kevin wasn't my father, Mom."

"Every man is your father," she said bitterly. "What's the difference?"

"I think you're tired."

"What's that you say, Mrs. Robinson? Joltin' Joe has left and gone away. Hey, hey, hey." She had begun to twirl around the room.

"Come on, Janey, stop," I begged, trying to take hold of her. But she only resisted, knocking me out of the way as she continued to sing the song that had once been our inside joke about her and Kevin and now only served as a reminder of what a fool she'd been.

I kept trying to stop her. I was afraid she'd fall. But she wouldn't stop, couldn't stop, until I fell first.

I lost consciousness after I crashed through the glass table. But the blood made my mother snap out of it. My blood, not Blanche's. Not another daughter.

She called the ambulance and held my hand the whole way to the hospital. I left with twenty-three stitches in my back, but I lived, thankful that I'd cushioned my mother's fall, relieved that she didn't have a scratch on her, angry that her scar would always be bigger than mine. Mother-daughter scars—I can't say Kevin never gave us anything. Perhaps the one on her heart and the one on my back, combined, would make some sort of pretty design. But I guess I'd never know. All I knew was that on Halloween morning, 2002, Kevin packed his suitcases to chase a dream while my innocent mother cried over another bloody daughter in the back of a speeding ambulance, fearing that her life had come full circle. And the whole experience had left both of us scarred.

My mother signed the divorce papers when they came. She had no reason to contest it. Her husband was gone. And he wasn't coming back. No one ever came back. Lightning had struck hard, and it had struck more than once. She really had seen Kevin as the start of a brand-new life, to wash away or at least help ease the pain of her past. But if he could slip away, if she could lose happiness a second time, then nothing was meant to last. My mother spent the next year and a half on antidepressants and sleeping pills—always waiting, always watching, always fearing for lightning.

By leaving my mother, Kevin managed to achieve the impossible: he'd reversed time. Time had played its healing hand in soothing wounds, old wounds that didn't need reopening. But in his cruel and sudden departure, he had reached in with his pitchfork and scraped the layers back, exposing her raw center of pain and forcing her to bleed fresh, only this time with three things to mourn instead of two and with very big bolts of lightning to fear.

But even from the deepest trenches of her darkest and bloodiest battle, my mother maintained that Kevin must have had a side. That the man who'd split her down the middle without so much as an apology in his measly six-sentence goodbye must have had a reason for doing it. A reason less selfish than going West to chase the desert. I understood why my mother would have thought so. Normal people, people with consciences, *did* have real reasons for their behavior. And if it had been anyone but Kevin, I would've wondered what his side was, too. His *real* side, barring the bullshit about painting the desert. But it *was* Kevin, so I never wondered much. Until now.

My legs quivered as I dialed, remembering their petrified witch's dance right in the middle of the airport. But this time, there was no glass table to look through, to fall through. Just a shaking heart and a scar that was more than two years old. And only an ocean stood between my quivering legs and the truth.

"Hello?"

"Emily, it's me." I took a long, deep breath. "Tell me his side."

London Calling

The phone call. The transatlantic phone call on that dark December morning we'd remember for the rest of our lives. It woke me at 4:00 a.m. and, immediately, I thought of Katherine. She was on her fourth pregnancy since Eli. The last three had ended in first-trimester miscarriages, but this time, she'd made it into her sixth month—the closest she'd come to carrying her baby to term in nearly five years—and we were all keeping our fingers crossed. Emily obviously didn't care about the name anymore. She just wanted her father and Katherine to have the child they'd been wanting so badly for so long. But now, this phone call. Could it mean that…

"Katherine's fine."

"Oh, thank God," I said, my eyes still adjusting to the light of my nightstand lamp.

"I don't think we are, though."

"What are you talking about?" Emily started to cry. "Emily, what is it? Come on, tell me what happened."

"I don't know where to... We always said we'd be best friends no matter what, right? Always and no matter what—I mean, that's how the saying goes, isn't it?"

"Yes, of course. Emily, what is this about? You've been in Europe for six weeks. What could you have possibly—"

"Well, you know I've been spending most of my time in Dublin—helping Anna with the new boutique and everything..."

"But, you're in London now, aren't you? Wasn't last night the premiere?"

"Yeah, I'm still here...Stella, I—"

"Well, how did it go?"

"Stella, you're not listening to me."

"I'm listening. I'm just not understanding you. What's wrong? Did something happen at the show? Did something happen in Dublin?"

"Dublin," she said quietly.

"Well, tell me, then. Whatever it is, you can tell me. I can't help you if I don't know what's wrong."

"You tell me," she pleaded.

"Tell you what?"

"I don't know! That I'll always be Tinkerbell. That you'll always be that girl I knew who got her first period in gym class... Just promise me, Stella. Promise you'll never forget us."

"Emily, you're not making any sense. If you tell me what happened, then maybe I can—"

"I'm getting married."

"*What?* But...you're not even seeing anyone."

"I am," she said. "I mean, I've been."

"Well, *who,* Em? Why haven't you told me? Why all the secrecy and drama?"

"It's Kevin, Stella."

"Kevin who?"

Kilbride. Kevin Kilbride. Kevin kills brides. It was sometime during the awful articulation of his name that my entire world flipped on its side like a dead fish. My ex-stepfather. The man who'd sent me crashing through glass. The man who'd tried to rape me on my bed. The man who'd given me nightmares for over a year. The man who'd made my mother weak. My ex-stepfather who had been born in Ireland, a fact lost easily in his New England accent and tendency to refer to Boston as "back home." As for his real homeland, he'd rarely discussed it, and not once in his entire marriage to my mother had he ever mentioned returning to his roots. Stupid, stupid me for almost forgetting he was Irish, for never considering that a nearly forgotten fact might one day become so important.

For two years, I preferred to think of Kevin as the devil who'd gotten lost in the desert. Writing him out of our lives that way helped to fictionalize him, making him a permanent joke that could never touch us again. But I should've known better than anyone that nothing lasts forever. I just never would've guessed that the devil had made a life for himself in the place where he'd been born, a life that would lead him to Emily. I never would've guessed he'd use that opportunity to prey upon the one part of *my* life he hadn't scarred yet.

Kevin had been residing in Dublin for a year now, Emily said. He'd moved there to live with his cousin, Liam, an Internet café owner, and his wife, Kyla, a fashion columnist for a popular women's magazine. Liam had provided Kevin with steady work as well as a place for him to showcase and sell his paintings, and one day, one of his pieces caught the eye of a buyer from a local art gallery. Kevin had since quit his day job and was making a living as a professional painter. He no longer lived with Liam and Kyla, either, but often stopped by the café to catch up. That's where he was when he saw Emily's face on some news magazine program that was playing on the office TV set. She was talking about a fashion show that weekend. Responding to his cousin's mesmerized stare, Liam told Kevin that Kyla would be covering the show and could probably get an extra pass if he was interested in getting a better look at the designer. Kevin explained that he'd *known* that designer in another life but couldn't quite explain why he was so intrigued. He did call Kyla, however, and ended up face-to-face with Emily after the show. That's when he told her about the office TV, his conversation with Liam, his inability to express what it was that had brought him there. All he knew was that his past and his present had united in one very familiar face—a beautiful face of a girl, a woman, who'd really done wonderful things for herself in the last couple of years. He was proud of her.

"Well, thank you," Emily said, "and if that's all, I need to be going."

"It's not all," Kevin said, taking hold of her arm. "Look, I know I've been a bastard to the people you love. And I can't erase what I've done to them. But I've really changed since then, honey. I have. And I'd really like the chance to see you while you're here in town." Emily glanced down at her arm and Kevin released his grip. Then she gave him a piece of her mind.

"You *have* seen me," she said. "Twice, actually. Once on TV and once tonight. So, consider yourself blessed. I'll be sure to send your regards to Stella. She'll be just thrilled to hear I ran into you. Oh, and Kevin?" she added, walking away. "*Don't* call me 'honey.'"

That was the first week Emily was in Europe. We'd spoken several times since then, but needless to say, she'd never sent his regards. She said it just wasn't the kind of bombshell she thought she should drop from more than three thousand miles away. Understandable. If only she'd known how explosive that bombshell would grow to become.

Kevin called around and found out where Emily was staying, and soon she began receiving flowers with cards inviting her to dinner so that he could explain how much he'd changed. Emily dismissed his attention at first, but Anna encouraged her to see what Kevin had to say. She said it would be healthy to clear the air and that, if nothing else, he might prove to be a good contact in the art community—he was, after all, related to Kyla Kilbride, a voice that people were really beginning to pay attention to in the world of fashion.

"But it wasn't all about networking," Emily explained. "I mean, Anna has a way of phrasing things, but she didn't mean it like that. She was just trying to give me another reason to see him. She knew he was a painful memory from my past—well, from *your* past, I mean. But you know what Anna's always said about us."

"That we share the same heart."

Emily was quiet for a moment. She was probably thinking the same thing I was—how could we share the same heart when I hated the man she loved? "Anyway," she continued, "Anna knew the attention was starting to wear at me. The flowers, the cards—all those reminders that he was around—were just dredging up things from the past I really didn't want to remember, like your accident and your mom's depression and—"

"I know what Kevin put us through."

"I know you do. I'm sorry. The point is that I began to realize Anna was right. I figured I'd get it over with once and for all and he'd be out of my hair. So, I agreed to meet him for a drink in my hotel lobby, just to see what he had to say."

"And?"

"Truth?"

"No. Lie to me, Emily."

"Well, it's just that I know you're gonna find this hard to believe."

"Probably."

"He's changed, Stella. He really has. I found myself having a wonderful time, which, of course, I felt completely guilty about. But it was the strangest thing—I had to keep *reminding* myself of why I was supposed to hate him because he just didn't seem like the kind of man we would hate at all."

"But he is."

"*Was,* Stella. He *was.* And you know, it's not like he was trying to cover anything up. He was so honest and apologetic about everything. He sincerely feels horrible about what he did to your mom."

"And you actually believe that?"

"Yes, Stella, I do. And if you had been there, you would've, too."

"I honestly doubt it."

"But how do you know?"

"Believe me, Emily, I just know."

"He told me why he left. He said he—"

"It doesn't matter. Let's just keep this about you."

"But don't you even want to know his side?"

"All I want to know is how the past six weeks went on behind my back."

"Stella, I didn't mean for it to—"

"But it did," I said. "So keep going. What happened after the drinks?"

"He said he wanted to see me again."

"And?"

"And I told him I'd had a really nice time, but I couldn't. And then I went back to Anna's room and cried in her bed for three hours."

"Why didn't you call me, Emily? We could've talked about it. You could've tried to make me understand."

"Because *I* didn't understand. I couldn't piece it all together to have it make sense to another person."

"But you were able to talk to Anna. And since when do you and I have to make sense around each other?"

"We don't, Stella. It's just that Anna was impartial. I was afraid that if I told you, you'd flip out on me. And I just couldn't handle a blowout with you from this far away. I knew how you felt about him. And I was scared of the way I felt about him—after just one night. I couldn't put it into words, exactly. All I knew was that he'd gotten to me—this man who'd known me since I was eighteen, dating Jason Neeley and getting ready to graduate from high school. And now, all of a sudden, here we are in Dublin ten years later and I'm living my dream. In a way, he *had* seen me grow up and change, and there was just something comforting in that."

"Not perverted?"

"He wasn't *my* stepfather. And besides, we're not eighteen anymore. I admit, it would've seemed perverted then. But things are different now. I'm twenty-eight, and Kevin's forty-one. These kinds of relationships happen all the time."

"Kind of like your father and Katherine?"

"Okay, I know I gave them a hard time in the past, but I've come to accept that age doesn't matter. Only love does."

"But, why, Emily? So, Kevin saw you mature. Big deal. Is that it?"

"No, that's far from it. It wasn't just the fact that he knew me when I was a kid. It was something in the way he sees me now because of that. I don't know…it's comforting, it's inspiring. I almost feel like it was destiny that we *should* meet again."

"Oh, Emily, please."

"I know it sounds ridiculous. But if you had been in my shoes, Stella…" She sighed. "I can't tell you how good it felt to be sitting across from someone who just made everything inside of me click and fly…. If it weren't Kevin, I would've thought I'd met the perfect guy."

"But it *was* Kevin."

"And that's why I cried—because it was all so complicated. You know how with every great guy you meet, there has to be a catch? With Rob, it was the cheating thing, with—"

"Yeah, yeah, I get it."

"Well, with Kevin, it was the fact that he was married to your mom. The catch was his past."

"That's a big catch, Emily."

"I know. And that's why I figured I would just immerse myself in my work and forget about him. I mean, it was one night, a few drinks. I figured I could eventually put it behind me. I wasn't willing to risk our friendship for a gut feeling that just wouldn't go away."

"So, what changed?"

Emily started to cry again. "I'm sorry, Stella! I really *am* sorry! I kept thinking I'd figure things out—that I'd sort it all through—and confess everything when I came home, once it was all over. I mean, even when the feeling was nagging at me, even when I was crying to Anna, I never thought…"

"You never thought what?"

"That I'd fall in love with him, Stella! You and your mom have been everything to me since I was thirteen. Do you honestly think I would ever plan to fall in love with the person who hurt you?"

"No, of course you wouldn't plan it. But the fact is that you *did* fall in love. You can't just sit there and act like you stumbled into the whole thing blindfolded."

"I don't mean to come across like that. If anything, I was determined to keep my eyes wide open so I *wouldn't* get swept away. I'd made a conscious decision to do what I thought was right, and I was really trying to stay focused on that. But he kept showing up—at parties, shows, my hotel. And every time, it got harder and harder to say I wouldn't go out with him."

"So, he was stalking you?"

"He wasn't stalking me, Stella. He was in love."

"After *one* night of drinks in your hotel lobby?"

"Sometimes one night is all it takes. But it was more than that. Every time he'd show up somewhere, my 'no' would last as long as some dates do. We'd spend an hour just talking, but he'd always end up leaving with a decline. I knew I'd never pursue him, but I got used to seeing him around. And as horrible a person as I feared it made me, I liked it."

"Well, it's natural to feel flattered when you're being pursued."

"Are you hearing me, Stella? I liked it because I was falling for him."

"Even if it made you a horrible person?"

"Do you think I'm a horrible person?"

"I think you've made a horrible mistake. But, go on. I'm assuming you eventually said yes to a date?"

"In Paris."

"He followed you to Paris?"

"He was persistent. Anna and I were doing a show there, and he booked a room in our hotel. That's when I threw in the towel and said I'd have dinner with him. It was after that dinner that I knew. I mean, all the signs had been pointing in that direction, but I'd been resisting, fighting them because of my loyalty to you and your mom. But after that dinner, I just knew I was beyond fighting because it really wasn't something I could control. I just knew."

"You knew *what?*"

"That I'd met him—the one." That was it. I'd had enough.

"Emily, you do realize we're talking about Kevin Kilbride, here, right? The man who sent me crashing through a glass table just a couple of years ago?"

"He's *changed,* Stella. And besides, it wasn't Kevin that pushed you."

There was a heavy spell of silence as I tried not to snap. "So, you slept with him in Paris, then?" I asked finally.

"It wasn't about sex." I couldn't help but snicker. "It wasn't, Stella. You might not think much of Kevin, but you should think more of me. Do you really think I'd risk what is most important to me in the world for sex?"

"So, you didn't sleep with him that night?"

"No, actually I didn't. But you'll forgive me if I don't see how that's relevant."

"And you'll forgive *me* if I'm having a bit of trouble understanding how my 'best friend,' whom my mother practically *adopted,* by the way—"

"Is that what I've been to you all this time, Stella? Some kind of white trash charity project?"

"Of *course* not! Where are you even getting that from?"

"I don't know. I'm just upset."

"And you think I'm not? My mom's gonna be absolutely *destroyed*. She's finally off all the medication, and now…" My head was spinning. "Can you even see past the drama and butterflies of this *Romeo and Juliet* affair to comprehend its effect on the people you claim to love? This is about more than Tinkerbell and first periods and some stuff my sister used to say a long time ago. 'Always and no matter what'—Emily, we're talking about the rest of your life! Of both of our lives—*and* my mother's! Am I getting through to you at all?"

"Yes!" she cried. "But can't *you* understand how serious this is to me if I'm sitting here completely terrified that the rest of my life might not *include* you and your mom?"

"So, you'd choose a man over me? Is that what you're saying?"

"I'm saying *please* don't make me choose. I've loved you since the day we met, Stella. If you were to cut me from your life tomorrow, there'd be a hole inside of me forever. No man could ever fill that."

"And if I asked you to cut him out of your life instead?"

"I'd always resent you. I'd know why you did it, but our friendship would never be the same."

"It's not going to be the same now, not if you marry him."

"It *will,* Stella. In time, I know it can. It sounds crazy now, and selfish, too, and I'm sorry. But I can't lose either of you. I just can't. Kevin isn't making me choose. *Please* don't be the one to—"

"Wait a second, Emily. Kevin isn't making you choose because he has nothing to fear. What the hell does he care if I come back into his life? Don't turn me into the bad guy by comparing us. *I'm* not the one who walked out on a marriage. *I'm* not the one who…" I stopped myself just short of going too far, and my heart pounded from the closeness of the call. I couldn't believe I'd almost said it. I'd almost told her about the night Kevin attacked me.

"What?" Emily asked. "You're not the one who what?"

I couldn't say it. It had been more than eight years and the secret was buried in a dark place I never wanted to visit, not even now when it might have the power to save a friendship.

"Nothing," I said. "Just go on. When did he propose?"

"Thursday night. He wanted to do it before I left for the Emmie premiere here in London. He really wanted to go with me, but had to stay in town to attend some big gallery opening with his art dealer."

"He actually has an art dealer?"

"Yeah, she's great."

"She?"

"Orla."

"And how old is this Orla?"

"Thirty-six. Why?"

"Is she attractive?"

"She's pretty, but if you're implying that Kevin skipped out on the Emmie premiere so that he could—"

"I'm not implying anything. But if you're suspicious of Kevin this early on in your relationship, then maybe you shouldn't have agreed to marry him."

"I'm not suspicious of him, Stella. You put those words in my mouth. Kevin hated that he couldn't come to London with me, so he took me out for a really nice dinner on Thursday night, and that's when he proposed."

"In the middle of the restaurant?" I asked. "Just like Rob?" It was a nasty question, intended to illustrate that this second engagement could end just as disastrously as her first, but Emily missed the point.

"No," she answered simply. "He waited until we got outside."

"And obviously your answer was yes."

Emily sighed. "Stella, at first I was so incredibly happy, and then it was like this gigantic weight came crashing down on me because I thought of you. And ever since then, it's been eating away at me. It's like this tremendous elation followed by this horrible fear and guilt, over and over again, like an endless cycle."

"But shouldn't that tell you something? That maybe you're not one hundred percent confident in your decision?"

"But I *am* confident. It's you and me that I'm worried about. As for getting married, I couldn't be any more sure."

"But, Emily, you hardly know him."

"I've known him as long as you have. And even if I'd only just met him, the heart knows what it knows."

"A few minutes ago, you said we shared the same heart."

"And I still believe that. You're everything to me."

"Then don't marry Kevin."

Emily started to panic. "Oh, God, Stella, no, please don't tell me that! I can't let go now, Stella! *Please* don't make me choose!"

"Would it be simpler if I chose for you? If I just...stayed away?"

She was crying again and didn't seem to understand my question. "What do you mean? For how long?"

"Forever."

"No!" she wailed into the phone—desperately, hysterically, like I'd never heard her cry before, and I felt my body break into a million pieces. It was a stupid thing to say—to scare her with threats of forever. "Stella, no, please, no! My mother *died* when I was three. Your mom really *is* the only mother I've ever known. And she *did* take me in, and you both changed my life. And look what I've…but I *love* him, Stella, more than I'm able to explain. If I didn't, would I be… Oh, God, Stella, please don't leave me! I never pictured you not being there at my wedding. I never thought I'd have to cut my heart in half this way! Just—"

"You don't," I said. "I mean, you changed my life, too." I felt the tears welling up in my own eyes, but was afraid that if I started crying, I might never stop. "When's the wedding?" I asked instead.

"Friday, six days from today."

"*What?* What's the hurry? Why so soon?"

"Kyla put in for a transfer at her magazine, and she got it. She and Liam are moving to New York next Saturday. They even sold the café."

"Well, what does that have to do with you?"

"Kevin wants Liam to be there when we get married, so we need to do it right away. It's going to be a really small affair as it is. Technically, I know we could wait. I mean, Liam and Kyla could always fly back for it, but this way, the wedding kind of doubles as a send-off party for them. And it gives us all the more reason to do it sooner rather than later."

"Yeah, but what's wrong with later? I mean, a wedding should be a *wedding,* not part of someone else's 'good luck in America' party. And what's wrong with America, anyway? Why do you and Kevin have to get married there?"

"Why do you think?"

"You're not gonna tell your father, are you?"

"I can't, Stella. Not with Katherine pregnant again—and so close this time. I wouldn't want to deliver any news that might upset her."

"Then why not wait until you can be honest with *everybody?* Don't you want that for yourself—on your wedding day?"

"In a perfect world, of course. But you can't choose who you fall in love with. And besides, we may as well have our wedding in Dublin since that's where we'll be living, anyway."

"Wait...you mean, you'd be giving up your entire life for him?"

"I'd be *starting* my life. Dublin is where Kevin's career is. I don't expect him to leave, not now when things are just starting to really take off for him. And it's not like I'd have nothing to do. There's the boutique. And my line is international now. As for Katherine and my dad, I'll just say I've got some more business to take care of over here, and I'll tell them about Kevin and me after the baby is born—well, you know, God willing and everything.... Look, we're not going to have much support from anybody back home. I was just really hoping for yours."

"Emily...I'd miss you."

"We'd visit each other. And it wouldn't be forever."

"It feels like it. This whole thing—it just feels like the end of something."

"Don't say that. You're just shocked. And upset. I understand. But don't say it's the end. You and I—we'll never end. We can't...we're bella donnas." She was quiet for a second. "Remember?"

I thought back to that night in my sister's room when we were fifteen.

There she is, Emily confessed to thinking long before we ever spoke. *My bella donna. My beautiful woman.*

I could still hear our voices—so young, so innocent, so remarkably unaware that our lives were about to change forever.

And for what it's worth, moon sister, you can be my bella donna, too.

"Stella?" she asked. "You remember that, don't you?"

"Of course, I remember."

"See? I share more memories with you than with anyone else on this planet. And because of our history, that's never gonna change. We understand each other, Stella. No one understands us the way we understand each other. No one *loves* us like we love each other. Nothing is strong enough to kill that. Not even this."

"But you're not leaving Europe for a month. Why not just wait a little—"

"Because I *can't* wait, Stella. Because waiting is the death of dreams. There might not always *be* tomorrow. People don't always live to be thirty. All we have is right now. So, why not seize the moment when I know it's right?"

"Okay, okay. All I was saying was that you *do* have time, you know? You're young."

"My mother was young."

"All right, Emily. I get it." My best friend was having her midlife crisis at twenty-eight. "When are you flying back to Dublin?"

"We're leaving here in less than an hour. Why?"

"Why do you think?"

Happiness entered Emily's voice for the first time that morning. "Oh, Stella, I love you! You never have let me down." She paused. "Promise me something, though? Don't say anything to anybody, not even Alison. Just say you're coming to visit me or something. You're off for winter break anyway, right? So, it's feasible that you decided to come see me on a whim."

"Because everyone knows how impulsive I am."

"Then say I called and invited you—like a spur-of-the-moment thing. Okay?"

"Don't worry about it. I won't let anyone know why I'm coming. Alison will be easy. She and Anthony left for the mountains last night. They'll be skiing all weekend, so I can just leave her a note. As for my mother, I'll have to blatantly lie."

"I'm *sorry,* Stella."

"I know you are. Let me go, though, okay? I need to start packing."

"Okay," she said. "I love you."

"Me, too. Now, fly away, Tinkerbell. I'll call you later from the airport."

I could actually see the relief on her face as I hung up the phone—in the dim light of my room and from more than three thousand miles across the ocean. But I could see it—the guilt washed away, the burden lifted. And now, the greatest burden was on me.

I walked over to my light switch and the room was suddenly bright. Within seconds, my shirt was on the floor and I was looking at myself, topless, in the mirror, wanting to turn around, but afraid. Kevin, the devil on my shoulder, the scar on my back—I couldn't believe I had to face him again. I turned and confronted the marking slowly. It wasn't so ugly, and it didn't hurt anymore. But I did.

Sympathy for the Devil

I was ready. Sitting at the airport, replaying everything in my mind, had given me no choice. I needed to know why Kevin left my mother.

"Emily, it's me…tell me his side."

"Are you sure?" she asked. "You didn't want to know about it this morning."

"I was still in shock this morning. But I've been sitting in this airport for hours, thinking about…everything. So, tell me his side."

According to Emily, my now penitent ex-stepfather walked out on my mom because one day he found himself locked into a life he wasn't built for. Although he thought he'd reached a settling point by the time he met her, it had really only been a crossroads. It hit him one day during their fourth year of marriage that there were two paths he could have taken back in 1995. But his love for my mom had blinded him to the choice. He hadn't *seen* a choice because he *had* loved her—truly and with all of his heart.

But that love had become his imprisonment, closing him off from the world of opportunity that existed outside of being a Pennsylvania contractor. Though he had always liked his job, he'd once considered it temporary, something that worked well for him in the meantime while his options waited safely within reach for future fulfillment. He didn't know exactly when that future would be, but just knowing it was there was enough. Until he realized that those options were slipping farther and farther away, that marriage had put a wall between him and his dreams, making him a slave to an ordinary life he never would've chosen had he predicted the trap. But it was a trap. Marriage was a trap, and as soon as Kevin realized this, he began to drown. He'd been standing at a divide back in 1995 and had chosen the shiny and unfamiliar path because he'd been a drifter for so many years and it finally seemed like time. But, for what? Because now time only seemed to stand still. And his wife and his life and his job had nothing to do with the person he was in his twenties or the person he knew he was meant to be. He was a painter, an artist, a free spirit. But he had no one to blame for his entrapment but himself. He'd chosen the wrong path.

"But why couldn't he have asked my mom to travel the 'right path' with him? I mean, if he loved her so truly and everything? It could've been an adventure for both of them."

"Because that wasn't the kind of life he wanted," Emily said. "Kevin didn't want to be tied to anyone or anything. He'd realized he'd made a horrible mistake. He just didn't know how to undo it. He wrestled with his feelings for three years before he finally found the courage to leave."

"Emily, you make it sound like he was a battered wife."

"Stella, come on, try to have a little understanding."

"Understanding? Are you *kidding?* I'm sorry, but I just can't seem to find sympathy for the devil."

"*Sympathy for the devil?* Who are you, Mick Jagger?"

"No, but if the phrase fits..."

"The devil? Come on, sweetie. Don't you think you're being a little harsh? I mean, I can understand your hostility to a certain extent, but be logical—marriages break up all the time. I agree that the way he ended things with your mom was shitty. But, the *devil?* Come on, Stella."

Her lecture embarrassed me. I'd never told anyone how I really felt about Kevin. For years, I'd even tried to make myself believe he was just a man who'd made a mistake. A mistake I could almost wish away. But I couldn't wish away fear. And after all these years and miles, I was still scared to death of the son of a bitch. The devil. Lucifer. It made me feel like I hadn't grown up at all.

"Okay, he's not the devil," I told Emily. "I had it all backward. He's an angel. God probably gave him his wings when he left my mother."

"Look, do you want me to finish this story or not?"

"Continue."

Kevin thought the clean break would be better for both of them. But in retrospect, he wishes he'd handled things differently. My mother deserved more than a note—he knows that—but he was afraid that if he'd said goodbye in person, she might've tried to talk him into staying, and because of how much he cared for her, he was afraid he just may have stayed. And that would've been awful because he really was dying inside on the East Coast. He did end up going West, after all, and he did paint the desert. But after a year of indulging in travel, art, wine—and anything else that could help compensate for the seven years he'd lost—Kevin realized that he was no better off.

Leaving my mother had been the right thing to do. He didn't miss that life. But he was running out of money in his new life and had begun to grow lonely. He was starting to crave a place that he could call home. That was around the time that a phone call from his cousin Liam in Ireland changed the course of his life. Liam had received a rambling letter from Kevin and was concerned about his middle-aged cousin's relapse into the drifter lifestyle of his twenties. He thought it might be good for him to return to his roots, a place where he could not only settle but also find new inspiration for his art. He offered him a job, a place to live, and a forum for showcasing and selling his paintings. Kevin booked his flight to Dublin that very same day.

For the past year, especially since he began painting professionally, Kevin has been living the life he knows he was meant to live. The sense of peace has given him a chance to reflect on all the roads traveled along the way, all of the bumpy spots, all the mistakes. His regrets, his wrongdoings, the things he wishes he could go back and change because they hurt people.

"So, what was my mother?" I asked. "A road traveled, a crowded intersection, a dead end? I just want to make sure I've got it all straight."

"She was a road traveled, Stella."

"Oh, okay, that makes sense, considering you can still see the tire tracks."

"He *knows* that. He knows how much he hurt her. And he wishes he could go back and change it. He's a different person now. He really is. He feels horrible about what he did, but if he hadn't done it—if he'd gone on living with your mom in Scottsboro—he would've suffered some kind of nervous breakdown in the end." There was a sudden pang of silence between us, and I knew that she was thinking of my father.

"It's okay," I said.

"I didn't mean that."

"You did. But it's okay."

"No, I mean...I didn't mean that your mom makes people crazy, because she doesn't. It was just a coincidence about Kevin and...well, it was just a bad choice of words."

"My mom got a letter from him yesterday."

"From Kevin?"

"From my dad."

"Your *dad?* You mean...he's still alive?"

"That's what I said."

"It's been...what? More than ten years since you've even heard anything from him? I was there, wasn't I—when your grandmom called?"

"Kurt Cobain had just died," I said. "We were seventeen."

"Whoa... What happens to time?"

I don't think she expected an answer. I couldn't have given

her one, anyway. I was too busy remembering the little girl with the shoes who was sitting across from me that morning while my mother read the letter. The girl with the father. I was crying.

Life Goes On

A lot had happened since Kevin's cruel disappearing act of 2002. As Flight 287 lifted me away from all the memories that had kept me company in Philadelphia, I thought of how much my life had changed since that Halloween morning when I fell through the glass.

First, there was Izzie. He was extremely attentive after my accident and even skipped out on a couple of his Guys' Days. I thought it was a turning point in our relationship, that however unfortunate, my fall had brought us closer together, making us like Alison and Anthony—one of those couples that just couldn't be kept apart. But after a while, we settled back into our old routine—Izzie gone on Saturdays, me waiting patiently to be consumed under the pathetic shadow of loneliness. Though I do admit to missing him, it wasn't so much the fact that he spent his Saturdays with Marcus and Adam that bothered me at this point. I'd gotten used to that. What I did worry about was the fact that the only time my boyfriend seemed passionate about me was *after* those days were over. That was what made them so lonely—knowing that what I looked most forward to in my week, my main event, was merely his finale before bedtime. I didn't think Izzie was using me for sex, though. How could he be? We hardly even *had* sex anymore. By the time our one-year anniversary rolled around, it was pretty much just those Saturday nights. We still had the friendship, but even that seemed a little distant. Or did it only seem distant because I was ready for more? Because I was always comparing us to Alison and Anthony? I didn't know. Analyzing things only made them worse. And I couldn't talk to Izzie about it. The one time I tried, I hated the sound of my own voice. I felt like one of those women who have everything, but can't ever be happy unless they're *unhappy,* so they must find something to nit-pick. Besides, Izzie seemed to think we were fine. But fine wasn't perfect. Then again, what was? Here I had an adorable, talented, almost-live-in boyfriend who hadn't broken my heart yet. What more did I want? The world?

But then came the muggy summer night when Izzie said he had too much work to do and wouldn't be able to see me.

"Well, I'll just come over and kiss you good-night before I go to sleep, then," I said.

"Don't," he told me. "I mean, seeing you would be too much of a distraction and I can't afford it. I love you, though. I'll call you tomorrow." It was the first night we went without seeing each other in more than a year.

A week later, the same thing happened again. When I asked him why he wasn't finishing his work during daytime hours like he used to, he said it was hard to explain to me because I wasn't an artist.

The third time it happened, I went down the hall and knocked on his door, terrified of what I might discover, only to find Izzie, Marcus and Adam listening to music and acting the same way they had the one time I intruded upon Guys' Day—nervous, paranoid, and like they couldn't wait to get rid of me. Izzie said that Adam and Marcus were going to the bar soon and that he was just taking a little break from his work while they were still there. That was the night I made the ungodly mistake of asking Adam what he was doing up from Center City on a Wednesday. Izzie completely reprimanded me for it over the phone the next day, saying I should never interrogate his friends like that.

"It's embarrassing, Stella. And it makes people anxious."

I apologized and told him I'd meant nothing by it, but at this point, I knew that everything wasn't fine. Sometimes, I worried that he was cheating on me. But why would he pick on me like that if he were cheating? Wouldn't he be extra nice because of the guilt? But if he wasn't cheating, what *was* his excuse? Why was he pulling away from me? Why was he acting so different? Why would he be completely excited to hear from me one afternoon, talking a mile a minute about his day, and the next afternoon not answer the phone at all? I told myself he was just busy with his cartoon column—because that's what he told me. And I never did catch him with another woman. How could he be cheating if there was no other woman? I found out in August that there *was* another way to cheat, that Izzie had been cheating since we started. Only now the affair had gotten too big to hide. Izzie's mistress was cocaine.

Alison was the one who told me, after Anthony told her, after Marcus told him. It all happened at a party we threw for Emily. Two weeks earlier, Anna had decided to drop the "Anna by Emily" label in exchange for "Emmie," which meant more recognition—and more money—for our friend, and was definitely something worth celebrating. We hadn't had one of those crazy, drunken bashes in an exceptionally long time, considering that Alison's and my idea of bliss had changed considerably since we'd settled down with our McIntyre Suites boys. But it was fun recapturing old times, and it warmed my heart to see Emily so happy in light of what was going on with Katherine, who'd suffered her third miscarriage since Eli just three days after the good news about Emmie came along. But at least she had Damien by her side for this one. Yes, for the first time in a long time, my best friend was actually dating somebody who seemed worthy of her. Damien Esposito was thirty (a mere four years senior to our twenty-six but more than twice the man Rob Sellers had been), lived in Fort Lee, New Jersey, and worked as a computer programmer for a major software corporation in Manhattan. He met Emily when he accidentally cut in front of her in the deli line on his lunch break. It was her lunch break, too, but she didn't mind—she liked the view from behind. And he liked the way her face lit up like a tomato when he turned around to apologize and caught her staring at his butt. They ended up getting a table together and exchanging numbers. That was around Christmastime. They'd been together ever since.

Even Warren liked Damien, and he was always critical of the men Emily showed interest in. But then again, how could he not be after seeing the whole Rob thing blow up in her face for a second time? Besides, Warren was like Emily's New York dad. If he endorsed the guy, I knew he had to be quality. And Damien definitely was. My only wish was that I knew him better. I'd only hung out with him three times in the eight months he'd been dating Emily. But that was because he did so much traveling on the weekends and was rarely around on the Sundays that Izzie and I came up to visit. Emily said Damien really liked me, though, and that I should never take it personally when he wasn't around, like the night of Alison's and my party, for instance—the one we threw in honor of Emmie. I didn't take it personally. Damien was an actual businessman—a mature and welcome change from the likes of Emily's past. And besides, all that really mattered was that she and Warren were there. That's what made the party feel so much like old times.

I was the warm-fuzzy-tingly kind of almost-drunk, sitting on the couch with Warren and Emily, gushing something to the effect of how much I loved them, when from across the room, I saw Alison and Anthony having some sort of huddle. It looked serious, but I figured it was none of my business. Adam had come to the party, and he, Marcus and Izzie were on their way to the door. Izzie called out to me that they'd be right back. They were going down the hall to grab a CD he wanted to play.

"It takes three people to carry one CD?" Emily asked once they were gone.

"Well, Adam probably just felt weird staying here without them," I said. "And Marcus and Izzie, I don't know…maybe it's a cousin thing. Where one goes, the other follows."

"Hey, Nelly Whiteman used to say that about us in high school and we're not cousins. *We're* S&M."

"I remember that!"

"Uh, I don't," Warren said. "But I'd like to."

Emily shoved him away. "Did you hear that she had a baby?"

"Nelly Whiteman had a baby?" I asked.

"I ran into Fred Corrie at the train station yesterday, and he said she had a baby girl last year."

"Oh, my God! That's so great! Is she married?"

"Okay, remember that twenty-seven-year-old lawyer she started dating after we graduated?"

"The one we thought was *so* old?"

"They've been married for four years."

"Wow," I said, a sudden wave of sadness washing over me. "And I can't even tell you why my boyfriend needs six hands to carry one CD."

By this time, Alison had drifted over to the couch. She asked if she could speak with me privately, and we went into her bedroom.

"Honey, Izzie didn't go back to his apartment to get a CD. He and Marcus and Adam…they do coke. Adam comes up on Saturdays to deal to them, and they just spend the whole day getting high. That's what Guys' Day is, Stella. That's what it's always been." I remained quiet as she explained, my eyes full of tears about to fall. I wasn't as shocked as I should have been. It all made sense now. Everything. Their nervous energy the times I intruded, Izzie's mood swings, the distance. "Izzie's gotten more into it lately," she said. "It used to just be a weekend thing, and now he does it almost every day. He says it helps him work." Skipping nights together, not answering his phone in the afternoon, talking a mile a minute when he *would* get on the phone with me. The distance—I'd never really known him at all.

I started to cry pretty wildly—raw, runny tears of distress—and Alison cradled me against her shoulder. "I had to tell you, sweetie. Anthony wanted to have a talk with Izzie first. He said he wanted to give him a chance to get his act together, and that if he didn't, then I could tell you. But how could I know something like that about the person you love and not tell you?"

"How long has Anthony known about it?"

"Marcus just told him tonight. He actually invited him back with the three of them to get high."

"What? What did Anthony say?"

"He was shocked. You know Anthony doesn't really know Adam that well, so even before me, he never did that whole Guys' Day thing. But for the past three years, he's considered Marcus his best friend. He can't believe he never knew what he was doing. He said Marcus talked about cocaine tonight like it was nothing. He got defensive, though, when Anthony acted weird about it. He said it was no big deal and that he only does it on Saturdays and 'special occasions.' And then Anthony asked about Izzie, and...I'm so sorry, Stella. Anthony thinks the only reason Marcus invited him along tonight was because they've drifted apart since we started seeing each other. He thinks he was just reaching for something to bond them again."

"So...he tried to get Anthony hooked on drugs? Alison, that doesn't make any sense! Why is this happening?"

"I don't know, honey. I don't know. Anthony feels awful. He says if he'd paid more attention to his friends, then maybe he would've—"

"It's not Anthony's fault," I cried. "It's mine! I'm so stupid!"

Alison held me tighter as I continued to sob. After a few minutes, I asked her to go get Emily, who burst into tears as soon as she came into the room and saw what a hysterical mess I was. It was then Alison's job to comfort both of us, which she was still doing when Anthony and Warren knocked at the door, wanting to know if everything was okay. I could tell by Warren's face that Anthony hadn't filled him in on what was happening, so I decided to do it myself.

"My boyfriend is a coke addict," I said. And for the first time since the discovery, I felt angry. There, ringing back at me, straight from my very own words, was the undeniable truth of how badly I'd been deceived. My boyfriend was a coke addict and I'd never had any idea. But instead of feeling hurt by his betrayal, I suddenly had the desire to hurt him. "I'm going over there."

"I'm going with you," Warren said, and I could see by the look in his eyes that there'd be no changing his mind.

"I'll go, too," Anthony said. "I'll wait outside if you want me to, Stella. I just want to be around in case things get out of hand."

The three of us walked down the hall and stood knocking at the door, but nobody answered. I knew they were all in there—cleaning up the lie—and it wasn't long before I'd had enough. I tried the knob and found the door unlocked. Izzie jumped up from his desk to greet me, sniffing hard as he wiped rigorously at his nostrils with the back of his hand, his nose bouncing from side to side like rubber. His grin was goofy and transparent, and I hoped his damn nose would start bleeding right in front of me just so that obnoxious grin would falter, just so he'd know I wasn't buying it. Marcus and Adam disappeared into the kitchen almost immediately, and Anthony and Warren followed them. When Izzie and I were face-to-face, he hugged me, kissing my cheek with an intensity that would have seemed like passion if I hadn't known he was on drugs.

"I've missed you," he said.

"Then why didn't you come back to the party?" I asked, pulling away from him.

"I told you—we were getting that CD to bring back."

"And how long does *that* take?"

"Oh, baby," he said, hugging me again. "Did you miss me?"

This time, I pushed him away—hard. "What's the matter with you?"

"You have to ask?"

"Am I supposed to be able to read your mind? I know you pretty well, baby girl, but I don't think I know you *that* well."

"And I don't know you at all."

"Come on. What are you talking about?"

"What do you, Adam and Marcus do on Saturdays?"

"I told you. We watch movies, play video games...you know it's the one day a week I get to be with my friends." He took my hands. "Does that bother you? Because if it does, you just say, 'Izzie, I need you to spend more time with me,' and Izzie will spend more time with you."

"And if I say, 'Izzie, I need you to stop doing cocaine'?" Izzie let go of my hands and looked down. "You can't deny it, can you?"

"Shh," he said, still looking down.

"What?" I asked, raising my voice.

"Shh, Stella, come on," he pleaded, lifting his eyes to meet mine.

"Does that mean 'be quiet'?" I yelled. "Are you telling *me* to be quiet? Well, fuck you! How *dare* you lie to me for a year and three months about who the hell you are and then tell *me* to be quiet?"

"I didn't lie to you," he said softly.

"You didn't *lie* to me? Izzie, what fucking world are you living in?"

Izzie took my wrist and started leading me toward the bedroom. "Just come here, Stella, please. Can't we just talk in private?"

"Let go of me! I don't want anything to do with you anymore!" But he didn't let go. "Get off of me, Izzie! I swear to God, I said let go!"

Just then, Warren rushed out from the kitchen. "She said to let go of her, Izzie."

"If you don't mind, I'm trying to have a conversation with my girlfriend," Izzie told him, never taking his eyes off of me.

"I'm not your girlfriend, Izzie," I said, freeing my wrist. The look in his eyes made me cry. I had hurt him, just like I'd wanted. But it didn't feel good. "I don't want to see you anymore," I said. "You made a fool out of me for way too long." Warren came over and stood beside me. He put his hand on my shoulder.

"You're moving in kind of fast there, buddy," Izzie snapped.

"It's not like that!" I cried. "You don't even know what the hell you're talking about! Warren is the only guy who's ever bothered to stay in my life and be there for me, no matter what! You know, I was actually dumb enough to think you'd joined that exotic group of one. Shows how little I knew about things."

"So, you're just gonna leave me, then?" Izzie asked, raising his voice at me for the first time that night, and the first time ever. "I make one mistake in a year and three months, and you're gone? That's pretty fucking compassionate of you, Stella!"

"Hey," Warren cautioned. "You wanna calm down?"

"Sorry, boss."

"Izzie," I said, softening a little as I realized for the first time that he truly had no concept of how much he'd hurt me. "It wasn't one mistake in a year and three months. It was a constant *series* of mistakes—of *lies*—over and over again, the entire time we were going out...I don't even know who you are."

"Someone who loves you."

"That might be true," I said, looking down. When I looked up again, there were tears in his eyes. I turned to Warren. "Would you mind if—"

"I'll be in the kitchen if you need me," he said.

As soon as Warren was gone, Izzie started to cry. "Please don't do this, Stella. I can't lose you. *Please.*" He moved to hug me, and this time, instead of pushing him away, I hugged him back. "You're the only thing in my life that's real."

"That's sad, Izzie," I said, rubbing his back. "That's really sad." He looked at me questioningly. "*We* weren't real, Izzie. Do you even realize how much you hid from me? A relationship surrounded by that much deceit isn't *real*. Izzie, I care about you, and there's going to be a huge void in my life now, but I can't be with you. And if you see that as me being a heartless bitch because you think you only made one mistake...well, Izzie, that's like cheating on me with another woman for over a year and calling it *one* mistake. I'm...I'm sorry, Izzie." I started to cry again. "I don't want you to think I don't love you anymore because I do. But I have to leave you. And I know that because, one, people who say they're going to change rarely do. And two, because not *once* during this entire conversation did you even *offer* to give up drugs."

"Drugs aren't a problem for me."

"Well, obviously they are," I said, breaking away from him. "Because they just cost you the only thing in your life you thought was real."

"Wait," he said, pulling me close again. "I'm sorry."

"I'm sorry, too. I'm sorry it has to end this way. I thought you were gonna be the one, Izzie. I really did. You were supposed to be the one."

"I was never good enough for you," he said. And that killed me. "I think I've always known that. But I loved you more than I've ever loved anyone. You can call me a liar all you want, Stella. But you can never say it wasn't love. No matter what you think of me after tonight, don't ever wonder if I loved you. Okay?"

"Okay," I whispered. And then we hugged for a while in silence until Warren came out of the kitchen and asked if I was ready to go. I told him I needed another minute.

"You deserve to be happy," Izzie said once we were alone again. He nodded toward the kitchen. "If I couldn't do it for you, maybe the boss can?"

We both smiled sadly. "Don't make fun of Warren," I said. "He's just protective. And besides, it never would've worked with us. I was never in love with him. And he's long since gotten over me."

"Yeah, well, maybe he could help me out with that. It's gonna be hard—getting over you."

"Likewise." We were quiet for a few seconds. "Listen, Izzie, I'm not gonna be able to do the whole 'just friends' thing with you. It would just be way too hard, and I don't want to get sucked back in unless you've really changed."

"I kind of figured this was it."

"All right," I said, hugging him one last time. "If you ever decide that drugs *are* a problem for you, and you think you want help, call me. Just because we won't be hanging out doesn't mean I wouldn't be there if you needed me."

"Thank you, Stella. And don't forget me, okay? I mean, don't try so hard to forget me that you can't remember what was good about us."

"I'll never forget you," I said. "You were supposed to be the one. Remember?"

And so we broke up. Marcus and Anthony didn't speak much after that. As far as Anthony was concerned, Marcus had lied to him and, in the process, had helped contribute to the destruction of something extremely precious to me. As far as Marcus was concerned, Anthony had betrayed his trust by telling other people about Izzie, and it didn't help that he'd acted like Mr. High and Mighty, either. Besides, they hadn't been close in a long time anyway. Things had ended pretty disastrously for the five of us. Alison and Anthony remained unscathed, and of course, Marcus and Izzie still lived together, but as for that group of five that had been such good friends for two years, it was over. Our close-knit pseudo-family had died. And we'd never be together in McIntyre Suites again.

Izzie and I saw each other every once in a while, but it was always by accident—running into each other outside of our building or in the hallway. And we never talked for very long. It wasn't that it was awkward. It just hurt too much to stand there and look at each other knowing what had happened not only to us, but to everybody. And then December came.

I'll always remember the night he knocked on my door to say goodbye. He'd gotten a job at a Seattle newspaper and was moving to Washington. Marcus was going, too. They were leaving the following day—my twenty-seventh birthday.

Of course, I invited him in. Alison was upstairs with Anthony, but it didn't matter about being alone. I was sad to hear he was leaving, even after all those months apart, and I wanted to spend some time with him, no matter how much it hurt. But to my sweet surprise, it didn't hurt. Being alone with Izzie again felt natural and right, as if no time had passed at all since we'd been in love. And that's because we still were. Only Izzie appreciated it more now, this love we felt that was real, because he was clean. At first, he had quit cold turkey, thinking it would be easy since drugs weren't a problem for him. But when cold turkey proved too hard, he sought help from a professional drug counselor at a rehab clinic. He said Marcus still dabbled occasionally, but never in his presence.

"I can't tell Marcus what to do with his life," he said. "And besides, he was never as out of control as I was. I needed to get clean. It's the best thing I could have done for myself."

"I'm proud of you," I said. "I'm really, *really* proud of you."

"Well, since you said that, I guess I'll give you this." Izzie reached into his pocket and held out a small velvet box.

"What's that?"

"It appears to be a box, Stella."

I leaned forward on the couch, shoving him playfully. It was the first time we'd touched since the breakup. Before I had the chance to settle down again, Izzie leaned forward, too, and gently took hold of my face, kissing me softly. We were both smiling when he pulled away.

"Happy birthday," he said, handing me the box.

"You remembered?"

"Of course I remembered. The drugs didn't fry my brain *that* bad. You're thirty-seven, right?"

"Ha-ha," I said as I opened it. The ring inside sparkled so much, it made my eyes water. Or maybe it was him. I didn't want him to leave.

"You don't have to count them. That's twenty-seven blue topaz stones, and the pink sapphire in the center is your one candle for good luck."

"For good luck?"

"Well, I won't be here to have cake with you tomorrow, so... Work with me here, Stella. I was trying to make an analogy."

"It's a beautiful analogy," I said, kissing his cheek.

"Thanks."

"Thank *you*."

"You're welcome."

"Put it on me."

"Put *what* on you?" he asked, smiling.

"The *ring,* Izzie." After he'd put the ring on my finger, he continued to hold my hand, anyway, just because. "You know, I never stopped loving you," I said.

"Likewise." He paused to lend a teasing grin to the expression. *It's gonna be hard—getting over you,* he'd said the night we broke up. *Likewise,* I'd told him. And obviously, it had been harder than we thought because four months later, here we were—not over each other at all. Not even close. He rubbed my hand as he continued to talk. "In a lot of ways, I'm glad you broke my heart, though. That was what motivated me to get my act together. I resisted for a little while, told myself you were wrong, that I didn't have a problem. And then I realized—if I'd lost you, I had a problem. There were no two ways about it."

"I broke your heart?"

"Like you didn't know."

"How's your heart doing these days?"

"It misses you."

"Yeah? Oh, Izzie," I said, sighing, "why didn't you tell me about all of this before?"

"You mean about getting clean?"

"*That* and moving away..."

"All right. Hold on. First of all, I know you said I could come to you for help, but I didn't want to drag you into that whole mess again. I wanted to do it on my own and impress you."

"Well, you *have.* But why wait so long to tell me about it?"

"What was I gonna do, call you that first day and say, 'Guess what? I've been clean for six hours?' I wanted to give it time. The last thing I wanted was to make you proud of me and then screw up again."

"But this Seattle thing..."

"It's a great chance for me. And I haven't known for that long. Things have been insane since I found out and I've been wanting to come by, but I didn't know how you'd treat me or what you'd say...I don't know. I realize now that I wasted a lot of time that could've been spent with you. I just didn't realize things could be this easy between us again. But at least we've got tonight."

I shrugged. "Who needs tomorrow?"

"Let's make it last."

"Let's find a way."

Izzie leaned forward. "I have to say, this is really turning me on. How come you never talked Bob Seger to me while we were going out?"

"I'm doing it to you now."

"Now? Really? I know it's been a while, dear, but I think I remember how you 'do it.'"

"Is that right? Well, then I guess you don't need me to show you."

"Is that an offer?"

"You remember where the bedroom is, don't you?"

It's a good thing Alison was at Anthony's because we didn't exactly make it into the bedroom—the first time. But eventually, we did, and Izzie spent the night. He left early the next morning with the sweetest kiss and a promise to call from his new apartment in Seattle the following week. One month later, he died.

Izzie's overdose invented a brand-new way to break my heart. I *gave* him my heart and he died. And a piece of my heart died with him.

We were supposed to get together soon. We talked every night on the phone, but hadn't seen each other since his last morning in Scottsboro, making love at sunrise on my twenty-seventh birthday with the birds chirping outside my bedroom window. We'd made plans, though, finally, for the first weekend in February. I couldn't wait—I missed him so much. He died on January 6th.

Marcus was the one who found him—in the middle of the night, facedown in a pool of blood and ink at his desk. He'd been working on his new column when his life passed through him. I wondered if his final moments had contained any thoughts of me.

No one had any idea that Izzie had relapsed until the night

he died. The experience scared Marcus into strict sobriety and helped ease the bad blood that existed between him and Anthony. After somebody dies, grudges can seem pretty pointless. They'd gone almost five months thinking that their friendship was over. But when tragedy hit home, Anthony was the first one Marcus turned to. And he was there. Alison had the most unfortunate task of breaking the news to me.

I had to take a leave of absence from work. It wasn't too long—only a couple of weeks. I spent those two weeks at my mom's place because I needed to feel like a little girl again. After all those years of feeling like I hadn't grown up as fast as everybody else, that I was somehow lagging behind, I now felt like I'd grown up *too* fast—my peers were already starting to die. But then again, shouldn't I have been prepared? Even as a girl, I'd known what others didn't. How many ninth graders have to bury their seventeen-year-old sisters? But, Blanche was different. Blanche was…another life. Yes, Blanche was the end of innocence, of childhood, of taking things for granted. I'd never taken Izzie for granted. Izzie wasn't supposed to die. Young people weren't supposed to die. Lightning wasn't supposed to strike twice. Though, it had for my mother. And now I understood her fear. Only my heart bled too heavily to fear much of anything. My greatest fear had already been realized. The man I was in love with had died. What difference did anything make now?

Izzie's body was flown back to Pennsylvania for the funeral. Emily and Warren came down for the service, which was so horrible, I promised myself I'd never think about it again. Not that such promises ever take. Emily spent the next few days at my mom's with me. She couldn't stop crying. It was all right, though. It's not as if I expected her to come up with any magical speeches that might heal me. I just liked having her around. The morning my mom left to drive her to the train station, I sank down by the front door and just lay there, watching my tears collect on the floor. Two hours later, when my mother returned, I still hadn't moved.

Marcus stayed with his mother for a while, too, and then he

moved back into McIntyre Suites. At first, that surprised me. I didn't know how he could do it—all those memories of Izzie. But then I realized that *I* was still there, and memories of Izzie filled every inch of my apartment. Marcus just wanted to surround himself with what was comforting and familiar. There was no life for him in Seattle without his cousin. But here in the building, there was Anthony, Alison and me. The old group that had always been so close. Minus one.

Marcus and I spent a lot of time together. Without him, I don't know how I would have gotten through those first few months without Izzie. He says the same thing about me.

We both felt guilty and confused. Neither of us could understand how we *didn't* see the signs that Izzie was using again.

"But maybe it was just the one time. Just that one night, I mean," Marcus said. "To get him through his work."

"That only makes it sadder—to think that one time could—"

"And if I hadn't been so casual about cocaine, myself, maybe I would've known something was—"

"You can't blame yourself."

"You're blaming *yourself.* You were all the way on the other side of the country, and you think you should've been able to notice a change in his behavior?"

"I'm blaming myself because I was so damn judgmental the first time. Izzie would've been afraid to tell me if he'd slipped."

"You weren't judgmental, Stella. You were right. You've never heard of tough love?"

"A lot of good it did me."

"Well, for what it's worth, my cousin loved you more than anything in this world. He was even talking about moving back here because he couldn't stand the distance from you."

"For what it's worth?" I asked, trying not to cry. "It's worth everything. What else do I have?"

A lot of my conversations with Marcus would end with unanswerable questions like these. There were no answers, I suppose. None that would cast a healing spell on our suffering. All we could do was be there for each other to lend the perspective and understanding that no one else, no matter how much they cared, ever could. Sometimes, we just watched TV, ate pizza, said nothing. The point was that we didn't go through it alone. We were partners in grief, Marcus and I, and after a while, when the heavy veil of mourning lifted, we realized we'd become incredible friends—independent of the group that had once bound us together, and able to tell each other anything.

By June, my sorrow had become less persistent, and I was actually able to go about life without the constant awareness of a gaping hole in my heart. Marcus had begun seeing somebody, and I was thrilled for him—he deserved the happiness. There was just no way I could picture myself having that kind of happiness again, at least not for a while. I certainly was the odd one out in that regard—romance was everywhere. Emily and Damien had been riding along blissfully for a year and a half without a single bump on the road. Anthony and Alison had just gotten engaged. And even Warren was seeing someone, his first girlfriend since Giselle. Tina Betts was a twenty-two-year-old waitress-actress whom Warren had met one night when third-wheeling it with Emily and Damien at a Mexican restaurant in Midtown. Unlike Giselle, Emily and I really liked Tina. She was cute, bubbly and completely *not* obnoxious about being cute and bubbly. In fact, she didn't put on any airs at all. Tina was completely herself at all times. She even talked openly about Warren's undying attachment to Emily and me.

"I know that his ex-girlfriend was bothered by it," she said, "but I think the fact that he's so loyal to the two of you, and so protective, says something about his attitude toward women in general. Maybe I'm weird for not being jealous, but if you can't trust a guy like Warren, who *can* you trust?" Did I mention how much I liked Tina?

Things seemed to be going pretty well for everyone that summer. As for me, the sun would shine brighter someday. And at least I was moving on with my life. By the time school started up again in September, I felt ready to make a fresh start. It had been eight months since Izzie died, and I still missed him, but things felt new in a positive way for the first time since my birthday, for the first time since Izzie and I made *our* new start. Maybe it was the new school year or the new season about to break, but I could feel that sun beginning to shine on me again. And its wonderful rays felt like hugs.

Unfortunately, September didn't bring good things for everybody. Emily got her phone call in September, a phone call that none of us had been sharp enough to predict. It was a Saturday morning and Warren was at an audition with Tina. Emily was alone, unsuspecting, just drinking coffee, when she heard the ring.

"Hello?"

"Hi. This is Melanie Esposito…Damien's wife."

A friend had spotted Damien having what appeared to be a romantic lunch with another woman a few weeks earlier. Since then, Melanie had been searching for evidence, and finally, last night, she had found it. Damien was taking a shower when Melanie came home and saw that he had one new message on his cell phone. Maybe he'd planned to check his voice mail before she arrived, but if that had been the plan, he was too late. For while Damien was in the shower, washing away his secrets and sins, his wife, who had always been faithful, was in the very next room, confirming the fears her friend had planted weeks ago—her husband was, in fact, having an affair.

Did Emily have any idea what it was like to be married to a man for seven years and hear another woman telling him she loved him and was sorry they couldn't spend the night together? *Seven years?* Yes, married seven and together eleven, since college. But in the past two years, she'd been doing a lot of traveling during the week, for business. She had just returned from Denver when she saw the new message light blinking on Damien's phone. Maybe it was partly her fault—for being gone so much. Maybe this was her punishment for wanting a career. But at least she never traveled on the weekends. That had always been her rule. The weekends were for Damien and the kids. *Kids?* Yes, two. A boy and a girl. Jeffrey and Amanda, ages four and six. They spent a lot of time at their grandmother's house during the week because Damien put in such "long hours at the office." Only now that she knew her kids had been losing time with their father because he'd been having an affair, she was appalled.

"And on those occasional weekends he says he's had conventions, I'm willing to bet any amount of money he's been with you."

Emily was pretty sure Melanie Esposito would've won that bet, considering that in all the time she'd been with Damien, it had only been the occasional weekend they'd actually gotten to spend together, when he "wasn't" traveling on business. Apparently "conventions" were code for whatever life he felt like living that weekend. Usually, they meant family time. And every now and again, he stole away from the family in Fort Lee and escaped to Manhattan to live a lie in the arms of the other woman. Emily was appalled, too. Appalled that she had been so naive. Appalled that Damien had gotten away with lying to her for so long. Appalled that the news had broken her heart even more than it had disgusted her.

Emily apologized to Melanie, assuring her that she never would've gotten involved—or stayed involved—with a man she knew was married, let alone married with children. Melanie said she believed her, and they both wished each other luck.

On Monday, Emily sent Warren to Damien's office with a letter saying that she knew he was married, that they were completely finished, and that if he ever tried to contact her in the future, she'd seek a restraining order against him. But the tough act was only that—an act. On the inside, she was devastated. How could she have been so stupid as to say she was in love with someone she'd never actually known? Her words reminded me of my own the night I confronted Izzie about the cocaine. Only this was different. I'd told Izzie that it was like he'd been cheating on me with another woman for over a year, but I was confused when I said that. Because it wasn't the same thing. Izzie had a drug problem. Drug problems are far different from not being able to keep your so-called manhood in your pants. Being lied to always hurts. But Izzie wasn't a cheater. Rob, Kevin, Damien—*those* were the faces of cheaters. Not Izzie. I wished he were around so I could tell him I'd realized the difference.

"Some guys just cheat," I told Emily. We were on the phone, discussing Damien for the second time that day. "And some guys never would. It all depends on the situation, I guess. But it certainly wasn't *your* fault."

"He didn't love me," she said. "The same way Rob didn't love me."

"I'm sure they *both* loved you, Em. Just not the way you deserve to be loved."

"Maybe I *don't* deserve to be loved—by any man."

"Now, that is completely untrue, and you know it."

"Is it? I gave my heart—and my virginity—to Jason Neeley in high school. He dumped me as soon as he got to college and found somebody better."

"Moron."

"And Rob..."

"Fuck-up."

"Damien?"

"Pig."

"So, what else is there? *Who* else is there?"

"Emily, I can assure you, you haven't dated every man in the world yet. You *will* meet somebody great, and probably sooner than you think. Just give it time."

Emily was quiet for a second, then said, "What if I think I've already met somebody great, but I can't have him?"

"Another gay brother?" I teased.

"Straight brother."

"No."

"But there's always been that thing between Warren and me. And for four years, I've been suppressing it because of our friendship, the fact that we were in other relationships, blah, blah, blah..."

"Yeah, well, 'blah, blah, blah' is very important."

"Stella...I never told you this, but do you know how much self-control it took not to try anything with him when we were both single—before I met Damien?"

"You were just horny."

"No. I think Warren could be the one. Why are you so against this?"

"Have you forgotten about Tina? Sweet, innocent Tina who trusts you? Warren really likes her, Emily. Don't mess that up because you're on the rebound and not thinking straight again."

"This has nothing to do with being on the rebound. It has to do with feelings and clocks."

"Clocks?"

"Mine is ticking, Stella. I'm gonna be twenty-eight in less than two months. It's time to stop dicking around. It'd be different if I were still *looking* for him, but I *know* who he is. It's Warren. And I like Tina. I really do. But I can't fight this feeling anymore."

"All I'm saying, REO Speedwagon, is that you might just want to slow down and breathe so that we don't end up with another Nick situation on our hands. That's all I'm saying."

"Is that all you're saying?"

"That, and I really think Tina's the best thing that's happened to Warren in as long as I've known him."

"But when will the best thing happen to *me?*"

"Give it time," I told her. "Your clock's not ticking that fast."

Three weeks later, Anna surprised Emily with an invitation to join her for ten weeks in Europe. She and Warren celebrated the news with a bottle of wine during dinner. Tina had landed a part in an Off-Off Broadway comedy and was going straight home after her waitressing shift to rest up for an early-morning rehearsal. It was Warren and Emily's first night alone together in months. They didn't come close to finishing the wine. They found their way to the bedroom all on their own, completely sober.

It had been eight and a half years since their last "roll in the hay," but this was different, much different. Emily described it as magical. She said she'd never felt safer with any other man in her life. The night had been perfect, and she wouldn't have changed a thing.

Warren told me it was a mistake. He was afraid he'd taken advantage of her trust.

She said he was sweeter, sexier and more attentive afterward than she ever would have imagined, even knowing the way he was last time and the way he is in his everyday life.

He said he was scared to death when it was over, just waiting for her to flip out on him for letting things go that far.

She said it was just what she'd needed, but that it couldn't happen again—at least not until he took care of his situation. That is, if he wanted to be with her. And if he didn't, she would understand. She'd be hurt, of course, but she could never hate Warren. He'd given her the greatest night of her life, and he'd always be her friend. Sex could never change that.

He said this was the *last* thing he'd needed and it definitely couldn't happen again. Sex screwed everything up. Now he had a situation on his hands and he didn't know what to do about it. His biggest fear in the world was losing Emily as a friend.

I said I refused to get in the middle of it. I told them they had to talk.

They said they would let what happened between them be what it was—one magical moment between two old friends who loved each other a lot and had gotten carried away one night. One magical, well, *mistake* that couldn't be repeated because of the, um, situation. Tina! Her name was Tina! Though, I seemed to be the only one who could remember that after Warren and Emily consummated their platonic living situation.

I did feel bad for Emily. I knew the "mutual" decision they'd reached hadn't really been all that mutual, that she'd merely followed Warren's lead, accepting his views because she trusted his judgment and never wanted to become a burden to him. But at least she had Europe to look forward to. Preparing for the trip helped take her mind off of things. And by the time she said goodbye to Warren in November, they were back to, at least, *acting* platonic. As for the way they felt, neither of them discussed it with me, so I assumed the magical mistake was to be kept hidden in the past—far from where that situation named Tina could ever find it.

But Warren's guilt—and his time away from Emily—soon got the best of him. Being alone in the apartment gave him time to think things through. Emily had been gone for five weeks when he finally came clean to Tina.

She called me in absolute hysterics, catching me completely off guard. Warren hadn't prepared me at all.

"I don't blame either of them," she sobbed. "I blame myself. I've been so *stupid!*"

"Don't blame yourself, Tina. You don't deserve to be cheated on."

"But I should've known what I was getting myself into. I mean, you're one thing. But, Emily…I know I said I wasn't bothered by it, but deep down, how could I not have been? The way he looks at her…God, it was *so* obvious!" Had I missed something? "I always knew he thought of her as more than a friend. But to have your boyfriend flat-out tell you that he's in love with somebody else, that he's been in love with her for years… How is that supposed to make me feel? What purpose did I even serve?"

"Warren said that to you?" Despite Tina's misery—and she really was a nice girl—my entire world had just gotten several shades brighter. You would have thought *I'd* just found peace and happiness. But in a way, I had. It all made sense now. All those trips into Manhattan he'd made to "check in" on her. Dropping Giselle without any regrets so they could be roommates. His critical suspicion of every man she showed interest in. Warren and Emily—all these years, all that resistance, and for what? They were in love.

"Cheating on me is one thing," Tina was saying, "but I was ready to forgive him. I mean, how often does a guy like Warren come along?"

"Not often," I said, glowing inside for Emily. "Not often enough. Listen, Tina, I'm sorry to do this, but I have to go. My mom's waiting for me. We had plans to go out today."

I felt bad for lying, but I knew I'd never see Tina Betts again, sweet as she was. And I was sure she'd find someone who appreciated her, eventually. It just wouldn't be Warren. Because

Warren loved somebody else. All this time—why the hell hadn't he told me? I couldn't wait to get him on the phone.

"Hello?"

"So, you're in love with Emily?"

"You've spoken to Tina, I take it."

"Answer the question."

"Of course I'm in love with her. Are you telling me you never noticed?"

"It seems I've been a little thick."

"Yeah, well, you're like that."

"Oh, thanks."

"No. With me, I mean. I kind of have to hit you over the head with things."

"Huh?"

"See what I mean? Anyway, I feel like shit about Tina. Did she sound really bad?"

"You don't want to know. Why'd you bother with her, anyway? Was it just a sex thing?"

"Not at all. I really liked Tina, and I was always looking for more to grow out of that. I guess I was trying to get over Emily, too. I didn't want to be in love with someone I could never have. I tried that before. Remember, Andie?"

I smiled as if he were there in the room with me. "Oh, come on, Duckie. You know we were destined for this."

"This?"

"You know, whatever *this* is."

"A brother and sister with an incestuous past?"

I laughed. "That's about accurate. What about Emily? Do you think of her like a sister, too?"

"*Fuck,* no! What do you think I am, some kind of pervert?"

"Sorry. Emily and I have a thing about gay brothers and straight brothers, and I think it's warped my senses."

"Well, you two have always been weird. But, anyway, what happens now—with Emily, I mean? Do you think she'll want to like..."

I knew she would *definitely* "want to like," but how could I speak for her about something this important? That was the wonderful and terrible dichotomy of being in the middle. I had access to privileged information, but had to keep everything I knew to myself. "You know I can't speak for her, Warren."

"You're loyal to a fault."

"And you're not?"

"Well, we all have our faults. Listen, do me a favor and don't say a word to her about Tina. Okay? Promise?"

"I promise. I figured you'd rather tell her yourself."

"Yeah, but I want to wait. When Emily and I talk about this, I want it to be face-to-face, not when she's off in Europe and I'm more than three thousand miles away in New York. Does that make sense? Or do you think I'm just being a big coward?"

"No, I think it makes perfect sense. This is definitely a conversation you need to have in person. But you have to really *do* it, Warren, once and for all. Set aside a night as soon as she gets back. And be serious about it. Your clocks are ticking."

"We're twenty-eight."

"And *how* long have you known each other?"

"I see your point. I've been kind of slow about things."

"Well, we all have our faults. Hey, listen. What are you doing next Saturday?"

"Are you asking me out?"

"I miss you. I feel like I haven't seen you in forever. God, I can't even *remember* the last time we got together by ourselves."

"It's been a while."

"And besides, I want to talk about this some more. Like, really *really* talk about all the things you've been keeping from me all these years."

"I didn't mean to keep things from you, Stella. It was just a strange situation. I don't know—maybe I didn't want to put you in the middle."

"You had no problem doing that when you slept with Emily two months ago."

"Well, that was a crisis."

"I see."

"I can always come to you in a crisis, Stella. It's different from setting aside time for spilling your guts about love and feelings. Guys don't actually do that too often, contrary to what you see in the movies."

"Really? And I thought life was just like the movies."

"Sorry to disappoint."

"You never disappoint."

"Well, I aim to please. Anyway, you were asking me out."

"Right. Here's what we'll do. We'll go out to dinner first and talk about bullshit, and then we'll come back here and get drunk so you can spill your guts about love and feelings."

"Sounds like a plan. Mind if I start now? With something about you, I mean."

"By all means, go ahead. It'll make good practice for next week."

"All right...Stella, despite our incestuous and ambiguous past, and the fact that I never came to you with a heartfelt monologue about the Emily thing, you really are the best friend I've ever had. And I can't think of anyone in the world I'd rather emasculate myself in front of than you."

"Aw, Warren..."

"Consider that your sneak preview. I'll call you next week before I leave for the train station."

"Saturday, right?"

"Saturday. We're on."

Saturday. Here it was. Only, I was on an airplane, and Warren was back at his apartment in Manhattan, pretending not to be hurt that I'd broken our plans. And worst of all, I hadn't even been able to tell him why. *Emily invited me to come see her on a whim*. Warren deserved a real explanation. He deserved to know how something that just one week earlier had seemed so important could suddenly slip my mind.

That whole day, I'd been thinking about my life and how much everything had changed over the years. It wasn't until my flight touched ground in Washington, D.C., that I realized just how much everything had changed in a single week. One day.

Timing Is Everything

I hadn't meant to stare at the man in the jolly seasonal sweater. I'd actually planned on using my four-hour layover at Washington Dulles International to sleep. The guy in the festive cardigan was just something to focus on while I faded. But then he reached for his book. I lurched forward and froze the moment I saw the cover. It was *Bloodlines* by John Lixner.

I found myself watching him as he read, burning with this completely nonsensical need for him to look up and make a connection—any connection—between the author and me. Maybe it was sleep deprivation, but I actually believed it possible that at any moment, Mr. Happy Sweater Man would look up and see that I was the novel's leading lady, Camille. That I was the one who'd put the passion in John's pen. That I was just the kind of woman the author would've moved to San Diego for. And he did look up eventually, but not for any of those reasons, I presume. I'd been staring at him for at least ten minutes, and he probably thought I was deranged. Either that, or I had a thing for middle-aged men in well-intended, yet flagrantly unfashionable Christmas wear.

"I don't mean to stare," I apologized. "It's just that the author, he's..." How could I describe John to a total stranger? "A very old friend of mine."

"Oh, no kidding? That's terrific! Are you aware that he's here in town today?"

"...Today?" My heart had stopped for a second. But now it surged with new life—Kevin, Dublin and all my exhaustion had suddenly disappeared. All that mattered was this news.

"He's doing a signing over at Gordon Books. I just came from there, myself."

Mr. Happy Sweater Man. Guardian angel. Same difference. The next thing I knew, I was in a cab on my way to see John for the first time in almost nine years.

I always thought I'd have advance notice for my next meeting with John. It never occurred to me that we'd both end up in D.C. on a day that in many ways felt like the end of the world. But our nation's capital was one of two stops on my connecting journey to Dublin. And since it was the holidays, John was probably in town visiting his parents. Logically, it all made perfect sense. His being there. My going to him. But in my heart, it seemed like fate. If I hadn't gotten Emily's call that morning, I never would've gotten in that cab that afternoon. And even though it had been nearly nine years and I'd had no formal preparation, I wasn't nervous. John had always had the ability to calm me, and now, on this crazy day, with everything that had happened and all I was going to face, I needed that feeling more than anything. Nine years—but I had never let go of the memories.

On the way to Gordon's, I thought of the rain—the way John looked standing in the storm the night before he left for Yale. That was the night he said he wished he could marry me. But he was only seventeen. I thought of the way he held my hand on the couch after Kurt Cobain died. I'd thought they looked so much alike, John and the man whose voice filled my bedroom the night we shared our first kiss. "The Man Who Sold the World." We kissed to it, we swam to it in dreams. But there was no soundtrack for that week we spent in bed. Just John, naked with a nosebleed in the hallway. Just John and his hair that smelled like apple shampoo.

But people's lives go in different directions, and even those who love each other go their separate ways sometimes. John and I were young and careless and we fell out of touch way too easily. It had been four and a half years since we'd even e-mailed, not counting that one message I sent him when *Seventeen Stories* came out. At the time, I'd considered it for the best that the message had been returned. Things were different then. Izzie. But when *Bloodlines* hit the shelves in October, all my old feelings came rushing back. Maybe it was the story, those silly little wishes that I was Camille. Maybe it was the pain of realizing that John and I hadn't been close in years, that the author whose face I saw on the back of the book was merely someone I *had* been close to…once. But pain and wishes and feelings—that all means something, doesn't it? And if Izzie's death had taught me anything, it was never to let another opportunity for love slip away.

Of course, I knew there was always the chance that John was seeing someone, but I also knew I'd *never* know unless I went for it. And even if he was involved, just the thought of having him in my life again, of grabbing the second chance and not letting go this time, seemed like a blessing on this last day of the world. All my hours of waiting and thinking—about Emily, Warren, Alison, Anthony and Marcus—had left me with an unprecedented appreciation of the importance of holding on to friends. And regardless of what John and I were to each other over the years before we lost touch, I never questioned whether or not he was my friend. In fact, I'd always considered him one of the best, even when he was breaking my heart.

The sunset was cold but sweet as I stood there, watching him through the bookstore window. In many ways, he looked so different from that fifteen-year-old boy who walked into my physics class on that first day of school in eleventh grade, and in so many ways, he was the same. His hair was darker, shorter, and he had the body of a man. But his smile, his eyes, they were just like I had left them. There was one highly significant change, however, illuminated in that very precious moment that our united past and separate ways had brought us to. And that was his confidence. John was a twenty-seven-year-old bestselling author. He wasn't that scared little boy in the rain anymore. And I felt honored to have known both sides of him and to recognize, still, in his smile, a striking resemblance to that genius of a lab partner who used to give me butterflies back in 1993. Without even looking at me or saying a word, he was doing it all over again in 2004. I took a deep breath and went inside.

The gathering in front of John's table had cleared by the time I approached him. But he had bent down to retrieve something from his briefcase and didn't notice me standing there. Stella and John, finally, after all these years, separated only by furniture, and he didn't even know it. There was something so cute about that. I got ready to shock him.

"Just sign it, 'To the man who sold the world,'" I said.

I don't know if it was my voice, the song, or some combination of both, but John knew it was me before our eyes met. I could tell by the way he lifted his head, by that little pause before he turned to face me—that moment of sheer disbelief, as if perhaps he had imagined my being there. But then, he did turn around—to behold that it wasn't a dream—and surprise seized control of him in a very visual way. His eyes grew to twice their normal size. His jaw dropped. He put his hand to his heart. And then a giant smile overwhelmed his face, and he laughed, shaking his head.

"Say something!" I blurted, laughing, too.

But he didn't, at least not yet. Instead, he got up and ran around the table to hug me. It was the greatest hug I'd ever gotten from him—or anyone else in my life. He held me as though I might not be real, as if he let go, he could lose me. When he did pull away, he kept his arms around my waist.

"Stella..." He took a break after saying my name and just smiled—that warm, genuine John smile. "What are you doing here?"

"I came to see you."

"How'd you know I was here?"

"The man at the airport told me."

"What man at the airport? Wait—why were you at the airport? Where are you coming from? Where are you going?" He was still smiling, and he hadn't let go of me yet.

"It's kind of a long story," I said. "How much time do you have?"

"For you?" he asked. "Forever."

John and I went for coffee next door as soon as his signing was over. As it turns out, I'd made it to Gordon Books just in time. If I'd arrived only twenty minutes later, I probably wouldn't have caught him at all.

"God, to think we've gone almost nine years without seeing each other, and just when I'm finally about to change that, I could've missed you by *twenty minutes.*"

John lowered his head. "I was such a jerk to you, Stella."

"What do you mean? No, you weren't."

"*Yes,* I was. I thought life was about getting straight A's and being in all the right academic clubs...." John smiled. "I was a *dork,* basically."

"You were young, John. You were sweet."

"Well, I was a young, sweet dork, then."

"They're the best kind."

John laughed. "Stella, you have no idea how many times I just wanted to say fuck the Ivy League, fuck my parents, but it really wasn't any one else's fault. *I* was the one who turned myself into that weird, obsessive freak, not them. I just had this compulsive need to be the best and to keep topping myself. I mean, back in high school, everyone always acted like I was so different because of what a 'genius' I was supposed to be, and then I found myself at Yale where no one actually *gave* a shit about any of that. I'd always resented being treated differently, and then, there I was in college—having absolutely no idea how to cope with being average."

"John, you were *anything* but average."

He smiled. "I loved you more than you knew. I just couldn't handle the kind of relationship you wanted."

"I always tried not to pressure you."

"And you didn't. *I* pressured me. Everything was all or nothing. I knew I couldn't be everything to you, so in a way, I guess, I chose nothing."

"That's not true. We stayed friends. We didn't see each other a lot, but—"

"And that was my fault, too."

"It was *both* of our faults. I remember one summer you kept inviting me up to New Haven and I kept coming up with reasons not to visit. I was afraid I'd get in your way."

"You were always a welcome distraction, Stella. I guess that's why I couldn't afford to see you too often. I couldn't afford to let myself get too distracted."

"And I kind of lied just now." John raised his eyebrows. "I said I was afraid I'd get in your way, but the truth was I worried that somehow my visit wouldn't measure up to the visit you made to Scottsboro that spring."

"Oh, you mean where we…"

"Mmm-hmm."

"And you punched me in the nose?"

"I didn't *punch* you. I accidentally bumped you with my head."

"Like there's a *difference.*"

"John…"

"I'm kidding, Stella. You know what I remember most about that week?"

"What?"

"Watching you sleep."

"You watched *me* sleep?"

John laughed. "I know I was a zombie for those first couple of days, but after we, you know, realized we could do *that*…well, every night, I would just lie awake afterward watching you sleep."

"You know what's cute? You can write all those passionate scenes in your books, but you can't say the S-word."

"I can say it."

"Say it, then."

John leaned forward. "Have I mentioned how good you look?"

"You have not. But you may."

"You really do look beautiful. I hardly even recognized you without the braces and glasses and all that acne you used to have."

"John…"

He smiled. "Wasn't you?"

"Must've been some other girl you did the S-word with. And you still can't even say it."

"Gotta save something for next time."

"So, we'll do this again?"

"Maybe not exactly this. But we'll see each other. It's ridiculous that we ever lost touch in the first place. I hate it, Stella. I really do, and if I could go back and change it, I would."

"Well, we can't change the past. And there's plenty of good stuff there, too—with you and me. A lot of it, kid stuff, but good stuff."

"Hey, since when is sex 'kid stuff'?"

"Ha! You said *sex!*" I teased. "But, seriously—the physics labs and how when we dated junior year, all we ever did was kiss and take naps together."

"We were wholesome."

"Puppy love. But then I fell *in* love with you the summer before you left for Yale. You were my first love, John. And I don't think that qualifies as 'kid stuff.'"

"Well, it depends on how long the feeling lasts." Was that a question? Was I supposed to tell him how long the feeling had lasted? That it had never gone away? Neither of us said anything for a few seconds.

"I tried e-mailing you when I first found out you were writing." There. That was my answer. Two years after we lost touch, more than six years after our last meeting, I still had feelings for him. Whether or not it was love, well, I still hadn't asked him who Camille was.

John looked surprised. "You did? I never got it."

"I know. It was returned to me."

"Oh, that's right—I changed accounts a few months before my book came out. Fuck, I was an idiot for not giving you the new address."

"Well, we hadn't e-mailed in two years, John."

He shook his head. "What was wrong with us?"

"Timing?"

John shrugged his shoulders. "All I know is that this feels like a dream. You're not gonna believe this but I've actually fantasized about you showing up at one of my signings. Just like you did today. Except in my fantasies, I act a lot cooler and we're usually having sex in some dirty motel room by now." His words gave me hope. He wouldn't talk like that if there was some other woman waiting in the wings back in San Diego. But I had to keep playing it cool.

"Wait, are you saying the sex would be dirty or the motel room, itself, would be unclean?"

"Any way you like it, as long as there's sex."

"You're a lot more forward than the boy I used to know."

"The boy you used to know grew up."

"Quite nicely."

"Is that a compliment, Ms. Gold?"

"I believe it is."

"Is that what your students call you—Ms. Gold? You're still teaching, aren't you?"

"Yes and yes."

"Forest Hills?"

"Yes."

"God, this feels good, Stella," he said, rubbing my arm. "I can't believe I never had the balls to make this happen."

"Hey, I didn't, either. At least not until today."

"So, tell me about your life in the last four and a half years. What else have you been up to, besides teaching and growing balls?"

I laughed. "Well, I have an apartment with Alison, my roommate from Penn. But she's getting married in—"

"Are *you* seeing anyone?" He cut me off! He actually cut me off with a question about my love life. He *couldn't* be involved with any so-called California cunt named Camille. Unless, of course, that so-called cunt was me. Unless his heart had never let go of us, either. "Last I remember, you were all about being single, but that was…"

"A long time ago."

"So?"

"So…"

"So, do you not want to talk about this? I mean, is this weird?"

"No. I can talk about it." I would have to tell him about Izzie. "I was actually single for a while, and then I got pretty serious with this guy, uh, Izzie." I hated saying his name aloud. Thinking it didn't hurt as much as it used to, but saying it hurt more. Each time I said his name, it sounded more and more hollow, farther and farther away from being attached to any kind of living being, and that's because it was. Izzie had been gone for almost a year now.

"Are you still together?" John asked innocently. I shook my head and seeing that I was upset, he reached across the table for my hand.

"I'm okay," I said. "I mean, I want you to know about him." And so I told the first love of my life about the last, including the overdose and everything I'd learned from it.

"Holding on to friends is so important, no matter what stupid arguments you might have, no matter how much time and distance come between you. It might sound trite, but when you've lost someone so incredibly close to you, it just becomes so true, and so valuable. I guess that's why I'm here now—with you."

"Is that the only reason?"

I looked down at our hands on the table and back into his crystal-blue eyes. Screw it. We were sitting there holding hands, flirting and sharing personal stories. I had a definite right to ask by now. "Who's Camille?"

"Who?"

"*Camille.* Beaumont."

John smiled. "Oh, I get it. I think that's a myth, though."

"What is?"

"That whole idea that every character in a book can be found somewhere in the author's actual life."

"Oh." I was relieved in one sense, but disappointed in another. Did this mean Camille couldn't possibly be me, then? "Well, then, why did you move to San Diego? It wasn't for a girl?"

"It was for a guy, actually." Uh-oh. I seemed to be having a Rob Sellers flashback.

"Oh, don't tell me—you, too."

"What?"

"Nothing. I'll tell you some other time. When there's more time."

"Can't wait to hear it. Anyway, I moved because Mike, my roommate from Yale, got a job out there after college, and every time I'd visit, I'd say I was gonna live there one day—it's such a great city. So, after I sold my manuscript for *Seventeen Stories,* I flew out and found a place. That's one of the best things about what I do now—being able to work from anywhere."

"I never told you how proud I was of you—about your novels, I mean."

"Well, thank you. I'm proud of you, too."

"So, let me get this straight. You're *not* seeing anybody in California at all?"

"Not in California and not at all." John leaned very close to my face, turning me on more than he probably realized. "Have I *mentioned* how incredible you look?"

"Not enough."

"I like this new confidence you have now, too. It's very sexy. You didn't always have that."

"It comes with old age. You have it, too. I noticed it when I was watching you sign copies of your book through the window at Gordon's."

"How long were you watching me?"

"A couple of minutes."

"Voyeur."

"Author."

"What?"

"I don't know. I couldn't think of anything else to call you."

"I've got a few ideas."

"I'll bet you have."

I'm not exactly sure where this conversation could have gone, but like John, I had my fantasies. None of them, however, included the waitress coming over and interrupting things with the bill. Though that is precisely what happened in real life. But I suppose it was good to remember the time. John said he'd drive me back to the airport.

When we got outside, he asked about my mother.

"How is she? Still Janey?"

"Still Janey."

"And Kevin?"

I turned around to face him. We were standing by the passenger side of his car, and he was about to let me in. "He left her," I said. "A couple years ago. That actually has something to do with why I'm going to Dublin."

"That's right—you said it was a long story, but all you told me back at Gordon's was that you were going there to see Emily."

"Well, you were busy wrapping things up. And that *is* the short version."

"Well, what's the long version? I'm sorry we got so sidetracked at the coffee shop—I would've asked you sooner. It sounds complicated." Even in the dimly lit parking lot, John saw the tears welling up in my eyes. He cupped my face in his hands. "Stella, you can tell me anything. You always could."

And so I did. I told him everything, not just everything about Emily and Kevin, but everything about Kevin and me.

It was the secret I'd vowed to take to my grave, and under any other circumstances, I may have never told. I'd had plenty of serious, alone, adult moments with Izzie, like the night he told me he'd die for me and I saw God and heard Vivien Leigh, and still, I didn't tell. I'd never tell. But now, I had. And I didn't feel disgusting. And I didn't feel ashamed. But only because I was with John. In D.C. Under these faint, little lights. On this last day of the world. Or first night of the world. Or whatever it was. He made me feel so protected. And he held me until I stopped crying.

"I can't believe I actually told you about Kevin and me," I said as we stood there hugging. "It's been more than eight years. I thought I'd die without ever telling anyone what he did to me."

John squeezed me tighter. "You should've told me when it happened. As crazy as I was back then with school and everything else, I would've dropped everything to come be with you. I hope you know that."

"I just wasn't ready to talk about it then."

"Maybe that's a good thing. I wasn't very mature in college. I probably would've killed him."

"Oh, yeah?"

"Not alone, though. I wasn't strong enough. But I'm sure if Warren Blakemen had known about it, he would've helped me." I giggled softly. "What's so funny? You don't think we could've taken him?"

"I know you could've. But I just got this image in my head of you and Warren flying in like superheroes to beat up Kevin."

"Were we wearing tights?"

"You were."

"Gee, thanks." John was quiet for a minute and I could sense that he wanted to ask me something.

"What is it?" I asked, pulling back a little.

"Are you and Warren still friendly?"

"Yeah, why?"

"How friendly?"

"Best, but strictly platonic."

"You never…S-word?"

"We S-ed once." John looked completely disappointed, which made me feel wickedly gleeful. Though, I immediately felt guilty about it. "It was forever ago, John. Sophomore year. Honestly, he's like a brother to me now. And unlike some people, I do *not* go lusting after my brothers."

"Another story for another time?"

"You've got it. But my point is that you shouldn't even be thinking about Warren and me like that when it's Warren and *Emily* who are really in love."

"Emily? But she's—"

"About to marry Kevin in Dublin. Believe me, I know. But she and Warren have been living together for more than two years."

"Living together?"

"Well, they've kept it platonic. Well, almost platonic." John breathed an enormous sigh of relief. "What was that for?"

"Warren was always the one I feared you'd end up with, you know. Not some guy you'd meet in college or later in life, but Warren. I knew he cared about you like I did, but at the same time, he actually had his shit together and knew how to treat you... Warren Blakemen. Holy shit, was I jealous of that guy."

"That's so funny."

"I'm glad I could amuse you."

"It's funny because the whole time you were jealous of Warren, he was jealous of you."

"What for?"

"Because I was in love with you."

"He knew that?"

"*Everybody* knew that."

"And you're telling me I wasn't a jerk?"

"We were both jerks," I said. "How about that?"

"How *about* that?" he teased.

"How about..." I couldn't think of anything witty to say. I just wanted to kiss him.

"Stella?"

"Yeah?"

"Don't think."

And that's when he kissed me. Not one of my fantasies since the age of nineteen could have prepared me for how amazing that kiss was—a kiss that could wash away pain, birth hope, and make even the purest of physical pleasures seem dull by comparison. A kiss that was sex, therapy, exercise, ecstasy, and nothing if not everything I'd been waiting for. A kiss that could validate myths: I was *definitely* Camille.

And for the record: his hair still smelled like apple shampoo.

I slept the entire way to London. Before boarding the plane, John made me promise not to see Kevin alone and to call him as soon as I was back in the country. By the time we said goodbye, we'd exchanged e-mail addresses, phone numbers, both home and cell, and I even had his parents' number in D.C. We'd thought of absolutely everything.

"I'm not going to let you slip away again," he said.

"You can't. You still owe me a signed copy of your book."

"Well, then it's a good thing I don't have any on me. It means you'll have to see me again."

"Well, if I absolutely *must.*" John smiled and kissed me. It felt so good to be standing there with him. But why were we always saying goodbye? "I hate leaving you."

"Don't phrase it that way. Things have changed. We're older. We have balls now, remember? Now, hurry up and get on that plane so you can come back to me."

One day, I thought as I boarded. In one day, I had seen what I thought was my entire life threaten to shatter spectacularly to pieces. And then, here was this sweet surprise—a new life, rising brilliant and bright from an old love that had never faded away. How one's life could come together and fall apart in a single day…I fell asleep before we even took off.

The layover at Heathrow was brief and, finally, I was on my way to Dublin. Calmed the whole way there by thoughts of John, I realized that this trip was just the thing the term "a blessing in disguise" was invented to describe. I'd gone from the end of the world to a brand-new beginning, and all because of Emily's phone call, all because of Kevin's twisted life. In a way, I owed everything to Satan. The son of a bitch had finally given me something to write home about, other than scars.

Face-Off

"You and John," Emily said, smiling. "I always had a feeling you'd find each other again." We were sitting on the couch in her hotel room in Dublin and had been artfully avoiding the subject of Kevin since I'd arrived. Which was fine—for now. I much preferred the topic of John, anyway. "How did he look?"

"Amazing."

"Does he still remind you of Kurt Cobain?"

"A little bit, yeah. There's still that resemblance in the face."

"It's kind of weird, isn't it?"

"What is?"

"Well, John was a year younger than us, so he's twenty-seven, right?" I nodded. "And Kurt Cobain was twenty-seven when he died."

"That's morbid."

Emily shrugged. "I just think it's weird." She was quiet for a second. "Did you tell him about Izzie?"

"Yeah. He was really sweet about it."

"Stella? What if Izzie were—"

"Still here?" Emily nodded. "I don't know. I loved him with all my heart, but it wasn't enough. He destroyed himself, anyway. And John…I…"

"You've always loved John. I know." I smiled, relieved that I never really had to explain things to her. "Hey, remember your condom collection?" she asked, trying to lighten the mood. "How many were there—seventeen?"

"Nineteen," I said as the chills ran through me.

"Nineteen," she echoed. "I'll never forget when somebody violated your sacred stash and stole that whole handful."

"Ten."

"You remember the exact amount? God, Stella, you *were* obsessed with John!"

I took those because…well…because I knew they were there.

"It has nothing to do with John," I said, gathering my nerve. "If you're planning to marry Kevin, I think you have a right to know something."

"What, Stella?"

"He cheated on my mother."

"I know," she said quietly. "He told me."

"And you still want to marry him? Knowing full well that you could become the next Melanie Esposito? Checking your husband's cell phone messages like a detective, always wondering if he is where he says he is?"

"It wouldn't be like that with Kevin and me. He isn't anything like Damien. He cheated on your mother *one* time."

"One time? Is that what he told you? My mother called it an affair." I could tell by the reaction on her face that she'd never doubted his version of the truth. Why did she have to be so damn trusting all the time? And why did opening her eyes feel like stealing toys from a child? "It wasn't even just that one woman he cheated on her with, either. Unless he was seeing her for four years."

"What do you mean?"

"I never even told my mom this, but he cheated on her back in '96. The affair she knows about happened only a couple years before he left her, putting it somewhere around the fall of 2000."

"So, what happened in '96?"

"Remember those ten condoms that were missing from my little collection?" She nodded. "Kevin admitted to taking them."

"Yeah? So? He took them to use with your mom," she rationalized. "Big deal."

"Kevin and my mom didn't use condoms. She had her tubes tied when I was twelve. In fact, that's how my mom caught him in the affair he actually admitted to—she found a condom in his pocket."

"So, he never admitted to this other affair you're accusing him of, then? The one in '96?" Her question irritated me. How had Kevin suddenly become the victim?

"I'm not *accusing* him of anything. I was simply stating a fact."

"How is it a fact if he never admitted to it?"

"He admitted to taking the condoms! It was one and the same!"

"How do you figure that? Maybe he took them for a friend."

"A *friend?*"

"Why not? Is it so hard to fathom? I've borrowed condoms from my friends before."

"Yeah, maybe in college!"

"What does college have to do with it?"

"Because college is young and crazy. In college, a person might not have any left at the last minute, so they'll ask their roommate or their friend down the hall. But, come on! A thirty-two-year-old man? Do you really think his friends were asking him for condoms? Why wouldn't they have just gone to the store?"

"Why didn't Kevin?"

"He said he took them because he 'knew they were there.' Maybe he had to get his quickie in and didn't have time to stop at the store first. Regardless, do you really think he was stealing condoms from his stepdaughter's bedroom to give to his *friends?* What do you think he was, some kind of underground contraceptives dealer?"

"Oh, *that's* funny."

"I'm not trying to be funny, Emily. I'm trying to make you realize just who it is you're marrying."

"And you don't think I know? Believe it or not, I *have* thought this through. People do learn from their mistakes. So, if you came here with a little prepared speech about all the bad choices I've made, you can save it. I know I'm a joke to most people."

"You're not a joke."

"Oh, really? I think my high school boyfriend and I are gonna end up just like my parents. Instead of a diamond ring, I get a dildo, just before he dumps me for somebody else. Then, the guy who actually *gives* me the diamond ring turns out to be 'taking it' from behind, courtesy of his male roommate, the entire time we're together! *Then,* sweet, saintly Emily takes him back only to find him fucking one of her closest friends in the shower. But along comes a knight in shining armor to take her away from all of that. Finally, a perfect example of what a man should be. Only, he turns out to be married—with kids!" She paused to look at me. "How am I doing here?"

I smiled. "Better than I could've done. But you forgot about Nick."

"Right. The gay guy she could never have, but insisted on pursuing, anyway." Emily leaned forward. "Stella, can't you see? Kevin isn't gay, ambiguous, married—"

"And Warren?"

A dark cloud seemed to pass over her face and she looked down. "What about him?"

"You didn't mention him, either—in your speech, I mean. Do you consider Warren a mistake?"

Emily lifted her eyes to meet mine again. She was crying. "What does it matter, Stella? My life is here, now. He chose *her.* Warren decided for us. *He* said it was a mistake."

"And if he hadn't?"

"What does it *matter,* Stella? Life goes on. I'm with Kevin now. And I'm happy. Why do you always have to throw the past in my face?"

I waited for her to calm down. "Don't you at least think you should tell Warren what's going on, then? So, he can start looking for another roommate?"

"I will…soon. I'll tell him soon." She saw the knowing look on my face and sighed. "Stella, would you stop it? This is not a rebound thing. I would *not* just decide to get married on the rebound, let alone to someone you despise so much. I mean, Warren and I didn't even date. We slept together once. Twice, if you count college. He's my friend, Stella. I only cried because…" She started to well up again. "I only cried because I felt weird about the way we left things." And then she burst into tears. I held my arms out and she put her head on my shoulder. "I only cried because… I miss him!" Inside, I shook with relief. Kevin hadn't diminished her feelings for Warren at all. If anything, suppressing them all this time had made them stronger than ever. And I had just taken the lid off of Emily's volcano.

I would do it. I would break my word to Emily and let Warren in on her plans. I had to. She loved him and he loved her. People who belong together should *be* together. I was tired of seeing my best friend screw up her life—over and over again—with the wrong men. If they didn't have the balls to make this happen for them, I did. Not that Warren knew any better, sitting at home in their SoHo apartment, having no idea that the love of his life was about to become the next bride of Satan. But I knew. And I would have to tell him, so that he could fly out here and tell her—to her face—what she's meant to him, all of these years, once and for all. If I told her about him and Tina, it would sound like too little too late. It needed to come straight from the horse's mouth, straight from the mouth of the man whose name, just days before her wedding, could bring her to tears.

We must have fallen asleep that way, with Emily in my arms on the couch. I only vaguely remember the phone ringing and her saying something about meeting Anna at the boutique. I must have moved to the bed because that's where I woke up—to the sound of my own name, repeating and repeating through my dreams. I'd been dreaming of John. I opened my eyes.

"Stella." It was Kevin, calling to me from the couch. I'd promised John I wouldn't see him alone. But we were alone. And I didn't know what the hell to do. "And so we meet again," he said, standing up.

"How long have you been watching me?"

"Not long." He smiled. "You must have been tired. Emily said she woke you up at four o'clock yesterday morning." He came over and sat down on the bed. I shot up right away, but not in time to gather the blanket so that I could cover myself. I'd wanted a shield between us, but he was sitting on it. The damn bastard was sitting on my shield. "Relax," he said. "I won't bite."

"How'd you get in here?"

"I guess Emily didn't tell you I had my own key to the room?"

"I guess she didn't think there'd be any need to." He looked confused. "Why didn't you call, Kevin? You knew I would be here. Emily probably didn't tell me you had your own key to the room because she didn't think you'd be rude enough to barge in when I was visiting." Wow, that felt good. I really *had* grown balls in my old age.

"I'm sorry. I should've called first, but I knew you wouldn't see me."

"Gee, whatever gave you that idea?"

"Stella, please. I'd really like to take this time alone to talk to you. Do we have to be hostile?"

"Do we have to be alone?"

Kevin smiled. "Well, Emily's not here. There's not much I can do about that."

He was waiting for some kind of witty retort, but I didn't have one. "Go ahead," I said finally. "I'm listening."

"I had an appointment this afternoon with my art dealer—"

"Orla?"

"Emily told you about her?" He seemed pleased.

"*Is* there anything to tell?"

"What do you mean?"

"I mean, we know how faithful you were to my mother."

"Look, I'm sorry about that. I feel horrible about the way things turned out with your mom and me."

"Yeah, you look miserable."

"*You* look wonderful." His eyes traveled straight down to my chest when he said it. And then he smiled, knowing how uncomfortable he'd made me. I folded my arms defensively, refusing to squirm. "Oh, come on. I've known you since you were eighteen. Was I really such a bad guy *all* of those years?"

"Most of them."

"Stella, be fair."

"Fair?"

"I always tried to be like a father to you."

"What?"

"But it was hard," he said, looking down at the bed. "I always felt like you were judging me. You can be pretty judgmental at times, Stella. You do realize that, don't you?" He gazed back up at me pleadingly, as if deep down he was hoping for…an apology?

"You are *not* going to put this on me."

"I'm not trying to put anything on you. I'm just telling you how I felt. Anyway, when I got home from my appointment with Orla, there was a message from Emily saying she'd be tied up at the boutique for a few hours and not to call the room at all because she'd left you in here sleeping. I knew you were tired, but I also knew it could be my only chance to come and set things straight with you before I married Emily."

"Wait a second. You mean, Emily specifically told you not to call and instead you came over? You came over knowing full well she wouldn't be here?"

"Stella, making peace with you is really important to me."

"Important to *you?* I'm supposed to care about what's important to you after what you did to my mother?"

"It's important to Emily."

"Emily has no idea what you're really like!"

"And you do?"

"I know more than she does."

"Is that a fact?"

"You wanna test me?"

"Look, Stella, given your perspective, it might be hard to believe that I've changed, but I have. It wasn't just a line I fed Emily."

"So, you don't lie anymore, then?"

"I've been honest with Emily from the very beginning."

"So, telling her you only cheated on my mother once when we both know it was a whole lot more than that means you've told her the *truth?*"

"Emily knows what she needs to know. The past is the past. It doesn't matter."

"But you just said you've been honest with her from the very beginning."

"About the things that matter."

"Oh, I see. You forgot to clarify. You know, you're right, Kevin. You have changed. You've gotten even better at conning people."

He shook his head, dismissing my remark. "It doesn't matter what you think, Stella. I love her, and I'm not going to let you screw it up. I thought I could come in here and be civil."

"You thought you could come in here and shut me up."

"What do you want? What would satisfy you? Do you want me to make a list of all the women I slept with when I was married to your mom and then show it to Emily? Would that be honest enough?"

"So, you admit it was more than one?"

"What—are you wearing a wire?"

"I wish I was. Then Emily could hear how you act when she's not around."

"You're really pushing me, Stella."

"So, what are you gonna do…rape me?"

I couldn't believe I'd said it and neither could he, but I wasn't afraid. I *wanted* to dare him—to see what he could possibly say for himself now, after all these years, to justify that night. I wanted to reach across the bed and claw his face off.

"*What* did you just say?"

"You heard me."

"I heard you. I just don't know what the *hell* you're talking about."

I leaned forward. "Think *real* hard… My bedroom. The air-conditioning was broken. My mother wasn't home."

Kevin reached out to touch my cheek, and I let him—to show that I wasn't afraid. "You wanted it," he said. "You may have fought me—"

"And screamed."

"But you wanted it. I read the diary. I knew what a dirty girl you were."

"They were dreams. I was just a kid."

"You were as legal as any adult, my dear. And living together in the same house like that—it was bound to happen."

"But you were married to my mother."

"There are always obstacles, Stella. The point is that *you* invited me into your room that night. You knew as well as I did that your mother wasn't home."

"I wanted to talk to you…I…" I'd lost my edge. He was too close to me. This was all too real. The thrill of intimidation was gone. I *was* afraid. "You were my *stepfather.*"

"What were you doing dreaming about your stepfather, then?"

"I don't know," I said, the tears welling up in my eyes.

"You don't know?" I shook my head. "It's okay not to know, Stella. You don't have to get upset about it. But you shouldn't go accusing innocent men of rape. How could it be rape when I never finished?"

"I don't know," I whispered.

"Sounds like you don't know much," he said. And then he pointed his finger in my face. "I'll tell you one thing *I* know, and that's if you ever say a word to Emily about this—" Suddenly the door slammed.

"Emily already knows." And there she was, standing in front of the bed, facing us, ready to pounce on Kevin. I jumped up and ran over to hug her, crying and shaking from the confrontation. "Why don't you go wait in the bathroom, Stella? I need to talk to Kevin alone for a minute."

The empty tub just looked so inviting and safe, so that's where I sat, rocking myself back and forth as I listened to them fight. She said it was a good thing she'd forgotten those sketches—she might've never believed what a bastard he was had she not heard it with her very own ears from the doorway. How long had she been listening? Long enough to know what a fool she'd been. He said it wasn't as bad as it sounded—that she couldn't see my face, the way I was coming onto him, the way I'd come onto him when he was married to my mom. But Emily dismissed all of his excuses. She said he was only making things worse, and that if he really wanted to do her a favor, he'd get out of her life and stay there.

"You know what? I give up!" Kevin yelled. "The two of you deserve each other! Why don't you just make yourself happy and marry Stella? No man is ever gonna be good enough for either of you!"

"I'd *rather* marry her—or any woman, for that matter—than any of the shitbags I've dated! And you're so high up on that list, it's scary."

"Well, she's *all* yours. Every ounce of emotional baggage *and* her crazy mother!" I heard a slap. "Oh, that's real nice, Emily. Hit me. Here—just take your fucking key and I'm outta here. It was great knowing you."

When the fight was over and Kevin had left our lives for good, Emily joined me in the bathroom. And together, we cried like babies in the tub.

Joyride

"I miss her," I said. Emily and I had made it out of the tub and were sitting on the bathroom floor, with our heads against the wall, watching Blanche's *yahrzeit* candle burn on the sink.

"So do I." She reached for my hand. "I used to think it would be the three of us, you know? For the rest of our lives."

"Yeah, me too." We were quiet for a while.

"I'm sorry I made you come out here."

"Hey, if I hadn't, you may have ended up with Kevin, and John and I wouldn't have met up again the way we did."

"Are you thanking me, then?"

"I don't know if I'd go that far."

We were still holding hands and neither one of us had taken our eyes off of the flame. Our voices had become monotone. We seemed to be in some sort of trance now that all the commotion had died down.

"Stella?"

"Hmm?"

"You're in Europe with me." I smiled. "What should we do?"

"Let's order room service."

While we ate, we watched a tape of one of Emily's fashion shows. When she came out onto the runway with her models at the end, I couldn't keep from laughing.

"What?" she giggled. "Do I look stupid?"

"No, it's just that when I see you doing these adult things, it cracks me up. No matter how hard I try, I'll always see you as—"

"The girl who helped you put your first tampon in?"

"Something like that."

"And you'll always be that raven goddess in the locker room whom I was oddly attracted to even though she wore Milli Vanilli T-shirts."

"Okay, it was *one* shirt, and I remember you saying you liked it."

"I was only trying to make you feel good about yourself."

"Well, I guess that's okay because I lied to you that day, too. I said I was conceived during that famous part of *Streetcar* where Marlon Brando stands outside screaming 'Stella!'"

"Not true?"

I shook my head. "At least not to my knowledge. And even if it were, you know my mom. What are the chances that she'd share that kind of information with me?" Emily walked around to my side of the table and sat on my lap. "What are you doing?"

She kissed my cheek. "I forgive you."

Later that night, as we lay on our sides in bed, talking with the lights on, I asked Emily how she knew about Blanche's *yahrzeit*.

"I don't even have a clue about the Jewish calendar," I said. "My mom always lets me know."

"Your Zayde Max and I are tight. He calls me every year."

Her answer shocked me. "What? He never said anything. Why'd you guys keep it a secret?"

"I don't know. It's not exactly a *secret*. It's just always been something between him and me. He knows I never wanted to bother your mom about it. It's just something I always want to make sure I do."

"Emily, that's really..." I didn't know what to say. It was beyond sweet.

"You don't have to say anything. I do it because you're my family—you, Blanche, your mom." She stopped suddenly, and her eyes grew wide with concern. "You're not gonna tell her about Kevin and me, are you, Stella? I mean, now that it's over?"

"Of course not. What would be the point in hurting her? You came to your senses before it was too late. That's all that matters."

She shook her head. "I don't know what I was thinking. This has got to be the stupidest thing I've ever done."

"Probably."

"It's just that..."

"What?"

"Don't you ever worry? About time?"

"Time?"

"I just thought it *had* to be Kevin, you know? I mean if Jason wasn't the one, and it wasn't Rob, Damien, or Warren, then..."

"What? What are you thinking?"

"I hated lying to Warren about what was happening over here. It was almost as hard as lying to you," she said.

"I think you should have a talk with him when you get back."

"About how he rejected me?"

"About how you feel. Can you honestly tell me you'd have chosen Kevin over him?"

"If Warren had wanted to be with me after that night we spent together, I don't think I ever would've come here."

"He would have made you come."

"Yeah, he's pretty good at that," she said, flashing a naughty smile.

"Always with her mind in the gutter," I teased.

"Would you have me any other way?"

"Oh, it doesn't matter what *way.* As long as I could have you."

Emily was impressed. "Very good, Stella! I've taught you well."

"Just do me a favor?"

"What's that?"

"Try to stay out of love for the rest of your trip?"

"Do *me* a favor?"

"Hmm?"

"Answer my question. Do you ever worry about time?"

"You mean growing up?"

"I mean dying before we've ever had a chance to do anything. My mom was my age when she died, Stella. *My* age, and she was already married with a three-year-old child. She was robbed of the life she could've lived, but at least she'd found love and had started a family. At least, she'd made some kind of mark that could say she was even *here.*"

"Well, you've made a mark, too. Look at Emmie. Look at Warren. Look at me."

"Look at Katherine. Do you realize she was only twenty-nine when she and my dad started trying? Twenty-nine, and it was already too late for her. Well, we're twenty-eight, Stella. Our clocks aren't magic. We're only human. Don't you ever worry?"

"Emily, our clocks may not be magic, but it doesn't mean they're ticking in time to Katherine's, either. Everyone's different. And your life is not your mother's. I'm not saying wait until you're fifty to have kids. But, every bad thing that happened to your mom and Katherine is not going to happen to you. Look, we've seen a lot of tragedies in our lives. And you should never forget your mom or what Katherine has gone through, just like I'll never forget Izzie or my sister, but that's not all there is. It's not even close to all there is. For all we know, Katherine *will* have this baby, and if she doesn't, your father told you they plan to adopt. You can't go rushing into marriages because you're afraid of time. Emily, I *know* you're going to be a good mother, but what good would it do your child if you arrived at motherhood out of fear?" I stopped for a second, suddenly aware of my own hypocrisy. "Sorry," I said. "Who am I to speak out against living in fear?"

"You're the bravest person I know."

"Me?" I could think of many ways to describe myself, but "brave" had never graced the list.

"Stella, look at everything you've been through. If you'd turned out to be even half the person you are today, I'd call it amazing."

"I never knew you felt that way. I always thought *you* were the brave one."

"Well, you never give yourself enough credit for anything that you are." She paused for a moment. "Can I ask you something?"

"What?"

"How come you never said anything—about what Kevin did to you?"

I shrugged my shoulders, smiling sadly. "I just wanted to pretend it never happened. Talking about it would've made it real. It was real enough in my head, but if I didn't talk about it—if no one else knew—then I could almost pretend like it was just a bad dream."

"So you never told anyone, not even your mom?"

"*Especially* not my mom. I'd never want her to know, not even now. It's like the stuff we knew about Blanche and the boys at Keith Shay's house. If my mom knew about Kevin and me, it would only upset her. She'd probably end up blaming herself. She doesn't need that after all she's been through. You and John are the only ones that will ever know."

"So, you *did* tell someone else. You told John."

"Not until last night."

"Last night? You mean, after all that time apart, you just came out and told him? What did he say?"

"That if he'd known about it when it happened, he would've killed Kevin."

Emily giggled. "Your superhero."

"That's what I said."

"Really?"

I reached out to rub her arm. "Don't be upset, okay? That I told John something you'd never known about me. Last night was just different. The circumstances with John made telling come so naturally—it didn't even feel like a decision. But afterward, I don't know…I just didn't want to dredge it all up again. I mean, if it had actually come down to the wire with you and Kevin, I would've told you. It's not as if—"

"It's *okay,* Stella," she said, smiling. "I understand."

"Are you sure? Because I'd never want you to think my telling him had anything to do with not trusting you."

"Well, I can't say I'm not jealous. It's a weird possessive thing I have with you. What can I say?"

"I'm your bitch."

"Well, as long as you still know it. But I'm glad you felt close enough to John to tell him all that. That really says a lot, Stella. That after all this time, you could still talk to him about something you couldn't even tell your—"

"Bitch mistress," I supplied.

"Ooh, I like it! So, is there anything else your *bitch mistress* doesn't know?"

"If there is, you'll find out eventually," I said, thinking of Warren. "I promise."

"What does that mean?"

"It means turn out the lights, baby. I'm tired."

As we lay there in the dark, I remembered the events of those last two days, the years, our lives. The people we had loved and lost. The ones we'd found and held on to. I thought of Laura Nyro and mourning for Emily's chastity at the prom. The week we spent together after Katherine lost Eli. Foam pancakes, purple dildos, midnight rescues, Stevie Nicks. Crying in the tub like babies. I thought of the way Emily had been there for me through everything I'd ever gone through that mattered, right down to that very first tampon lesson when she'd told me we were sisters of the moon.

Welcome to the crazy train that was our lives. The scenery was constantly shifting, and new passengers were always getting on board. But Emily and I had been sharing the same seat since we were kids. And not even the devil himself could change that. As long as there was a track to travel, we'd be there—together, just like always, no matter what the future held.

"Stella?" Emily whispered, long after I thought she'd fallen asleep.

"Yeah?"

"Anna already started working on a gown for me."

"Well, you can tell her what happened tomorrow. I'm sure she won't kill you."

"How about I just have her finish it and we get married, instead?"

"We, who?"

"Stella," she said as she reached for my hand under the covers, "will you do me the honor of becoming my wife?"

"I thought you'd never ask," I told her. "But I *do* hope you know that I intend to stay a virgin until our wedding night."

"Oh, goodie. I always hoped I'd find me a virgin to marry. It is kind of a pity, though ain't it?"

"What is?"

"A couple'a pretty young things like us, alone in the dark, and we can't even go for a test drive."

"It's tragic."

"And you look like just the kind'a gal who could get my motor runnin', too. Now, I hope you don't think I'm gettin' fresh. Sweet busty dames like you must get lotsa come-on's. But I've loved you since you was just a flat-chested ninny in braids, milkin' cows on your daddy's farm."

I had no idea what she was talking about, but it was good to hear her acting like her silly old self again. Emily was too full of life to waste her energy obsessing about clocks.

"Em?"

"Yeah?"

"You're gonna be okay, you know? With time. We both are."

She was quiet for a second. "How can you be sure?"

"Come on, a couple'a pretty young things like us?" I said. "This is only the beginning."

"Stella?"

"Hmm?"

"Do you ever think about how our lives would've been different if we'd never met?"

"I try not to."

"Maybe we should send Mrs. Wilder's thighs a thank-you note."

"Or at least a postcard from Europe to let them know how we're doing."

"Hey, Stella?"

"Yeah?"

"Do you *really* plan on staying a virgin until our wedding night?"

I laughed. "Good *night,* Emily."

She rolled over onto her side. "Sleep well. The past fifteen years have been one hell of a joyride, but you ain't seen nothin' yet."

New Beginnings

Emily and I never did get married in Dublin, but we did have our European vacation. And in a way it was like a honeymoon, as we reveled in our rediscovery of the fact that nothing could break us apart. I guess that makes our union stronger than a lot of marriages. At least half of them, anyway, since heaven knows that Emily and I will never get a divorce.

Three months have passed since her 4:00 a.m. phone call sent me to the airport in a flood of fear and sadness, three months since my life fell apart, came together, and the world stopped and started fresh, all in the matter of a weekend. Now, it's spring. But only according to the calendar—it's still pretty chilly in Scottsboro. John misses the California weather, but says that's what plane tickets are for. We're flying out to visit his friend, Mike, in San Diego next week.

We did try the long-distance thing, but only in the interests of "taking it slow," which only lasted for a few weeks before we got honest. The honest truth was that we felt lucky to have found each other again and didn't want to live apart. So, John moved in with me. He knows how attached I am to the little town I once termed "the symbol of my stagnation." And like he said, one of the best things about his job is being able to work from anywhere. We can always visit San Diego.

Alison jumped at the chance to move in with Anthony sooner. Although she'd been spending every night at his place, anyway, she hadn't planned on making the transition permanent until they were married. But I think she was only doing that for my sake, to give me more time to put off looking for a roommate. John turned her bedroom into an office. He's in there writing every day until dinner.

At least once a week, we eat at my mom's. About a month ago, she set an extra place at the table. It was for my father. They'd been in touch ever since that letter he sent her, but that was the first they'd seen of each other—that morning, actually, at my Grandmom Betty's funeral. She was laid to rest next to my Grandpop Eddie in the same cemetery where Blanche is buried. I was sorry to hear she'd passed away, though I have to admit, it didn't break me—I could barely remember what she looked like. I hadn't seen her since I was little. But that's not why I didn't attend the funeral. I was speaking at a teacher's conference in Harrisburg that morning. Though that's not why, either. I could've gotten out of it. I just didn't think a funeral was the best place to reunite with my estranged father after twelve years apart. But I had to see him while he was in town. Experience had taught me that there was a big difference between evil and illness. Kevin was evil. My father had been sick. He deserved the chance to overcome that. And I owed it to my mother—and Blanche—to give it to him.

Of course, our reunion was not without its awkward moments, but I expected that. What I didn't expect was for him to look so old. He was forty-three the last time I'd seen him, and now he was fifty-five and almost bald. But he was still my father, and as the night wore on, I began to see hints of the man whose memory I'd buried beneath a gross exaggeration of what he eventually became. This was not the wolfman, but the guy I had known for the first fifteen years of my life—*before* my sister's death ripped our family in half. I hugged him goodbye before John and I left.

"I'm sorry about Grandmom," I said. "Goodbye, Dad." My mom says the look on his face when I called him "Dad" almost made her cry.

He's still living in Florida and hasn't been back since then, but we've spoken a couple of times. And we e-mail about once a week. It's not ideal—it can be downright embarrassing when I mention something he should know about and he has absolutely no idea what I mean. That's when it hits me that he missed out on a dozen years of my life. But he's trying and I'm trying. And we're getting more comfortable. The most important thing is that after all this time, I actually have a father again. I may have said I didn't need one, but I must admit that having one feels unexpectedly nice.

As for my parents, I have no idea whether or not they'll ever get back together. They talk every day—about what, I don't know. Though, I will say that their friendship has given me an odd sense of security. With my father's return from the virtual dead, it seems my mother has realized that good things can actually happen to her and she's finally stopped living in fear of lightning. I haven't seen her this relaxed in years, and that's what gives me security—to see her enjoying life again. If those daily phone calls from Florida are the reason, then I guess I have my dad to thank.

Alison and Anthony are in Florida now. Walt Disney World—"a heavenly spot for honeymooners," or at least that's what Alison wrote on the postcard that arrived in the mail yesterday. The wedding was beautiful. Marcus was Anthony's best man, and I was a bridesmaid. It was John's and my first big event as a couple. Warren and Emily's, too. I wasn't surprised when they started seeing each other. I already knew how each of them felt. Emily, on the other hand, was shocked. She couldn't believe Warren had kept his love a secret for so long, and she *really* couldn't believe I'd withheld such valuable information at her critical hour of need in Dublin.

"I gave you as many hints as I could!" I said. "But I promised Warren I wouldn't say anything. Don't you think after all those years, he deserved to be the one to tell you how he felt?"

"You're loyal to a fault, you know that?" It was the same accusation I'd gotten from Warren when I told him I couldn't speak for Emily. I guess they really *are* two of a kind.

Warren and John have been getting along surprisingly well for two people who hardly knew each other, but spent years feeling as if they were in some sort of competition. But it's not really all that odd, considering they're both smart and giant-hearted with wonderful senses of humor, not to mention that they've got to be at least a little alike to be so remarkably understanding of me. It only stood to reason that they'd get each other's jokes and have things to talk about when the four of us got together. But it wasn't until the wedding, when Emily and I heard them teaming up to make fun of us to complete strangers that I realized they were actually becoming friends in their own right. We thought it was absolutely adorable.

Warren and John. Who would've ever guessed? But then again, that's the way things happen sometimes. We find friends in the least likely of people, love in the least likely of places, and every once in a while, we look up and there's a miracle. Katherine gave birth to a seven-pound baby girl two days after the wedding. With my mother's consent and blessing, they named her Blanche.

That just about brings me to yesterday. John was out shopping when I walked in with Alison and Anthony's postcard. I put it on the fridge next to the note he'd left me saying he was out buying some things for dinner. He cooked for me—because he felt like it, he said—and after we ate, he reached under his chair and handed me a copy of *Bloodlines.*

"You finally signed it for me?" It had been a running joke between us since he'd moved in that he could write two best-selling novels but couldn't figure out how to sign a copy of his book for his girlfriend. He kept saying he wanted to come up with something special.

John smiled. "Open it."

I gladly complied and looked down at the page. And staring straight up into my eyes, unmistakably, were the words, *Will you marry me?*

"John!" I was so taken aback, his name emerged as a whisper.

He got up from his chair and knelt down on one knee. "Stella," he said, removing a small velvet box from his pocket. "I knew it when I was seventeen. And in all that time we were apart, I never stopped knowing it. You were always the one. And now that we've found each other again, I want it to be forever. I want you to be my wife. So, Stella…" He opened the box. "Will you marry me?"

Staring into his eyes, I started to cry, oceans and rivers of happy tears, and at the same time, I laughed, like a demented hyena. I was overwhelmed.

"Are you *kidding?*" I asked him.

"Apparently not," John said, smiling as he glanced down at the ring—the beautiful square-cut diamond ring that mysteriously transformed me into a babbling idiot.

"No, I didn't mean are you kidding about the proposal…I meant are you kidding to think I wouldn't… Yes, okay? Yes! I mean, yes! And I'm not just saying that because of the ring. Well, you know that, obviously. I mean, you *do* know that, right? Wait, what am I saying? Can I start over?"

I was completely killing the romance of the moment, but it didn't matter. John's eyes were glowing—he loved me, anyway. And that was the best part of all. To be with someone who loved you, anyway. And to know the rest of your lives were starting right at that very table.

John slid the ring onto my finger and stood up to kiss me. "I love you very much," he said, drying my tears. "And you don't have to analyze your reaction later, okay? It was perfect."

To be with someone who really knows you and loves you, just when your lives are starting, is the greatest feeling in the entire world. Especially when his eyes are blue and his hair never did stop smelling like apples. I think I'll be riding this cloud for a while.

Emily's already talking about designs for my dress. We haven't even set a date yet. But we're thinking early fall—before it gets too cold. Of course, Emily will be my maid of honor and Warren will be one of the groomsmen, and there will be oceans and rivers of happy tears, just like last night, only more. And my father will be there to walk me down the aisle. Aside from actually marrying John, I see that as my proudest moment—having my dad there to give me away. Just how I imagined my wedding would be when I was a little girl. It's hard to feel anything but lucky when things actually work out like you dreamed.

Engaged. A second-grade school teacher. Still living in Scottsboro. Happy. That is me now. At twenty-eight. And that's how people will see me this summer at Summit Valley's ten-year reunion for the Class of 1995. Warren and Emily will be there. Emily. Live-in boyfriend. Internationally known fashion designer living in New York City. Centered. People will pigeonhole us like that, pasting us into neat little categories, not at all caring what we've gone through to get there. And we will do the same thing to them. Fortunately, John will be there to hold my hand. I'm not sure if he'll receive an invitation since he spent his senior year out in L.A. and didn't actually graduate with us, but he'll be there because I'll be there. And together, John, Warren, Emily and I will brave the barrage of stares and questions that are part of the territory of reunions.

I can't believe it's been ten years since high school. Or fifteen years since Emily and I shared that moment after gym class. The moment that neither of us could exactly describe, but would always remember. Because it changed our lives and spawned other moments, memories and times that would stay in our hearts long after Milli Vanilli T-shirts went out of fashion. Long after tampons were anything new. But Emily and I would never change, not where it really counted. We'd never forget those thirteen-year-old girls bonding over thighs, talking about their mothers, knowing they'd found a friend. And she will always be Tinkerbell. And I, her raven goddess. And no one will know what we're talking about half the time, with our gay brothers, straight brothers, and that thing about bitch mistresses, but that's okay. Because we are bella donnas. A pair of pretty young things whispering in the dark. Whatever we need to be, we are. Sad, bad and sometimes crazy. We're prom queens without their crowns invoking Laura Nyro. We're babies crying in the tub. Sisters of the moon. Best friends on a crazy train, sharing a seat through shifting scenery and the test of time. Together forever since the moment our lives changed. Always and no matter what.